◇◇◇◇◇◇◇◇◇◇◇◇◇◇◇

# Love's Surprise

### By

## Charlotte Kent

### The Fourth Novel in the Series

## Captain's Point Stories

◇◇◇◇◇◇◇◇◇◇◇◇◇◇◇◇◇◇◇◇◇

To Rose Nectar, for her unfailing support and encouragement
as well as her valuable feedback and input.
This one's for you, Rose!
Annie Acorn

To my husband, John, the love of my life.
Juliette Hill

Charlotte Kent is the pseudonym used by
Annie Acorn and Juliette Hill
when writing their collaborative contemporary
women's fiction/family saga series
Captain's Point Stories

You may contact and/or follow the authors at:
charlottekentromances@gmail.com
@CharlotteKent20

This is Max's fifth starring role in a work of fiction.

The true story of his actual rescue can be found in
Annie Acorn's *Chocolate Can Kill*

The novel, *Love's Surprise*, is a work of fiction. Any resemblance to real people or events is completely accidental. A few literary liberties may have been taken when it comes to geographic locations, medical treatments, sailing terms, tidal charts, and helicopter rescue protocols in the interest of creating great literature.

# CHAPTER I

Jack Jefferson, award-winning, internationally read author and noted musician, turned his Mercedes SUV into the driveway of The Cove and let out a sigh. Nothing could've looked any better to him at this moment than the welcoming lights shining through the windows of the sprawling Victorian-era house spread before him.

His in-laws, Anders and Elizabeth Chesterton, had welcomed friends and family to their home for a fun-filled New Year's Eve celebration ever since their marriage decades before, and knowing that their second daughter and grandson were part of the crowd inside made his destination even sweeter.

Had it been less than two days since the call had come that had taken him away from his wife Susan and stepson Daniel?

"Jack?" Jules's tenor voice had come over the line. "I've called to ask you a huge favor."

Cellist in the acclaimed chamber music group String Flings, Jules Fauré had done everything but offer to pay for a world cruise for Jack and his new wife, if the author would agree to substitute for the group's lead violinist the following evening.

"I wouldn't bother you at this time of year if it was a tour engagement," Jules had pleaded, "but this is a huge charity event, which is right up your alley. Pierre's appendix is probably being removed at this moment, and you're only a few miles away on Maryland's Eastern

Shore. Besides, we're already on record as playing your own *Alpine Spring* as one of our two numbers."

Asking for a moment to confer with his wife, he had excused himself, and Susan had immediately agreed that he should go. Daniel and she would remain behind in Captain's Point, where they would continue to enjoy a holiday visit with her elder brother Andy and his family.

Still harboring mixed feelings, Jack had made Jules's day by agreeing, with one contingency, and had flown to D.C. in his personal helicopter an hour later, arriving at the hotel in time to practice with the group for the concert that had been held that afternoon.

"Daddy!"

As he entered The Cove's foyer, Jack felt the thrust of his stepson's five-year-old body striking his knees before he even heard the word.

"There you are." He hoisted the boy skyward, settling him onto his hip and giving him a bear hug as the child snuggled against his chest.

"We've been so worried about your flying back and forth in the helicopter, but now you're home," Daniel stated solemnly, no doubt repeating words his mother had spoken as was his habit.

"Your mom didn't say she was worried about my flying the copter up there," Jack responded.

"Aunt Kate asked her why she hadn't told you," his mole continued, filling him in.

"So why hadn't she?"

"What business is it of ours to tell a grown man who never asks for anything for himself what to do?" Daniel repeated what the author recognized as exactly the sort of thing his new wife would've said, readily putting his wishes before hers.

"Let's keep this conversation between us, okay?" Jack stepped into what had once been a formal parlor, but now served as a comfortable family room, filing away for later thought that he had once again taken a wrong step as he learned how to be married. Obviously, his primary New Year's resolution should be to work even harder at being the best husband for his wonderful wife.

"Sure," Daniel agreed, again drawing his attention before shifting his weight slightly in order to better address the crowded room. "My daddy's here!"

"He certainly is." Chase Sheffield, owner of the Sheffield Place Inn next door and Jack's wife's law partner, sent the author a welcoming grin as the lawyer's wife, the former Adrianna Montgomery, smiled her own greeting.

"Glad you had a safe trip." His cousin-in-law Larry Chesterton looked up from the puzzle the three of them were working at a large round table, along with his own sister Kate, who blew him a kiss.

Noting that Kate's hand rested under Larry's on the financial advisor's thigh, Jack wondered if the two of them realized that passersby could see what was going on beneath the table's edge, since neither of them had yet made their developing relationship public.

Not that it mattered. No one at the party this evening wished the budding couple anything but the best, and Kate's uncontested divorce from what's his name would be final in just three more months.

"Mama's in the music room with Grandma," Daniel whispered into his ear, and Jack opened the door that led to the next room, struck immediately by how tightly his wife was holding onto her mother's hand.

"Jack!" Susan cried, disrupting the playing of a show tune on the grand piano by the gray-haired Edmund Robinson, a former professional musician who, with his wife Marissa, managed the Sheffield Place Inn.

Not surprised when his wife flung herself at him, Jack held her tightly with his right arm as he allowed his stepson to shimmy down his left side. "I missed you so much," he whispered into his Susie's ear as he wrapped his other arm around her.

"I missed you, too." She raised her beautiful blue eyes to his dark ones, and he bent and kissed her long and deep with no thought whatsoever as to onlookers in the room.

"How did the concert go?" she asked once he released her.

"Great! Playing *Alpine Spring* for an audience of that size and hearing their applause was amazing," he shared. "I wish you could've been there."

"Are you hungry?" Susan asked as she took his hand and guided him back into the family room. "If so, I'll make you a plate, and then we could work on the puzzle with the group."

"I was in a hurry to get back, so I didn't stop to eat," he filled her in. "You save me a place at the puzzle, and I'll grab some food and join you."

"Heading my way?" Chase walked beside him as he started for the kitchen. "Elizabeth made sure some of everything was left for you, and I can show you where it is."

And as he followed one of his two best friends in Captain's Point to the kitchen where he knew a feast awaited him, Jack couldn't help but be filled with gratitude for all the people who surrounded both his sister and him on this, their first New Year's Eve celebrated with a real family.

## CHAPTER II

Removing the makeup she had worn to the Chestertons' family-oriented, somewhat rambunctious New Year's Eve party, Adrianna Montgomery Sheffield brushed her dark waves from her face and met her brown eyes in the mirror. What a wonderful evening it had been!

Recalling the fine buffet, snippets of conversation and the grin on her husband Chase's face when he had located the final piece of a difficult puzzle, she quickly slipped into a comfortable pair of drawstring pajamas, knowing he would be waiting for her.

"There you are." He smiled as she entered their octagonal bedroom lit only by the glow from the fireplace, and as she took in how well his crisp, blue and white-striped pajamas hung on his tall, lean frame, setting off his dark hair and deep blue eyes, she wished she had chosen her slinky blue gown instead.

Taking her hand, he gazed down at her with the soft look she loved in his eyes, but instead of taking her into his arms as she had expected, he studied her face.

"You're so beautiful." He traced the line of her jaw with his finger, sending a shiver along her spine as her mind recalled that he had said and done exactly the same thing before their first kiss. Only this time, his face reflected his deep love for her, instead of an inner struggle.

Holding her as if he were afraid she might break in the crook of his left arm, he slipped the fingers of his right hand through her hair, supporting her head as he kissed her tenderly.

Expecting him to lift her into his arms and carry her to their half-tester bed as he was so often wont to do, she was disappointed when he didn't.

"Come here." He led her by the hand instead to one of the Queen Anne chairs by the hearth, where he took her onto his lap, and she snuggled her head against his shoulder.

"Do you realize that we've been married nearly six months?" he asked, amazement rooted in his voice. "It doesn't seem possible, does it?"

Thinking of all the delightful, laughter-filled times they had shared – entertaining friends in their new home, renovating Sheffield Place and turning it into an inn, riding their horses along the cliffs here in Captain's Point – she, too, wondered at it not having been longer.

Sensing he wished to ask her something important, she straightened and pulled back slightly against the arm of the chair, so she could take in his facial expressions. "No one can say that we've wasted the time," she stated, understanding his need for reflection.

"I agree, my queen." His eyes twinkled. "It's been a great ride."

Surprised, she watched as he diverted his gaze. "It struck me this evening that we were witnessing the birth of a new year." He bent and kissed the hollow of her neck.

"And?" Adrianna found herself confused by his mixed messages, pleased when he again faced her directly.

"Do you think it might be time for us to consider having a child?" He again searched her face.

As was her way when asked such an important question, she considered before giving him her answer. Was there room in their love for each other for another? But then, the vision of a little Chase rose in her head, and she smiled up at him.

"Yes, I can see a little fellow with dark hair and blue eyes sitting here in front of the hearth on a rainy day, toys from the cabinet in the dressing room spread around him while I knit," she answered honestly, surprised by the joy that filled his face.

"I'm not sure I wouldn't prefer a little Adrianna." He lifted her chin with the tip of his finger. "I remember a charming little girl with dark curls and huge, trusting brown eyes that I once had to rescue from the woods behind the gazebo."

"Perhaps we should settle the matter by having twins." She smiled shyly, suddenly filled with an unexpected feeling of tenderness.

"Do you see us with two children or a brood?" Chase's face took on an expression of forced seriousness.

"Oh, a brood." She joined him in his fun. "I've always seen myself as a strong, strapping farm wench."

"A delightfully pert wench, yes." He chuckled. "Strapping – not so much. Not, of course, that I'm complaining."

"It matters not." She kept their game going. "You're strapping enough for the both of us."

"You think so?" He sent her a boyish grin, genuinely pleased, but then his expression sobered. "So we're agreed? As of this date, we are childbirth bound?"

"Definitely, you'll make the best of all fathers."

"My little bride becoming a mother..." He spread his hand on her flat abdomen in which their future child would grow and once again lowered his lips onto hers.

Coming up for air, Adrianna saw immediately that his mood had changed, laughter now filling his eyes.

"Strapping you said? We'll just see about that." Chase stood with her still in his arms and carried her to their bed as she had been hoping all along that he would.

But he surprised her yet again, making love to her with the oh-so-gentle sweetness she had known only once before, on their wedding night, and Adrianna wished it could go on and on.

# CHAPTER III

In the master suite of Blue Wolf Manor, three houses away, Jack flipped the bed covers back from where he sat propped against their pillows, allowing Susan a cleared place upon which to sit as she set her MP3 player to a soft tune before joining him.

"I can't tell you how lucky I feel to be entering a new year so blessed," he said, surprised when his wife burst into tears.

"I'm afraid you're blessed more than you know," she whispered, her face averted as she dried her eyes on the sheet's corner.

"That I haven't been," he assured her, gently kissing her belly within which he had long since determined new life was growing.

"Oh, Jack!" She lifted her face to his when he straightened. "How did you know?"

"I was pleased when you filled with happiness and contentment after we were married," he shared, "but then a new glow emanated from deep inside you. I wasn't doing anything to preclude our having a child, and no one could say that we haven't made use of our opportunities to create one."

"No, they couldn't." Her blue eyes sparkled. "Some of us don't seem able to get enough of you."

"And others of us are more than glad to oblige." This time his kiss was filled with desire.

Later, as they lay satisfied in each other's arms, once again propped upon the pile of pillows behind them, Susan turned to him.

"We never discussed whether or not you wanted a child," she broached the subject hesitantly, "and I didn't meet my responsibility to protect against it as well as I should have."

"Two things." His voice took on an uncharacteristically firm edge. "One, if I hadn't wanted another child in our lives, I would've told you before I proposed, and two, if I hadn't wanted another this soon, I would've seen to it myself that we didn't conceive.

"I won't have you thinking that the life growing within you as a result of our love for each other is in any way a product of something either one of us has done wrong." Then his voice softened. "Were you seriously afraid that I'd be displeased, Susie?"

"Not seriously, but I wasn't sure what you would think," she admitted. "Even I was in shock when Janie told me. I had no idea I was pregnant. I hadn't been paying attention, and I hadn't been sick. I'm not completely immune to how many times your pleasure at being newly married has been interrupted by Daniel, though."

"Not by him, but by his open, easy, unconditional love for both of us." Jack's face filled with an expression of utter amazement. "No one else has ever offered me their love so fast. One minute we had just met, and the next minute he was snuggled against my shoulder.

"I can't explain it. At that moment, I knew he and I were destined to be connected forever, and he never wavered. Each time I called at The Cove or ran into you two somewhere else, he welcomed me into his little world as if I'd been there all along – openly, eagerly and comfortably. You'll never know how much that has meant to me."

Susan placed her hand against her new husband's cheek. "Do you blame him?" she asked. "You've filled a great void in his life. You're everything to him that his birth father never was and never will be. Dad tried, but while he's a fabulous grandfather, Daniel recognized that was Dad's role, still leaving a huge hole.

"Then you came along – tall, strong, the right age, full of interesting tales, doing for him and saying to him exactly those things that his father always should've done and said, but never did. The only surprise would've been if Daniel hadn't cast you in the role that clearly had been written for you. Do you have any idea how glad I am that you were willing to audition?"

"Willing?" Jack laughed. "I jumped at the chance. It would've broken my heart to put distance between me and that little guy. Thank goodness I'd already fallen for you on the boardwalk. What a mess I would've been in, if I hadn't already adored his mother."

"That would've been a bother." Susan chuckled, even as she remembered how needlessly worried she had been as to whether or not the two men in her life loved one another. They had been way ahead of her in that department.

"And now, we've been blessed with this new little soul to cherish and nurture." He placed his hand gently on her stomach, joy filling his face. "I'll never know what I've done to deserve such happiness in one lifetime.

"Here I sit, married to the most beautiful woman inside and out that I'll ever know – truly the love of my life, whose child has chosen to love me instead of reject me and make my life miserable, and now our love has blended and formed into this tiny being inside of you. What more could a man want?"

"I can think of only one thing." She lifted her face to his, pleased when he drew her to him, wondering yet again how such a passionate man had held his desires at bay long enough for her to find her way to him.

## CHAPTER IV

Edwina Foster flipped on the fireplace logs in the cozy living room of Montgomery House's former dependency and then joined her handsome suitor, the gray-haired artist Arthur Stern, where he waited for her on the sofa.

"I should go home and let you rest." He reached forward and took one of her homemade, oatmeal raisin cookies from a china plate, belying his words.

"There's no rush," she assured him. "I don't know if it's the Chestertons' champagne or the coffee I drank after dinner, but I'm not at all sleepy."

"Me either." His faded brown eyes met hers. "Now that we've seen in the new year, I've discovered a second wind, and there's nowhere I would rather be than in this room with you."

"It was a nice party, wasn't it?" She took a cookie for herself. "Edmund and you had us in stitches with your childhood memories. I'd be hard-pressed to determine which of your mothers could've claimed that her son was the worst troublemaker."

"Probably mine." He sent her a boyish grin. "I was a real handful. That's why my parents gave me sketching lessons in the first place – a desperate attempt on their part to keep me still in one spot for more than ten minutes, and miraculously, it worked."

"I would hate to think of a world without your art in it." Her eyes traveled to the large seascape that now held pride of place over her mantel – his Christmas gift to her. "I find it so easy to lose myself in your paintings."

"Would you do me a favor?" he asked as his expression sobered.

"Anything." She straightened in response, wanting him to know that he had her full attention.

"Let me paint your portrait, full-length in the blue dress you wore to Montgomery's the last time we went to dinner." He took her hand where it rested on the cushion between them. "My hope is that this will be a special year for the two of us, and I want to capture your beauty as I know it at this moment – your lovely hair, your sweet face, the soft look in your eyes when they meet mine."

"It's been a while since my portrait was painted." Memories of her deceased husband's art studio filled her mind. "Time has taken its toll."

"Nonsense." Arthur shifted his position. "Time has merely recorded upon your face the life you have lived well, and it has left you all the better for its passage."

Gently, he lifted her chin with the tip of a slender finger, studied her delicate features for a moment with his artist's eye and then lowered his lips onto hers.

Four miles away, Kate Sinclair stood at the front window of the two-room and a bath suite she rented in the home of Jewel Parkerson in Captain's Point's historic district and gazed at the full moon, her right hand gently covering the bracelet on her left wrist.

"This is our year," Larry had whispered into her blonde curls, hugging her to him in The Cove's converted carriage house that now served as a garage before driving her home.

"I love you so much," he had continued. "Let's do what we're able to insure we can move forward quickly once you're free. Seeing you only at work and in group situations has been a necessity so far in order to keep you from being uncomfortable, but it won't be for long."

"No, it won't be for long," she had repeated his words, finding it hard to believe that she had come to Captain's Point only to attend her brother's wedding last fall and consider a move to the small town, as a first step towards making a new life for herself.

Ten minutes into the rehearsal dinner at Montgomery's restaurant, she had looked across the room and discovered a blond-haired, blue-eyed Greek god conversing with her brother.

"Let me introduce you to my cousin." Susan had guided her towards them.

And then, this handsome man had smiled down at her, and she had known in an instant that he was the love of her life.

It had been a simple matter to remain near him in the small gathering of family and close friends. Observing his interactions and listening closely to his words, she had seen and heard nothing that had changed her mind.

Three weeks later, she had returned to stay with her brother and his new wife until she was able to find a home of her own.

It had been Larry who had located her current abode, Larry who had offered her a position at Chesterton and Chesterton, the brokerage firm he owned with his uncle Anders, and Larry who had filled her thoughts until, finally, he had declared his love for her on the broad porch of her brother's home that overlooked the Atlantic.

Christmas Eve, they had left Blue Wolf Manor and detoured to Larry's luxurious condo over The Cove's carriage house to exchange gifts, laughing like two teenaged lovers who had snuck away from their parents as they rode up in the elevator.

First, he had opened her present – the driftwood carving of a sailboat that she had purchased for him at Drifters on the grounds of Montgomery House, and then he had surprised her.

Unwrapping the distinctive paper that signified Captain's Point's most expensive jewelry shop, she had revealed a long, flat velvet box, but he had placed his hand over hers before she could open it.

"You know that I love you," he had said, "but circumstances at this moment keep me from giving you the gift I would want you to have. Instead, I'm offering you this token of my affection, in hopes that your wearing it will be a sign between us that you're promised to me as soon as we can make our feelings for each other public."

Once opened, the box had revealed a delicate sapphire and diamond tennis bracelet that he had removed and clasped around her wrist, as she had fought back tears.

"I love you, too." She had smiled at him. "I agree we should make the best use of the time left. Your patience and understanding deserves to be rewarded as soon as it's in my power to do so."

And then, he had kissed her, and once again, she had fought the desire to accompany him to his bed, allowing him to drive her home instead.

Whether he believed in her decision not to date while still entangled in her non-marriage to Samuel Meriweather Sinclair V, she didn't know, but Larry had certainly respected her choice – never asking her to rethink her position.

Either way, he had already sacrificed too much for her to change gears, despite how good it felt to be held in his arms, wrapped in the heat emanating from his body as the light scent of his aftershave wafted around her.

Thank goodness, as he had said, it wouldn't be much longer now.

## CHAPTER V

In her own room along the hall, Jewel Parkerson turned off her bedside lamp. Her mind completely oblivious to the bedroom she had shared with her husband Bruce, who had died as the result of a mid-life heart attack three years previously, her thoughts centered instead on their friend since childhood, Herb Stuart.

Who would've thought that someone like Herb would suffer even a minor myocardial infarction? After all, the man had built Captain's Point's premier landscaping service from the ground up with his bare hands, and despite having passed the half-century mark, his abs were still as hard as rock.

Her Bruce now, he had always been a Type A personality, burning his candle at both ends even after Dr. Thompson warned him to slow down, eat better and exercise more. On the other hand, Herb had always been a quieter, gentler soul, spending his evenings with his wife Nancy and their son Jeff until her death from cancer two years before.

Now Herb's wife was gone, and Jeff had attained his majority – a handsome young man, who had looked to her for advice when his father had lain in a hospital bed connected to a plethora of tubes.

"What am I going to do with him, Aunt Jewel?" he had asked, using the name he had called her as a boy as a token of their families' friendship. "You know how he is. He has his pride, and he won't want me fussing over him, even if I can figure out what to do with the new diet and everything."

"Don't worry," she had assured the young man who reminded her so of his mother. "I'll be there for both of you. I still have a key to your house. Is it okay if I use it?"

The look of relief that had passed over Jeff's face had been all the answer she had needed.

When Herb's son had brought him home the next day, she had greeted them both at the door along with the aroma of roasting chicken. Fresh sheets had awaited the patient in his bed, bottled water was close at hand, and a comfortable chair had been shifted into a better position for his visitors.

For weeks now, she had rolled out of bed in response to her alarm before six and returned home after dark, but it had been worth it as they had spent the comfortable days together. Color had returned to Herb's cheeks, and she had watched as his spirits lifted. Tonight, though, he had surprised her, despite her own developing feelings.

Jeff had escorted Becca Tate to a young people's party at the church, leaving his father and her alone in the Stuarts' third bedroom that served as a den. Listening to old favorites playing softly on the stereo, they had completed several rounds of Hand and Foot at the game table, their scores almost even.

It had been Herb's turn to shuffle and deal, but instead he had placed the gathered cards in a stack to the side and had taken her hand in his.

"Thank you for everything you've been doing," he had begun. "I've hit my old stride again quicker because of the care and good food, and everything's been easier on Jeff because of your efforts."

"My pleasure," she had assured him. "Besides, we go back too far for me to have done any less."

Then silence had fallen over the room as he had gathered his thoughts, his thumb gently passing back and forth across her knuckles.

"Do you remember the morning you invited me in for fresh-baked cinnamon rolls?" he had asked, seemingly bringing the memory out of nowhere.

"Yes." She recalled how good it had felt to have him sitting in her kitchen.

"I said your Bruce was the closest thing to a brother I'd ever had, and perhaps, we should consider that a bit more in the biblical sense," he had reminded her.

This time, he hadn't turned and left the room, though, like he had on that earlier fall morning. This time, he had held her gaze, and she had felt the warmth of a blush filling her cheeks.

"I want to remind you that my thoughts were heading that way before this little medical blip," he had said.

"Okay." She had found it impossible to say anything else.

"As long as my Nancy was alive, I never looked to another woman, but I've loved Bruce and you all my life," he had continued.

"And we both loved Nancy and you," she had stated simply, once again on solid ground, not wanting her strong emotions to show through.

"Recently, my feelings have shifted." His gentle, gray eyes had locked onto hers. "The fact is, Jewel, I don't just love you anymore. I'm in love with you, and I recognized last fall that I'd been so for some time. The doctors say that if I take care of myself, I'll live to a ripe old age, and I want to share the years I have left with you."

She had opened her mouth to speak, but he had held up his free hand and stopped her.

"I know Bruce left you in a difficult financial position, and you've handled the situation well. Still, Larry Chesterton's a fool if he doesn't cement things with that pretty renter of yours as soon as he can, and I've never questioned that young man's intelligence.

"Stuart's Landscaping Services is a growing concern thanks to both my and Jeff's efforts, and I've got a pretty penny set aside. We're opening a whole new division in partnership with the Sheffields, Chestertons and Jeffersons in the new year, but keep that under your hat. My boy's never complained, but I know he could use an office here in the house.

"Marry me, Jewel. I love you, and I believe you have feelings for me," he had concluded. "We're both certainly lonely, and good marriages grow best from good friendships.

"I'll move into your house and give Jeff free rein of this one, so you won't have to leave any of your things or happy memories behind. You can feed me what the doctors have ordered, and I can watch out and care for you as we grow old together. Like they did in the olden days in the Bible, I'm asking to be allowed to marry my brother's widow. Will you have me?"

"Yes, I will." She had heard her own voice as if it had come from another.

A look of pure joy had filled the face of the man she had promised to marry as he had stood and drawn her into his arms, kissing her softly at first as they had felt their way along this new path before he had allowed his passion to show through.

Now, as she lay in the dark beneath the covers of her own bed, the memory of that single kiss once again washed over her.

"The doctors have assured me that I'll be able to satisfy all of your needs as your husband." He had held her to him, and she had been overwhelmed by how hard she now knew it would be to wait for him to do so.

Four blocks away, Becca Tate stood in the shadows on the porch of her family's large Italianate Victorian and hugged herself to keep warm as she watched Jeff Stuart drive away, her heart full and her mind reeling.

Tomorrow she would leave him and Captain's Point behind as she drove to Virginia where she would finish her undergraduate degree in history before heading to graduate school. Part of her knew this was what she must do to fulfill the dreams that had been her focus for many years, and part of her wondered if she could do it.

Thrown together since they were babes in their church's nursery, Jeff had been her friend – teaching her how to fish, standing up for her against the class bully and encouraging her to make the best of her talents. Recently, though, their relationship had shifted.

He had filled out in all the right places, muscles rippling beneath his T-shirts as his face had morphed into that of a man.

Suddenly, she had found herself looking forward to their lunch meetings in the community college's cafeteria in a new way, even as her banker father and social-climbing mother had made it clear that their plans for her lay in quite a different direction.

Slipping out of their home during her parents' pre-Christmas open house, she had met him by the fountain in the backyard where they had exchanged presents.

Surprised when he gifted her a gold heart pendant, she had been astounded by his declaration of love, pledging he would always be waiting for her and asking nothing in return, even as he had sealed his words with a kiss that had sent sparks flying through her body.

Ever since that evening, he had left no stone unturned as he had sought ways for them to be together, silently understanding that it would be best if he didn't ring for her at the front door, although this evening had been a close call.

Her parents had ordered food to be delivered at precisely the time she was expecting Jeff to arrive.

"They're here!" She had rushed out the front doorway and hurried down the steps, motioning him to get back into the car and then telling him to "Take off!" as soon as she had closed her door, not happy that they had to sneak around in such a way.

"It's okay." He had run his arm along the back of the seat and stroked her long hair until her breathing had calmed. "We're not doing anything wrong, and it's easier for you if they don't know."

"I hate it!" she had stated with a vehemence that caused him to pull into the deserted paved area behind a local business where he had turned off the car.

"Come here." He had kissed her hard and deep, his desire to possess her shining through, and she had responded in kind.

"I'm perfectly willing to end this cloak and dagger game, whenever you want." They had separated. "I can't stand seeing you this upset, though."

"I won't give you up." She had met his gaze head-on. "You're five times the man my father is."

"Good." His expression had softened, and he had kissed her again gently. "You hang onto that thought."

Once at the church, they had enjoyed a nice time surrounded by friends they had known all their lives – never touching, but nonetheless communicating silently all evening as his eyes never left hers.

Then the ball had dropped in Times Square on the flat screen in the Fellowship Hall, and he had somehow managed to maneuver her into a darkened Sunday School classroom for a long New Year's kiss.

A few minutes later, they had left, and he had once again pulled into the abandoned parking lot on their way to her home.

"I want you to know that I wish you the best." He had cupped her face in his hand. "I'll never ask you to give up your dreams for me, and this is your first step. Down the road, we'll find a way if you want me, okay?"

And all she had managed had been a shake of her head in agreement as she had fought back tears until he kissed them away.

The red of his vehicle's taillights disappearing around the corner, Becca let out a small sigh and turned the knob on the front door. Tomorrow she would take the first step towards her dreams like Jeff had said, but at what price?

## CHAPTER VI

Susan took in the fact that her husband's arms held her and the house around them was quiet as she woke slowly the next morning, surprised when she opened her eyes to find Jack smiling down at her.

"How long have you been awake?" she asked.

"I've been watching you sleep for about half an hour." His expression softened. "I'll never tire of finding you in my bed, and this morning, I remembered first thing that now there are two of you beside me."

"Are you hoping for a boy or a girl?"

"A girl," he answered with no hesitation, surprising her. "Obviously, I want most for our child to be healthy, but I've never felt the need for a carbon copy of myself and the Jefferson name has caused me more problems than pleasure.

"Besides, I already have the best of all sons," he pointed out. "Although, I would like to watch a little Susie grow up. Uncle Ivan said you were the cutest thing in pigtails he'd ever seen."

"Your Uncle Ivan always spoiled me." Memories of time spent with her husband's deceased relative on the broad back porch of their home rushed through her mind. "Any more thoughts on the subject?"

"You didn't tell me when the baby's due," he replied, "and I was wondering when we should tell Daniel."

"Based on information recorded in my file and her own observations, Janie set a tentative date of July 15, although ultrasounds may give us a better picture since I hadn't kept track like I usually do."

"In other words, we conceived this little one soon after we got married." He chuckled.

"We created plenty of opportunities for it to happen." She grinned back at him. "And no one can say that you aren't a man in your prime."

"Compliment accepted." He planted a firm kiss on her lips. "Know that I'm on yellow alert anytime you need my services. Now what about Daniel?"

"What do you think?"

"The sooner the better." Jack surprised her again. "Your mother knows about my suspicions, which means Anders knows, too, and I wouldn't be surprised if Larry's been brought into the fold as well."

"Which would mean that both Chase and your sister would be told to keep it to themselves, but…" Susan let out a small laugh. "I'm surprised Adrianna hasn't already asked me for confirmation. Why did you advise my mom of your suspicions?"

"Because we were having so many of our holiday meals at The Cove, and I wasn't sure you'd realized that you were pregnant," he explained. "As our hostess, she was the only one who could ensure that you weren't served alcoholic beverages."

"So that's why we only had your grandmother's fruit punch and soft drinks offered to us with Thanksgiving dinner." Understanding dawned on her. "And yet, champagne was served last evening."

"Yes, but by then you had already refused wine on three occasions when I knew you would've usually accepted a glass, so I assumed you had figured it out and were keeping it to yourself for some reason," he filled her in. "Although I provided plenty of sparkling apple and grape juice, so it was there for you. Anyway, I didn't want to take chances with our little treasure."

"I love you, Jack Jefferson." She cupped his cheek as she heard their son playing with his two canine friends, Casey and Lady, in his room.

"I love you, too, Mrs. Jefferson." He covered her lips with his, leaving no question in her mind as to his intentions for later.

"Mommy! Daddy!" The sound of footsteps running along the hall punctuated the words before the door to the master bedroom was flung open. "We're awake."

"So you are, Charger," Jack greeted their son as he swung his legs off the bed and reached for his jeans. "Glad to see that you're dressed and ready to go. Let's give these dogs a run, and then we'll all have some breakfast, after which your mom and I have something we'd like to discuss with you."

"I'll put on my coat." Daniel gestured for his furry shadows to accompany him downstairs, and the room grew quiet.

"I've promised to help the little guy string chunks of bread on the Christmas tree for the birds sometime this morning, so we can get it off the porch." Jack bent to tie his tennis shoes. "Want to join us?"

"No, you two go ahead," Susan replied. "I have bills I should take care of if I don't want the payments to be late."

"Payments?" He glanced up surprised. "You mean you have ongoing financial responsibilities? Why didn't you tell me?"

"Because I didn't want to bother you," she explained. "Besides, now that we're married, I can apply more of my salary to them. They'll be gone in no time at all."

For a moment, silence filled their room as Jack cleared his head of the emotions that were running through him. How could he have been so stupid? How worried had she been about these responsibilities?

Pulling himself together, he took her hand.

"Susie, once we've eaten breakfast and told Daniel our news, but before I do the tree with him, you and I are going to retire to the library and pay off those bills." He fought to keep his voice calm. "Then we'll have a long overdue conversation about the state of our joint financial affairs, so that you'll understand how unnecessary it is for you to pay interest on anything, okay?"

"But…"

"No, buts." He heard the firmness in his tone. "Please."

"If that's what you want," she agreed, much to his relief. "Remember, though, Chase and Adrianna are expecting us at Montgomery House to watch the football games."

"I'm sure we'll have time for me to give you an overview," he stated, but then he noticed the way her fingers were picking at the top sheet and rolled back onto the bed, drawing her to him.

"I'm not upset with you." He stroked her cheek. "If anything, I'm upset with myself. Now you freshen up and join us downstairs, where I'll have started breakfast. After all, you're eating for two, and from this day forward, I'm concentrating all my efforts on spoiling you."

# CHAPTER VII

"We're here!" Daniel called out as soon as he entered the foyer of Montgomery House later that afternoon.

"Yes, you are." Adrianna hurried from the home's kitchen to greet her guests as Chase appeared on the landing above them.

"Pre-game's been rather boring," the latter announced as he headed down the staircase. "Still, watching New Year's Day football is a tradition that should be continued."

"Absolutely!" Jack sent his friend a high-five, then turned and gave his son one as well.

"We've only invited you three, Larry and Kate," Adrianna filled them in as her husband took their guests' coats. "The tower room doesn't hold that many people, and it seemed like we'd spent our time recently in one large gathering after another."

"A quiet evening sounds good to me," Susan stated, and something in her tone caused Jack to glance sharply from where he was retrieving a container holding two of his wife's lemon meringue pies from the foyer table.

Thinking they might need to cut their evening short if she appeared to be tiring, he vowed to keep an eye on her as he followed the group towards the Sheffield's kitchen, breathing in the aroma of chili that was emanating from the large room.

"Shhhhh!" Daniel stopped traffic by turning in the doorway and blocking the others' way, before repeating words he had heard from the adults who surrounded him.

"Cousin Larry is kissing Aunt Kate, and we should give them their privacy."

"Sounds to me like there's more simmering in that room than a pot of chili." Chase grinned down at his wife.

"Careful, Sheffield, that's my sister you're talking about." Jack worked to keep a straight face.

"And my cousin," Susan chimed in.

"Who are doing what they're doing in my kitchen," their host stated, building his case.

"Children are often best seen and not heard." Larry turned his gaze onto his short cousin.

"Not this one." Kate sat on her heels and opened her arms, gesturing for the boy to come and receive a hug. "Daniel is free to speak his mind in my presence whenever he wants. It's just that we'd prefer to keep this a secret amongst ourselves, okay?" She kissed his cheek. "Can you remember?"

"Sure, I can." He nodded in agreement. "It's the same as with our family's other secret."

"Your other secret?" Kate shifted her gaze to her brother, who was now standing in the doorway – his wife's pies sitting on the counter beside them, his arms wrapped around Susan from behind with his hands resting on her belly, a slow smile taking up residence on his face.

"You're pregnant!" His sister stood and hurried forward.

"Pregnant? Who?" Larry turned from where he had been stirring the chili.

"I'll say one thing for you, Jefferson." Chase extended his hand for a congratulatory shake. "You certainly get things done fast."

"Even we were surprised by this." Susan accepted a kiss on one cheek from Adrianna and on the other from her law partner.

"My brother is a man in his prime." Kate grinned up at the object of her teasing who was hugging her to him with his right arm, while still encompassing his wife with his left.

"That's exactly what Susie was saying this morning." He beamed down at the two of them.

"Congratulations, Tiger!" Larry scooped Daniel into his arms. "I was afraid you would end up an only child like me, but now you're going to be a big brother like your uncle, Andy."

"We'll probably put our baby in the room next to Aunt Kate's," the youngster informed the group, referring to the guest room his aunt had used when she had first arrived in Captain's Point.

"Sounds like you have everything figured out." Larry moved forward in line, first kissing Susan on the cheek and then shaking Jack's hand. "When's the new one due?"

"Janie's set the date as July 15 as of now," Susan filled them in, "but please keep it to yourselves, except for my mom and dad who already know. July's a long way off, and I don't want to be pestered by questions from well-meaning friends yet."

"Mum's the word," Chase agreed. "Although you might want to let Penny and Otis into the secret. As often as you two are here, they're almost bound to overhear something sooner rather than later." He interjected the Sheffield's housekeeper and her husband, who had managed the Montgomery Properties since Adrianna had been a child, into the mix.

"You're right." Jack nodded his agreement after a quick glance in Susan's direction. "Feel free to tell them next time you see them."

"Believe me, they can both keep a secret," Adrianna spoke up from where she was unloading bowls of potato salad and heavenly hash from the refrigerator.

The timer on the double oven let out a firm ding, and Chase answered its call, donning an oven mitt and removing two pones of cornbread the tops of which he spread liberally with butter.

"Looks like we're going to enjoy a real feast," Jack uttered his approval. "Is there anything we can do to help?"

"No, we're serving buffet style from here on the island," Adrianna stated. "If everyone will get themselves something to drink and fill their plates, we have places set at the round table in the morning room."

"Good friends, good food, football, a new baby on the way, and renovations on Montgomery House starting tomorrow." Chase gestured for Jack and Susan to go first, understanding their need to take care of Daniel as well. "The new year has gotten off to a great start."

# CHAPTER VIII

Something was clearly wrong with his wife, Jack realized later that evening as he watched her move about their room, straightening a lamp and then rearranging an afghan where it lay ready on the back of the couch.

True to her word, she had allowed him to pay off the remaining year on her car loan that morning, along with the next quarter's fees for Daniel's kindergarten and a much larger than he had anticipated balance on her single credit card from before their marriage.

Her explanation of how the charges on the latter had accrued had appalled him, as his dislike of her ex had grown even deeper. The fact that she had stayed with the other man as his wife for so many years he now recognized as a cautionary tale of how much she would subjugate her own wishes for another, even someone she no longer loved and viewed only as her child's father.

As they had shifted to an overview of the financial dealings he had brought with him to their marriage, she had given him her full attention, but her face had shown no indication as to her reaction with two exceptions.

When he had pointed out that Blue Wolf Manor and the farm he had inherited from his uncle were now owned jointly by the two of them, so she would never be parted from her favorite view of the ocean, she had kissed his cheek.

"Thank you," she had said in a soft voice. "That was thoughtful of you."

Thoughtful? He had turned over her word choice in his mind. Why would he have done otherwise, loving her as he did?

Then he had moved on to the seven-figure trust fund he had set up for Daniel prior to their marriage, as well as the fact that two of the farms he had purchased since taking up residence in Captain's Point, both of which backed onto their home's property, would pass to their son.

"Oh, Jack…" She had been unable to continue her sentence as she had buried her face in his shoulder, and he had held her tightly in his arms as she had cried.

"I couldn't have done anything less for our boy now, could I?" he had asked once her tears had been spent.

"His own father hasn't even paid his child support," she had explained, "and yet, you do all of this out of the goodness of your heart."

"No, I did this because Daniel's my son in every way that matters," he had corrected her. "I'll do the same, but no more for our little treasure as soon as he or she arrives on the scene. As far as I'm concerned, the two of them will share equal positions in my heart, second only to yours."

When he had asked what, if anything, she was doing about the missing child support, she had shared that her ex-husband had lost his job, as a result of a restructuring at the agency where he had worked, three weeks after their divorce had been finalized.

The jerk was still unemployed, and she preferred not to pursue the unpaid support given their history, much to his own relief.

Being limited by his promise to Daniel about the Christmas tree and their plans with their friends, they hadn't talked about handling their monetary affairs going forward.

The discussion had ended with his giving her the two credit cards he had ordered for her prior to their marriage – one he preferred and another that was more widely accepted – and her agreement to use the cards going forward whenever she purchased groceries or everyday household items.

"Susie?" He attempted to look nonchalant as he set his tablet on the bedside cabinet beside him. "Do you remember the communication exercise in your women's magazine that we did one evening not long after we got married – the one that involved threads of conversation for which there would be no repercussions?"

"Yes?" She looked up from where she was reorganizing the contents of a small desk drawer, her eyes filled with a haunted look that he hated to see there yet again.

"Would you be willing to take a few minutes for another couple of threads?"

"You want to sit cross-legged on the bed, hold hands and ask each other questions?" she asked, her tone illustrating her disbelief.

"For a thread or two." He gestured for her to join him as he stood, straightened the covers and then took the required position, relieved when she obliged.

"You first." She took his larger hands in her slim ones. "It was your idea this time."

"It's about our discussion this morning," he began, immediately aware of her body tensing across from his. "I may have been a bit overbearing, and I want to make sure that I haven't offended you.

"It's just that the old-fashioned romantic you're always saying you love in me would have a hard time looking in a mirror, if I didn't provide for Daniel and you in the way that I feel I should," he sought to explain. "You're not angry with me are you?"

"Angry with you?" Surprise filled Susan's face, even as her body visibly relaxed. "Because you want to take us under your wing in such a wonderful way? Of course, not."

"Not at all?"

"Not at all."

"So we're completely okay," he persevered, "and you're not upset about anything?"

"I'm not upset," she reassured him, but then a small crease formed between her brows. "I'm afraid, though, that I've disappointed you terribly by bringing a financial mess into our marriage."

"I'm not disappointed," Jack interrupted her. "I can honestly say there hasn't been a single moment since we met when I would've used that word to describe my feelings towards you. What made you think that I was?"

"I knew you were an extremely successful author, both with your Anderson series and your literary novels, as well as an exceptionally talented musician and composer," she replied. "I also realized you were astute when it came to real estate investment, particularly in regards to leasing out your grandmother's farm in Virginia and the three farms on the other side of the lake here.

"Still, I had no idea how actively involved you were in the business world. The few times you've mentioned the drilling equipment firm, you made it sound as if you merely collected ongoing checks as a result of a lucky investment you made years ago to help out a friend. In point of fact, you hold a corporate position and are actively involved in major decisions."

"Only on a flexible, part-time basis," he reminded her.

"In addition, the fortune you've accrued from your investments probably amazed even Larry," she point out. "It certainly amazed me.

"You must think I'm an idiot to have ended up with my debts, especially since I could've liquidated some of my own investments and eliminated them myself." She studied his face. "The fact is I didn't want Larry to know I owed the money, because he would've wanted to take care of my bills for me."

Feeling as if his left leg was going to sleep, Jack adjusted his position.

"Why don't we plump up the pillows, and I'll fill you in more about my corporate responsibilities?" he suggested.

Once they were resettled a few moments later, her head on his shoulder and his arms around her, he continued, "First and foremost, I know full well that you're an intelligent woman, and I recognize that you merely did what you had to do in order to survive and then arrange for your and Daniel's escape from the disastrous situation in which you found yourself. Frankly, I'm proud of you for pulling it all off as well as you did."

"Are you really?"

"Absolutely!"

"I'm just glad I found the courage to do so." She faced him. "Otherwise, Daniel and I would've missed out on all this." She made a small gesture with her hand that encompassed the room around them.

"I'm not talking about the money, you understand," she continued. "I'm talking about our living in this big, happy house, as Daniel puts it, and our being cared for by you in the way that I recognized we would be when I only knew you as the marina manager. Can I share something that may sound a bit silly?"

"Be as silly as you wish," he encouraged her to go on, relieved she sounded so happy and relaxed.

"Ever since you first showed me this room, I've held an image in my head of you as some sort of magical, golden bird that swooped into Captain's Point and set about preparing his nest, before taking up a position on the boardwalk and keeping an eye out for a suitable mate."

A hint of pink entered her cheeks. "Then along came Billy Spooner, who snatched my purse and gave you the perfect opportunity to show off your power and good looks to the first single woman who came along."

"To the most beautiful woman that I'd ever set eyes on," he corrected, even as he fought to get his brain around an image of himself as some sort of golden bird.

"Anyway." She brushed the compliment aside. "I already loved the downstairs of the house and the view of the ocean, but the minute I stepped foot in this room I knew I'd come home to our nest. I know it sounds ridiculous, but there it is."

"I'll never comprehend a woman's thought processes," he admitted, "but I'm perfectly willing to consider you as my lifetime mate, especially as we've already created a little one in this room who's now growing inside of you."

His hand covered their unborn child as he drew her closer for a kiss that led to another that deepened, until all thoughts of his corporate position vanished, and by unspoken agreement, they left their conversational thread behind in deference to a more pleasurable physical pursuit.

# CHAPTER IX

As he had always done as a child on the first day of school, Chase awoke in Montgomery House's tower suite bedroom before the alarm was set to go off the next morning, his thoughts focused on the renovations that were scheduled to begin in two hours.

While part of him was dreading the dust and the mess, another part of him couldn't wait to see the remodel completed.

First and foremost in his mind were the new dressing room and connecting bath with steam shower that would be formed by combining the existing upstairs hallway bath and a small bedroom.

The fact that this would necessitate his sharing the tower suite bathroom with Adrianna for a few weeks had not bothered either of them. In fact, she had gone so far as to point out that their sharing a shower on a more frequent basis offered up all sorts of possibilities beyond the mere application of soap and water.

Reflexively, he tightened his hold on her slightly and she snuggled closer in such a way as to set his blood racing.

Not wishing to disturb her sleep further, he forced his thoughts onto the elevator that would run from an unneeded storage room next to the kitchen to the third floor, where several servants' bedrooms would be converted into a media and games room.

Here Adrianna had insisted, rightly, that he expand his original idea to include a full kitchenette and serving bar with a dumbwaiter running alongside the elevator shaft.

Watching movies or the Super Bowl with their friends would soon be an entirely different ballgame to what it had been.

How lucky he was to have found the woman he loved at precisely the moment that he had done so. Life had taken its toll on him, but her warm, giving heart had turned everything around, softening his hardened edges.

Now he treasured every minute of their lives together – her shy smile, their home-based routines, the feel of her in his arms. The only things needed to complete the picture were the children whose laughter would ring forth in the new rooms that would be added during this and the second wave of renovations planned for later.

The alarm ringing forth, Chase reached over Adrianna and turned it off, not surprised when she slid her arms around his neck in response and drew him to her.

Never one to waste an opportunity, he gave himself up to the moment as thoughts of sharing future showers with his wife once again filled his head.

In his master suite an hour later, Larry's hand found the button on his alarm a moment after it jerked him awake from a warm, fuzzy dream in which Kate and he were snuggled on the couch in the front room of Chesterton and Chesterton watching a football game. Where in the world had that one come from?

Rolling onto his back, he forced his eyes to remain open as he slid his arm along the cool sheets to his left, wishing with all of his heart that the woman in his dreams had been resting there.

Three more months, only a few weeks, not all that many days remained until she would be free so he could make her his own, and he was finding it harder and harder to wait.

Throwing back the covers, he flipped on the bedside lamp and made his way to the bathroom, where he paused beside a wall calendar showing the first three and a half months of the year, picked up the pen that hung with it and crossed off New Year's Day.

The good news was that, in a little over an hour, he would pick up his Kate at her front door and work beside her all day. The bad news was that he would have to return her to her own home.

Maybe, just maybe, she would accompany him to his place first, where they could cook and eat dinner together, finishing off the evening listening to music while they snuggled on the real couch in his den.

At almost the same moment the warm water of his shower hit Larry's broad shoulders, Becca Tate opened the drapes in her dorm room, let in the morning sun and examined the college campus spread before her.

Filled with the feeling that this was the first day of the rest of her life, she couldn't ignore the ache in her heart. Life without Jeff in it suddenly seemed empty.

What was he doing at this moment?

Like her, he would head for his first class of the year at some point during the day, but he might put in several hours on jobs for the landscaping service first.

No, wait. This was the first day of renovations at Montgomery House, and the Sheffields had asked him to make himself available as much as possible.

Feeling slightly better now that she could envision him going about his activities, she opened her sweater drawer determined that, as soon as she returned to her room, she would send him a first email.

In her home, a few minutes later, Susan stepped into her clawfoot bathtub and slid beneath the warm, bubble-topped water she had prepared, her eyes resting on the antique rose-covered, hand-painted tiles her husband had secured for her pleasure even before she had heard his proposal.

How wonderful it was to be loved by a man like her Jack, who was even now in their kitchen – feeding the dogs, fixing their breakfasts and spending a few minutes of quality time with their son over his cereal.

Closing her eyes, she called forth the memory of the joy that had filled her husband's face as they had discussed their new pregnancy, so different from the disdain and indifference that had accompanied her carrying Daniel.

With hindsight, she wished she had left her disastrous marriage even earlier, but at the time, the task before her had seemed overwhelming.

Downstairs, Jack placed a small stack of printed papers on the kitchen table, each sheet carrying a single column of rectangular boxes running from top to bottom.

"You understand what we're doing, right?" He picked up the top sheet and put it in front of his son, who held a mechanical pencil tightly in the fingers of his right hand.

"We're counting down the days until our baby will be where we can see it," Daniel replied.

"That's right." Jack took the seat next to him. "According to my calculations, we have 195 days to go, so you will enter this number in the top box on our first page."

He pushed a sticky note with the number of days showing on it into a better position for his stepson to see.

"Tomorrow, we will enter that number minus one in the next box down the row and cross out the day before," Jack explained further. "Does that make sense?"

"I think so, but we're doing this together, right?" A somewhat lopsided 1 gradually took shape in the top box beneath the little guy's fingers.

"We'll do this and a lot of other things together," Jack assured him.

He lifted the boy's hand and placed the tip of the pencil lead in the right position to begin the 9.

"The way I look at it, we men have to stick together, and while your mama has the primary job in all of this, it's our role as her coaches to support and encourage her." He overlooked his stepson's progress.

"Like on television last night?" Daniel added a tail to his carefully drawn, oversized circle.

"Exactly." His stepfather again placed his hand in the right spot to begin the next number. "By counting down the days, we'll be helping her judge her progress. We'll also encourage her to rest, eat well and take it easy. Basically, we're going to pamper your mama."

"Does the baby know that we're doing this?" Daniel asked.

"Not now, but I think we'll keep our crossed out sheets, so we can show them to him or her later, if you agree," Jack suggested.

"Then they'll know we were looking forward to their coming." The box now held three figures, the 5 at the end looking a bit more like a 6.

"Very good." Jack gave his approval. "I'm glad we started writing your numbers last fall when you turned five. Now, why don't you hang this on the refrigerator door with a couple of your magnets, and then we can take it off and fill in the next box in the morning."

"Mama!" Daniel turned away a few moments later from his chart where it now hung on the stainless steel door. "We're tracking your progress."

"You are?" Susan lifted one finely formed brow in the direction of her husband.

"Daniel's combining his number writing skills with some elementary subtraction," Jack explained, "and I've started working on a list of things that we'll need to do to get ready."

"Such as?" She took a seat at the table where her place setting and glass of juice were already waiting.

"Furnish the nursery, purchase new car seats, buy clothes and diapers, order birth announcements, and interview nannies for starters." Jack broke four eggs into a bowl.

"Dear me." Susan let out a small laugh. "All of that, and here I was thinking we could relax and take our time, since we have over six months to go."

"Jack says 195 days will rush by really fast," Daniel informed her, "so we're going to encourage you."

"What I need most this morning is a big hug from both of you." Susan turned to her son, who slid his arms around her neck and squeezed.

"Now you." She held out her hand to her husband, who crossed the room and drew her into his arms. "I love you, Jack Jefferson," she said.

"I love you, Susie Chesterton." He dropped a kiss on her nose.

"Like Daniel, how lucky our child will be to have you as his or her father." She smiled up at him.

"And you as their mother." He found her lips and kissed her thoroughly as the knowledge of exactly how blessed he was filled him.

## CHAPTER X

In the breakfast room two properties away, Chase covertly observed his wife over the rim of his coffee mug as she rechecked the demolition To Do List she had been working on for weeks. How was he going to leave her and Montgomery House this morning?

Susan had offered to switch her working from home day with his, but that would've just meant that he'd have to go into the office tomorrow. Hopefully, by taking a long lunch hour and leaving for home early, he wouldn't miss too much of what would probably be an uneventful process.

Getting his mind around that part of the problem, though, didn't resolve the entire issue. These last two holiday weeks spent at home with his wife had flown by too fast, and what she had done this morning had inadvertently made it more difficult for him to leave her.

Responding to her invitation, they had started their morning with a slow, easy lovemaking before recapping their plans for their day. Wanting to discuss a couple of items with Otis before leaving, he had left their room to get dressed for work as she had busied herself with making their bed.

A couple of minutes later, she had joined him in the hallway bathroom.

"I wanted to return your jersey," she had said, the problem being that she was wearing it – only it.

"Oh, you did, did you?" he had teased, rubbing his shaving cream covered jaws along both of her cheeks.

"This is the first room in which we showered together." She had sent him a shy smile, and he had felt his throat tighten. "It seems sad that we're going to demolish it without some sort of send-off."

Gently, he had wiped the cream from her face with a hand towel and then held her to him until she had snuggled against him in a way that freed his hands, so he could finish his shave without injury.

"So…" He had rinsed off his razor and set it aside. "Exactly what sort of send-off did you have in mind, Mrs. Sheffield?"

One thing had led to another until no one could now say that the old-fashioned shower stall hadn't been sent-off in style.

Now, here she sat next to him, wearing little or no makeup, a chartreuse T-shirt that set off her eyes and a pair of old jeans, and all he wanted was to bundle her back up to the tower suite and make love to her over and over throughout the day – his need for her a never-ending constant in his life.

"You'll be late if you don't hurry." She put her clipboard aside as he tossed back the rest of his coffee. "I'll call you if anything unexpected happens – anything at all."

"I know." He stood and planted a firm kiss on her lips. "Promise me that you'll be careful. There will be plenty of men available for the heavy work. Your role is to supervise along with Otis."

"I promise." She placed her hand on his cheek, and his heart skipped a beat. "Please don't worry."

"And you'll wear this?" He reached to the side table and retrieved a bright pink hard hat, plopping it onto her dark waves at a rakish angle that allowed him the access he needed for a second, deeper kiss.

"Whenever I hear your voice in my mind telling me that I should," she stated, and he went in for a third, wondering why he was doing this to himself, even as he couldn't stop.

"Chase." Adrianna pulled the brim of the hardhat to a horizontal position. "I hear Otis in the mudroom."

"Otis?" Her husband looked at her through glazed eyes.

"You remember Otis." She grinned. "My property manager and now our business partner in the new venture. I'll go fetch your overcoat, while you ask him the question about the elevator that Jack and you discussed last evening."

"Jeff is accepting delivery of the larger dumpster as we speak." The object of their conversation appeared in the doorway to the kitchen where he absentmindedly smoothed his grizzled hair. "The crew is gathering their tools."

"Glad you're here," Chase stated as his other half slipped from the room. "I have a quick question."

Two minutes later, Penny interrupted the men's conversation as she handed the lawyer his overcoat. "Your wife said to tell you she would see you at lunch," their housekeeper passed on the message. "She's greeting the crew."

Making her way through the kitchen garden with Max, the couple's Chihuahua/Beagle mix rescue, on his leash by her side, Adrianna let out a small sigh.

At thirty-four, her husband was too young to retire, and no one could spend every waking moment in bed – day after day, week after week, year after year – no matter how pleasurable it was although, if it was worth a try, it would be with her Chase.

Hopefully, this new real estate venture they were putting together with their friends would provide a middle ground for him as well as a meaningful occupation for her.

Turning left, she was greeted by Montgomery House's black-and-white, outdoor cat Nip at the entrance to the vine-covered tunnel leading to the converted carriage house that would be designated as construction central over the next couple of months.

For a moment, she recalled similar situations during the early days of her residence at Montgomery House almost a year earlier, although then she had only just met Chase Augustus Sheffield, Attorney at Law, and had no idea of the fabulous future that stretched before her.

Reaching her destination, she paused and took in the front of the large, gray granite home that had been built two centuries earlier, complete with its three-story, octagonal tower and slate roof, by the sea captain Jebediah Montgomery.

"Watch over our progress today," she whispered to her ancestor, into the wind coming off Captain's Point from the ocean that he had loved. "Something tells me that the house has a lot more secrets to reveal."

# CHAPTER XI

"I've found it!" Kate Sinclair's crystal blue eyes sparkled with excitement as Larry came around the front of his Mercedes SUV to open the passenger door, picking her up on his way to work.

"Found what?"

"The first property for our newly formed Sheffield and Montgomery Enterprises, Inc., to buy and flip or rent out," she filled him in.

"Here?" He glanced along Tuttle Avenue, the quiet street in Captain's Point's historic district where she lived, unable to discover a For Sale sign.

"Look over my shoulder at the bungalow next door to Jewel's house." She kept her own back to the property, not wishing to draw attention to their interest. "The one with the sagging gutter and cracked window."

"Sarah Ridgewell's old home," he stated. "A young couple bought it from her about the same time that Bruce passed away, when Sarah moved to North Carolina to be near her son and daughter-in-law."

"That's right." She beamed at him. "I knew you would have the particulars filed away in your brilliant mind. According to Jewel, the house needed updates to the kitchen and bathrooms, but otherwise, it was in good repair when this couple bought it. The boiler is fairly new, and the roof is less than ten years old."

"Sounds like something we should consider," he agreed, "but it doesn't appear to be on the market."

"Which means we may be able to purchase it directly from the owners and save a realtor's fee, if we hurry," she pointed out. "The couple has done some demolition inside since moving in, so the house won't show well. He turned out to be a jerk, has had at least two affairs, and they're getting a divorce."

"What put you onto all of this?"

"I was ready a bit earlier than usual this morning, so I took a quick walk around the block." She absentmindedly slipped her gloved hand into his. "When I returned, the woman was crying by her mailbox."

"So you offered to help, and one thing led to another," he picked up the story.

"Exactly."

"Sounds to me as if the ball's in our court."

Instead of opening the SUV's door as he had planned, Larry led his fellow investor in Adrianna and Chase's new financial venture along the sidewalk, excitement building within him.

"Renovations are starting on Montgomery House as we speak, and your brother's probably making eyes at my cousin over their breakfast," he reminded her. "Let's you and I check this out and indicate our interest."

"Without an appointment?" Kate hurried to keep pace as he headed up the bungalow's front walk.

"This way, we'll see the thorns as well as the roses." He grinned as his finger found the front doorbell.

"Yes?" A bleached-blonde in her early twenties peered at them through a crack she had made in the front doorway, as she pulled a thin cardigan sweater together across her chest.

"My name is Larry Chesterton, and I believe you met Kate this morning." The broker nodded towards his partner in crime. "I understand you're thinking of selling your house."

"I'm selling it alright." The woman's eyes narrowed. "I want my share of the money we put in it. Why?"

"It happens that I've been considering the purchase of a home in this neighborhood," Larry explained. "Do you have a realtor I should contact in regards to a showing?"

"I'm thinking of selling it myself." The crack in the doorway widened. "Why don't you come inside?"

A mixture of stale cooking odors and unattended cat litter greeting them in the foyer, Kate caught Larry's gaze, but he sent her a silent warning and reached into the inner pocket of his suit coat.

"My business card," he stated as he passed it to the home's owner. "As a financial advisor, I would encourage you to sell the home on your own, thus saving the realtor's fee."

"Gee, thanks." The woman's face softened. "Chesterton and Chesterton. I've seen your office on Main Street. My name's Hannah Smith. My cheating, soon to be ex-husband has moved out, and I've started packing, so you'll have to excuse the mess."

"I like the way the rooms flow from the foyer," Kate spoke up. "So often in these Craftsman bungalows, you step directly into the living room."

"That's exactly what I told Rick when we first saw the house." Hannah gestured for them to proceed into the main living area. "We wanted to turn all of this into open space, but my husband only tore out the kitchen before he started making his way through the female population of Captain's Point."

Noting the original, stained-wood moldings and built-in china cabinet in the dining room, Kate raised an eyebrow. If nothing else, the home needed to be rescued.

"I've been doing dishes in the upstairs bathroom for two and half years now." Their hostess added a whine to her voice. "Up and down those stairs, carrying tubs of dirty dishes, for two and half years."

"You understand that having no kitchen in place will devalue the house, don't you?" Larry didn't wait for an answer. "I would require a current appraisal of value, the same as a mortgage company, although mine would be a cash purchase."

"Cash?" The homeowner's thin features brightened, then fell. "An appraisal would cost me, though, wouldn't it?"

"A good appraisal runs anywhere from two to four hundred dollars in this area," he filled her in. "My partners and I could cover the cost that would be subtracted from the purchase price, enabling you to set an asking price. This would save you from incurring an out-of-pocket expense."

Behind their hostess, Kate glanced into the kitchen and sent him a negative nod. "Might we get a quick tour of the upstairs?" she asked.

"Go ahead." The younger woman gestured for them to reenter the foyer.

Left to themselves, the two interested buyers made their way to the second floor, where they were appalled by the mess that greeted them, but pleased with the overall layout.

"You're a treasure." Larry threw his arm around Kate as she reentered the master bedroom from the ensuite bathroom that had surprised them with its presence. "This is a real opportunity for our new firm."

"I'm glad you're as excited as I am." She smiled at him and received a quick kiss as a reward.

"So much so that I think we should detour to Montgomery House on our way to the office." Larry steered her towards the hallway that led to the stairs. "Way to go, girl. I've said it before, and I'll say it again. We make a great team. Together, we can pull off anything."

## CHAPTER XII

Adrianna felt a tug on Max's leash moments before Chase's overcoated arms wrapped around her from behind. "I'm barely out of the house and you already have another man coming to see you." He kissed her temple removing the sting from his words.

"Who?" Adrianna swung her gaze away from her home's façade.

"Our architect has decided to pay you a visit." Chase nodded towards a Marlborough and Company van that was making its way up Montgomery House's long drive. "I'll wait a minute to make sure you don't need me."

"We weren't expecting him today," she reminded her husband. "Montgomery Properties is acting as subcontractor when it comes to the demolition."

"Good morning, folks." Pete disembarked and hurried around the front bumper as soon as he had brought the van to a stop, his thick, auburn hair lifting in the breeze. "Looks like we're having a good first day weather-wise."

"The crew is already assembling," Adrianna addressed the new arrival. "Did you stop by out of interest, or has something come up?"

"Mainly out of general interest," the young architect, who had won this major opportunity after completing reconstruction of what was now the Sheffield Place Inn to the owners' satisfaction, admitted. "Although I did wonder if you've stumbled over the original house plans."

"Not yet, and between us we've given the house a good once-over," Chase stated. "I'm headed to my office, but I wanted to run something by you in regards to the elevator. Would you mind taking a minute to walk with me to the garage?"

"Not at all." Pete waited as the lawyer gave his wife a quick squeeze, his mind immediately traveling to the chestnut hair and amber eyes of Julia Henderson, his firm's historically accurate interior designer.

It had only been a few weeks since he had recognized his growing feelings for the woman he had known since she was in grade school, and now his thoughts were filled with her as he strove to match Chase's longer strides along the sidewalk towards the relatively new structure.

Left to themselves, Adrianna entered the open bay in the carriage house accompanied by Max, who immediately worked his way through the men, receiving an absentminded pat from this one and a last bite of sausage from that one before taking a seat on the floor by his mistress.

"There you are," Otis greeted her from where he was pointing to a large blueprint spread across a sheet of plywood supported by two sawhorses.

"Have I missed much?" she asked.

"I was explaining to the crew how we're dividing into two teams," her property manager stated. "Team One will work with me, demolishing the hallway bath, and Team Two will start on the third-floor rooms. Once the easier part is done, we'll work our way from the top to the main floor, opening up what will become the elevator and dumbwaiter shafts."

"Does everyone understand their role in this?" Adrianna glanced around the group of familiar faces, receiving a mixed response of nodding heads in the affirmative. "As before, if you have any questions, please ask Otis, Jeff or myself before moving forward. In the long run, that usually saves time and money."

A murmur of agreement made its way through the group.

"Also, you'll be working inside of my family's historic home," she continued. "We've done what we can to cover and protect the inside surfaces, but please take your time, watch your step and limit the opportunities for collateral damage."

"We'd also appreciate it if you would clean as you go," Otis interjected. "Chase and Adrianna, as well as Max here – he pointed to the dog, who looked ready for work in his gray sweatshirt stamped with the words Construction Consultant – will still be in residence. Use the vacuums we've provided to cut down on dust as much as possible, and we've already discussed how we want plastic barriers installed as a first step."

"In addition, if you should uncover anything of interest, anything out of the ordinary at all, please call one of us or Pete Marlborough to look at it immediately," she added.

"Did I hear my name being taken in vain?" The architect entered through the open bay.

"Adrianna was pointing out that we want to be advised of anything out of the ordinary," Otis repeated her words.

"Absolutely," Pete agreed. "There's no telling what we may find in a fine old home like this one. Interesting items being used as insulation, unusual construction methods and even dated signatures of previous persons of skill who worked on the home have turned up in other renovations I've dealt with. If nothing else, we would want to document these for the record."

"Okay, guys, if there are no more questions, let's get a move on." Otis carefully rolled up the blueprint and replaced it in its storage tube.

Inside the house, Adrianna and Pete remained in the foyer, now emptied of its large octagonal table, as the teams began the laborious process of hanging the plastic dividers.

"I see you've shut off as many rooms as possible." The architect nodded towards the mahogany pocket doors that were closed where they led off the foyer into the first and second parlors as well as the formal dining room.

"Penny and I have spent hours taping white sheets over the soft furnishings as well," Adrianna filled him in. "Needless to say, it's going to be messy, but it'll be worth it in the end. Chase and I are both thrilled with the tiles and fixtures that Julia found for the refurbished bath, and her plans for his dressing room are amazing."

"I envy him that," Pete admitted. "He'll enjoy both rooms for years to come."

Sounds of hammering now coming from the third floor signaled that Team Two had begun the painstaking removal of the original wood moldings in a way that would allow them to be reused in the new spaces.

"I've shut off the water to the hallway bath," Chuck Rolfe, the master plumber whose work had been admired during past projects, informed them as he descended from the second floor. "Everything else is still usable."

"I appreciate your handling that yourself," Adrianna stated. "Plumbing in a house of this age can offer up surprises."

"You can say that again." Chuck sent her a grin. "Pete and I could both tell you some stories, I can assure you. Let me know when you're ready for me to return and see to the new installations."

He shook hands with the architect and then headed towards the kitchen, where Penny had set up a large basket of oversized blueberry muffins on the end of the island with a hand-printed sign that stated: *Help Yourself!*

"We have our first find," Jeff Stuart said as he appeared at the top of the stairs.

"What is it?" Adrianna hurried forward and met him on the landing.

"It rolled out from under a molding running along the floor in the first bedroom as we pulled it away." Jeff set a small, cool object in the palm of her hand as Pete peered over her shoulder.

"A gold ring," the architect stated, his voice filled with excitement.

"Set with what looks to be a tiny, but real ruby," Adrianna added. "It certainly belonged to a slender woman." She slid it onto the little finger of her right hand. "Or it could be a child's ring. You'll have to excuse me. I want to enter this in a notebook I'm keeping, and then I have to call Chase."

# CHAPTER XIII

"Hello?" Larry called out as he and Kate entered the foyer of Montgomery House a few minutes later.

"You'll find Adrianna in the library," Pete informed him as he joined them from upstairs. "We just had our first find, but I'll let her have the joy of sharing it with you. I need to head to my office."

"Actually, if you have a minute, our news might interest you as well." Larry pushed aside one of the pocket doors that he knew allowed access to the home's library through the second parlor, carefully closing it behind their small group before following the others past the sheet-covered furniture.

"This is a surprise," Adrianna greeted them from where she was working at the long table that served as a home office desk for both her and Chase. "To what do I owe the pleasure?"

Larry gestured to Kate that it was her story to tell, and she beamed at the other two. "We may have located a property for our new firm to purchase and renovate," she filled their partners in.

"Actually, Kate discovered what I agree is a golden opportunity." Larry strove to keep the record straight.

"But you were smart enough to gain us entry into the house and save us a realtor's fee," she insisted, giving credit where credit was due.

"Is it a house we would know?" Pete asked.

"Probably," Larry stated. "It's the Arts and Crafts bungalow to the right of Jewel Parkerson's place. Sarah

Ridgewell's home until about three years ago." He gave them the details.

"It sounds exactly like the sort of place that we're looking for," Adrianna agreed, "and it's in the right neighborhood. Where did you leave things with the current owner?"

"I explained how the demolition they'd done would decrease the value, so we would need an appraisal," Larry stated. "I told her ours would be a cash purchase and we would pay for the appraisal up front, subtracting the cost from the purchase price at closing. My goal there was to keep us realtor fee free, although I hope I didn't overstep my bounds."

"Not at all," Adrianna assured him. "Chase and I have retained a controlling interest in the firm to insure that we'll be the tie breakers, but everyone involved is a professional of one sort or another. There are bound to be times when an opportunity such as this will arise, and unless it gets out of hand, we'll save money by all of us feeling free to commit the firm to some degree."

"I appreciate what you're saying, but speaking for myself and, I believe, Julia as well, we'd probably be more comfortable going forward if we had some sort of guidelines in place," Pete pointed out.

"As a newcomer to the group, I would as well," Kate added her two cents worth. "While I was impressed with Larry's take charge attitude and I certainly agree with everything he did, I wouldn't have proceeded on my own in the same way, which ultimately would've cost the firm money."

"I'm making a note on the agenda for our Wednesday evening meeting right now." Adrianna's fingers moved across her keyboard. "This one's at your condo again, right, Larry?"

"Right," the broker confirmed after a quick glance towards Kate. "We'll expect everyone to arrive around six o'clock."

Not sure which thing had left her more excited, finding the first property for their new joint venture or hearing Larry refer to the meeting as theirs, Kate savored the moment as Pete excused himself, promising to fill Julia in on the new property when he arrived at his office.

"We were told that you found something interesting this morning," Kate said as soon as the architect left them. "Is it something we could see?"

"Sure." Adrianna pulled the small ring from her finger and handed it to her friend. "I'd like your opinion."

"I'm not an appraiser, of course, but it looks old to me." Kate passed the tiny treasure over to Larry. "It's been worn enough that the underside is thinning, which would denote both age and a higher karat."

"I knew you were the right person to ask." Adrianna sent her a smile. "I hadn't picked up on either one of those things. What about the stone?"

"With the naked eye, it looks genuine," Kate gave her opinion. "It's certainly a sweet, historic piece."

"The real value to me would be its history," the ring's new owner stated. "My great-aunt might've been able to shed light on the subject, but unfortunately, she's now gone."

"Sometimes you can tell who once owned a piece by finding a photo of them wearing it in a family album." Kate accepted the ring from Larry and passed it back to Adrianna.

"That's a good idea," he agreed. "Penny could probably guide you to where you might have the best luck."

"Hadn't we better be getting to the office?" Kate asked. "After all, you may be an owner, but I'm an employee. Your uncle may need me for something."

"Right again, girl." He gave her a quick squeeze. "You see how she keeps me on the straight and narrow," he addressed their hostess.

"We women have to do that a lot with our men." Adrianna sent Kate a knowing look, as she escorted the two of them to the foyer. "Chase will be home for lunch, and I'll fill him in on the house you found as well as Otis, Penny and Jeff, who are all here."

"I'll call Jack and let him know," Kate volunteered, "which will put Susan in the loop, too."

"I love doing business in a small town like Captain's Point." Adrianna laughed as Larry opened the door in such a way as to allow Kate to pass through the doorway first.

"I wouldn't want to be anywhere else," he stated and then took his leave.

Left alone in the foyer, sounds of demolition coming from upstairs, Adrianna couldn't help but think how blessed her life had become in only nine months – a home of her own, a wonderful husband, great friends, a new business venture to run, and the possibility of becoming a mother to look forward to.

What more, she wondered, could a woman want?

## CHAPTER XIV

"So what would you like us to serve for dinner Wednesday evening?" Kate asked as Larry headed his SUV along the drive, not sure if it was the overall excitement of the day or the devil in her, as her mother had often stated, that had caused her to ask the question as her companion brought their vehicle to a halt.

"What did you say?" He turned in his seat and faced her.

"Have you given any thought to what we'll serve for dinner Wednesday evening?" She obliged him, relieved as he threaded the fingers of his right hand through her blonde curls at the back of her neck and pulled her gently to him, kissing her long and deep as traffic passed on the main road into town right in front of them.

"Do you realize that's the first time you've referred to an *us*?" he asked, his blue eyes darkened by love.

"I'm sorry." She reached up a gloved hand and touched his cheek. "I didn't deliberately hold back the word. I'm just feeling my way forward until my divorce."

"I want to hear that word, feel that word and, most of all, live it," he assured her. "I want *us* to be the reality of every moment in both of our lives from now on." He kissed her again, this time pulling away at the sound of a vehicle approaching theirs along the gravel from behind.

A glance in the rearview mirror alerted him to the approach of Paul Lynch, the young minister who rented the old caretaker's cottage on the Montgomery property, and

Larry signaled his turn onto the main road, his day now complete.

Lunchtime came and went with no sign of Chase at the house, a phone call from him advising Adrianna that his eleven o'clock appointment had run over, but if he sent out for a sub sandwich and worked through lunch, he could come home early.

"Do that," she had agreed. "Nothing else out of the norm for a demolition is going on here."

Now, as he entered the home's kitchen through the mudroom a bit later than he had intended, he found all to be quiet – work finished for the day.

Making his way upstairs, he took a quick tour of the construction area, pleased with the care that had been taken and the progress that had been made. Otis and Adrianna had put together a great crew.

Once changed into casual clothes, he began a swift search for his wife in the tower rooms before heading downstairs, where he located her, sitting on a thick Chinese carpet in the Captain's study, surrounded by old family albums with Max looking on.

"I hardly have any pictures of my parents or childhood," she shared with him, once Chase had joined her on the floor, received a welcoming kiss and run his hand along the dog's back.

"Penny thought there were some in albums in here, but I've only found one or two photos that were taken when I was visiting as a little girl," she continued. "Sometime, I'd like to sit down together and see if you can put names to these faces."

"Anytime you want," he agreed. "We could look through some of them after dinner this evening."

"The frustrating thing is that my father often snapped pictures of my mother and me or had someone else take a photo of the three of us," Adrianna continued. "There were three albums that my mom kept with us, but they weren't sent to me with their other things. I followed up at the time, but all I reached were dead ends."

"I only have a few of pictures of myself growing up," he filled her in. "My father never bothered, and my mother didn't put herself to the trouble of keeping up with a scrapbook. The photos I have were taken by Augustus at major events, such as when I became an Eagle Scout or won an athletic trophy. He kept them in a small album that he gave me before his death."

"I'd like to see those." She slipped her hand into his, clearly reading the hurt emanating from him. "All we can do now is document our lives together going forward."

"Including keeping scrapbooks for our children, so they won't share our experiences." He drew her into his arms, needing her close. "Should we purchase a quality camera sometime this weekend?"

"Definitely."

"I don't need photos of the past to know what's important to me now," he whispered into her ear before his lips traveled along her neck to a spot where it joined her shoulder.

"Neither do I," she breathed as he traced the collar of her V-neck top towards its point with feathery kisses. "All I need is your love."

"That you have, my queen." His eyes locked onto hers. "As well as my body and soul."

In the living room of his home on Tuttle Avenue, Herb Stuart glanced up from the evening paper as he heard his only child close the front door. "So how did it go today?" he asked.

"Great!" Jeff sent him a grin. "And we may have located the perfect house for our new firm's first project per Adrianna – the bungalow next door to Aunt Jewel's, who I assume is here cooking our dinner again, since I smell the aroma of pot roast coming from the kitchen."

"Is that Jeff?" Jewel called, as the room's occupants heard her footsteps approaching.

"One and the same." The younger man threw an arm around her as she joined them and planted a kiss on her cheek. "I'm hungry enough to eat an elephant, and if I'm not mistaken, you've already gone a long way towards taking care of that."

"Come and sit down, Jewel." Herb indicated the seat next to his on the couch. "Son, you sit for a minute, too. There's something we'd like to share with you."

Hopeful that he had already guessed what was coming, Jeff obliged, giving the other two his full attention once he was settled in a slip-covered armchair.

"I'm sure you know that, as long as she was alive, I never had eyes for anyone but your mother," Herb began.

"Yes, sir."

"The fact is, Son, that I've fallen in love with this wonderful woman and have asked her to marry me," his father continued. "Through some miracle that I don't understand and for which I can, therefore, only be grateful, God has blessed me with her being willing to have me."

"Congratulations!" His son's face lit up with pleasure.

"We hope to be married in a quiet ceremony in a week or two," Herb filled him in. "Just the two of us, you and Jewel's brother – after which, I intend to move to her house, leaving this one to you."

"I do have one question," Jeff responded, surprised to see Jewel's hand tighten her hold on his parent's.

"Yes?" His father attempted unsuccessfully to hold his gaze that Jeff shifted to the woman who would soon be his stepmother as he quickly rose, strode to the couch and sat on his heels at her feet, taking her free hand in his.

"You've been so much more to me than a mere aunt for some time," he stated. "Would it be okay if I call you simply Jewel from now on?"

## CHAPTER XV

In Montgomery House's dependency the next afternoon, Edwina Foster stood in her unlit kitchen across from its over-the-sink window, her back to the wall opposite the opening formed by her U-shaped counters.

Hoping to remain unobserved, she watched as Arthur Stern paused on the sidewalk in front of his retail space, Artful Soul, at the far end of Montgomery House's former carriage house and engaged the much younger Michael Wolford, the co-owner of Drifters, in conversation.

How tall and straight her Arthur looked, more like a man in his prime than one in his seventies.

Her Arthur…

There was no denying that was how she now thought of him, but where was it all going? Where did she want it to go?

True, they had only known each other for a little over six months, but her body responded to his kisses in a way that recalled earlier times with her Hamilton.

Still, as much as Arthur spoke of them as a couple and despite the special effort he had made to include her and her grandson Jason's family in his own family's plans during the holidays, there had been no mention between them of the word love.

Was it possible that, although his first wife Sylvia had been dead for several years now, he wasn't ready for more than casual dating? And what about her?

Certainly, she enjoyed dressing up in her best outfit and being taken out for a fine meal in the company of a good-looking man, whose conversation she found agreeable. Visiting with the artist in his gallery cum studio or sharing lunch with him in the property's gazebo overlooking the ocean when the weather was nice helped to fill her days in a pleasant way, too.

Recently, though, Arthur had referred to this being a special year for them on several occasions, and for the first time since her previous dating experiences over half a century before, she wished that her father was still here to run interference for her.

Like her Ham before him, Arthur had shown himself to be a passionate man although, except for his kisses and holding her hand, he had so far kept his impulses in check.

So, what did he mean when he spoke of their special year? More of the same, marriage, or an affair, and exactly where amongst these choices did her own conscience and wishes reside?

One state away, Becca Tate switched on the light in her dorm room, glad to dump some of her books before she grabbed a quick supper and made her way to the library for several hours of studying.

As she gathered what she would need, her fingers brushed her smaller laptop case, and she paused. Had Jeff answered her email from last evening?

Moving to her designated desk, she keyed in the password on her larger computer, willing to take the seconds it would require for her to find out. A few quick keystrokes revealed that a reply from him had arrived, and opening it eagerly, she read:

*Hey, girl –*

*Great news! My dad and Jewel are getting married, but keep it between us for now. They're planning a quiet ceremony in a couple of weeks, and then Dad's moving in with her, which means I can have an office here at home.*

*Didn't you have Bernard for Soc 103 when you took it? Any pointers?*

*I so wish you were here, Becca. Campus isn't the same knowing there's no chance I'll catch up with you. Still, you're where you need to be.*

*How's it going with your classes so far? Are you finding the professors any better?*

*Miss you!*

*Jeff*

With a small sigh, she closed her email and logged off. She would send him a reply later.

In the meantime, History 301 called along with Political Science. Jeff had been right, though. No campus was the same without him.

Back in Captain's Point, Julia Henderson swiveled her desk chair in what had once been the music room of an Italianate Victorian and now served as her office at Marlborough and Company.

"It's about time you showed up," she greeted Pete through the archway that separated her room from his in the original second parlor, sending him a smile.

"I stopped by Montgomery House again and then spent most of the day at the farmhouse," he explained.

"How are things at the former?"

"Fine." He hung his coat on a mission style, oak hall tree. "The demo's gotten off to a great start, although they haven't located any original plans for the house yet, which is disappointing."

"That's a shame."

"I do have a bit of news, though, that I forgot to mention yesterday." He lounged against his desk. "Kate and Larry have located a first property for us to purchase through the new venture, and we're discussing guidelines at the meeting tomorrow evening."

"That was fast."

"It's the bungalow to the right of Jewel Parkerson's over on Tuttle," he filled her in. "Sounds like it'll mainly be updating, and some of the original character's been maintained. They'll need your help with staging fairly soon, I would imagine."

"Not a problem," she assured him.

"Why don't we ride together to the meeting tomorrow?" he suggested as he straightened. "That way I can make sure you get home safely."

"Sounds good." Julia turned back to her computer, hoping that her pleasure at his concern for her wasn't apparent.

Relieved when Pete began working, she couldn't keep from glancing his way. Ever since Thanksgiving things had been different between them.

He no longer cautioned her before each assignment, seemingly more confident in her abilities, but there was more. He'd always been good to her, ever since they were children growing up in the same neighborhood, she the kid sister of his best friend, but now his actions had softened further.

This was the third time he had suggested driving her somewhere and mentioned her safety as if he were truly concerned for her well-being, even though Captain's Point wasn't exactly a hotbed of crime even in its worst areas.

Twice during the holiday period, he had surprised her by suggesting that they go out for lunch, and when her family and his had spent New Year's Eve together, he had stuck to her like glue. When the ball had dropped in Times Square, he had even given her a brief kiss on the lips and wished her well.

There was no doubt about it. Their relationship was morphing into something more than a working one spread over a layer of lifetime friendship. It would be interesting to see exactly what this new year had in store for them.

## CHAPTER XVI

"Done!" Chase hit Save on his laptop and looked along the length of the library table to where Adrianna was working on her own computer. "Where do you stand?"

"I've been finished with my demo notes for ten minutes or more," she admitted. "This is the bones of a grocery list."

"The ingredients for a batch of your molasses cookies wouldn't happen to be on it, would they?" he asked.

"No, but they could be, if you'll give me a moment."

"A moment I can spare, but then I want you here on my lap." He grinned, holding his arms open and gathering her to him as she obliged.

"I love your work-at-home days." She snuggled against him. "Is it working as well for Susan and you as you both had hoped it would?"

"So far so good." He dropped a kiss on the top of her head. "I don't see any need to go back to things as they were, and I was glad I was here today with the demolition going on. It's one thing to learn second hand that a stash of old movie posters had been used as filler in a bedroom wall and another thing to be present when Jeff first shouts the news down the stairs."

"What would you say to our having them framed and displayed in the new media room?" Adrianna asked.

"It'd be a great way to showcase them and would add ambiance to the space." He lifted her face to his with one finger. "Do you have any idea how sexy you are when you talk decorating?"

"Really, Chase." She giggled. "There simply isn't anything sexy about framing a few old movie posters."

"There is if it's you doing it," he insisted as he covered her mouth with his.

A few minutes later, Larry locked the front door of Chesterton and Chesterton, while Kate waited beside him.

"That's it for the day." He shortened his stride to match hers as the two headed towards his SUV where it waited in a nearby parking lot. "Would you mind if we stop at my place on the way to Jewel's?"

"Not at all." She smiled at him, as part of her did a jig across her heart at the thought of getting to spend a little more one-on-one time with him.

"Good, because our hosting the dinner meeting got me thinking, and I set up a couple of things on my way back to the office from my appointment with Mrs. Madison," he filled her in.

A few minutes later, Larry brought the Mercedes to a halt in front of his normal bay in the bottom level of The Cove's former carriage house, turned the engine off and shifted in his seat so he could face Kate.

"I've arranged for Marissa to make us a large pan of lasagna for tomorrow evening," he began, referring to the wife of the Sheffield Place Inn's General Manager. "In addition, Sissy will make us a pan of her world famous brownies."

This time, Kate recognized the name of the woman she had replaced at his firm, when Sissy had agreed to provide Chester's, his family's crab shack at Montgomery Marina, with a never-ending supply of what were deemed the best chocolate-iced brownies most folks had ever eaten.

"You and I will throw together a couple of salads, set up a drinks area and arrange some rolls, sliced bread and butter on the island," he continued. "We'll serve vanilla ice cream alongside the brownies for those who want it, and

Penny has volunteered to make us a pitcher of homemade hot fudge to drizzle over it."

"Sounds like everything's under control," she responded, "but I wasn't concerned about whether or not you could handle organizing things, when I asked my question yesterday morning."

"I know you weren't." He reached out and ran the tip of his finger along her left cheek. "The thing is, both the lasagna and the brownies may need to be picked up."

"I'd be glad to handle one or both of them," she volunteered.

"But how would you get them upstairs, if you were to arrive first?" he asked the question that had started him thinking in the first place.

"It would only be a few minutes before you'd get here yourself," she pointed out. "I'd simply wait in my car."

"And possibly freeze to death if we believe the weather report." He opened the console between them and withdrew a black, rectangular object that she couldn't make out in the dim evening light.

"I have the use of the four bays on this end of the carriage house," he explained. "I keep the truck in the far right one. The two middle ones remain empty, unless I have guests, and I've been using this one on the far left, that's closest to the elevator, for the SUV."

"The one in front of which we're now parked." She nodded in agreement, not sure why he was explaining what she already knew.

"This is a second garage door opener that's programmed for all four bays." He handed it to her. "I want to make sure that you understand how it works, and then we'll install it in your car once we get to Jewel's place. It'll only take a couple of seconds."

"But..."

"No buts, Kate, please." His eyes begged her. "No one will know, except you and me. From now on, I'm going to park in the next space over, so this one will be free for you."

He again reached in the console, this time handing her a small plastic sign designed to be hung from a car's rearview mirror, on which the initials MM were printed in gold inside a deep blue circle.

"What's this for?" she asked as he handed it to her.

"The sign allows you to park in any of the three reserved Montgomery family slots at the marina, as long as you slip it onto your mirror," he explained. "Adrianna gave me this one for you and one each for Jack and Susan this afternoon. You can use the one at the Chester's end of the boardwalk tomorrow, if you pick up the brownies, although Sissy may bring them by the office."

"That was nice of Adrianna."

"Actually, she apologized for not having thought of it sooner, but that's our Adrianna all over." He chuckled, but then his face sobered. "I'm also giving you this key that unlocks the stairwell to my condo, and I've written down the new security code for the elevator. I want you to test both of them while we're here, and then we'll slip the key onto your key ring."

"Oh, Larry..." She held the key to her heart. "Are you sure you want me to have this right now?"

"I want you to have it and use it, whenever you need or merely want to." He held her gaze. "I want this to be the key to your home as well as mine, but we can't say that it is until after your divorce. Still, there's no reason why you shouldn't have full access to the condo. You already live in my heart."

And with that, he leaned over the console, his kiss making no secret of how much he wanted her.

## CHAPTER XVII

Finding the half-tester bed in the tower suite empty except for himself, when he awoke the next morning, Chase immediately felt bereft, even as he supposed that Adrianna had wanted an early start along with the crew.

After all, today they were scheduled to channel their way through the three floors as the first step in preparing both the elevator and dumbwaiter shafts.

Still, this was the first morning since their marriage that he had awakened without her in his arms, and it was a firm reminder of how much he relied on her. As was their custom when she was there, he took a moment and reviewed the day ahead in hopes that it would help him stay organized.

Its being Wednesday meant that his work day would begin with his leading the weekly staff meeting at the firm – part of his role as managing partner.

Then he and Susan would spend a few minutes alone in his office discussing whatever either of them thought the other should know, since this would be the only day in their week during which they would both be in the office.

After work, he would head back to Montgomery House, receive a tour of the day's accomplishments on the demolition and then accompany his wife to the board meeting for their new venture in real estate development over dinner at Larry's condo.

All in all, he thought, his day stretched before him filled with a variety of interesting undertakings, two of which would involve Adrianna. Slowly, but surely, his life was morphing into more what he had hoped it would be, and his wife was the key.

With a start, he remembered a commercial that had aired on the kitchen television the previous evening and had reminded him that Valentine's Day was heading their way. He needed to think of something really special to do for his queen.

Flinging back the covers, he exchanged the mattress for the floor, where he completed a number of sit-ups, push-ups and cross-abdominal curls.

Finished, he made the bed and headed through the dressing room into the tower suite's bathroom, where he discovered there were no towels in evidence and he had left a newly purchased, economy-sized bottle of shampoo on the dressing room vanity the previous evening.

Retracing his steps, he grabbed the shampoo and then crossed the small room, where he opened the cabinet door beneath the larger one that held Adrianna's childhood toys. As he reached for a fresh towel, though, the heavy bottle slid from his hand and landed with a loud thud on the cabinet's floor, shifting it slightly and exposing what at first appeared to be the corner of a sheet of paper, browned with age.

"Well, who would've thought?" he addressed Max who had joined him, sensing a note of excitement in the air.

Three properties away, Larry let himself into the foyer of Blue Wolf Manor, announcing his presence by calling out, "Anyone home?"

"In the kitchen," Jack's strong baritone replied at the same time that Daniel flung himself through the doorway into the breakfast room, heading for their visitor's knees.

"Only 193 more days until our baby will be able to see us," the youngster announced as he was lifted into the air and given a bear hug.

"How's your mama doing?" Larry headed with his short cousin in his arms towards the kitchen.

"She looks a bit peaked, but we're encouraging her," Daniel filled him in.

"Brought you these." Larry set two Montgomery Marina parking placards on the kitchen table.

"What are they?" Susan leaned forward, receiving the same explanation that Kate had heard the previous evening.

"Now that is nice," Jack responded. "Can you join us for coffee or breakfast?"

"No, I'm on my way to pick up Kate." Larry remained standing. "We want to leave the office early, since the dinner meeting this evening is at my place."

"Will it be okay if we bring Daniel with us?" Susan asked.

"Sure, we can tuck him under a blanket on the couch in the den after we eat, and he can watch one of his movies as long as he behaves." Larry tickled the boy's stomach.

"I always behave at your condo," Daniel insisted.

"Actually, you do, don't you?" Larry set him on his booster seat at the table. "I'll let myself out." He bent and kissed Susan's cheek. "Take care of yourself."

Left to themselves, Daniel finished his bowl of cereal, Jack broke four eggs into a bowl and Susan took a third bite of dry toast, chewed it thoroughly and forced herself to swallow.

"I'll brush my teeth, and then I'll be ready." Daniel placed his bowl in the sink, before addressing his two canine shadows, "Come, Casey and Lady."

Reaching into a lower cabinet for a skillet, Jack glanced up in time to see his wife hold her hand to her mouth and rush from the room, not surprised when he heard her close the powder room door.

Knowing she preferred privacy in such instances, he turned off the stove and made his way slowly across the foyer and along the hallway that led to the garage, relieved to hear the flush of the toilet when it came, followed by the sound of water splashing against the sink.

"Susie, it's me." He tapped lightly on the powder room's door. "Are you okay?"

Turning the crystal knob, she let him in, her face blotched with red by the efforts of the previous couple of minutes and her eyes filled with tears. "It's just morning sickness," she advised him.

But, as the woman he loved more than life itself washed the sour taste from her mouth, Jack recognized it was his actions that had put her in this position, and yet, amazingly, she still welcomed the pregnancy and loved him, where his own parents hadn't.

His heart filling with adoration as she turned off the water, he pulled a fresh hand towel from the rack, drew her to him and gently dried off her face.

"I love you, Susie," he said as she slumped against his chest for support, and he hugged her to him. "More than you can possibly know."

## CHAPTER XVIII

"So, what's on our agenda for today?" Chase put down his paper when his wife joined him in their breakfast room the next morning. "Or are we in limbo on the demolition until the engineer gets here?"

"Otis found a source for the steel beams to provide the extra support that's needed in the shafts, so we'll begin as soon as they're delivered." She glanced at the regulator clock on the wall. "Which should be in about an hour."

"I suppose it was inevitable that we'd run into at least one problem in this old house," he commented.

"Frankly, I'm glad we haven't run into more." She chose a blueberry muffin from the basket on the table and cut it in half. "Speaking of old houses, I was relieved last evening when everyone voted to proceed towards the purchase of the bungalow on Tuttle Avenue, weren't you?"

"It's always nicer when there's a consensus," he agreed.

"Thank goodness Larry and Kate will continue the negotiations as the firm's agents." She tore off another bite of muffin. "I'd have my hands full handling that, Montgomery Properties and the renovations right now."

"I'll go ahead and give Gary Butler a call, when we're done here." Chase referred to one of the new associates at his firm, who had previously indicated an interest in handling work concerning the National Register of Historic Places.

"If I understand him correctly, the Governor's Consulting Committee only meets three times a year. We'll want to get the house submitted for consideration as quickly as possible, since acceptance can mean eligibility for both Federal and State tax credits."

"Do you know how sexy you are when you speak legalese?" She surprised him by reversing their normal banter as she rose from her seat and plopped onto his lap, where she proceeded to drop tiny kisses along his neck.

"Why Adrianna Montgomery Sheffield." Chase attempted a shocked look, which she patently ignored. "And here I was thinking you were a good girl."

"Oh, I am," she whispered into his ear, surprising him even further. "I'm very good indeed, and if you have time, on this your work-at-home morning, to join me upstairs for a few minutes, I'll be glad to demonstrate how good I can be."

At almost the same moment the younger couple shut the tower suite bedroom's door behind them, Jewel Parkerson opened the oak door of her Victorian home to find Herb Stuart standing on her porch.

"Come in." She stepped back and allowed him to enter. "It's so good to see you getting out and about more."

"I thought I'd take a look at the closet and drawer space that I'll have here, so I can judge how much to bring and what to leave in Jeff's old room back at the house," he explained, surprised when his new fiancée's face fell.

"I'm afraid we have a bit of a problem there," she stated, as he made his way past her and started up the stairs.

"Nothing we can't take care of, I'm sure." He kept on going. "There are bound to be things that need fixing in these old homes from time to time, and you'll find that I'm handy to have around."

"It isn't exactly a repair." She hurried to keep up with him as he headed along the hall to the master suite, where he paused at the door.

"Is it okay if I go in?" he asked.

"Sure." She gestured for him to go ahead, unable to hold off the inevitable as she watched him open the door to the spacious walk-in closet.

For a moment, the room filled with a pregnant silence, but then he turned to her, a concerned look on his face.

"Why didn't you tell me, you couldn't bring yourself to dispose of Bruce's things?" He took her hand. "I would've helped you a long time ago."

"I didn't want to bother you with it," she explained as well as she could. "I knew I should do it, but the house was so lonely without him and, somehow, having his suits still around helped. Besides, putting his things into plastic bags for the charity center felt too much like throwing him away with the trash."

"It was easier for me with my boy in the house," Herb stated calmly. "Even so, when it came time to clear out Nancy's closet and drawers, he helped. I still have three of her dresses that I couldn't bring myself to part with hanging at one end of my closet and her jewelry set aside for Jeff's wife someday if she wants it."

"You do understand." Relief filled her face.

"Of course." He smiled at her. "Now, why don't I pop over to the storage center and pick up some nice fresh boxes for us to pack Bruce's things neatly in, while you decide which three items you want hanging on your side of this closet? That way, once I move in, we'll always have a little bit of the other two with us." He lowered his lips onto hers, his question not requiring a reply.

And, as the man who now held her in his arms kissed her in a way that denoted nothing but tenderness, Jewel's heart filled with a grateful certainty that she had never been happier than she was at this moment and the loneliness would be gone as long as Herb remained in her life.

## CHAPTER XIX

Julia Henderson sat on the window seat in her bedroom and absentmindedly smoothed her hair, as she watched Chestnut Street where it passed below her for any sign of Marlborough and Company's familiar white van.

"I'll pick you up between nine-thirty and ten in the morning, and we can run by Montgomery House," Pete had stated when he'd dropped her off the evening before, his breath leaving a white cloud in the chill air where he stood holding the passenger door open for her. "We've both been working long hours, and tonight's dinner was a business meeting, no matter how much fun we had. Sleep in, and enjoy a relaxed breakfast."

Part of her had been pleased that he'd noticed the long hours she had put in at his firm, while part of her had resented his assumption that she could put her work plans for this morning aside. Still, here was another example of how he was increasingly keeping her close by.

"So what's up with Pete and you?" her brother had asked over dinner in their parents' dining room downstairs on New Year's Day.

"Same old, same old," she had replied, unable to meet his eyes as she had reached for the scalloped potatoes.

So what was up with Pete and her? Was she reading too much into things? After all, it was possible that he had merely found a way to accept her professional abilities as being intact and moved on.

For a moment, scenes from her childhood growing up in this neighborhood, the only girl in a bevy of boys, flashed through her mind.

"Aw, let her come, too," Pete had insisted more times than she could count. "She sticks to us like glue, so we won't lose her."

How lonely her childhood would've been without his intervention, and during those early years, she had latched onto his hand more often than not, not wanting to be left behind.

"The Rigby's house, now that's a Queen Anne." He had pointed across the street and down one as they had sat side-by-side on the porch swing one summer evening, the other boys playing poker for pennies on the steps. "Rumor has it that Jeremiah Rigby lost the family's fortune in the Crash, shrugged his shoulders, bought a cart and made another fortune selling produce."

Her professional path would surely have been different if he hadn't made the historic homes around them come alive, igniting her imagination in ways that simply would not die.

For years, she had hero-worshipped him, and then he and her brother had started high school, driven away in secondhand cars, held part-time jobs and survived first dates.

By the time she had reached the hallowed halls of Captain's Point High, they had left town for college, and she couldn't have said which one of them she missed more, her entire existence geared towards their holiday visits home.

Not that she hadn't enjoyed her own high school years, she had, but no one had ever captured her imagination or heart in the same way as Pete Marlborough.

Finally, it had been her turn to leave Captain's Point for college, where she had achieved a double major in fine arts and design, even as she had struggled to put memories of her brother's best friend out of her mind.

Then, on the same day that she had received an email offer of a dream job from a famous L.A. design firm, she had come home and learned that Pete had returned to Captain's Point and would be opening his own company.

"He'd like to talk about your working with him as a designer," her brother had dropped casually during a television commercial. "Stop by the old Brickman place sometime tomorrow morning, if you're interested. Pete's bought it to fix up and use as his home and office for the time being."

All night long she had tossed and turned, debating whether or not to walk the two blocks to the new offices of Marlborough and Company the next morning, but in the end, Pete had made the decision for her, showing up at their door while she was still in the kitchen eating breakfast.

"I wasn't sure your crazy brother would remember to give you my message." Pete had sent her a lopsided grin as she had poured him a mug of coffee and fixed him a plate of pancakes to go with it. "I can't think of anyone I'd rather hire than you."

And, as she had looked into his amber eyes, she had mentally written her refusal to the L.A. firm, knowing she couldn't drive away from Captain's Point and leave behind the man who was wolfing down syrup-covered bites of pancake in a seat across the table from hers.

The first months of their working partnership had been somewhat rocky, and now she was receiving mixed signals.

There were days when she wasn't sure what she wanted, and times when she wanted nothing more than for him to lock the front door of the Brickman's old home, turn the Open sign to Closed and lead her by the hand to the suite of rooms he had constructed for himself upstairs.

Was it possible that Pete didn't know what he wanted either? After all this time, was she nothing more to him than his best friend's kid sister, who happened to be a designer?

Perhaps, he needed for her to make a first move. Although how she would do so while still living with her parents in their home, she didn't know. Somehow, someway, Pete must truly see her, not as the girl she had once been, but rather as the woman she had become.

A flash of white caught her eye, and a familiar coil tightened within her as she reached for her purse.

Good, bad or indifferent, he was here now. At least, she could have her coat on and be ready. After all, no matter what their feelings might be for each other, Pete paid her a good salary and deserved her best in return.

"He's here," she called to her mother who was in the kitchen, starting something in the crockpot for their dinner.

"Have fun," her mom responded in the same way she had for years, but their visit to Montgomery House wasn't about fun. It was about work.

Although, truth be told, any time spent with Pete Marlborough for her had always been about at least one of three things and often all three put together – laughter, sharing and, most of all, her love for him.

# CHAPTER XX

"Let's stop by Montgomery House and tell them on the way in," Larry suggested to Kate as he signaled a left turn onto Captain's Point's Main Street.

"Fine by me," she agreed. "After all, those that can do so may want to join us at the Tuttle Avenue house when the appraisal is done next Wednesday. Julia, for instance, might welcome the opportunity to take measurements, and Pete will be interested in the historic details."

"Would you mind calling Glenda and letting her know?" He referred to the administrative assistant whose time he shared with his uncle at Chesterton and Chesterton.

"Not at all." She reached for her phone as Pete, coincidentally, completed a left turn and kept pace behind them.

"I think that's Larry and Kate up ahead," he commented to Julia, who looked up from a small spiral notebook into which she was sketching the outline of a loveseat with tall arms that curved outward.

"You may be right." She returned to her work, still basking in the warmth of his compliment about her new sweater as he'd held the van's door open for her.

"I wonder if they stopped by the Tuttle Avenue house," he commented, signaling their turn into Montgomery House's driveway and then following the familiar Mercedes SUV.

"I have no idea, but there's no time like the present to ask them." She stuffed her notebook into the oversized purse she carried when working.

Pete opened the passenger door of the van and offered Julia his hand that she absentmindedly took, her focus on the fact that Larry had opened the thick oak door to the granite mansion without so much as a knock and was holding it ajar for them.

"Morning, Chesterton, Kate," Pete greeted the other two as they entered, and Julia marveled at how at ease he appeared to be as he gestured for her to enter the large foyer first.

Small functions at historic Montgomery House had been sprinkled throughout her girlhood, the result of Martha Montgomery's active involvement in the Girl Scouts. Each time such an august occasion had presented itself, she had received a series of stern warnings from her mother.

"Hold your head up, don't slouch, remember your manners," her mother would say, sending her tomboyish daughter off with a tentative smile and an anxious look on her face. "Martha Montgomery will expect you to be at your best."

Reflexively, Julia straightened her shoulders in silent homage to Adrianna's now deceased great-aunt, even though she had been the guest of the current owners several times during the past couple of months.

"Visitors here." As was the custom amongst members of Captain's Point's leading families, Larry led their small group along the hallway towards the kitchen, from which came the aroma of freshly baked chocolate chip cookies.

Following behind, Julia kept her eyes open for their hosts, unable to overcome the feeling that they were trespassing.

"I see we've arrived in the nick of time." Larry dropped a kiss on the cheek of the middle-aged Penny and then lifted three cookies from the cooling racks on the island.

"Help yourself." Penny rolled her eyes at the broker, the grin on her face belying the tone of her words. "If I'd known you were coming, I'd have made a triple batch. The rest of you grab a couple before this one here goes through them."

Never one to turn down a warm cookie, Pete helped himself to three, passing one to Julia, who sent him a smile as Kate accepted the two Larry handed her, understanding he would welcome the return of one later if she offered it.

"Is everyone upstairs?" Pete asked the housekeeper.

"I think so," Penny answered. "Unless you want Chase. He's working from home, so he may be in the library."

"Give me a sec." Larry strode through the doorway into the breakfast room as he called over his shoulder, "These are delicious."

The library having proven to be empty of inhabitants and Julia feeling even more like an interloper, the group made its way to the foyer, where she dropped slightly behind, surprised when Pete slowed his pace as well. Placing his hand on the small of her back, he guided her forward as they headed upstairs.

Sounds of sawing mixed with several male voices, as they passed through first one and then another plastic wall that had been erected against the onslaught of demolition dust.

"Hello?" Larry called out.

"In here," Adrianna responded. "Hurry! We've found something, but be careful."

Entering the first bedroom on their right, Pete drew Julia's attention to the gaping hole in the ceiling. "You can see the support beams the engineer required from here," he pointed out. "It cost the Sheffields a chunk, but structurally, it was necessary."

Then he surprised her by taking her hand as they stepped carefully over the construction debris that littered the floor.

"The bed was sitting right about here." Chase outlined a large rectangle with a pointed finger.

Approaching the area where the cut was to be made into the first floor storage room, Julia was relieved to discover sheets of plywood set over the original hardwood flooring, some of which the crew had been removing prior to sawing through.

Work had halted, though, and a one-foot square trapdoor had been lifted, revealing a shallow hidey-hole.

"This is the diary of one Serepta Montgomery," Adrianna filled them in as she thumbed through the first pages of a small book bound in faded red leather, where she kneeled beside the opening in the floorboards. "I know of two Sereptas – my great-aunt Martha's aunt and that Serepta's grandmother. Hopefully, reading the entries will reveal to which one this belonged."

"What's the larger volume?" Larry peered over their hostess's shoulder, his arm wrapped around Kate's waist as she, too, leaned forward.

"We're not sure yet." Chase bent, reached in and retrieved what appeared to be a ledger, opened its front cover and worked to interpret the faded spidery handwriting as he read:

*This is a listing of those persons of color who have made their way northward through our cellars and the dates during which we provided them sanctuary.*

*If my brother and I have been imprisoned or hung for aiding and abetting them and you are an abolitionist, please burn this if you cannot guarantee its secrecy.*

*If you differ with our opinions and intend to pass this information onto those who will use it against these now free men, women and children, may your soul burn in hell.*

*Serepta Montgomery*
*1849*

Chase closed the book softly and his gaze traveled around those gathered in the room, including the members of the construction crew.

"Please keep this to yourselves," he requested. "I know I speak for Adrianna as well, when I say that we would prefer to tell Elizabeth Chesterton ourselves. As a leading authority on the Underground Railroad, the contents of this book, adding to the discoveries we've already made in the cellars, will add substantially to her research."

Glancing up, Julia was surprised to find Pete's attention on her, his amber eyes sparkling with the excitement of the new find as he let go of her hand, reached around her waist and gave her a quick hug – her day now complete.

## CHAPTER XXI

"Your number ones look much neater," Jack commented to his stepson the next morning in the kitchen of Blue Wolf Manor.

"Only 191 more days until our baby can see us," Daniel announced to his mother as she joined them.

"My, how time flies!" Susan watched with pride as he reattached his countdown sheet to the front of the refrigerator.

"We're having waffles for breakfast," he filled her in as he climbed into his booster seat in the chair beside hers.

"Only frozen ones, I'm afraid," Jack apologized as he set a glass of orange juice in front of her. "Although I do have fresh blueberries to sprinkle on them, if you're interested. I thought we could drop off Daniel at school on our way to the lab and dentist."

"You're going with me?" Susan didn't hide her surprise.

"I'm going to all of your medical appointments," he tossed over his shoulder as he buttered the first round of toasted waffles. "It's important for pregnant women to pay attention to their dental care, and I want to understand everything I need to know in order to help you."

He set Daniel's plate in front of him and hurried back to the counter, arriving in time to snatch the next batch from the toaster.

"You do realize I've been pregnant before," she reminded him. "I kept up my cleaning appointments and drank plenty of milk. Nothing else was required, and my teeth came through fine."

"That was then, and this is now." He handed her a plate that contained two waffles smothered in blueberries and drizzled with syrup under a dusting of powdered sugar.

Thinking one would've been quite enough, Susan resolutely dug in, aware of Jack's ever-growing concerns about her eating plenty for two. What would he think when she no longer fit into any of her regular clothes once the baby was here?

"Isn't this nice?" Her husband took his place at the head of the table and beamed at the other two diners. "I love it that, even though we're a modern family, we take most of our meals together."

"Who else would we eat with?" Daniel asked, his eyes widening.

"Some families are too busy or have schedules too different from each other's to allow them to share their meals, so they end up eating alone in the kitchen, grabbing a bite on the run or dining in front of a television," his mother explained.

"Like when we lived in the apartment," her son mumbled, but then looked up at his stepfather. "He wasn't like you."

"I know, Charger." Jack covered the boy's hand with his. "Trust me, it was your birth father's loss not to spend more time with you and your mother, and now, you're both here with me."

"We're a family in our big happy house, where we'll all stay forever," Daniel continued the thought as if to make sure.

"I'm certainly not leaving," his stepfather stated emphatically and then sent his gaze to his new wife. "How about you?"

"Wild horses couldn't drag me away." Susan made her position clear.

"And our baby's going to live here, too," Daniel added. "We need to get that nursery ready."

"It's on the list," Jack assured him. "Maybe we could look online at baby furniture this evening, so we can get an idea of what kinds of things are out there. Then your mom can decide what type she prefers."

"Can we, Mama? Please?" Daniel slid from his seat, picked up his now empty plate and carried it to the counter by the sink, before crossing back to her.

"If you'd like." She ran her fingers through his wavy blond hair, smiling as he headed along the table.

"I'm glad I gave my mama to you to marry," Daniel muttered into Jack's neck as his stepfather gave him a bear hug, understanding the hurt the child had felt in his earlier years.

"I'm glad you both were willing to be a family with me." Jack rubbed the boy's back. "Now, go brush your teeth and grab your backpack, so we can head out."

Once they were alone, Susan stood and retraced their son's footsteps to her husband's side. "I'm glad we married you, too."

She put her arms around his neck and held his head to her chest, absentmindedly running her fingers through his thick black hair in the same way that she had with their son's. "No one else would ever love the three of us as well as you do."

Jack scooted his chair back and took her onto his lap. "Maybe, just maybe that's because I love the three of you so much. No one, other than Kate, has ever loved me like you and Daniel do."

"Then they were fools." Susan again made her position clear as she rose, so he could finish eating, gathered her dishes and began rinsing them at the sink.

"There." She dried her hands on a dishtowel when she finished. "Now, if you'll excuse me, I'll brush my pregnant teeth, so we won't shock David Eskar, D.D.S., too much when we get there."

## CHAPTER XXII

Thirty minutes later, Daniel delivered to his kindergarten class on time, Jack turned his SUV onto the road that would take them to the lab that was their first stop.

"There's Arthur Stern." Susan waved at the artist, where he waited for a light to turn from red to green, his Buick signaling an intended right turn into the parking lot of a medical professional building. "He must not have seen me. Either that or he has a lot on his mind. I hope everything's all right."

"He probably has a routine appointment the same as you do." Jack covered her hand with his. "I thought I was the fiction writer in our family."

"And a very good one you are," his wife stated emphatically. "Not that I have strong opinions on the subject."

"No, of course not." He ached to draw her into his arms.

"I hope you don't think this is silly of me to tag along with you." He changed the subject. "It's just that this is our first pregnancy, and it may be our only one. I don't want to look back someday and wish I had done anything differently."

"I love that you're so thrilled and involved," she assured him. "It certainly wasn't the same when I was carrying Daniel."

"Speaking of the little guy, is there anything else I could do that would ease his concerns?" Jack turned their vehicle into a parking slot and brought it to a stop. "It bothers me that, while he seems happy enough, he still doesn't feel secure. You'd tell me if there was something I was doing wrong, wouldn't you?"

"You're doing everything right for both of us." Susan cupped his cheek in her hand. "No one could do any more. Daniel is happier with you in our lives than he's ever been, and his understanding that your commitment won't waver will come with time."

"I love you, Susie Chesterton." He leaned forward and kissed her.

"I love you too, Jack Jefferson." She sent him a smile as he opened the driver's door.

In the sun-brightened breakfast room of Montgomery House, Chase lowered his copy of the morning paper at the sound of Adrianna's chair moving against the floor, surprised to find her standing still and looking at him as opposed to gathering her dishes to take to the kitchen.

"Is something bothering you?" He drew her to him, pleased when she sat on his lap and snuggled against his shoulder.

"You've always say that our money is mine to do with as I please, as much as it is yours," she began.

"Yes, and I mean that." He tightened his hold on her. "Is there something you want to buy for the house?"

"No, I want to do something much bigger."

"Then do it."

"You don't even know what it is." She sat up and met his gaze. "I'm talking about spending a chunk of money."

"I still say do it," he repeated. "Just out of curiosity, what is it that you have in mind?"

"When we weren't able to take Elizabeth the ledger last evening, it gave me some time in which to think." She concentrated on straightening his tie, which suddenly needed her complete attention.

"And now you've had an idea."

"Elizabeth's trying to get grant money to add a small wing onto the college's history building that would house the two rooms used by the Underground Railroad, when they're moved from our cellar to the campus." Adrianna smoothed the collar points on his shirt.

"Grant money is hard to come by these days, and I wondered if we could provide some funds for the addition with the stipulation that it be named the Walter and Sophia Montgomery Museum in honor of my parents."

Chase nudged her chin gently with his finger until she raised her face to his. "Why would I have an objection to that? It's a wonderful idea. As a matter of fact, I've been thinking of something similar as a way to give back."

"You have?" Her face brightened. "What did you have in mind?"

"Steve McKinney works with underprivileged youths." He referred to their new accountant. "Before Men's Group at church last month, he told Jack, Larry and me that he believes Captain's Point needs a youth center, probably hoping Larry and I would get the City Council involved. Anyway, I thought we might underwrite part of the center in memory of my cousin."

"Two minds with the same generous thoughts." She smiled at him, even as her heart filled with a sense of peace at the realization that he could now speak so easily of his cousin's loss.

"So, we're agreed?"

"Yes, let's tell Elizabeth tonight when she and Anders join us for dinner at Montgomery's." Adrianna started to rise, but felt his arms tighten.

"Do you have any idea how sexy you are when you spend large sums of money?" he asked.

In the parking lot of the medical professional building, where he had spent the regulation fifteen minutes with his general practitioner, Arthur closed the driver's door of his

Buick and took a deep breath, feeling a bit shaky from the report he had just received.

Resolutely turning the key in the ignition, he headed the car towards his gallery on the property of Montgomery House, but instead drove by and turned beneath the wrought iron arch that marked the entrance to Captain's Point Cemetery.

Bringing the car to a halt, he disembarked and crossed the grass to the granite bench that stood alongside his Sylvia's grave.

"What do I do now?" he whispered into the chill air once he had taken a seat, but he wasn't surprised when, this time, no response came.

After all, the only one who could answer his question was Edwina, and he couldn't bring himself to ask her.

## CHAPTER XXIII

"That's the last of them." Herb hung a gray tweed sports coat on what would now be his side of the master bedroom closet in Jewel's Victorian. "Jeff's bringing two more boxes on his way home this afternoon, but those things will go in the drawers."

"I can't tell you how much this has meant to me," his fiancée stated. "Both to have your help with Bruce's things and to see your possessions filling the space. The latter's made our getting married seem real."

"Not having second thoughts are you?" He crossed the short space between them and took her hand.

"I haven't experienced a moment's hesitation," she stated firmly. "I love you, and you love me. People who love one another should be together."

"I couldn't agree with you more."

"Father Thompson is available next Saturday morning, and the small chapel is free," she continued as they made their way towards the stairs. "Everything's falling into place. The only item left on my list is to tell Kate our plans sometime tomorrow, when I'll have an opportunity. I hardly spot her during the week."

"I don't see why she would object, do you?" he asked. "After all, her suite of rooms is self-contained, and I don't think she'll be living here much longer anyway. They're trying hard not to show their feelings for each other in public, but it's clear as a bell that she and Larry Chesterton are deeply in love."

"Kate couldn't do any better than Larry, and he'll do well with her." Jewel held Herb's gloves as he put on his heavy winter work jacket. "Hopefully, wedding bells will ring for those two as soon as her divorce finalizes. From the little she's told me, that girl deserves a whole lot better than she got with her soon-to-be ex, and it's time Larry settles down."

As Jewel closed her front door behind Herb, Becca opened her laptop in her dorm room, pleased to spot a new email from Jeff in her Inbox that she immediately opened and read:

*Great news about your A on your history quiz. Way to go, girl!*

*I'm enjoying the landscape design class I chose as an elective. Hopefully, some of what I'm learning will help me to fulfill my part of Dad's and my obligations on the Tuttle Avenue project.*

*Everyone that can is meeting at the house next Wednesday afternoon, when the appraiser is coming. Because of the wedding, Dad's asked me to do the lion's share of this one. Talk about diving right in.*

*That crazy song about the duck came on the radio, when I was driving home today, and I started singing and quacking along like we used to. It wasn't the same without you.*

*Miss you!*

*Jeff*

Sounds of laughter came from her suitemates' room, and a television blared across the hallway. Still, Becca suddenly felt lonely, her finger touching the screen before her as if somehow she could feel a connection through it to the man she had left behind in Captain's Point along with her heart.

"Last one." The object of her thoughts looked up from where he was tying closed an oversized yard bag.

"I appreciate your helping me." Jack swung the bag over his shoulder and headed towards the driveway of his home. "Getting this area cleared is the first step towards the rose garden I want to put in for Susan when spring gets here, but keep that under your hat. Do you have a few minutes to come in? Susie's still working, so I'm free."

"Sure," Jeff agreed, always glad to spend time with the older man whom he now thought of as a friend.

"Soda, lemonade or something hot?" Jack asked once they had hung their coats on the backs of two kitchen chairs.

"Coffee, if it isn't too much trouble." His helper took a seat.

"How are things going?" his host asked.

Jeff hesitated. "Depends on how you look at them."

"Go on."

"Dad and I are pleased about this new business venture with you." Again, he hesitated.

"But…" Jack put a mug of coffee in front of his guest and took his own accustomed seat at the table.

"All of my life I've thought what I wanted most in the world was to be a journalist, but now, between Stuart's Landscaping and this new business, I don't see any way I'll ever be able to leave Captain's Point. Then, journalism itself has changed dramatically over the past years, and there's more."

"There always is." Jack sent him an encouraging smile. "Is this about the girl you bought the necklace for at Christmas?"

"Yes." A slight flush entered the younger man's cheeks.

"Becca Tate?"

"Yes."

"You've proven yourself to have good taste." Jack lifted his mug from the table.

Jeff's head came up sharply. "Am I aiming too high?"

"Don't be absurd," Jack admonished him. "When a woman truly loves a man, it isn't because of what he's accumulated, it's because of who he is deep down inside."

"You really think so?"

"Susie wasn't even aware of John Jeffers, internationally known, award-winning author, as the media refers to me, when she accepted my proposal. I was no more than the manager of Montgomery Marina, whom she'd grown to love."

"Eventually, Becca plans to earn a PhD and teach at a major university, while I no longer want to be a journalist. I'd still like to use my writing skills in some way, though. So what do I do?" He hoped the man before him would offer some sort of solution.

"Keep the lines of communication open," Jack suggested. "Take advantage of opportunities to cement your relationship, when she comes home to visit. If your feelings stand the test of time then, at some point, one of you will switch gears or you'll come up with a way you can live part-time here and part-time somewhere else."

"What about the writing?"

"Don't put it off." The author relaxed in his chair. "I started writing my Anderson series as a diversion, when I was working on my MBA. Think about what you find entertaining, and write the book you'd like to read in that genre. Get three chapters completed, and I'll give you a critique."

"Thanks." Jeff sent him a grin. "That's a great idea." But then, his face sobered. "I'm not looking forward to the next couple of years without Becca close by."

"Actually, I have a couple of ideas about that as well." Jack crossed to the counter, returned with the coffee pot, topped off their mugs and resumed his seat.

"Anything you can suggest would be a relief."

"From where I sit, there are two opportunities coming up that you can't afford to miss." Jack's words couldn't have surprised Jeff more.

# CHAPTER XXIV

David Eskar looked out the kitchen window of the white frame home in which he had grown up, enjoying a few minutes of peace and quiet before he returned to his self-contained dental practice that resided on the west side of the house.

How happy and in love Jack and Susan Jefferson had seemed this morning, both obviously pleased about her pregnancy. Each time he interacted with the author, he found himself respecting the other man more, even as he filled with jealousy, but all it would take was his own marriage to Karen to resolve that.

Jefferson and Edmund Robinson's plans for the new Captain's Point Chamber Music Group would further his cause, as he and Karen's father had both indicated their interest in playing with the group as violinists. Hopefully, her father would consider him worthy of his intended, once the older man knew him better.

And this other idea of Jack's… Amazing!

What an opportunity, although how the author would pull off such a plan without his wife knowing was more than he could imagine. It would be interesting to watch Jefferson make the attempt, and he might learn a few things along the way.

As David turned from his kitchen window, Edwina looked through hers, relieved to see Arthur's Buick pull into a slot in front of his gallery. It was about time.

"I won't be available to lunch with you tomorrow," she had mentioned to the artist on Monday. "I have my yearly medical exam scheduled with my doctor at eleven-thirty, and she usually runs late."

"Sylvia kept our appointments up," he had shared. "Maybe I should make one for myself. I haven't seen my general practitioner since her death."

Realizing this meant her Arthur hadn't been examined for years, she'd been aghast. No wonder married men lived longer than unmarried ones.

"Call his office now," she had encouraged him, trying not to appear too pushy. "It's the sort of thing one easily forgets, no matter how well-intentioned."

To her relief, he had obliged and secured an early appointment for this morning. Hopefully, things had gone well, but the fact that he carried a small, white paper bag resembling those given out by Captain's Point Pharmacy and that there was a crease in his brow didn't inspire confidence.

Slipping into her winter coat, she lifted an insulated bag from the counter that held a lunch of homemade potato soup and roast beef sandwiches she had prepared a few minutes before in hopes that Arthur would appear.

Two slices of chocolate pie made in a homemade graham cracker crust with whipped cream ready in a container to top it would finish their hearty repast and, hopefully, set anything that was worrying him to rights.

Entering Artful Soul a few minutes later, Edwina realized that she had interrupted the gallery's owner in the process of taking a pill.

"Edwina," he greeted her, his eyes sliding from her to the pill bottle that sat open on the antique desk he used as a counter. "I see you've brought lunch."

"I hope you didn't eat on the way back from the doctor's." She headed for a work table in the back.

"And miss one of your meals?" He peered over her shoulder eagerly. "Not on your life. Should I get us bottled waters?"

"Please."

"Just what I needed." Arthur set the top he had unscrewed from his container of soup aside and added generous portions of grated cheddar cheese and bacon bits Edwina had placed within his reach.

"So how did it go this morning?" She watched his face carefully.

"Not as well as I had hoped, I'm afraid." He focused completely on straightening the lettuce in his roast beef sandwich.

Edwina stilled his hand with her own. "Tell me."

"My blood pressure was 140 over 95, and I've been put on medication." He met her gaze, his faded brown eyes full of worry.

"And...?"

"That's all."

"What did the doctor prescribe?" she asked, not surprised when he named the same drug that she used.

"I only have to take one tablet per day," he pointed out. "Plus one enteric coated baby aspirin each night before I go to bed."

"Next time ask him to order the generic version of the beta blocker," she stated. "It'll save you a lot of money over time. It does me."

"You have high blood pressure?" Arthur's spoon stopped halfway to his mouth.

"Ever since my mid-fifties," Edwina filled him in. "It runs in my family, but like you, one tablet per day has kept it well under control. You must be in very good overall health if this is the first regular medication you've ever taken."

"You really think so?" he asked, his face relaxing before her.

"Absolutely, but I'm not surprised." She sent him an encouraging smile. "After all, you're lean and well-muscled, and you stay active on a daily basis."

"Thank you." He took her hand in his, even as he fought to get his head around a vision of himself as well-muscled. "You've eased my mind. I was afraid you would think less of me, if you knew I had a health concern."

"Arthur, listen to me. We have both passed our three score and ten," Edwina said. "God has given us a great gift, bringing us together at this time of our lives, but while we should take care of our health, we mustn't dwell on it. Both of us know what it is to love and suffer loss, but neither of us would be any happier if we had never known those loves at all."

"What is it that makes you women so wise?" he asked.

"Probably, the fact that, left to your own devices, you men wouldn't take care of yourselves." She laughed as she returned to her soup.

And, as he took a bite of one of the most delicious roast beef sandwiches he had ever eaten, Arthur reveled in the fact that the woman before him had chosen to take care of him in her spare time.

## CHAPTER XXV

"Good afternoon, gentlemen," Jack greeted Herb and Jeff Stuart as the three of them gathered before their new firm's prospective Tuttle Avenue project the following Wednesday afternoon. "Looks like Larry and my sister are inside with the appraiser." He nodded towards the broker's Mercedes SUV that was parked in front of his own.

"Is Susan going to join us today?" Herb asked.

"No, she has an appointment with a client this afternoon, but Chase is on his way with Adrianna," the author filled them in.

"I think I'll pop over and ask Jewel if she could come over for a few minutes," the older man stated. "She may be able to provide some insights, since she spent so much time in the house when Sarah Ridgewell owned it."

"Good idea." Jack turned to the landscaper's son. "The yard seems neglected."

"Yes, but the Ridgewells always kept it neat," Jeff replied.

"So what are your thoughts as to how we should put it back to rights?" The author crossed to where an overgrown holly bush stood at the front left corner of the house.

"The first step would be to clear it of weeds and debris." The younger man absentmindedly reached down and pulled a green onion plant from what had once been a bed of annuals. "The grass needs to be aerated and treated with a mixture of seed and weed controller as soon as it's warm enough, and every tree and shrub on the property could use a good pruning."

"I agree."

Jeff led them around to the backyard. "There used to be a nice patio with a small wall fountain," he stated as they turned the last corner.

"It's still here, although it needs a good cleaning," Jack stated. "It'll add value when you get it fixed up. What about new plants?"

"None of the bushes or trees appear to be dead or diseased at first glance," Jeff pointed out. "We may need to invest in some new edging material and, of course, everything should be mulched. After that, some well-placed perennials would add long term seasonal color, and we could put in a few annuals prior to our initial showings."

"Those could go into large pots on either side of the front porch steps to add another architectural element," Jack suggested. "Sounds like you have everything under control. Let's step inside and see what the rest of them are up to."

As the two of them approached, the front door opened, and a stocky, middle-aged man dressed in jeans and a sweatshirt stepped onto the porch.

"I'll fax you the figures as soon as I complete my comparisons, Mr. Chesterton." He shook hands with the broker who had followed him into the fresh air.

"We'll look forward to seeing what you come up with." Larry paused at the top of the front steps and waited for his business partners to approach.

"Otis is giving everything the once over as we speak," he advised them. "So far, nothing too horrendous has cropped up. Basically, we have to replace the kitchen and update both of the bathrooms. The floors also need sanding and refinishing, but the Ridgewells had always taken good care of the property."

"Jeff's been filling me in on his ideas for the outside," Jack spoke up. "It's mainly elbow grease, plus some standard yearly maintenance. Overall, things are neglected, but in place."

"The other ladies are in the kitchen or what's left of it, if you want to join them," Larry greeted Jewel with a smile as she came up the front walk, with Herb walking proudly beside her. "I'm sure they'd welcome any input you could give them as to how it looked before the demolition."

"I may be able to do more than that," Jewel stated. "I can probably pull together photos that show every room in this house."

"That would be a big help." Pete Marlborough came to a stop at her elbow, along with Julia. "Is it okay if we go inside?"

"The appraiser just left." Larry gestured for all of them to go on ahead, not surprised to see Jewel make her way along the hall to the former kitchen from which women's voices could be heard.

"The plumbing's already in place for a basic triangular workflow pattern," Penny was saying to Kate as the group crowded into the room.

"Sorry we're late," Adrianna stated as she appeared in the doorway they had all just passed through. "Chase had a little trouble getting away. What's the verdict?"

"Everything's checked out as anticipated," Otis filled her in. "The electricity was updated approximately five years ago when the new boiler was installed. We need Julia to put together some updating plans for the two bathrooms upstairs and work with Penny on the kitchen. Pen also suggested that we utilize the small box room for a first floor powder room, since there will still be storage under the stairs."

"Sounds like a good idea," Chase said from where he stood behind Adrianna with his arms wrapped around her. "It certainly wouldn't hurt resale value. Can you work up some quick figures?"

"Sure," Otis agreed.

"Jewel was just saying that she can provide pictures of the kitchen that was removed," Herb filled the rest of them in. "What had you been thinking, Penny?"

"While I wouldn't have demolished the existing kitchen, it seems the current owners have done us a small favor." A slight pink tinge entered the housekeeper's cheeks as she found herself center stage. "There appears to be a hardwood floor beneath all these layers of tile and linoleum, and I wondered if we might utilize it. If so, we could match the new cabinetry to it."

"I believe you're right." Pete sat on his heels and lifted a corner of the current flooring material. "What do you think, Julia?"

"I agree with Penny. Properly treated, it would hold up well against use, and it would restore the home to its original condition."

"Speaking of original condition, we've lucked up with the built-in china cabinet in the dining room and the fact the moldings have never been painted," Pete added. "Why don't you and I go check out the upstairs?" he addressed his designer.

A half an hour later, everyone regrouped in the living room, where Penny made sure she returned Otis's metal tape measure to him, having taken all the kitchen measurements that she would need in order to draw up a plan once she reviewed the photos Jewel had promised to provide.

"Now that everyone's had a chance to look over the property and get a general idea of what's involved if we make this our first purchase, I suggest we take a vote." Adrianna drew everyone's attention. "Do I hear a motion to move forward with a cash purchase of this property as soon as the appraisal is in?"

"I move that we go ahead with the purchase," Jack said.

"I second my brother's motion," Kate added.

"All in favor, please raise your hands." Adrianna cast her gaze around the room. "It appears that we all agree. Motion carried. Larry, will you let me know as soon as we have the appraisal, and we'll call another meeting to consider our offer."

And as everyone prepared to take their leave, Herb smiled at his intended, thinking how nice it would be when the two of them could host a meeting of the group as a couple in the Victorian next door.

## CHAPTER XXVI

Half awake, Susan made her way back to bed after what was morphing into the first of two nightly trips to the bathroom with her pregnancy, glad that she hadn't experienced any morning sickness during the previous day for the first time in two weeks.

"I want to make love to you so badly, Susie." Jack's warm breath caressed her neck as she rejoined him. "Will you have me?"

"Now?" she whispered, already slipping towards a deep sleep, but then he kissed her, his answer clear.

"Will you carry me along with you?" she asked.

"Always," he promised, his voice husky with need.

"I'd be a fool then not to come along for the ride." She faced him, her curves softening further as she became shifting silk to his hot wall of strength.

Three hours later, freshly returned from her second trip, Susan automatically ran her hand over Jack's chest as she snuggled against him and let out a small sigh.

Recognizing that his beautiful wife was awake in his arms once again, Jack tightened his hold and kissed her. "I can't believe I need you so badly after what we accomplished a little while ago," he whispered into her ear.

"No problem." Her hand continued its exploration of his body. "As long as you're that gorgeous hunk of a man that my secretary's always going on about – the one who turns my insides into jelly with his kisses and makes me wrap around him like a satin ribbon, then I'm in."

"Woman, I had no idea where your highly intelligent mind journeyed when we were engaged in this type of pursuit." He chuckled softly. "I can't promise that I'm him. Still, I'm willing to take you for a spin, and we'll see whether or not I measure up to your standards." Once again, his lips found hers in the dark.

"Oh, yes!" Susan breathed, when they separated. "I'm quite sure that you'll do."

"Thank you for last night." He graced her lips with a soft kiss when she awakened to their room now filled with sunlight.

"I have to tell you that I feel a bit cheated this morning." She fought to retain a blank expression.

"Cheated?" Surprise filled his face.

"You didn't offer me one of your famous encores after that last round." She attempted a forlorn look.

"Not a problem." His voice deepened, his need for her ignited as wonder filled him at how her pregnancy seemed to make her even more receptive to his advances. "Consider the time we spent sleeping in each other's arms as nothing more than a long intermission."

Three properties away, Susan's law partner, whose day it was to go into the office, this being the third Friday of the new year, lay collapsed on his own wife in the half-tester bed in the tower suite of Montgomery House.

"That should send you off in good style," Adrianna teased as she ran her fingers through her Chase's thick hair.

"Sleep…I need sleep," he objected as he tightened his hold on her. "Can you give me fifteen minutes of snooze without dozing yourself?"

"I can certainly try." Hearing his breathing deepen, she nuzzled her head against the bend in his neck where it met his strong shoulder, reveling at how pleased she was with the new work arrangements that he and Susan had set in place.

As much as she wanted him to keep working, she still appreciated his willingness to bring flexibility into their marriage. So far, he had attended all of their new business venture's meetings, while still maintaining his duties at his law firm. Hopefully, they would continue to form their new life together as a couple in such a wonderful way.

Dutifully nudging Chase awake when it was time, Adrianna wished she could let him sleep on, not quite ready herself to be removed from his warm embrace.

"Do you have any idea how hard it is for me to leave you?" He gazed at her with eyes filled with love.

"Well, you must." She rolled out of bed, threw open the drapes and began her Tai Chi routine. "It's time for you to kill a mammoth and drag it back to the cave for our supper."

"Kill a mammoth for our supper?" He chuckled as he, too, rose and stretched. "Just the sight of one of those would send our Max into shock."

"Then, maybe, you should concentrate on a small bear." She brought her arms down and out in one graceful motion.

"Mammoths and bears," Chase mumbled on his way to the shower. What, he wondered, would his wonderful wife come up with next?

Once she had seen her husband on his way after breakfast, Adrianna called for Max to join her in the kitchen.

"Elizabeth Chesterton was jogging over to their farm as I was walking up the drive this morning," Penny informed her employer, who was attaching the dog's leash to his harness. "She asked if you could stop by The Cove sometime today. If that doesn't work, then she'd like for you to call and arrange a time. She has something she wants to give you."

"What a nice surprise!" Adrianna slipped into her pea coat. "She won't mind if I have Max with me, so I'll swing by after I take our little guy to see Jim Laidlaw for his shot." She referred to their veterinarian who, she remembered with a start, still had no one special in his life.

Her antenna now fully extended, she sent her housekeeper a last smile before heading with Max towards her car. A matchmaker's work, she thought to herself as they made their way through the walled kitchen garden, was never done.

# CHAPTER XXVII

"Good morning, fellow," Jim greeted one of his favorite furry patients a short while later. "How are you?"

Max's only response being to lick the vet's nose, Adrianna thought it best to enter the conversation.

"He seems to be doing fine." She set the hunter green car coat she had removed from the rescue a moment before on the chair that already held her purse. "We're only here for his shot. Your office sent us a notice."

"Well, then, we'll give you a quick once over and a small prick, followed by a treat before we send you on your way," the vet again addressed his patient before turning back to the dog's owner. "How are the renovations going over at your place?"

"Really well, so far," she replied. "We're making good progress, and we've had some interesting finds, including a small ruby ring that a diary we found later revealed had been passed down through the women in my family for generations."

"Neat!" Jim sent her one of his characteristic grins. "If you'll hold our fellow here for just a minute…" He picked up a syringe from a handy counter, took care of the reason for their visit, and then continued, "I've heard rumors that you've started a new business venture as well. Are they true?"

"Guilty as charged, if you're referring to our investing in some rundown properties in the historic district to turn them around," she admitted.

"I applaud your efforts in that direction." He gave Max a good scratch behind the ears. "I've always agreed with Chase and Larry's take on the way to head Captain's Point towards the best future."

Recognizing that their time was over, Adrianna slid Max's front right leg through one arm of his coat and then lifted his front left paw to do the same.

"We'll have to invite you, Bev and the rest of the gang back for another dinner, once the renovations are done and the dust covers are off." She slipped into her own coat as Jim lifted Max down.

"Always willing to accept an offer of a free meal at Montgomery House." The vet opened the exam room's door. "Tell Chase not to be such a stranger. I'm up for a game of squash anytime."

"Will do," she promised, thinking that perhaps she and Chase should plan a dinner out with friends one evening soon.

Closing the door behind them, Jim leaned against the exam table in the empty room for a few moments of quiet reflection. Even Adrianna, it seemed, considered Bev and him to be a couple, so why didn't his intended?

Growing up in the same neighborhood, they had been best friends until high school, when his feelings had morphed into more. A new driver, he had made an error of judgment on the night of the prom, and she had refused his advances from then on. By the time he had returned to Captain's Point to set up his vet practice, she had already been married and widowed.

Time after time, he had approached her in small ways and large, and each time he had been rebuffed, quite unfairly in his estimation. Why, he wouldn't even be a vet if they hadn't discovered her pet canary dead in its cage one afternoon during the summer after the ninth grade.

She had burst into tears, and he had held her in his arms as she had cried her heart out over the dead bird, his teenaged hormones racing as he had vowed to learn how to stop such incidents from happening to her in the future.

Maybe, if he had been in Captain's Point when her husband had been killed by a drunk driver, things would be different. Maybe, if he had held her in his arms then and let her cry her heart out on his shoulder in the same way as before, she would be his wife now.

Frankly, the way he had caught Bev looking at some of the other couples at the dinner at Montgomery House last fall, he wondered if she still had more crying to put behind her. Perhaps, that was the problem.

The room's door opened, revealing the concerned face of his plump, middle-aged office manager. "Your next patient is waiting in Room 4," she advised him. "Are you okay?"

"Who is it?" he asked, avoiding her question.

"Clara Madison with her aunt's budgie."

And then it hit him. Valentine's Day was only three weeks away. What a golden opportunity!

"Tell Clara I'll be right with her." He threw his arm around the woman he had known all his life and planted an uncharacteristic kiss on her cheek. "You're a dear!"

At the same time that Jim Laidlaw was whistling his way along the back corridor to Room 4, Arthur took a drink of orange juice and washed his morning blood pressure pill down his throat.

Catching a glimpse through the kitchen window of a small V-formation of geese flying overhead, the older man smiled. They, too, were probably enjoying what had so far been a fairly warm winter.

Returning his pill bottle to the cabinet by the sink where it was now stored, he couldn't help but remember how his concerns after his visit to the doctor during the previous week had been eased by his luncheon companion.

What would he have done throughout his life without his Sylvia, his precious daughter-in-law and now his Edwina? For that was how he now thought of the latter.

His Edwina…

Was it really only eight months since they had met? He couldn't imagine life without her sweet smile, tasty lunches and stimulating conversation. Each moment they spent together left him feeling more alive, the years after Sylvia's death having left him bereft, lonely and, if he admitted it, sometimes a bit depressed despite his family's best efforts on his behalf.

Meeting Edwina had changed all of that as she had reintroduced laughter and perspective into his life. Yes, he now had to take a prescribed tablet every morning, but where he had seen himself poised at the top of a downward slope, Edwina had congratulated him for being in such good overall health.

And then, there were the times when he held her in his arms and her kisses – her wonderful kisses. Oh, what those kisses did to him!

That had been the first thing that had entered his mind when he had been given the news about his blood pressure. When asked, the young doctor he now used had hidden his surprise fairly well as he had assured his worried patient that there were no concerns in that area.

On his way to his car, he had thanked God that he wouldn't have to give up Edwina's kisses, because he didn't think that he could. The warmth of her in his arms and the soft feel of her lips on his were like a drug to him, and he was more than addicted, grateful when she returned his advances in such a passionate way at their age.

She was right. Neither of them was dead yet, and they would be dead long enough when they were. Now, though, was a time for living, and he intended to make the most of it with her for as long as she would let him.

A bright red heart pinned to the message board by the back door caught his attention. Valentine's Day was coming in a few weeks – their first. He would have to do his best for his Edwina.

Pete Marlborough sat at his desk in what had once been the second parlor of the Victorian and tried not to glance through the archway that connected it to the former music room where Julia Henderson sat working, fighting the new feelings that rose within him. What was wrong with him?

Ever since he had kissed her on New Year's Eve, she had lived in his mind, the feel of her lips against his a never-ending memory. As each day passed, he found it harder to keep his hands off of her, his best friend's kid sister, and he had no idea what she thought of him. Would she even welcome his advances?

How well did he really know the woman who sat before him? True, they had grown up together, rarely separated for more than a few hours, but then he had left for college, limiting their time spent together to large gatherings during which their two families met to celebrate the holidays.

She had surprised him by seeking his advice when offered the opportunity to invest in Adrianna's new venture, she had seemed willing to accompany him out to lunch and to business appointments and they worked well together. Still, that didn't mean she would be thrilled by an invitation from him for a real date.

If he did ask her out and she rejected him, what would that mean from the standpoint of their business relationship? After all, it was usually just the two of them here in the office working together. Long silences could easily turn uncomfortable.

But then, he remembered that kiss and had to shift in his chair to assuage the feeling of discomfort that made itself evident within his jeans. Who would have thought that the tomboy he had known would grow up and become such a beautiful woman?

Even the way she stroked her pencil against the page as she sketched was a thing of grace, and when she walked away from him across a room or along the sidewalk to her parents' home, it was almost all he could do to let her leave him.

"Do you have a minute to look over these preliminary sketches I've made for the custom furniture we'll need when we finish the second stages of renovations at Montgomery House?" she asked, her rich voice calling to him way beyond what was appropriate to an employer/employee relationship.

"I'm supposed to meet with Adrianna to go over my final recommendations on February 14, but I want to be ready well in advance," she continued as he approached her desk.

Valentine's Day, his thoughts rushed forward. Of course!

## CHAPTER XXVIII

"Is my mama going to be okay?" Daniel's forehead wrinkled as he worked to cut the form of a half-heart from a piece of creased, red construction paper with a pair of blunt-ended scissors, several weeks later.

"Of course, she is," Jack answered, searching through the paraphernalia spread around on the kitchen table. "As bad as it seems to you and me, it's only morning sickness. Some folks consider it a good sign."

"Why do they call it morning sickness, when Mama gets sick after lunch?"

"Because most pregnant women get sick first thing in the morning, but some, like your mom, do so later in the day," his stepfather filled him in, as he placed the pattern for a slightly larger heart along the same crease in the paper to get the boy restarted.

"I'm glad it's only 152 more days until our baby gets here." Daniel set down his scissors. "I want my mama to feel better."

"Come here, Pal." Jack lifted the little guy from his booster chair onto his own lap. "I want her to feel better, too, but she would tell you, as she has me, that it's all worth it once the baby arrives. In the meantime, we can make your mom's days as easy for her as possible, and so far, I think we've done a good job of it."

"I mark off the days before I eat my breakfast." Daniel pointed to the fridge. "And I give her an extra hug every morning to encourage her."

"Exactly, and between us guys, we're getting your Valentine's box ready for you to take to school tomorrow, so she can lie down and rest." His stepfather twisted the cap open on a small bottle of school glue.

"Why don't you start sticking the hearts you've cut out onto the aluminum foil you've attached to your shoebox?" Jack suggested. "Then we can put the cards you and your mom prepared yesterday into it."

"Are you taking Mama out to dinner for Valentine's Day?" Daniel pressed a small heart onto the foil-covered box lid into which had been cut a long slit. "Heather's dad is taking her mom to Montgomery's."

"Not this year." Jack handed him a slightly larger specimen to glue on next. "I thought I'd do something special for her in the morning instead, but keep that under your hat, okay? It's supposed to be a surprise."

"Everyone likes surprises."

"Yes, they do, but you know what?" Jack slid another paper heart his stepson's way.

"No, what?" Daniel smeared a blob of glue over the heart and then pressed it onto the side of his box, getting almost as much glue on the visible side from what was left on his finger.

"I enjoy working with you on a project like this as much as I like surprises," Jack shared, glad that the child he now held accepted him so willingly.

"I like working with you, too." Daniel abandoned his task and locked his eyes on his stepfather's. "You don't yell at me like my other dad did. Why is that?"

"Perhaps, it's because I have enough sense to recognize a great little guy when I see one, and you're a special fellow to me." Jack forced the words past the tightness in his throat. "I'm certainly glad that you and your mom let me into your lives and chose to live with me here in our big, happy home."

Meanwhile, in the ranch house he had purchased from his parents, Jim Laidlaw lay on a faded beige couch in the living room and played with his phone. Half watching a basketball game on the old portable television that still sat in the room's opposite corner, his mind went back and forth as to whether or not he should follow through and call Bev.

On the one hand, if he didn't do something, there would be no further progress. On the other hand, she might tell him to bug off once and for all.

With a sigh, he brought her picture up on the small screen in his hand, thinking that looking into her smiling face might give him courage. Gently, he ran his thumb along her cheek as it appeared in the candid photo he had enlarged. How lovely she was, and how vulnerable.

Why had it taken him so long to figure out that she hadn't yet reached the point from which she could move on? After all, a downer part of his job as a veterinarian was to help owners of deceased pets find their way forward.

Resolutely, he thrust himself into a sitting position, called her cell number and adjusted the flattened end pillow behind his back as he heard her phone ringing, trying not to think of the space she had kept between them since that fateful evening in high school.

"Hello?" Her voice sounded distant, as if her caller only had half her attention.

"Bev, it's me…Jim," he began, thinking he could've done better.

"Oh, Jim." Her voice took on a businesslike tone, even as it came through clearer.

"I have something for you, and I wondered if I could bring it by your house tomorrow evening," he asked, making no mention of its being Valentine's Day. "I could stop by Armand's and pick up a pizza and cheesecake, if you want. That way, it wouldn't run us too late, since it's a work night."

"I guess that would be okay," she agreed, and he sensed a note of curiosity coming through. "I'll be here by six."

"See you between six and six-thirty then. Take care." He ended the call, giving her no opportunity to back out of their deal.

In her Virginia dorm room, Becca Tate tossed a deck of cards onto her roommate's bed. "You shuffle, and I'll deal," she said.

"So who's this guy that's coming to see you?" Angel Evans glanced up, her large blue eyes filled with questions. "Is this the one you're always emailing?"

"His name's Jeff Stuart, and he lives in Captain's Point." Becca placed a mug of hot chocolate on the bedside cabinet for her friend and retained one for herself.

"But he's driving over here as we speak, and you two are going out." Angel handed her the shuffled cards.

"That's right. He's staying overnight with some friends of a business associate, and he'll be here through tomorrow evening."

"So he's coming to spend Valentine's Day with you." Angel held the cards she had just been dealt over her heart. "How romantic!"

"He's doing Mr. Jefferson some sort of favor," Becca filled her in, minimizing her friend's visit. "Something to do with their making a trip next month to New York. Mr. Jefferson is an author, although he writes under the name of John Jeffers."

"Uncle Jack?" Angel's head snapped up. "He's one of my father's best friends. He's not my real uncle, of course, but I've always called him that. Isn't he a hunk? I wonder if Dad's aware he'll be in New York. How does he know your friend?"

"Everyone knows everyone else in Captain's Point." Becca discarded a red three. "Recently, though, Jeff's bought into some sort of business venture with Jack Jefferson and several other folks."

"He'll make money then." Angel discarded a ten, and Becca picked up the top seven cards from the rejects, melding most of the ones in her hand onto the bedspread.

"My father says Uncle Jack turns water into gold." Angel drew two more cards. "Your friend will end up a millionaire in no time at all, if he isn't one already. Didn't you say once that he owned his own landscaping business?"

"He and his father together." Becca wished they could stop talking about money.

"So, are you in love with him?" Angel's eyes filled with hope as her rosebud lips opened slightly in anticipation.

"I'm out." Becca fanned the rest of her cards onto the spread, neatly avoiding the question. "I'd better shower and get ready. I'm sure Jeff will be starving when he gets here."

She grabbed her robe and headed into the bathroom she and Angel shared with their suitemates, where she turned on the shower to drown out further questions that might flow from the mouth of her overly romantic friend.

What she had with Jeff was special, and she wasn't ready to share it with anyone. Nor did she want to talk it to death.

Part of her was afraid to meet with him in this new environment. Would she seem the same to him. Would he to her?

No one could say that he hadn't been faithful to their relationship, such as it was – emailing and texting her each day with bits of news and funny stories, even though they had never talked about dating exclusively.

Like her, he seemed reluctant to discuss their feelings for each other digitally, and their ever-changing schedules made it difficult to connect for a phone conversation.

Pouring shampoo into her palm, she felt a sick knot form in her stomach.

What if Jeff had found someone else? What if he was coming to Virginia to break up with her?

# CHAPTER XXIX

Jewel woke softly Valentine's Day morning and snuggled her head against Herb's shoulder, loving the warmth of his arms around her.

Had it only been a month since they had exchanged wedding vows?  Somehow, it seemed longer - almost as if they had always been married, their adjustment to living with one another practically nonexistent.

Of course, much of that was due to Herb's easy-going personality and his marvelous flexibility.  Whatever she wanted to cook or do was fine with him, as long as they could do it together, and if she did have plans in which he couldn't be included, such as her church circle meeting, that was fine, too.

"Good morning, Mrs. Stuart."  He smiled at her when she opened her eyes.  "Happy Valentine's Day."  His kiss was gentle and tender.  "I'm taking you out for breakfast, whenever you're ready, and then I thought we'd go to Tea, Crumpets and More later this afternoon.  I don't want you spending your special day working over a hot stove."

"I could get used to this, Mr. Stuart."  She touched his cheek with her finger.

"No doubt about it."  He once again covered her lips with his.

At the same time that Herb was starting his new wife's day off right, Jack was whistling his way up the stairs of Blue Wolf Manor.

"Your *petit dejeuner* is served, Madame."  He positioned a breakfast tray, on which sat a plate of scrambled eggs, a glass of juice, a cup of coffee and a single rose in a small vase, over Susan's lap where she was propped against the pillows of their bed.

"What a luxury." She smiled up at him, pleased when he stooped and graced her lips with a kiss. "I love it when I do work-at-home days."

"I love it, too." He perched on the edge of the bed beside her, reached over and lifted a mass of her blonde waves, allowing them to trail through his fingers. "Almost as much as I love you."

"Has anyone ever told you that you're an incurable romantic?" she asked as she spread homemade lemon curd on a bite of croissant.

"My wife has explained that to me several times over." He chuckled. "Although, she doesn't seem to mind it all that much."

"I can't imagine her minding anything you would do." Susan lifted his hand, kissed his palm and placed it against her cheek. "You're, quite simply, the best, and I hope Daniel turns out to be every bit as wonderful once he's a grown man."

"Speaking of our son." Jack wrapped her compliment away in his heart and moved on. "Did I tell you that he asked me to help him make a special valentine for someone named Heather?"

"That would be the Wolfords' daughter," she stated. "You know, Michael and Cheryl who own Drifters, the store that opened right before Thanksgiving in the old Montgomery carriage house. Were you able to put something together?"

"I think we made a fair job of it, utilizing some of the leftover red construction paper and a couple of doilies from our wedding reception."

Disappearing into his dressing room, he returned with three gift bags – one large, one medium-sized and one tiny one. "Ready to open your presents?"

"Oh, my!" Her face lit up. "Did you leave anything in the stores for the other husbands to buy?"

He lifted her coffee cup onto the bedside cabinet and moved the tray to their bureau.

"A few this and that's." He joined her on the bed, laying the two larger bags between them and retaining his hold on the smallest one. "Open them Papa Bear, Mama Bear, Baby Bear, if you don't mind."

Susan slipped her hand into the white tissue that filled the top of the larger bag, felt a squashy, cloth-covered item beneath her fingers and pulled, revealing a pink pregnancy wedge.

"How did you know I wanted one of these?" she asked, amazed that he would've thought of such a thing.

"Courtney told me you would appreciate it once the baby grows a bit bigger, especially when you're napping by yourself," he filled her in, referring to her sister. "Also, doctors recommend that you sleep on your left side after the first trimester, so we may need to sleep more like spoons going forward."

"You have been reading up on things." She blinked back tears that resided just beneath the surface now that her hormones were so out of balance.

"I want you to have everything you need or want and nothing but the best." He lifted her chin and kissed her tears away. "Promise me you'll tell me anything else that you wish to try, no matter how big or small. This is our child that you're carrying. Let me pamper you both."

"I'll do my best," she gave her word. "You have to understand that I kept such things to myself for a long time."

"That was then," he reminded her yet again, his voice filled with kindness. "This is now, Susie. You, me, our Daniel and this little one." His hand found her belly.

"Let me make the most of the gift you gave me when you agreed to marry me." He slid the second bag along the coverlet towards her. "Let's see how well I did here."

This time, Susan's fingers were greeted by the silky feel of satin, followed by soft cotton.

"You might want to dump the contents onto the bed," Jack suggested, which she did.

"They're lovely." She smoothed her hand across the first of two flannel maternity nightgowns, before lifting a third satin one, trimmed in lace, to admire its beauty. "They'll help me feel a little more normal."

"Pregnancy isn't abnormal," he reminded her.

"No, but it's how I feel," she said. "Everything's out of whack, and I'm stretching all out of shape."

"You're a beautiful woman, Susie, and I want to see you clothed in beautiful things, even now. There's another part to this that's still in the bottom of the bag."

Susan rummaged amongst the tissues and discovered a small notecard, which she removed from its envelope and read:

*This entitles the bearer to a shopping trip accompanied by Adrianna Sheffield and Kate Sinclair, during which at least one upscale black, pregnancy dress will be purchased before a girl's lunch out at Montgomery's.*

"I don't want this trip to include discount stores," Jack stated firmly. "Although, Kate, who has had a fair number of pregnant friends, suggested you might prefer a really nice, evening wear pants and top set instead of a dress, since your ankles may swell if you sit too long at a concert or over dinner."

"Thank goodness for Kate." Susan laughed, even as she marveled at how thoroughly he seemed to have interviewed family members and friends. "Are you sure you don't want to go with us and look over my shoulder as I'm checking for price tags?"

She hurriedly placed two fingers against his lips, so as to keep him from uttering the words of acceptance she sensed were well on their way. "You're bound and determined to fill that huge dressing room you've provided for me with designer clothes, aren't you?"

"Susie…?" He lifted one eyebrow.

"I promise I'll let you spoil me yet again. What's more, I'll enjoy doing it with my friends." She set the card on top of the nightgowns and looked at the tiny bag expectantly. "Are you having second thoughts about that one?"

"Not at all." Jack handed it to her. "There's no one else in the world I would rather have this."

Surprised by the weight of the bag, she carefully removed a two-inch square, slightly faded with age, velvet box from within it that, when opened, revealed a large, oval-shaped, antique gold locket suspended on a heavier-than-normal chain.

"This was my great-grandmother's," he explained as she opened it. "Both she and my grandmother cherished it, and the latter passed it to me. After the baby is born, I'll have a picture taken of me holding our little treasure to go in the left side, and for now, you have the one of Daniel and me on the right."

"Jack…" She couldn't utter anything further as her vision blurred with fresh tears.

"I love you, Susie Chesterton." He cradled her in his arms as he dried her cheeks with his thumbs.

"I love you, Jack Jefferson." She prepared to accept his kiss that she hoped was forthcoming, her heart full of gratitude for the man who loved her in such a thoroughly wonderful way, even as she was morphing into a beached whale.

## CHAPTER XXX

Edwina Foster opened her kitchen window to allow in some fresh air on what was turning into an unseasonably warm day and listened to the Atlantic waves crashing against the rocky shoreline. As seaside sounds blended with classical music from her radio, one faint memory beckoned, her thoughts drifting back through the years to past Valentine's Days spent with her Ham.

Wishing to retrieve a valued keepsake, she hurried along the hall to her bedroom, where she opened a dresser drawer, shifted her silk scarves and revealed an ivory-colored box that she lifted and carried to her bed.

Once seated, she raised the box's lid and pulled out a collection of worn, handmade valentines tied together with a red ribbon. Each one as special to her as the last, they represented the best of over forty years of celebrations with her dear Ham, and as she read her way through several of them, she allowed the depth of her love for her husband to once again fill her heart.

Not wanting to dwell too much on the past, she returned her focus to the present. This would be her and Arthur's first Valentine's Day together, and she had no idea what to expect.

How had he celebrated with his late wife, Sylvia? Always sentimental and thoughtful, right down to the last detail, surely these characteristics of his would carry over into a day centered on romance.

Even though she had developed strong feelings for this new man in her life as they teetered on the verge of something wonderful, neither had professed feelings of love to the other, only acknowledging that their relationship had progressed to the next level – their affections deepened.

Falling in love? Being in love? Was she ready for that?

Sometimes she felt that she was, but at other times, she preferred to leave things as they were, perfect in their own way.

Yesterday, they had shared Sunday dinner, taken a walk along the cliffs and then played a few games of cards. As he prepared to leave, Arthur had drawn her into his arms.

"Tomorrow is Valentine's Day, and I want to make yours full of pleasures – all that your heart could desire," he had whispered into her hair.

Returning to the kitchen, she breathed in the salty air as it filtered through the screen. What could he possibly have in mind?

Suddenly, the dependency's doorbell chimed, interrupting her thoughts.

"Edwina Foster?" a young delivery man from Beth's Buds asked, once she had opened the door.

"Yes?"

"Happy Valentine's Day, ma'am." He held out a long, white box that had been secured with a wide, red satin bow, and she accepted it before he handed her his delivery log and pen.

"Sign here, please." He pointed to the recipient's line.

Quickly, she scrolled her signature.

"Thank you. Same to you." She closed the door as he turned away, anxious to open her first surprise of the day that she set on the kitchen table before releasing and lifting the lid.

Pressing aside the green tissue paper, she discovered a perfect, long-stemmed red rose nestled within a cloud of baby's breath, a sterling silver vase tucked in beside it. Picking up the card, she read:

*To the beautiful woman who came to Captain's Point ten months ago –*

*This rose is a symbol of your steadiness, your strength, your faith in me and, most of all, your giving nature. You've brought a special happiness and joy to my life that had been missing for a long time.*

*Happy Valentine's Day, my sweet Edwina,*

*Arthur*

Touched by his words, she filled the vase with water, clipped off the bottom inch of the single stem and added it, along with its white background, to the lovely scroll-worked container.

Glancing at the microwave, she realized it was time to join her granddaughter-in-law Ginny at her recently opened shop, Needles and Thread, most of the morning now past.

Regretfully, she shut the window over the sink and hurried on her way along the sidewalk, eager to share in some of her great-granddaughter Lucy's first Valentine's Day.

Normally, she would've stopped by Artful Soul to thank Arthur for his gift, but he was meeting with a business associate about an upcoming exhibition at the other man's gallery most of the day.

Later, back at the dependency, Edwina sorted through her closet. Much as she loved surprises, she had no idea what to wear for dinner this evening.

"Please meet me at my studio at six sharp," was all Arthur had said the previous evening.

Once, Ham had surprised her, whisking her away to a ski resort in Wisconsin for the weekend. Was she ready to set aside those Valentine memories for good?

Ham was her family and her past. Arthur was her present. Was he also her future?

By three o'clock, she had narrowed her choices to two outfits, one casual – her gray pants suit with a red cashmere turtleneck sweater, and one dressier – her new rose-colored dress with its matching jacket.

Excitement filled her as the mantel clock ticked away the minutes. Whatever lay ahead, she was prepared.

Then it dawned on her. Her Arthur would've already taken care of everything.

She had been on her own for many years now and had mastered the art of independent living – a skill she valued. Still, it felt good knowing that Arthur had spent time putting her needs first. Would it be possible as their relationship developed further to somehow merge the two?

## CHAPTER XXXI

Promptly at three-thirty, Julia rang the front doorbell at Montgomery House, straightening her shoulders as the deep chimes reverberated in the foyer beyond the thick door.

"I'm looking forward to seeing what you've pulled together for us," Adrianna greeted her warmly, a smudge of what appeared to be flour decorating her left cheek. "Will we need a large space for spreading out, or will a smaller area do?"

"We shouldn't need too much flat surface." Julia nodded towards the design boards she had tucked under her arm. "Most of it's on these, and additional suggestions I have for the Tuttle Avenue house are in my briefcase."

"Let's sit in the breakfast room then, if you don't mind." Adrianna led their way along the hall to the kitchen. "Our library table is stacked. Besides, it's such a nice day out that I was enjoying a cup of tea overlooking the garden with the windows open. Would you like some, too? The kettle's still hot."

Ten minutes later, Julia felt they were ready for business, each now supplied with a mug of tea, two heart-shaped sugar cookies iced with pink, butter cream icing and several round wedding cookies covered in confectioner's sugar.

"I'm afraid I bake to relieve tension," her hostess apologized, glancing at their dessert plates and shaking her head sadly. "I made these for Chase, but he won't get home until later than usual this evening, which is a shame since it's Valentine's Day."

"Was your baking what first drew his attention to you?" Julia couldn't have said why she asked, except that Adrianna seemed in the mood to talk.

"No." Her hostess smiled shyly. "He told me later that he knew he loved me when he first saw me on the stairway in the foyer. He had asked me to dinner at Montgomery's in an effort to break the ice in our necessary business relationship under my great-aunt's will and to introduce me to John Thornburg." She referred to the former head chef and now owner of the restaurant.

"And did the relaxed environment help you to feel more comfortable with each other?"

"Yes, it did." Adrianna broke off a small bite of one of her heart-shaped cookies. "In the end, we barely spoke about business. He discovered I was quite different from the client he had anticipated, I saw a more personal side of him, and we both realized we could be completely honest with the other."

"You two were married only a few months later." Julia hoped the statement didn't sound too impertinent. "How did you know he was the one, if you don't mind my asking?"

Adrianna's matchmaker instincts suddenly sprang to high alert. "It was small things at first – a growing electricity between us, a desire to see a certain look in his eyes, wanting his approval. Am I making sense?"

"Definitely." The fact that Pete had the same effect on her swept over the designer.

"Then, Chase was called to Boston when his aunt had a stroke, and I realized he was constantly with me – in my head and in my heart," Adrianna continued. "That's when I knew I had fallen for him, but I had no idea what he thought of me. Up to that point, he had kept his feelings to himself, due to the terms of the will that lay between us."

"So how did it all get resolved?"

"Settling his aunt's affairs proved to be a huge project," her hostess filled her in. "Larry spent weeks in Boston with him, and finally, Chase asked Elizabeth Chesterton and me to join them for a short visit, so he could get opinions on some things that required our being in his aunt's home. The last evening we were there, the will no longer an issue, he revealed his feelings to me."

"How romantic." Julia wiped a last bit of confectioner's sugar from her fingers. "Anyone who spends time with the two of you can see how happy you both are."

"I can't imagine life without him." Adrianna sent her another shy smile. "Now, let's see what you suggest for the guest bedroom, and then I'm anxious to hear your ideas for the Tuttle Avenue project."

Relieved they were addressing the purpose of her visit before her hostess began asking questions of her own, the designer reached for her first board.

"When we discussed the guest room, you indicated your concern that it would appeal to both male and female guests," Julia began. "We're reusing the spool bed and vanity, which limits the number of decisions you'll have to make, but the furniture leans toward the feminine."

"I see you've included a comfortable chintz-covered chair on your board," Adrianna commented. "I like its profile."

"What you can't tell from the picture is that it's also a rocker," her guest explained. "Because of its arms, this particular chair would provide comfortable seating for anyone who wishes to read as well as for a nursing mother. It would also be easy to slipcover later."

"I like the blues you've brought into the color scheme."

"I've done the board utilizing chocolate brown, rich cream and a variety of blues, all of which lean toward the masculine." The designer pointed towards a fan of various fabric samples. "But we could substitute either a green or wine palette for the blues, if you would prefer."

"No, I like the blues you've chosen, and these fabrics are perfect." Adrianna met her gaze, relief clearly written on her face. "I can't tell you how glad I am to have this decision behind me. My parents and I moved constantly, often living in tents, and I didn't know where to begin. Your help means a lot to me."

"Believe me, it's been a pleasure," Julia assured her. "I love what I do at the worst of times, but you and Chase are receptive and relaxed clients. Frankly, it's been fun working with you two. If you don't have any questions about this board, then let me show you what your housekeeper and I came up with for the bungalow."

"Penny wanted to be here." Her client kept the conversation going as the designer switched boards. "Otis whisked her off to an inn for a long Valentine's getaway, though, and she could hardly push that aside."

"Certainly not," Julia agreed, wondering what it would be like to go somewhere for a weekend with Pete.

"Oh, my!" Adrianna's eyes widened. "That's not at all what I expected, but I love what you two have suggested. It's much more in character with the age of the home, but it's still functional."

"Penny and I both agreed that we wanted to keep things turn of the previous century," Julia filled her in.

"You've definitely hit your mark."

"Varying the heights of the standard cabinets we're using gives them a custom look," the designer continued. "Since we have a large pantry already available, we went with chunky table legs on the island because this isn't, strictly speaking, an eat-in kitchen.

"This gives the impression of a table while providing plenty of bar-type seating as well as drawer space. The drawers we've chosen are double deep and come with sliders that allow for more usable storage for such things as plastic containers and spices."

"Penny was certainly right when she suggested we refinish the original flooring."

"Yes, and if some of it needs replacing we can intermingle the original with new in such a way that you can't tell the difference," Julia assured her.

"May I ask you a favor?" Adrianna leaned forward. "I feel more like you're a talented friend than my designer, so I'm going to impose."

"I'll do anything that I can to help you." Julia wished her mother could've been a fly on the wall.

"Chase and I own other properties, including a home in Cape Cod that's quite large and needs work as well as a smaller property in Key West." Her hostess paused a moment. "The thing is, I don't want to disappoint Chase, and I meant it when I said that I have no idea what I'm doing in this arena. If possible, I'd like for you and Pete to travel with us to both properties at some point, but there are still going to be decisions that I'll have to make on my own."

"I'm sure we would both do our best to be available for a trip to either of those places," the designer assured her.

"Could we meet at the library on a Monday or Friday, while Chase is at work?" Adrianna's eyes filled with hope. "I'd like you to help me pick out some books to study. We could even drop by a store, if there are volumes you think I should purchase. I would love to treat you to lunch afterwards, and of course, I'd expect to pay for your time."

"Lunch out would be lovely," Julia agreed. "As your friend, I'll look forward to pointing you in the direction of some excellent resources at no charge – my pleasure. Pete taught me for free as my friend for many years, and this will give me an opportunity to pass his gift to me forward."

"I do love living in Captain's Point," her hostess stated. "Life is so much easier when one is surrounded by nice people. Let's set a firm date and time before you leave."

Thirty minutes later, Adrianna closed the front door of Montgomery House behind her guest and made her way upstairs to the tower suite to freshen up. Chase had said they wouldn't be going out this evening as he would take care of dinner, and she wanted to look her best for him.

In her mind, she envisioned the wrapped gift that waited for him in the library as doubts filled her about its suitability. Neither of them needed anything and rarely wanted more than they already had, so she had been thrilled when the opportunity had first presented itself.

Now, though, she wasn't so sure. What if he didn't like her gift to him on this, their first Valentine's Day together?

# CHAPTER XXXII

"Wish me luck," Jim Laidlaw addressed an aged gray cat as he paused in the foyer of his home, an open-topped, mid-sized, cardboard box in his hands.

Ignoring him completely, the cat continued to groom the underside of her left hind leg, and he shook his head slightly. There was no doubt about it. She was definitely losing weight and probably wouldn't last out the year – no surprise.

Quickly, he calculated how long it had been since his mother had brought the feline home as a kitten. Well, the cat had had a good run. She was at least nineteen years old, if she was a day, and twenty was definitely pushing it, even for one who had never ventured outdoors.

Still, although she had never shown him the slightest bit of attention or affection, she was something alive and warm to greet him when he returned home at the end of his day, even if all she wanted was her dinner. He would miss her presence when she was gone, which was all the more reason for him to keep on his present course.

How lonely had Bev felt all these years, coming home each evening to her empty house?

Shifting the box more onto his left arm, he headed on his way, surprised when he reached Armand's to find the restaurant's takeout service so busy. A lot of younger men, it appeared, considered pizza a reasonable way to offset their wife having to cook a Valentine's Day dinner.

Hurrying back to his SUV, he was pleased to see that it was just now six o'clock. Both when he hadn't shown up to take Bev to the prom because of the accident and when Dick hadn't returned the night he had been killed, she had sat waiting. It would never do for him to be late when she was involved.

A few minutes later, his finger pressed her duplex's doorbell, as he held a bag that housed two slices of cheesecake in individual containers and the pizza in its box. The cardboard container and the rest of the assemblage that would be required rested on the stoop beside him, just beyond the sight line of anyone opening the door.

He had brought no Valentine card with him, no chocolates and no roses. Merely getting to spend an evening with her and seeing to it that she wasn't alone, on what could still be a difficult holiday for her, was enough.

"Jim," Bev greeted him, a wary look in her eyes as they left his and moved to the pizza. "Come on in." She took the box and bag from his hand as he extended them, relief filling her face.

Lifting the carton, but leaving the rest where it sat, he followed behind, feeling a bit like a conquering hero who had managed to storm the battlements of some far flung castle.

Appreciating the open concept of her home's first floor after the chopped up configuration of the ranch he had left behind, he set his gift on the end of the kitchen area's peninsula.

"I've brought you a little something," he said.

"So I see." Bev moved a step closer to him and peered over the edge of the box at what was clearly an old beach towel that had been tucked in loosely around an eight by twelve inch container. "Okay, I'll bite. What is it?"

"Something I should've done back when." He paused until her gaze met his. "This has been a long time coming, and I apologize for that." He pushed the carton a foot towards her along the counter, and she took another step forward. "Go on. It won't bite, and neither will I."

"Oh, Jim," she whispered, once she'd lifted the towel and revealed the yellow canary that was perched in a hard plastic carry cage, her soft brown eyes awash with tears. "You remembered. Sometimes I think loss has been a constant in my life ever since the death of my bird."

"How could I forget?" He drew her to him, surprised but immensely pleased when she slipped her arms around his waist and hugged him. "Maybe it's time for you to start looking forward, instead of backwards."

"Maybe."

"I became a vet because, when your other canary died all those years ago, I wanted so badly to relieve the pain of your loss," he shared. "Did you know that?"

"No, I didn't. You've always been there for me, haven't you?" she asked, but then her eyes widened. "I don't have a cage or food or anything."

"Please." He attempted a shocked look. "I'm a veterinarian, remember?"

Reluctantly, he released her and retrieved a top-of-the-line cage and stand as well as a large bag of toys and supplies from the porch.

"You're such a pretty bird," Bev was cooing at his gift when he returned.

"Everything the loving owner of a canary needs, including a CD that claims to get them singing," he stated. "Compliments of the house."

"Thank you." She looked as if she might cry, and once again, he wrapped her in his arms.

"You're right," he said as he gave her a quick squeeze, knowing full well that he needed to keep things light at this stage of the game. "I've always been there for you, and I still am. Now, though, let's eat before that pizza gets cold. I'm starving. Then I'll help you get your new roommate moved in."

Taking a seat on one of the bar stools, he gave her some space. "I recognize these from your mom's house, when we were younger," he stated when she placed two vintage Fiesta plates side-by-side on the counter in front of him.

"She always claimed you were a bottomless pit." Bev laughed and held up a can of beer in one hand and a soda in the other.

"Beer for me." He opened the lid on the Armand's box. "Just out of the can's fine."

"I'm using my best napkins since I have company." She tore two paper towels from a roll.

"So I see." He placed a couple of pieces of pepperoni pizza on his plate and a piece of onion and spinach on hers, hoping that her tastes hadn't changed in the intervening years.

As they both munched in what he was surprised to find was a comfortable silence, he couldn't help but think about all the loss she had experienced in addition to the death of her canary. No wonder she had shut him out for so long.

First her father had deserted her and her mother, showing up only once, years later, with a wife who was younger than his daughter. Then, during their freshman year in college, her mother had been diagnosed with Stage IV cervical cancer, dying only a few weeks later, and her own husband had been killed shortly after their marriage.

Now she was head ER nurse at Captain's Point General. Even her off time was spent nursing injured animals at the Animal Rescue Center.

Viewing her more from this new perspective as opposed to his own selfish needs and wants, he doubted that she had ever allowed herself the time she needed to grieve, merely taking each new loss on the chin and plowing on.

"I wonder how many slices of Armand's pizza I've eaten over the past thirty-four years," he commented as he reached for another piece.

"I shudder to think how many I've eaten." She reached into the box, their arms brushing against one another. "Probably half a hip's worth."

"Trust me, there's nothing wrong with your hips." He sent her a lecherous grin, and she rolled her eyes at him, even though she seemed pleased with his compliment.

All in all, he thought as he took another bite, things were going better than he had hoped.

An hour later, the bird's cage assembled and organized in a safe spot that both of them agreed would minimize drafts and kitchen fumes in the wide open space, he determined it was time to leave, not wanting to push his luck by overstaying his welcome.

"Thanks again for everything," Bev said, when he paused by the front door.

"This was long overdue." Once again, he risked the progress he had made and drew her into his arms, snuggling her head beneath his chin. "I meant what I said earlier. I'm always there if you need me." He dropped a kiss on the top of her head. "You're not alone, Bev."

"I'll try to remember that going forward." She pulled back and sent him a somewhat watery smile as she opened the door.

Whistling his way along the walk, he was surprised when he reached his SUV to find her still standing in the doorway, silhouetted against the lights from beyond.

"See you soon," she called after him softly, and then, miraculously, she blew him a kiss.

# CHAPTER XXXIII

In the Montgomery House's dependency, Edwina marveled at how perfectly her new dress fit, accentuating every feminine quality she still possessed. Misting on perfume from a crystal atomizer, she glanced at the clock. Five minutes until six.

Lifting her satin evening bag from the table, she slipped tissues and lipstick inside the zippered compartment and then retrieved her special Valentine for her Arthur.

Her Arthur...

She loved the sound of the words, and tonight she wanted him to know just where he stood in her eyes.

More than a friend, not yet a lover, but still, he was a keeper. At this moment, she could feel forever, but is that what he wanted?

Personally, she was firmly planted in a state of awe that she had met another perfectly suited match as her life moved forward.

Draping a silk shawl over her arm, she stepped outside. Arthur was waiting.

Moments later, Edwina opened the door of Artful Soul and let out a small gasp.

"Happy Valentine's Day." Arthur hurried forward, very dapper in his best Sunday suit. "You look amazing." He extended his hands to hers as she stepped inside, her eyes floating around the sales floor, noting all his special touches.

Miniature white twinkle lights had been strategically hung throughout the space, accent lighting highlighted his paintings, and a round mahogany table was centered in the room, set with sterling silver candlesticks and a tiny arrangement of baby roses.

"How romantic." She smiled at him, amazed by the lengths to which he had gone to create this one-of-a-kind atmosphere. "Your paintings glow in this soft light."

"As do you, my dear. Now, let's get you seated." He held out one of the velvet arm chairs customers usually enjoyed as they made their selections, before handing her a glass of chilled chardonnay and placing a plate of stuffed mushrooms on the table. "Hors d'oeuvres? Montgomery's catering service has done us proud."

"Thank you." She lifted one of the roasted vegetables onto the small plate in front of her. "And thank you for your thoughtful gifts – my beautiful rose and vase and now all of this. I'm touched."

"You deserve the best." Arthur gave her hand a gentle squeeze. "It's been my pleasure."

As they enjoyed their appetizers, Edwina shared moments from her time spent at Needles and Thread, noting that he seemed genuinely interested. Dinner, when he served it, proved to be all her favorites – Lobster Thermidor, Caesar salad, and rice pilaf.

"Everything looks exquisite." Edwina prepared to enjoy the special treat he had provided for them.

"For dessert, we have individual pots de crème waiting in my little refrigerator," he filled her in. "I hope you don't mind that I chose to wine and dine you here, but this evening, I wanted you all to myself."

"I prefer being here tonight, too." She watched as he refilled their wine glasses.

"A toast." He lifted his crystal goblet to hers. "To the first of many Valentine's Days spent together."

## CHAPTER XXXIV

Who would've thought that he would be taking little Julia Henderson out for Valentine's Day?  Pete Marlborough tightened the new tie he had bought for the evening around his neck, approved what he saw in the mirror and reached for his suit coat that lay on the bed in the suite of rooms over his office downstairs.

It had taken him two weeks to make up his mind as he had waffled back and forth, debating whether the timing was right.  So much lay on the line – his and Julia's working relationship as well as their partnership in the Sheffield's new venture, and once he took this step, nothing would ever be the same again.

Then memories of their New Year's Eve kiss would enter his head.  Even after Chase had arranged for him to use the Montgomery table at the restaurant bearing the lawyer's wife's maiden name, it had taken him another week to put his plans into motion.

"I'd like to take you out for a nice dinner Monday evening."  He had lounged against Julia's desk the previous Friday afternoon, thinking as he had uttered the words that he had now cast the die.

"That would be lovely."  Her amber eyes had smiled back at him.

"Good."  His mind had suddenly gone blank, and he hadn't even mentioned that it would be Valentine's Day.  "Why don't I pick you up at your house around six-thirty?"

"I'll look forward to it," she had replied, and he had taken his leave, spending the rest of that day and this one at the barn-conversion project.

Not wanting there to be any doubt as to his intentions, he had ordered a dozen roses delivered to her home, including a card with them on which he had written simply:

*Looking forward to this evening.*

*Pete*

Hopefully, she wouldn't feel too pressured by his gesture.

That kiss…

Who knew that a single kiss could make such a difference? But then, it hadn't been their first kiss. There had been that other time eight years ago.

It had been Christmas Eve, and their families had once again gathered to celebrate, this time at his family's home. His mother had hung mistletoe from the lintel over the doorway to the den, and a comedy of errors had placed Julia under the dried arrangement at the same time as him.

Two of her young cousins had seen them and insisted that they should kiss, and in an effort to keep the youngsters from making their demands even louder, he had obliged. That was the last thing he remembered until he pulled away from her face and discovered her arms around his neck and his around her waist.

Appalled, he had excused himself, putting on his coat and taking a long walk in an effort to rein in his body's response.

He had been a graduating senior. She was a mere freshman and the kid sister of his best friend. In the end, he had written it off to hormones and stayed away from her.

Neither of them were kids anymore, though, and he wanted her in his arms, warm and willing. Ever since that

New Year's Eve kiss, she had traveled with him in his mind – to the projects he was overseeing, the grocery and, finally, each evening to his bed.

He wanted to take care of her, to know that she was okay and, yes, to love her. The question was did she feel the same?

Gathering his courage, he made his way to his car, drove the short distance to her childhood home and rang the bell.

"Give me a second," she said when she opened the door herself, leaving him to stand on the porch for only a moment while she retrieved her purse.

"You look amazing," he declared, and he meant it – the olive green of her knit dress playing well against her thick chestnut hair.

No one could say that Julia didn't have style. From the deep red and gold of the silk scarf she had draped around her shoulders to the designer heels on her slender feet, she could've stepped off the pages of any style and design magazine he had ever thumbed through, and tonight, she would be seen going out with him.

"Thank you for the roses," she started their conversation once they had left their neighborhood behind. "They're lovely."

"Beth's Buds always does a great job," he replied as if he ordered flowers for women all the time.

Having arrived at the marina, he placed his hand on the back of her waist and steered her the short distance to the restaurant where Raoul, the maître d', treated them like royalty, opening with the line, "Ah, yes. For you, sir, we have reserved the Montgomery table."

Sliding into the banquette seat beside Julia, he couldn't help but see her pleasure at the arrangements he had made, his heart filling with relief that he hadn't disappointed her.

"How did it go today at the farm?" she asked, once their orders had been taken.

By the time their cups of cream of crab soup had arrived, he felt himself relaxing. It might be a formal dinner at a fine restaurant, but it was still little Julia Henderson sitting beside him, the same as on the front porches of their childhood.

Julia, who had listened to his endless lessons about architecture. Julia, whom he had watched over as she had grown up, as he had felt a sense of responsibility for her even then. Julia, who shared his workdays so comfortably, who looked to him for advice and who might, if he was really lucky, even love him.

Finally, the meal over, dessert enjoyed and the sun set, their waiter delivered two glass mugs of Irish coffee, and it was time for him to make his position clear.

Reaching over, he took her hand in his, pleased when she turned from the view of the twinkling marina lights spread before them and gave him her full attention.

"You're probably wondering why I asked you to be my special lady this evening," he began.

"No." She smiled up at him, her eyes filled with nothing but warmth. "I'm wondering why it took you so long to do so."

## CHAPTER XXXV

Adrianna entered the library where the grandfather clock now resided, in an effort to protect it as much as possible from the dust being disturbed, precisely as the antique announced six-thirty.

Attempting to create a cozier ambiance and remove the slight chill in the high-ceilinged room, she lit the gas logs in the fireplace and then made her way to an arrangement of roses that stood in the middle of the long work table. Taking a deep breath of their scent, she recalled the note that had accompanied them:

*As always, my heart is with you.*

*Happy Valentine's Day, my love!*

*Chase*

Wondering how much longer he would be, she paced around the room's circumference to ease the anxiety that hounded her concerning her gift to him. After all, experience had taught her that whatever he had chosen for her would be perfect, and she didn't want to disappoint him.

Had he splurged on another beautiful piece of jewelry or planned a romantic getaway, such as the one Otis had gifted to Penny? Next to either of those, her lackluster present would pale in comparison.

"Adrianna?" Chase called to her from the kitchen.

"Coming." She hurried to join him, flinging herself into his waiting arms and responding to his kiss eagerly.

"That was quite a greeting." He beamed down at her. "Let me change into something more comfortable, and then we'll eat." He nodded towards a large picnic basket that now held court on the island.

A few minutes later, seated on a slipper chair in the spare bedroom her husband was still using as a dressing room, she admired the muscles rippling along his broad shoulders as he changed, and her mind traveled back to earlier that morning.

As usual, she had begun the day with her Tai Chi routine while he had taken first turn in the bathroom they were sharing. There he had discovered a Valentine she had left leaning against his shaving cream.

*You are my love, my life*, she had signed the card, and as she had stood in the light streaming through the bay window, she had felt his bare arms come around her from behind, her Valentine in his right hand.

"Do you have any idea how much I cherish you?" he had asked, and she had faced him, the thin fabric of her nightgown doing nothing to hide the fact that he stood before her clothed only in his boxers, his desire for her clear.

"Why don't you show me," she had suggested, sliding her arms around his waist.

In response, he had tightened his hold, his arm reaching out a moment later as they kissed, flinging back the covers on the half-tester and insuring that some time later they would start their work day all over again.

Seeing that he was now changed into his casual clothes, she rose.

"Where would you like to enjoy your dinner this evening?" he asked, as they made their way towards the kitchen.

"In the library, if that works for you," she stated. "The roses you sent me are in there."

"A picnic in front of the hearth it will be then, my queen." He stepped into the butler's pantry and returned with a wooden tray, upon which plates and silverware sat, along with two crystal flutes.

Adrianna realized she had been so busy with the renovations that she hadn't even noticed the preparations for their evening that he had left waiting.

"If you'll carry this, I'll bring our dinner and champagne." He handed her the tray and retrieved a chilled bottle from the fridge.

"I can't wait to see what's in the basket," she admitted, once she was seated beside him.

"John's put together a real feast." He unpacked signature Montgomery's containers. "The restaurant was full, and I wanted you alone with me this evening, here in the place that you make into such a wonderful home for the two of us."

"It's more of a mess than a home right now," she pointed out.

"No, it's not." Chase set the lid from a container of Caesar salad aside and took her chin in his thumb and forefinger, lifting her face to his. "All I need to feel at home is you near me, and you're as beautiful as ever."

His kiss when it came was tender, and Adrianna could've skipped dinner as her body reacted to him as it always did.

A while later, she relaxed against the back of the couch, memories of crisp salad, warm mussels and soft bread vying for position in her head. "Thank you," she said. "That was delicious."

"I'll make us some coffee, and then you can open your present while we sample John's dessert assortment," he suggested.

"I have something for you as well." She started to rise, but he held her in place with a touch on her shoulder.

"Let me," Chase volunteered. "I don't want you to lift a finger this evening. It's the gift on the table, right?"

Thinking her husband might surround the base of her coffee cup with a bracelet, Adrianna was surprised when he headed into the Captain's study and returned a moment later with a box that was even larger than the present wrapped for him.

"No peeking," he warned and left her for the kitchen.

He had set the box on the floor at her feet, and when she lifted it slightly, she discovered it was heavier than she would've thought from the way he had carried it into the room, balanced on one hand. Knowing he was due to return, she put it back like he'd left it, feeling something inside shift as she did so.

"Here we are." He set the tray with their drinks on the coffee table and placed an assortment of miniature desserts where they could both reach them.

"Open yours first," she said. "I distinctly remember leading at Christmas."

"If you insist." He sent her a boyish grin, and her heart melted as, for a moment, a younger, often ignored Chase sat before her making quick work of the wrapping paper and exposing the scrapbook she had spent hours assembling where it now sat on his lap.

"I'm not very crafty, but I did my best," she apologized. "Elizabeth sorted through all of their family photos as one of her New Year's resolutions, and when she was finished putting together albums for her three, she had lots of leftovers in which you were pictured."

"Look at all of these." Awe filled his voice as he turned pages of candid shots taken at Chesterton family gatherings as opposed to the more posed photos Augustus Chesterton had taken of him at major events. "It's like getting a lost part of my life back. You must've spent days organizing and displaying all of them like this."

"It probably would've taken Penny or Elizabeth an hour or two, but it took me time to get the hang of it," she admitted.

"Thank you." He threaded his fingers through her hair as he leaned forward and kissed her. "You did a beautiful job. What did I do to deserve such a wonderful wife?"

"All you had to do to get me was be yourself." She snuggled her cheek in his palm, but then she let out a small giggle. "Although I appreciate your appearing beside me in our bed every night."

"And most mornings," he teased her as he closed the scrapbook, retaining it on his lap with his hand spread across it as he nodded towards the box at her feet. "Now yours."

"I can't imagine what this is." She took care as she removed the broad white ribbon and thick, ruby red paper, revealing a plain cardboard box.

Opening the flaps, she found the top stuffed with moving paper, which she quickly removed. "How?" She glanced up at him, her eyes wide with surprise. "Where?"

"They were in your dressing room," he filled her in on his discovery. "The cabinet where you keep extra towels has a false bottom. I'll show you when we go upstairs. I dropped a heavy bottle of shampoo on it while getting a fresh towel, and the wood panel shifted."

"Do all the cabinets have false bottoms?"

"Neither of the ones on either side did." He lifted the first of three albums containing her family's photos from the box. "I checked right away."

Making a mental note to investigate further in her spare time, Adrianna took the album and opened it.

"See?" She drew Chase's attention. "That's me the first time my parents took me on a dig with them."

"You have your mother's hair and eyes, and your father's chin," he commented. "They both look even better on you."

"Don't be silly." She turned to another page.

"These were taken the same year that you found me in the woods and cleaned my knee where I'd skinned it." She sent him a shy smile as they recalled their first meeting years before.

"Your eyes drew me to you even then," he shared.

"There I am on Silver Queen," she referred to the Shetland pony on which her great-aunt's and now their property manager had taught her to ride. "See how young Otis and Penny look? Aunt Martha must've sent this one to my father."

"Otis is right. You always sat well in your saddle." He separated the next page for her.

"This was my parents' anniversary party at a local restaurant in Greece." She pointed at another photo. "How in love they were." Her voice broke.

"Just like us." Chase closed the album, lifted it and the others from her lap and held her close. "We have each other now, and soon we'll have a couple of little ones filling this house with their laughter as well."

Pulling herself together, she nodded her agreement into his chest.

"Don't you want the rest of your present?" he asked.

"There's more?"

"Only one thing." He lightened his hold, and she withdrew another album from the box, this one new and bound in leather. "It's for our memories going forward," he explained.

"Thank you," she whispered, her fingers tracing the intricate design in the cover. "Your gift and your love have soothed a hurt in my heart." She lifted her eyes to him. "You've given me the best Valentine's Day ever."

"And you've done the same for me." He once again drew her to him. "Neither of us is alone anymore, for which we can be grateful, and now both of our histories have been restored to us as well."

# CHAPTER XXXVI

"Those sure were good Valentine cupcakes your mom brought to your party at school today, weren't they?" Jack addressed Daniel who was sitting on his lap in the reading chair in the child's room as was their habit each night at bedtime.

"Jason took two of them, because Tiffany can't have sugar," his stepson responded, a solemn note underlying his words.

"Is this okay?" Susan lifted her fingers from an oversized Valentine he had received from Heather along with a kiss on his cheek that his parents had witnessed. "I thought you would prefer it on this chest by your bed."

"It's fine." Her son shrugged, and, not for the first time that evening, Jack and Susan exchanged worried glances.

"After you left, the other kids laughed at me," Daniel stated simply.

"Why did they do that?" Susan asked, a frown taking root on her face.

"We were supposed to list two special things that our best friend did well," he answered as if that said it all.

"So what does Heather do special that would've made the other kids laugh?" Jack fought the urge to return to the school the next day and demand a period of time out for the rest of the class.

"I couldn't use Heather, because she's a girl," Daniel explained as if he were a law professor lecturing to a group of preschoolers. "All the boys used boys, and all the girls used girls. I said that my best friend writes big books and plays the violin better than anyone, because it's true."

Jack heard his wife suck in her breath where she was turning down the quilt on the bed.

"Ah…" He frantically searched his mind for the right words. "Well, I'm not laughing. I'm honored. You're my best friend, too." He hugged the sleepy child to him and gently rubbed soothing circles on his small back, pleased when he felt the youngster's body relax.

"Thank you." Susan slipped her arm around her husband's waist as they made their way to their own room a few minutes later. "You handled that well. It never ceases to amaze me how cruel children can be to each other."

"True, but…" He steered her past their bed to the sitting area, where he pulled her onto the couch next to him, the silence between them lengthening until finally he said, "I'm not sure I should say anything."

"Whyever not?"

"Because I can't conjure up any way to say what I'm thinking that doesn't sound like a criticism," he replied.

"Of me?"

"You could take it that way, but I wouldn't mean it." For the second time that evening, he struggled to find the right words.

Drawing back slightly, she took both of his hands in hers. "No repercussions," she said.

"No repercussions?"

"None."

"Perhaps, this was inevitable," Jack began. "Think about it. Except for Sunday School classes and birthday parties that you say are mainly attended by girls, Daniel doesn't spend much time with boys his own age outside of school."

"Go on." A crease formed in her brow.

"I don't know what it was like in D.C., but given you were working full-time and had virtually no help with him, I would imagine that when he wasn't at preschool, Daniel was alone with you." Jack wished a hole would open in the floor and let him drop through it.

"You're right." Understanding dawned on his wife's face.

"Then you moved here to Captain's Point, and he was surrounded by the adults in your family and his cousin Lizzie, another girl," Jack continued. "Before I arrived on the scene, I bet he would've named Larry as his best friend."

"I agree."

"We've missed an opportunity by not inviting some of the boys in his class to play here or spend the night." He plunged ahead. "What do you think? You've been a mother a lot longer than I've been a father."

"But you're a smart man." Her eyes, filled with trust, locked onto his. "And you've added an outside perspective to the mix. Who do we invite over first?"

"Whoever Daniel wants." Relief washed over him at her acceptance of his theory. "Why don't we try a sleepover this Friday night? I'll take care of everything." His hand sought her swelling belly. "I don't want you overtiring yourself."

"I let him down, didn't I?" Susan averted her gaze.

"No, you've been a competent, loving mother to our boy, in what were often horrendous circumstances," he reassured her as best he could. "That's why he's the great little guy that he is.

"Circumstances have placed him primarily in the company of adults, recently for good reason. Now it's time to make sure he experiences everything he should during his childhood."

"Thank you," she whispered, her eyes still averted, and he drew her to him.

"I love you, Susie Chesterton," he said. "I love both you and Daniel, and I'm thrilled that our little one on the way will know you as his or her mother because, no matter what they have to face in their young life, you will always be there, guiding and loving them."

"I love you, Jack Jefferson." She hugged him tightly around his neck. "Even more, because I know they'll have the best father in the whole world."

# CHAPTER XXXVII

As the Jeffersons ended their discussion about Daniel with a kiss, the private elevator that had whisked Larry and Kate to his spacious condo on the top floor of what had been The Cove's carriage house opened.

"Okay, girl, let's get this train wreck rolling," Larry declared as they stepped into his luxurious foyer.

"What smells so good?" She took a deep breath, savoring the aroma of roasting meat and…apples?

"I started some pork loin chops and apple juice simmering, along with some sliced Vidalia onion and apple, in the crock pot this morning," he explained as he led them into the kitchen. "All we have to do now is put together some mashed potatoes and peas, and we'll have a veritable feast, including chocolate mousse topped with real whipped cream for dessert."

"My, you have been busy." She wondered if she would ever be able to cook as well or as casually as he did.

"I could hardly ignore our first non-official Valentine's Day now, could I?" He scooped her up in his arms and twirled her around in the middle of the large room.

"Larry Chesterton!" She laughed when he finally brought them to a halt. "What in the world has gotten into you?"

"You." He kissed her soundly. "You. You. You." He punctuated each pronoun with a light peck on the tip of her nose.

"I've never affected you like this before." Kate's crystal blue eyes widened. "If I hadn't been with you for the past nine hours, I'd think you had already started sipping on the chilled champagne you mentioned earlier."

"It's never been Valentine's Day before," he pointed out. "I woke up this morning, and the fact that I love you and you love me was the first thing that entered my head. Love, real love, is a two-way street, and I've never been in real love with anyone before.

"All of my life, I've been alone, even when I thought I was doing fine," he continued. "Now, though, I have you – the best gal in the world – and in a few short weeks, we'll be official. I've been waiting all day to get you here, alone, with me."

"I do love you, Larry." She cupped his cheek in her hand.

"I know." He beamed down at her. "And I love you, too. Isn't it wonderful?"

"Yes." She slid her arms around his neck. "It is."

"Ready for your first Valentine's gift of the evening?" he asked once he had turned on the pan of potatoes he had prepped that morning.

"But you've already sent me a dozen roses each to Jewel's and the office, and you gave me that lovely card and note when we went to lunch at Montgomery's." Kate's crystal blue eyes widened.

"So?" He grinned at her. "It sounds like you're forgetting that this is our first Valentine's Day together. Such events should always be treated as special. Now, if you're game, grab your tote bag so you can change into your casuals, once you've seen your surprise."

Placing his right arm around her waist, he covered her eyes with his left hand and guided her far enough along the hall that she was sure they were now in the master bedroom, where she believed they had taken a left before he brought them to a halt.

"Surprise!" He dropped his hand from her eyes, so she could see the big red, professionally formed bow that now hung suspended across the doorway of what soon would be her dressing room.

"You're always saying you don't have enough clothes to fill all of this closet space, and I always answer that we'll see to that once we're married." He loosened the tape on the two strips of ribbon that were securing the bow to the right side of the doorframe.

"So, I've taken a first step towards making sure everything's ready for you." He flipped a switch that turned on the chandelier suspended over the large island chest of drawers, and gestured for her to enter the room.

"Oh, my!" Her right hand went to her heart. "Where did you find them all?"

"Susan suggested that I order them online and helped me choose which ones to get." Larry watched with pleasure as Kate stepped forward and ran her hand along the first few feet of a lengthy row of padded satin hangers that now stretched like a rainbow along the bar on their right.

"I only did the one side, because my gorgeous cousin thought you would already have some for the left. We'll order whatever else you need closer to the time. Do you think we got the mix of regular and suit hangers right?"

"Definitely." She crossed the distance between them and slid her arms around his neck. "Thank you," she said. "That was thoughtful, and…" She searched for the right words.

"And…?"

"Somehow it makes my getting to stay here with you seem more real," she explained.

"Our being married and living here in our home together," he corrected. "I know what you mean. Sometimes, it all seems like a dream."

"A wonderful dream," she added.

"Yes, a wonderful dream." He wished as he kissed her that he could somehow fast forward time. "Now, I'm leaving you to change into your jeans, while I switch into mine."

He undid the other side of the bow and draped the whole over the island, then closed her into the dressing and bathroom area that would be hers, so she would have her privacy.

Not wishing to keep him waiting, she quickly changed clothes and hung the pant suit she had been wearing on a deep purple hanger, wondering as she did so what Maggie Daniels, who cleaned the condo once a week, would think of these new additions.

How this man pampered her – not at all like her soon-to-be ex who had patently ignored every Valentine's Day since their marriage, but it wasn't that Larry willingly spent his money on her that meant so much. It was the thoughtfulness of his gift, the way he wanted everything to be perfect for her and their life together.

Most men would never have considered that a woman might want such a thing as padded hangers. Even her brother, one of the most thoughtful, detail-oriented men in the world, hadn't remembered them when he had splurged on a dozen designer dresses for his new bride, although he had been thrilled when she had taken care of it for him, wanting the best for his Susie.

"I hope you don't mind, but I'm using one of my new hangers," she greeted Larry when he opened the door to his own dressing room and rejoined her.

"Mind?" He took her hand and drew her back to the doorway she had just passed through.

"They're for you to use, and I love seeing something of yours in its proper place." He made his position clear. "If I had my druthers, we'd move all of your clothes in here tomorrow, but I do understand and respect your sentiments about waiting. Now, let's get us fed before we both starve to death."

Ten minutes later, he was serving dinner onto their plates, but when he started to place hers on the table he paused.

"This won't do at all." He frowned. "I don't want you that far away from me, not tonight."

"You could slide your chair around to this longer side," she suggested.

"Still no good." He sent her a mischievous grin and positioned their two plates side-by-side at her normal place. Then, he shifted his silverware and champagne flute from the end of the table, pulled her chair out, sat on it himself, and gestured for her to sit on his lap.

"That should do it." He grinned at her when, giggling, she obliged. "Now I have your pert little self exactly where I want you."

"You are being silly tonight." She hugged his neck. "Now eat your dinner before it gets cold."

Taking a sip of her champagne, Kate couldn't help but compare time spent with Larry here in Captain's Point with the life she had left behind.

Complete trust was required before you could let down your guard and be ridiculous with someone else. There was no doubt about it. The man on whose lap she was now perched loved her deeply.

With a start, she realized she had probably laughed more during these past few minutes in his home than she had during any of her play dates as a child. Only with her brother had she let herself go like this.

"I'm so glad you're here." Larry nuzzled her neck in between bites.

"I am, too, and this is delicious." She took another taste of pork, being sure to include some of the sliced onion and apple.

"Let me stack these dishes in the sink, and then we can adjourn to the den," he suggested, once they had enjoyed their desserts, removing his left arm from around her waist.

"No, let's leave your kitchen clean, so you won't face a mess when you return from taking me home." She surprised him by objecting. "Besides, I love playing house in here with you."

"I can't wait to stop playing and start living the real thing." He planted a kiss on her lips that took root.

"That was quite an embrace, Mr. Chesterton." She rose from his lap once they'd separated. "I could get used to receiving one of those after dinner each evening."

"And a whole lot more of me, I hope." He followed her to the sink, his hands full of cutlery and flutes, where he noted that her face had sobered.

Placing the dirty items next to the sink, he took the dishcloth from her hand and turned her to him, thoughts of the stories she had told him about her husband's treatment of her on their wedding night and during the first weeks of their marriage filling his head.

"What is it, Kate? Memories?"

Without meeting his eyes, she nodded her agreement.

"Come here." He drew her tightly to him, not for the first time fighting the urge to track down her ex and deliver a swift upper cut to the other man's jaw.

"I know you experienced a tough time and a whole lot of disappointment, but not all men are callous animals," he sought to reassure her. "You only have to see Susan and Adrianna with their spouses to know that."

"I know," she whispered before adding, her voice stronger, "and you're kindness itself."

"We'll take things one step at a time," he promised her. "I'll never force or hurt you. You know that, don't you?"

"Yes." Trust shone from her eyes as she lifted them.

"I'll always know that it's you I'm making love to, Kate, and I'll never forget the honor you've bestowed on me by allowing me to do so."

"Sometimes, the past washes over me," she explained.

"One of my foremost goals is to erase those memories from your mind." He bent his face to hers, his kiss gentle with a touch of pleading.

"It isn't that I don't want to share your bed," she said into his broad chest a moment later. "Sometimes, I lie awake at night and think about how wonderful it will be when you make love to me."

"That makes two of us." Larry sent her a grin as he released her and turned on the hot water. "I'll wash the stuff that shouldn't go in the dishwasher, and you dry while I make coffee and turn on some music in the den."

Fifteen minutes later found them snuggled on the couch, mugs of coffee within easy reach and a Fauré CD he knew was one of her favorites playing in the Bose.

"I do have one more thing for you this evening." He made a deprecating gesture with his hand and then withdrew a black-velvet covered box from behind the end cushion to his left. "They'll go well with the dress you said you'd be wearing to Montgomery's this Saturday."

Nestled inside, Kate discovered drop sapphire and diamond earrings that matched the tennis bracelet he had given her for Christmas and glanced up, surprise and delight vying for position on her face.

"They're a little much to wear with your jeans tonight, but they'll look beautiful showcased with my favorite outfit." He bent and kissed her neck on a particularly sensitive spot beneath her left ear.

"I'm going to sound like Susan when Jack splurges on her, but I'm not used to being spoiled like this," she said, gratitude filling her that this wonderful man with whom she had fallen in love here in Captain's Point wanted her in return.

"Well, you'd better hurry up and adjust to the new position in which you find yourself," he informed her. "I've had nothing but time in which to plan how I'm going to spoil you rotten once we're married, and I intend to enjoy doing so immensely."

# CHAPTER XXXVIII

While Arthur cleared the table, insisting that she remain seated, Edwina set a white envelope at his place.

"What have we here?" He smiled at her as he withdrew her card, along with a decorative gold key designed to be slipped onto a keychain, and then read:

*Arthur –*

*Will you be my Valentine? You already own the key to my heart.*

*Edwina*

"Certainly," he replied. "I have something for you as well." He reached into the pocket of his suit coat and retrieved a leather jeweler's box that, when she opened it, revealed a heart-shaped garnet set in platinum that had been suspended from a matching chain.

"How beautiful." She lifted her eyes to his.

"May I?" He removed and secured it around her neck, then offered his hand and drew her from her chair.

"Will you join me for a short walk?" he asked. "With this unseasonably warm weather, we've been gifted with a lovely evening."

Sensing there was more to come, she took his arm as they walked along the sidewalk towards the gazebo Montgomery Properties had draped with twinkle lights several months previously.

"You're right about the evening." She gazed at the full moon that floated above. "It would've been a shame to waste it."

Arrived at the spot where they often shared lunch, she took her accustomed place on the bench seat next to him.

"It's so peaceful here," he began. "Almost as if we're alone in the world."

"You've made this a wonderful day for me." She drew his gaze. "You're a special man, Arthur Stern."

"We've known each other for less than a year, but we've shared so much in that time." He slipped his arm around her shoulders, and she caught a whiff of his aftershave. "I wish this night would never end."

Leaning closer, he kissed her tenderly before pulling back only slightly. "I love you, Edwina." He found her lips again.

"I love you, too, Arthur," she said, pleased by how natural it felt to form the words. "More than you'll ever know."

"And the best part is that we're just beginning." He hugged her to him.

In neighboring Virginia, Jeff Stuart opened the passenger door of his dad's Chrysler, where he had parked it in Becca's dorm's parking lot, and held out his hand to her.

"It's a lovely evening," he said, inadvertently mimicking the words of his older friend back in Captain's Point. "Why don't we take advantage of it and enjoy that park over there for a few minutes."

"Sure." She smiled at him as he shortened his long strides to match hers. "I'm glad you came. It's been a fabulous twenty-eight hours."

"I'm glad I came, too." He squeezed her hand gently. "You may think this is silly, but I was afraid big campus life might've changed you beyond all recognition."

"I felt the same way." She let out a soft laugh.

"Have I changed?" He held his breath.

"Only a little." She paused by a fountain. "Everything that's good about you is still there, but you seem, I don't know, somehow wiser." She searched for the right words. "Maybe it's this new business venture of yours."

"I'm learning a lot from it," he admitted, "and I've been doing a good deal of soul searching lately as well."

"About what?" she asked, as by unspoken agreement they continued along the paved path.

"My future, our future, journalism, big city, Captain's Point." He shrugged. "It's been a fairly long list. I even discussed some of it with Jack Jefferson, but there's one constant in all of it."

"And that is?"

This time he was the one who paused, turning her towards him.

"You, Becca." He slid his right hand along her jaw and then turned it upwards, allowing her long dark hair to trail over his palm. "You're my constant. I've loved you ever since grade school, and that's never going to change, no matter where our paths lead us."

"I love you, too, Jeff." She lifted her face to his. "I've realized since Christmas that I always loved the boy you were, and now I'm in love with the man you've become."

Wrapping his arms around her, he found her mouth, his tongue seeking admission, and when her lips parted, he tightened his hold and accepted her gift. She tasted of coffee, chocolate and honey, and he loved her.

"What do we do now?" she asked, once they resumed their saunter along the path.

"What we've been doing," he stated calmly, as they neared a bench set beneath an arch comprised of grapevines that the landscaper in him admired. "You're right where you need to be for the moment, and so am I." He drew her onto the seat beside him.

"I haven't changed my mind about my plans." She kept her eyes on their joined hands where they rested on his thigh.

He relaxed against the back of the bench and extended his long legs in front of him as his arm found its way around her shoulders.

"I don't expect you ever will," he responded. "On the other hand, I'm having second thoughts about journalism. That world's changing from the one I wanted to be part of."

"What are you thinking of doing now?" She wondered why he hadn't shared any of this in his emails.

"It's working with words that I enjoy," he explained. "Jack suggested I try writing some short stories or even a novel."

"And have you?"

"I've started on one of each," he admitted. "I write at least a few lines on the novel every day, and then, all at once, the plot takes off. It has a mystery component, and it's set in D.C. near where my aunt and uncle live. The main character's a computer geek."

"May I read it when you're ready to show it to someone?" Becca felt pride rise within her.

Her parents' choice of suitor for her had certainly never accomplished anything similar. What a Renaissance man her Jeff had become – landscaper, business owner and now writer.

"Sure." He twirled a lock of her hair around his finger. "I'll email you the first three chapters when they're ready. Jack's offered to critique them for me as well."

"Speaking of Mr. Jefferson, did I tell you that Angel's dad and he are good friends?" She snuggled her head against his shoulder, loving the feel of his firm warmth beside her.

"Really? That's great." He rested his cheek against the top of her head. "She lives in New York City, right?"

"That's right. Why?"

"Because I'm going there soon for something Jack's planning," he filled her in. "If it's during spring break, maybe you could set up a visit with Angel so we could all meet in the Big Apple."

"She's told me I'm welcome any time."

"Aren't you going to ask me for your Valentine's present?" he teased, changing the subject.

"No, I thought your coming to visit, the roses and all these meals out were your gift." She faced him.

"You thought wrong." Jeff grinned and reached into his pants' pocket, removing a box that once again declared itself by its signature wrapping paper to have come from Captain's Point's finest jeweler. "You deserve the best, Becca."

Carefully, she unwrapped a square, hunter green box. Lifting the lid, she discovered a gold charm bracelet from which was suspended a plump, heart-shaped charm.

"That's to remind you that my heart's always with you," he stated, as he removed the bracelet and fastened it around her wrist. "I'd give you the world if I could."

"Everything I want is right here." She drew his face down to hers. "Thank you."

"You're welcome." He found her lips once again, this time deepening their kiss.

She wrapped her arms around his waist and hugged him to her, wishing there was some way she could stop time and keep him here with her.

As if he'd heard her thoughts, he straightened and then held out his hand to her as he stood. "I'm afraid I'd better head out. I've got a long drive home and an early class in the morning."

"I know." She rose on her tiptoes and kissed him on the cheek. "I don't want you to go, but I understand that you have to leave. This has meant the world to me, Jeff."

"To me, too." He hugged her tightly to him and then released her, clutching her hand once again in his.

A few short minutes later, they arrived at the pavilion in front of her dorm, where he kissed her once more in the shadow of a tree, then lifted her wrist and pressed his lips to the plump, little heart that now resided there.

"Always," he said, turned and headed towards his dad's car where he paused, once he'd opened the driver's door, and sent her a wave, receiving a kiss blown by her in return.

As she watched his car's taillights leaving her behind yet again, Becca hugged herself against the slight chill that now filled the air and recalled all the meaningful times they had shared during his visit. Then it hit her.

Despite everything that he'd done, he still had asked nothing of her in return.

## CHAPTER XXXIX

Back in Captain's Point, Susan stood in her dressing room and debated whether to wear one of her new flannel gowns or the prettier satin and lace creation, not that it mattered. Each night, she slid beneath the sheets of their bed in her night clothes, and shortly thereafter, Jack took off whatever she was wearing.

Often she would retrieve her gown or pajamas on her way to her bathroom during her first nightly trip, only to have them removed again upon her return. She would then slip into them as part of her now habitual second trip, not wanting to be caught without clothes on should Daniel surprise them earlier than expected in the morning.

Sometimes, off they came yet again, her overactive hormones making her more receptive than ever to her lover's advances.

It was a wonder her pretty lingerie wasn't in pieces by now, despite her having spent very little time actually in any of it. Still, she thought it pleased her husband that she came to him looking her best.

As they lay in each other's arms some time later, her new satin gown discarded somewhere on the floor next to their bed and the gas logs in the fireplace casting a warm glow throughout their room, Jack amazed her.

"I have one more surprise for you, Susie," he began. "I hope you'll agree to it. I've already checked with Janie, and she's assured me there's no danger to the baby at this stage if you go. Chase and Bridgette have both stated that it wouldn't be any trouble for you to be away from the firm for a few days either, if you're willing."

"Whatever are you talking about?"

"Remember when I flew to D.C. and filled in for String Flings during the holidays?"

"Sure."

"They're playing in New York City next month, and they've invited me to join them," he filled her in. "It's a real opportunity for you to hear me play professionally and *Alpine Spring* performed by a group before an audience. I don't want to leave you alone right now, so I thought I'd take you and Daniel with me."

"Will we stay at your condo while we're there?" she asked, and he relaxed, relieved she was at least considering his suggestion.

"Not this trip," he replied. "I've lent our condo, as it now is, to some friends, so we'll stay in the drilling equipment company's suite at the Plaza.

"Daniel should enjoy that since it's the setting for one of his favorite books," he pointed out, "and you can take advantage of the amenities while I'm rehearsing with the group. I've asked, and they have a special massage table for pregnant guests."

"Don't tease me." Susan laughed, just the thought of a full body massage making her feel more relaxed.

"Scout's honor." He crossed his heart. "Promise me you'll take advantage of it. I've asked Jeff to go with us, so he can share a room with Daniel and act as the little guy's companion."

"As usual, you have everything planned down to the last detail," she stated. "I can hardly say no when you've gone to all this trouble now, can I? Will we be driving? I'm not sure I could take flying in the helicopter."

"Goodness, woman, do you really think I would subject you to that in your condition?" Surprise filled Jack's face. "The answer is neither."

"How will we get there then?"

"Gerald Tate's new runway at the airport is completed, so I'll arrange for one of the Lears to pick us up and bring us back. You'll hardly realize that we're off the ground before we'll have landed in New York, and the company's limos will be at our disposal while we're there."

"Limos? Are you serious?"

Susan wondered if she would ever get used to her husband's lifestyle and the perks that came with his part ownership of an international firm, especially since there was virtually no sign of them during their day-to-day lives.

Then again, having a Learjet and a limousine at your disposal would make travel when pregnant a whole lot easier.

"I know." Jack grinned at her in the soft light. "I'm spoiling you, but you and Daniel will come, won't you?"

"I wouldn't miss hearing you play and *Alpine Spring* performed for anything in the world." She straightened a stray lock of his black hair with her fingers.

"Thank you, Susie." He settled her head into the crook between his shoulder and neck with his hand. "I have no idea why you love me the way that you do, but I'm grateful for your love, just the same."

"Not as grateful as I am for yours." She snuggled against him. "Oh!"

"What is it?" He drew back, concern filling his face.

"Nothing's wrong," she assured him. "Didn't you feel that?"

"Feel what?"

"The baby moving. Right here." She slid her hand between what had once been her waist and his ribcage.

"No. Can you make our little treasure do it again?"

"Trust me, I have absolutely no control over it." She chuckled. "That was the strongest one that I've felt so far, though, so you should be able to feel movement soon."

"Really?" Excitement now flooded his face. "I thought it wouldn't happen for a quite a while yet. Daniel will be thrilled."

"You've done a wonderful job of making him feel a part of this," she thanked him.

"They say a newborn recognizes his or her mother's heartbeat." Jack again drew her close. "Do you think, if I held my hand over the place where the baby was moving, that it could hear my heartbeat through you?"

"I have no idea, but you're welcome to try it, Daddy." She sent him a smile, her eyes twinkling.

"You're laughing at me." He chuckled. "But, believe it or not, outside of hearing you say that you love me, Daddy is quickly becoming my favorite word."

## CHAPTER XL

As he pulled his SUV away from the curb in front of Herb and Jewel's house later that evening, Larry congratulated himself on the success of his and Kate's first Valentine's Day together.

It had been perfect – full of laughter, love and fun, but then, he had ridden down in the elevator with her and taken her back to her rooms once again, all the time wishing he had lifted her into his arms and taken her to his bed.

As much as he admired her for wanting to stick with her principles, it was killing him to hold himself in check day after day, week after week, he admitted. What if he was killed in some sort of freak accident never having made love to her?

After all, things like that happened every day, and he had learned only yesterday in an email that one of his pals from college had suffered a heart attack. If God would only allow him the opportunity to sleep with her in his arms for one night, at least then he would die a happy man if a tragedy should befall him.

At the same time Larry was turning onto the main road that would take him and his morbid thoughts back to his condo, Kate made up her mind and placed the tiny box that held the sapphire and diamond earrings he had given her into her lingerie drawer instead of under her pillow.

She couldn't envision a more perfect evening than the one they had just spent together. They had laughed until tears had flowed from their eyes, kissed until her desire for him had been overwhelming and then laughed even more about something quite silly.

How she loved this wonderful man. There was only one thing missing, and it was all her own fault. What had she been thinking?

Part of her admired and appreciated him for the way he respected her values, but another part of her wanted him to sweep her into his arms, carry her to his bed and make mad, passionate love to her.

If only God would allow them the opportunity to sleep in each other's arms for one night, she knew she could last through the rest of the time left until they could be married, without making his hard-earned sacrifice on her behalf worthless by her changing her mind and seducing him.

Three blocks away, David Eskar shut his laptop and turned off the desk lamp in what had been his childhood bedroom, his dark eyes gleaming with excitement.

What an amazing day it had been. No, what an amazing year it had been.

First, Jack Jefferson and Edmund Robinson had formed the Captain's Point Chamber Music Group. Excited as he had been about having a regular opportunity to play his violin with someone as talented as the famous author/composer, he had been even more thrilled to discover that Karen would be playing her flute with the group.

But then, her father had charged into the front parlor at the Sheffield Place Inn, ten minutes late and a violin case in his hands. Who had known that Ira Zobel played the violin the same as he did?

A major purpose of the organizational meeting had been to determine each player's position in the group. Managing to get the author aside by volunteering to help him bring in more chairs, he had begged Jack to name Ira second violin and not him.

The composer had looked at him strangely, but when they had returned to the room and he had sought out Karen as he often did, the other man had nodded at him with what he thought had been understanding.

Ira Zobel kept a tight rein on his family and business concerns, employing both his son and daughter in the latter, and it simply would not have done for him to have bested the older man he hoped would someday become his father-in-law.

Two rehearsals later, Jack had leaned towards him and Ira during a short break. "I need an extra violin to play in New York City with me in mid-March," the composer had said. "Would either of you two be interested?"

Ira had immediately declined the invitation, declaring in no uncertain terms that he was indispensable to the proper running of his furniture business.

Receiving the rebuff with his normal grace, Jack had then looked to him as third violin at exactly the same moment Edmund had called for everyone's attention, saving him from what could've been an embarrassing moment.

In the inn's parking lot, later that evening, he had accepted the composer's invitation. Between his father's last illness and working to grow his dental practice, he hadn't had a vacation in years. It was time to leave town for a few days and experience something new and different.

Then, two weeks ago, he had learned quite by accident that Karen often jogged mornings in a nearby park, taking advantage of the gym and shower facilities their synagogue had recently installed right next door.

Ever since, he had made it a point to be at the park most mornings, and on eight occasions, they had combined their morning runs, chatting as they did stretches and made their way around the paved paths. Asked what she thought of his plans to go to New York City with Jack, Karen had been thrilled for him, stating it was an honor to have been offered such an opportunity.

This morning, he had set his alarm earlier than usual, making sure that he was already doing his warm-up when she arrived. As she finished stretching, he had managed to slip a Valentine card from his gym bag into hers.

It had taken him hours to finalize the words he had written inside. He and Karen were good, long-time friends, and they often sought each other's company at their synagogue's young adult gatherings. Still, he had no reason beyond his own hope to believe that she would welcome further advances on his part.

Eventually, he had decided that less was better. Gathering his courage, he had taken pen in hand and added to what was already printed on the card only the few words:

*May this be your best Valentine's Day ever!*

*Yours,*

*David*

The next fourteen hours had seen him vacillating between thoughts that he had done the right thing and fear that he had ruined all progress made by his tentative advances. But then, he had retired to his room and checked his email, thrilled to find an uncharacteristic message from Karen in his Inbox.

Clicking on the line, he had discovered that she, too, had kept her words to a minimum as he had read:

*Thanks to your lovely card, it has been!*

*Yours, too,*

*Karen*

Rising from his chair, he paced to his bedside table where he once again set his alarm for earlier than usual before retiring for the night. There was no way he would be late for his meeting with Karen at the jogging path in the park tomorrow.

# CHAPTER XLI

Later that night, as spouses often do, Susan rolled towards Jack, and he reflexively gathered her into his arms. This time, though, she did not follow through on their normal routine by snuggling her head against his shoulder and returning to a deep sleep. Instead, she brought her left leg over his and raised her head from the pillow.

"Are you awake?" she asked, her mind still focused on a comment he had made earlier.

"Parts of me will soon be more awake than is conducive to sleep if you continue to rub your inner thigh against mine," he chuckled a reply.

"Do you have a minute?"

"I can check my calendar if you wish, but I seem to be free." Once again, his ribs moved beneath hers in laughter.

"It's only that I have a few things I want to say," she explained.

"Should I prepare for this discussion?" he asked, recognizing that she must have something serious on her mind for her to disturb their sleep in this way.

"No, I merely ask that you stay awake and really take in what I'm saying as I prattle along."

"Okay," he agreed. "I'm all yours, and I promise to listen carefully to whatever it is that you're sharing with me."

"Before we went to sleep, you commented that you don't know why I love you," she began. "It all started that day on the boardwalk when you rescued my purse. You looked into my eyes, and I knew I'd never meet anyone like you ever again. Then I discovered you playing your violin later that day, and I heard in it the call of my mate in a very visceral way."

"I have no problem with your need for me to fill that role," he assured her, relaxing as their conversation flowed in this direction.

"Then I surprised you here at the house, and when I shared with you that Bill had basically thrown Daniel and me out with the trash, you became angry on our behalf," she continued. "I knew then that you would always come to our defense."

"And I would." He tightened his hold on her.

"You asked me out to dinner, but when you arrived to pick me up, you found Daniel ill with an earache," she persevered. "Instead, of being irked, you eased his concerns and my burden, taking us under your wing and making sure both of our needs were met as if it was perfectly natural for you to do so. I knew then that you were kind, caring and generous, and I once again caught a glimpse of your fabulous sense of humor.

"As we met further, I easily shared my history with you, receiving no criticism or condemnation whatsoever, and you told me your story in return," she pointed out. "Because of this, I understood we could trust each other with anything, and I admired and respected the way you had dealt with your pain and moved on.

"Then you lent me your porch and made your home available for my use, having recognized that time spent in one of the outside rockers overlooking my view would result in my healing. You'll never know how much your unselfish actions meant to me.

"There simply is no one else like you, Jack Jefferson. No one else who will love and take care of Daniel, me and the child I'm carrying in the same way that you will. You're intelligent, talented, witty, kind, generous, unselfish, romantic and loving – besides being the handsomest man alive and a great lover, who can cook like a dream. What more could a woman want?

"So, for what it's worth, there it is," she brought her words to a close. "You never knew the love that you should've from your parents, but I felt you should know why I love you more each and every day, and why I will continue to do so throughout our lifetime honeymoon together."

"Thank you, Susie." His voice cracked. "Your love and the words you shared have filled a hole that has existed in me ever since I was born."

At which Susan felt a huge sense of relief, her goal of easing the pain her new husband had carried within him for so long now achieved, and lifting her face for the kiss she knew he would give, at the same time, she deliberately rubbed her inner thigh along his.

"Ah…" He rolled her onto her back, his dimples deep shadows in his cheeks in the dim light. "I wondered when we would finish with the tell portion of this Show and Tell session and move on to the show."

Later, as they lay limbs-entangled, Susan drew in a deep breath and then voiced her most overriding thought. "Wow!"

"That one may have been our best show session ever." Jack grinned down at her in the semi-darkness.

"How did I get so lucky and find someone like you to love me?"

"I don't know that luck had much to do with it," he replied. "After all, I'd been looking for you all of my life. No wonder my feet kept bringing me back to Captain's Point."

"Thank goodness they did."

"Finally, I realized my journey was at an end, and if I would stay where I was, my wishes would come true," he shared. "Then a miracle happened. Billy Spooner stole your purse, and there you were."

This time his kiss signaled his continuing desire, and she gave herself up to him, knowing his efforts would prove that luck could indeed strike one twice.

The next morning found Adrianna snuggled beneath the covers of the half-tester bed, listening to Chase as he sang in the shower, pleased to know he had awakened so happy.

He had certainly made their previous evening special, and their lovemaking had continued all through the night. Four times in fourteen hours, her mind did the math, each time more wonderful than the last.

"I love you," he had whispered when she had snuggled closer, and she had melded her body to his and sought the soft touch of his lips once again.

He had deepened the kiss and let out a groan as his hand had found her left breast. One touch, that was all it had taken for her to be on fire for him, and he had gladly obliged, taking them easily to the next level.

Sometimes, she wondered if she should be quite so obvious about her desire for him. Weren't women supposed to keep an aura of mystery surrounding them?

But then, he would kiss her or take her into his arms, and she was lost once again.

Perhaps, this time they had made a baby. She had wanted so badly to share with him last evening that they had conceived, but so far, she had received no sign of its being true.

The sinking sensation she had felt before reentered her stomach. Susan and Jack hadn't had any trouble getting pregnant. Why should she and Chase?

At first, she had been relieved when it hadn't happened right away with all that she currently had on her plate, but as the weeks stretched further into the new year, she had begun to be concerned.

Well, she wouldn't worry about it now. Last night had been spectacular, and this was a new day.

# CHAPTER XLII

"Hello, Mrs. Sheffield." Bridgette sent Adrianna a warm smile when she entered the main conference room at her husband's firm on Wednesday. "It's nice you could join us this morning."

"Chase felt I should make myself available to answer questions the junior partners may have about how our new business venture plans to utilize the firm's services," Adrianna explained. "For my part, I'm looking forward to catching a glimpse of exactly what this type of operational meeting generally entails."

"You may be surprised." Her husband's legal secretary laughed. "Although Chase does a great job of keeping everything under control. Both he and Susan are top grade professionals, but they all are really, each in their own way."

"I hope to spend a few minutes with Gary, once this is finished, discussing the National Register of Historic Places as it's administered here in Maryland," Adrianna filled her in, thinking how much more comfortable she was in this suite of offices today than she had been when she had first arrived in Captain's Point.

"There should be sufficient time for you and Gary to meet before your closing on the Tuttle Avenue property commences," Bridgette assured her. "Can I get you a cup of coffee or tea before things begin?"

Provided with a cup of tea, Adrianna looked on with pride a few minutes later as Chase, sitting to her left at the head of the long table, led the attorneys and their assistants efficiently through a lengthy agenda that covered a broad range of topics.

No wonder Susan preferred for him to deal with the firm's operational needs.  He obviously had the talent for it.

"I understand you have some questions for me in regards to the Register."  Gary approached Adrianna after the meeting, and she was impressed with his knowledge of the subject as they spoke.

"We shouldn't run into too many road blocks on this one," he eased her mind as Chase pointed to his watch, letting her know it was time to move into the smaller room where some of their business partners were already gathered.

"I'm glad you could join us," she greeted Jack, Larry and Kate when she entered the room where they sat – already supplied with coffee, tea and muffins Penny had sent along with them.

"I'm Adrianna Montgomery Sheffield."  She smiled at the young man and woman who were sitting stiffly at the other end of the table.  "I appreciate that we came to an agreement so quickly."

"The sooner the better as far as I'm concerned," the man snarled in response, and Adrianna took a seat next to Susan, thinking it best to ignore him.

"Has my wife mentioned to you that she and Daniel are coming to hear me play with String Flings in New York City in a few weeks?"  Jack leaned forward and addressed her.

"That should be fun."  Adrianna tried hard to sound surprised.

"Why don't you four join us?" the musician suggested, including his sister and cousin-in-law in the invitation.  "It would be nice for Susan to have company while I'm rehearsing with the group, and I'm sure Chase and Larry could find something they'd enjoy doing."

"Chase will spend his time at Tiffany's, if I don't warn him off." Adrianna laughed.

"I'd certainly pop my head in and see what they had on display." Larry sent Kate a grin.

"You two can't go there on your own," Jack stated firmly. "I insist on tagging along."

"I'll need a small room just to house my jewelry pretty soon." Susan let out a small sigh.

"That won't be a problem." Jack made a deprecating gesture with his hand as if every woman housed her jewelry in its own room. "All these renovations at Montgomery House have given me some ideas for our third floor. I'll just work something into those plans."

At which, Susan rolled her eyes.

"Looks like we're all here, if you want to get started, Brett," Chase addressed one of the firm's new associates as he entered the room and shut the door, before assuming a seat on Adrianna's right and taking her hand in his beneath the table.

Finding it hard to concentrate on the proceedings as her husband absentmindedly made gentle circles with his thumb against her palm, Adrianna strove to pay attention, this being the first real estate closing she had ever attended.

Much to her relief, Brett had done a good job of preparing, and everything proved to be relatively straightforward, relieving her concerns that she would do or say something that embarrassed Chase in front of his business associates.

"Congratulations on your new property." Brett handed her a set of keys a short time later and then shook her hand. "It's been my pleasure to assist your firm with its first purchase."

The previous owners soon departed – the husband exiting the room with a belligerent look on his face, while his soon-to-be ex-wife stopped briefly to thank Larry and Kate for their help in making a quick sale possible.

It now being lunch time, the six partners agreed to adjourn to Montgomery's for a celebratory luncheon, and each couple headed to their respective vehicle.

"I wasn't sure your brother could pull off this thing in New York City without my gorgeous cousin catching on to the bigger picture," Larry stated to Kate, once he had steered them from the parking lot. "At this point, though, I'm sitting back and taking advantage of the opportunity to watch a true genius at work."

"Jack's pretty amazing, isn't he?" she replied. "Susan will be so surprised."

"And pleased," Larry added as he reached over and took her hand. "You're pretty amazing, too, you know, and I'm really proud of your part in it as well. It's one more reason why your being my gal makes me the luckiest man in the world."

## CHAPTER XLIII

Saturday evening marked the fourth monthly meeting of the same three couples for dinner at Montgomery's – this time being Chase and Adrianna's turn to treat.

Following up on Jack's request, both she and Kate had accompanied Susan on a shopping spree that included a stopover at Tea, Crumpets and More for lunch, which they had enjoyed.

Giving way to her husband's wishes, Susan had shut her mind to all thoughts of cost or extravagance and had purchased several pregnancy pants suits for their upcoming trip, including a formal black one at the designer dress shop that had recently opened in Captain's Point.

Not to be outdone, Kate had joined in the fun, treating herself to two new cocktail dresses and a pair of heels, bearing in mind that she now had a whole room-sized closet lined with padded hangers to fill.

In line with the same spirit, Adrianna had splurged as well, buying a dress that she had slipped into easily before seeking her reflection in her dressing room's cheval mirror.

Comprised of a black flowing skirt, the dress came to mid-calf with flashes of red petticoat showing beneath the hem. One shoulder of black crossed over the deep red of the other creating a form-enhancing bodice that then carried around the back where it plunged into a low V.

"Whoa! You really should warn me," Chase teased her from where he now lounged against her dressing room's doorframe. "I believe you only need one thing to complete the picture."

He held out an index finger from which was suspended a tiny black and gold gift bag as he approached her.

"Again, Mr. Sheffield?" She attempted to send him a disapproving look, which failed miserably as her fingers withdrew a small, rectangular jeweler's box from within the tissue.

"Your emeralds won't go with this outfit," he pointed out as she lifted the lid and revealed an onyx and diamond dinner ring and matching drop earrings.

"You're so beautiful." He bent and kissed her. "And I want you to have beautiful things."

"I love them." She allowed him to slip the wide gold band of the ring onto her finger, then drew his face down to hers where she whispered against his lips, "But I love you more."

Bringing his SUV to a halt in front of Herb and Jewel's, Larry congratulated himself on the fact that only one more dinner like this was scheduled before he and Kate would be married.

Tonight she would wear his favorite dress and her new earrings as well as the sapphire and diamond tennis bracelet he had bought her for Christmas – symbolizing for the two of them their love for each other.

How had he survived all those years without this woman in his life? He wondered as he quickened his pace up the front walk. He certainly couldn't survive without her now.

Two more months…

Two more months until she would be his, living in what would then be their condo, working with him, sharing her life with him. There were times when he knew he no longer needed food or water or air, only her.

At the same moment that her cousin was pressing the doorbell at his destination, Susan felt her husband's eyes upon her, signifying his return from dropping Daniel off at her parents' for an overnight.

"I was hoping you'd make an appearance about now." She smiled a greeting from where she stood wearing a new pant suit, her thick blonde waves drawn into a twist. "I'd appreciate your help fastening the locket you gave me, and then I'll be ready."

"Not quite," he informed her as he stepped forward. "Kate and Adrianna have assured me that you'll look lovely wearing these." He presented her with a small velvet case that held a set of gold and diamond earrings to go with her Valentine's present.

"You're spoiling me again," she whispered, not quite trusting her voice further. "They're perfect."

"They're nowhere near as beautiful as their owner." He took in the way her outfit brought out the gold of her hair and the deep blue of her eyes. "Every time I think I'll never see you looking any lovelier, you prove me wrong yet again."

"Don't be silly," she chided as she secured the second earring in place. "I'm growing bigger every day."

"You're carrying my child." He drew her to him. "That alone would make you the most beautiful woman in the world to me, but it's more than that, Susie. There's a soft glow emanating from you. Once again, I'll be the envy of every man at Montgomery's this evening."

And with that having been said, he proceeded to kiss her with a tenderness that bespoke of his love and filled Susan with the belief that, at least in his eyes, she was still his beautiful wife.

Travel and dinners out when one was pregnant weren't all that bad, she realized, when one had a husband as tall, dark, handsome and loving as hers.

As Susan picked up her evening bag, Beth McIntyre, owner of Beth's Buds, Captain's Point's premier florist, sat at the dressing table in the master bedroom of what had been her grandmother's bungalow on Tuttle Avenue and searched her heart-shaped face in the antique mirror now speckled with age. Not bad for a forty-something spinster, she decided.

She had kept her figure, her brown hair showed only a few traces of gray and her dark eyes still sparkled in the right light. Anxiety before a date was something else to which she had clung.

Here she was, twenty years after her last evening out spent alone in male company, her stomach filled with butterflies because a kind man would ring her doorbell in a few minutes and escort her to dinner at Montgomery's.

Most women would've been thrilled. The single dimple in his left cheek would've seen to that. His soft brown eyes and velvety voice would've clinched the deal.

It was his wit and intelligence that drew her to him, though. That and the way he looked at her as if she had value beyond the fact that she could arrange a bouquet of flowers and cook a decent meal.

And then, of course, there was the fact that she had fallen in love with him in the space of only a few hours.

## CHAPTER XLIV

A little while later, a round of hors d'oeuvres having been ordered to share by the group, Jack settled against the Montgomery banquette at the family's table just as the elevator door opened and revealed Raoul, the restaurant's maitre d', escorting a handsome couple, one of whom he was surprised to recognize.

"Palmer?" He rose and hurried forward. "Is that you? Why I'll be a monkey's uncle. What hole did you crawl from?"

"Jefferson?" The middle-aged man's eyes widened with surprise, as he felt his hand taken in a strong grasp. "Why you old son of a gun. I'm sure the hole I crawled from wasn't located too far from the one you squirmed out of, if history can be relied upon. What are you doing here in Captain's Point?"

"I've made this town my permanent home since last June," Jack informed him. "And you?"

"I grew up here and just moved back after I retired from *Stars and Stripes*," Gabe Palmer filled him in, "as your friend Larry there could've told you if you had asked him. Have you met Beth McIntyre?" He indicated the petite, dark-haired, dark-eyed woman by his side.

"Certainly." Jack sent the florist a smile. "Beth saved my life when I only gave myself two weeks in which to plan my backyard wedding." He took his friend's arm in his hand and led the newcomers to the Montgomery table. "Gabe Palmer, I'd like for you to meet my wife, Susie."

"Nice to meet you." Susan smiled at her husband's friend.

"Susan…" Gabe's soft brown eyes narrowed. "You were formerly Susan Chesterton, weren't you? I remember those lovely eyes looking at me over the back of the Chesterton pew when I attended church with my aunt and uncle as a teenager and you were just a little thing."

"You're Joan and Charles Palmer's great-nephew," she replied. "I know they're pleased to have you back with them here in Captain's Point."

"They seem to be, God bless them." A twinkle now entered his eyes. "You have my condolences on your marriage to this rascal."

Gabe nodded towards Jack and then glanced to where Larry sat at the head of the horseshoe-shaped banquette, his face filled with a grin reminiscent of one found on any cat that had just licked all the cream. "Good to see you again, Larry."

"Gabe." The broker sent him a nod of recognition. "It's nice to see you, too, Beth."

"Thanks to some fancy financial footwork on the part of my advisor here, I'm now the proud owner of the *Captain's Point Gazette*," Gabe informed his old friend.

"Congratulations!" Jack slapped the newspaperman on the back. "It couldn't be in better hands."

"I agree," Chase stated as he, too, rose.

"Larry is my wife's cousin," Jack continued his introductions, "and Chase Sheffield here is Susie's law partner."

"Nice to meet you." Gabe shook the attorney's offered hand. "Have you met my date, Beth McIntyre?"

"I've known Beth most of my life," Chase stated, "but I'll always be most grateful for the kind way she helped me through my stuttering attempt to order a prom corsage for Susan during our junior year in high school. By our senior year, I considered myself to be an old pro.

"Now, of course, she's the one I rely on whenever I send a floral tribute to my wife, Adrianna Montgomery." He took a step back and placed his hand on her shoulder.

"Are you related to Martha Montgomery?" Gabe asked. "She was good to me after my parents were both killed in a car crash when I was in junior high, and I moved here to live with my aunt and uncle."

"She was my great-aunt," Adrianna replied, glad she no longer felt the jealousy she once would have at hearing how nice her Aunt Martha had been to another, now that she better understood her aunt's reasons for treating her in a harsh manner after her own parents' similar death.

"So you now own the restaurant in which we'll be dining this evening?" the newspaperman asked.

"Not anymore," the former owner explained. "Shortly after I inherited it, I sold it to John Thornburg, who had served as Head Chef and General Manager for some time, but Chase and John both insisted that I retain the privilege of the Montgomery table due to the cachet that it brings to the restaurant."

"Wise man." Gabe sent the attorney a nod.

"Last, but not least…" Jack drew his old friend's attention. "The lovely lady seated on the other side of my wife is my sister Kate, whose time Larry has been hogging for the past couple of months. I wouldn't be surprised to hear that he has single-handedly guaranteed the success of your date's shop for several years to come, given evidence I've seen with my own eyes."

"I object." Larry attempted an offended look.

"Overruled," Chase stated firmly before turning back to the new arrivals. "This evening's meal is on me," he explained. "Won't you join us for dinner? We've only ordered our hors d'oeuvres, which we're all quite accustomed to sharing."

Quickly glancing at Beth, whose eyes he found to be filled with only warmth and pleasure at the invitation, Gabe agreed, and Raoul immediately sprang into action, producing two more place settings seemingly out of nowhere.

Adrianna, Larry and Kate scooted around the banquette towards Susan, leaving room for Chase to slide further in and the newcomers to take their places directly across the table from Jack and Susan.

"I must admit that I have an ulterior motive for asking you to join us, beyond merely hoping to get to know you better personally," Chase admitted to Gabe once everyone had placed their dinner orders. "Larry and I have convinced Jack to run for the ad hoc city councilman position that will open up shortly, and it strikes me that you could be a valuable ally in our battle to secure the seat for him."

"Who do you think will be your primary opponent?" Gabe asked the future candidate. "Not that it makes much difference. I'll have to back you, if for no other reason than to keep you from blackmailing me over the sins of my youth."

"Gerald Tate, without a doubt," Jack informed him, his tone having reverted to a purely professional one.

"Then I'm definitely on your side," the *Gazette*'s owner made his position clear, "but please keep that under your hats until I make a public announcement of it in the paper at the proper time."

"Thanks, friend." Jack sent him a smile.

"Don't let your head grow too big." Gabe chuckled. "I'd support a cartoon character over Gerald Tate. I know for certain that he's tried to rob my Aunt Joan of her savings on two separate occasions, but the old girl has her wits too much about her to be taken in by the likes of him. How that man keeps himself one step ahead of the law is beyond me."

"Well, he does," Larry stated, disgust clearly running beneath his words. "Although he's walking a fine line.

One false step on his part, and I'll personally make it my life's mission to see him put behind bars."

"Not that you have any strong opinions on the matter," Kate spoke up.

"Hardly any at all." Larry's face relaxed as he smiled down at her.

Conversation interrupted by the appearance of their dinner meals, Adrianna couldn't help but notice how happy Beth looked as Gabe shared a quiet confidence with her.

She would have to invite the couple to join them the next time Chase and she had friends over for dinner, she decided, her matchmaking instincts going into high gear as she took note of how nicely Beth's hand seemed to fit within the grasp of the newspaperman's stronger one.

## CHAPTER XLV

Humming a nonsense tune, Beth McIntyre wrapped a container of chocolate and caramel swirl ice cream in foil and placed it into an insulated container that was open and waiting on her kitchen counter. Glancing at the microwave's clock to confirm she wasn't too late, she lifted a colorful gift bag filled with various food items from the table and headed to her car.

Saturday evening, on their way home from what had proven to be a wonderful dinner, Gabe had shared that he was spending most of his hours as editor of the *Captain's Point Gazette* alone in his office.

Putting two and two together, she felt this explained why he had arrived at Beth's Buds at the right moment to take her to lunch three times in the past week. Today, she planned to beat him to it.

Located two doors along the street from Chesterton and Chesterton, the newspaper's office was only five minutes away. She slowed her steps as she approached the door that now boasted a fresh coat of deep red paint, so that she wouldn't arrive out of breath.

"Beth!" A grin took up residence on Gabe's face as he rose from his desk and came forward to greet her. "To what do I owe this surprise?"

"I'm repaying you in a small way for all the wonderful lunch hours you've given me recently." She held out the bags she had brought with her. "I've prepared lunch for two, if you have time to share, or you could eat half today and half tomorrow."

"And miss a chance to enjoy your company for longer than a couple of minutes?" He looked aghast. "Not on your life. Option number one, please." He took the bags from her and gestured for her to join him at his desk.

"You've made some changes," she pointed out the obvious, once she had taken a seat. "I like the way you've maintained the original ambiance, while at the same time adding some modern touches."

"We have to appeal to a broader readership in order to survive," he informed her. "I'm hoping this will please everyone."

"What did you think of Jack Jefferson's suggestion that you bring on a younger, part-time reporter?" she asked, noting that a large peace lily she had sent as a congratulatory gift had been prominently displayed in what served as the paper's reception area.

"I thought it was a great idea." He watched with interest as she unpacked a number of containers from the gift bags as well as colorful paper plates, napkins and plastic silverware. "As a matter of fact, I've emailed a friend of yours to see if he might accept the position."

"A friend of mine?" She paused. "Who?"

"Jeff Stuart."

"He'll do a great job, if he has time to fit you in." The lid on a container of what proved to be potato salad yielded to her fingers.

"According to Jack, he's a talented writer and has an interest in journalism, so I'm giving him first refusal." He eyed what appeared to be some sort of fruit salad and fought not to lick his lips. "Just out of curiosity, what army are we feeding?"

"I may have gotten a bit carried away." Her gaze traveled over the spread she'd set before him. "Make sure you save room for dessert." She unwrapped the foil from a package of homemade fried chicken. "Dark meat or white?"

"Dark." He locked his eyes onto hers. "Have I died and gone to Heaven?"

"Not yet." She laughed, pleased with his response to her gift. "Now fill up your plate, and then I want you to tell me all of your impressions, now that you've been in business a full week."

"Are you sure about that Heaven thing?" he asked a few minutes later, after he'd swallowed his first bite of chicken. "This is delicious."

"Thank you." She speared a tiny cornichon with her fork, suddenly feeling shy in the face of his praise.

For several minutes, they ate in comfortable silence, but then Gabe took a break as he spooned seconds of several items onto his plate.

"The good news is that it's different here at the *Gazette* than at *Stars and Stripes*," he restarted their conversation. "The bad news is that it's different from what I'm used to. I love that I'm free to fill the pages with good news if I want to, but I've realized that I won't be satisfied if I don't report on some meaningful issues as well."

"Then maintain contact with Chase, Larry and Jack," she advised him. "Chase and Larry are city councilmen who represent a strong majority in Captain's Point that's striving to maintain all that's good about the town while acknowledging its now the twenty-first century."

"And Gerald Tate represents a minority that's more interested in making a profit from haphazard, shoddy development schemes?" He helped himself to another chicken leg.

"In my opinion, yes." Beth met his searching gaze head on, her chin lifting slightly.

"As I implied Saturday evening, I agree with you," he reminded her. "I'll have to feel my way carefully, during the first few weeks under new ownership, but long-term, you'll find an ally in the *Gazette*."

"I have no doubt whatsoever that you'll follow the best course." She rested her fork on her plate. "You're a good man, Gabe – an intelligent man. I'm quite sure you'll recognize a snake as opposed to a kitten when you see one."

"I'll drink to that." He lifted a plastic cup of the best iced tea he'd ever tasted – her secret, she had shared when asked, the use of brown sugar when sweetening.

"To the new *Gazette's* future." She raised her cup as well, tapping his gently over his blotting pad.

"Now let me get you some dessert – iced chocolate brownies with ice cream on the side." She patted his hand. "I'll leave the extras with you for an afternoon snack, since you've cleared your luncheon plate twice over."

# CHAPTER XLVI

A few days later, Chase relaxed in his chair where he sat at the table in the breakfast room before leaving for work and glanced at his wife.

"That was delicious." He sent her a smile. "Now where is that copy of our latest itinerary?"

It was hard to believe that seven months had passed since their marriage. Their departure for their postponed trip to Europe with Otis and Penny was now less than a month away.

All of his life, he had wanted to travel and experience more of the world, but except for his years away at school, he had been chained to responsibilities here in Captain's Point. Thank goodness, all of that had changed. Now, he was free to go and take Adrianna with him, which would make the experiences even more meaningful as they shared them.

"I've been working on my French between clients at the office," he admitted, as he took a sheaf of stapled pages from her hand. "That new software you purchased helps a lot."

"I'm glad." She sent him one of her shy smiles from where she stood next to him. "You'll find that most people speak English, but you can learn interesting things, when they don't know that you understand what they're saying in their own language."

She was glad they were taking this trip. Hopefully, it would calm some of the restlessness she still sensed in her husband.

His jumping from a helicopter had been a start, their trip to New York City would provide another new experience, but a month in Europe would take Chase whole new places. Besides, she was looking forward to revisiting some of their destinations and sharing them with him.

She had been afraid that, between Susan's pregnancy and Jack's New York concert plans, they would have to postpone their vacation even further, but then the author had surprised them by offering his apartment in Geneva for the four of them to use as home base.

Now all the evenings spent thumbing through travel brochures and surfing the internet with her new husband were bearing fruit. She had enjoyed sharing her experiences with him in their library, but she was excited about seeing Europe through his eyes.

"Everything looks great to me." Chase drew her onto his lap. "Do you know how sexy you are when you're planning a belated honeymoon trip?"

Three properties away at Blue Wolf Manor, the call, when it came, was taken by Susan as opposed to Jack, much to his chagrin, since she was covering his cell phone for him while he attended a virtual board meeting of the drilling equipment company.

"Is there anything you want to tell me?" she asked, when he joined her a few minutes later in the front parlor where she was working on her laptop with her feet elevated.

"No, the meeting was routine." He perched on the edge of her ottoman and began massaging her right ankle.

"I was referring to the delivery we'll be receiving any minute." She lifted an eyebrow.

"Ah..." He focused his attention completely on her left ankle, which for some reason was always more swollen than its twin. "I've bought a few things you and Daniel will need for our trip to New York."

"A few things?" She worked hard not to let a smile take over her lips. "The dispatcher informed me that our 'truck of goods' had just left the loading bay."

Their old-fashioned doorbell choosing this moment to ring, Jack hurried from the room, his mind rapidly searching for ways to justify his latest move.

"Leave them right here," he advised the young, sandy-haired driver, who handed the author an electronic tablet to sign as he wheeled in the first of several dollies.

Left to themselves sometime later, from the position she had assumed a few feet up the stairway, Susan passed her gaze over the cardboard cartons of various sizes that now filled their large foyer.

"Should I take the Louis Vuitton name that's stamped on most of these boxes as a possible clue?" she asked sagely.

"You're still using the luggage you took to college, Susie." Jack sought to explain. "And, while a cartoon character duffle bag is fine for a sleepover at one's grandparents', it hardly fills the bill when one is standing in the Plaza's lobby."

"Okay," she allowed him his point. "I'll agree, but exactly how many outfits do you think Daniel and I will need?"

"I locked in a discount." He offered his second best excuse.

"Oh, a sale." She attempted to add up the large figures that were running through her mind. "We could hardly pass on one of those now, could we?"

"It didn't seem so at the time." He sent her what he hoped was a charming smile. "Besides, you never know exactly which sizes will fit your needs best, so you might as well purchase a full set."

"So what exactly does a complete set of Louis Vuitton luggage designed for use by a five-year-old boy look like?" she asked.

"Exactly like mine, of course." His dimples deepened. "As I always tell Daniel, we guys have to stick together, so his is the black Utah that I always carry. Yours is the classic monogram that you've probably seen more frequently."

He headed up the stairs, took a seat two steps down from hers that placed them at eye level, and opened his mouth to speak. "Susie…"

But she surprised him and leaned forward, covering his lips with hers, immediately emptying his mind of all thoughts except those of her as he accepted her gift.

"Now," she stated matter-of-factly a few minutes later, as if the passionate embrace they had just shared had never happened. "Why don't you show me what Daniel and I have to choose from when we pack for our trip, and then you can tell me exactly where you think you're going to store all of this."

# CHAPTER XLVII

February had remained unseasonably warm throughout its twenty-eight days, but March chose to arrive in Captain's Point in the guise of a lion. For the entire first week, Jack paced the floors of Blue Wolf Manor as he waited to discover whether or not his family's upcoming flight to New York City would even be possible.

"There's nothing you can do about it," Susan reminded him over and over, unable to understand why he continued to worry, but then, he remembered, she didn't know the half of it.

On departure day, he awoke to bright sunlight and a clear sky, which he took as a good sign. He wanted so badly for everything to go well for his Susie.

At eight o'clock on the dot, Jeff Stuart rang the front bell, attired in one of three new suits he had purchased for the trip, along with a new overcoat. He held a pull case with one hand and a suit bag slung over his shoulder with the other. The strap of a small laptop case crossed his chest.

"We're taking our time, so Mama doesn't feel rushed," Daniel announced when he opened the door. "It's only 123 more days until our baby can see us, and it can't go by fast enough."

"Meanwhile, we're going to have a great time on our trip." Jeff deposited his luggage in front of the bombe chest, along with the computer, overcoat and his suit jacket, noticing a large, mixed collection of Louis Vuitton that waited beyond the doorway to the Jeffersons' library cum home office. "Have you had your breakfast yet, or should we fix you some cereal?"

"Jack made a spinach omelette for my mom, and I had oatmeal," Daniel informed him. "It was instant, but I'll live."

"I'm sure you will." His companion for their journey chuckled. "This is my first time in an airplane. Have you flown in one before?"

"Only in my dad's helicopter, and it's not the same." The youngster's eyes locked onto his. "You're not afraid to fly are you?"

"No, I'm looking forward to it," Jeff explained. "My family always took road trips, so I haven't had an occasion to go airborne before, although I have been to New York City."

"You should never miss out on a chance for a new opportunity," Daniel advised him. "I'm going to order off the Eloise menu at the Plaza."

"Neat."

"I thought I heard someone arrive." Jack appeared at the top of the stairs. "Susie'll be down in a minute. We shouldn't be long at the doctor's. Then we'll come home and let her grab a quick shower, before we head to the airport."

"I'm betting with you that it's a girl," the landscaper stated.

"We would've postponed the exam, but we're rather eager to hear the verdict," the expectant father filled him in. "Daniel and I want to start on the nursery. Don't we, Charger?"

"123 days will fly by really fast," his son agreed, calling on an old favorite.

"Is there anything I can do while you're gone?" Jeff asked.

"Not here, but you could make sure Daniel's electronics are in his carryon and turned off before we go airborne,"

Jack replied. "He has his Jitterbug, a tablet and a couple of educational games, none of which should be on."

"No problem." Jeff glanced up as he caught movement out of the corner of his eye.

"Thank you for coming so early," Susan greeted him as she started down the stairs, dressed in casual clothes that could be easily removed at the doctor's in preparation for her ultrasound. "Kate and Larry should be here shortly."

"Feel free to help yourself to some coffee or anything else you want," Jack said as he escorted his wife through the front doorway.

"Excited?" Susan squeezed her husband's hand as they made their way to his SUV.

"You bet." He grinned. "Remember, this is a first for me. Which do you think it'll be, or are you still undecided?"

"Honestly, I have no idea." She waited while he opened the passenger door, warmed by his interest in every detail of their pregnancy.

"Dr. Jackson is waiting for you in her office," the receptionist greeted them when they arrived for their appointment. "Go on back."

"We appreciate your allowing us to be your first this morning," Jack stated when they entered the small, but tidy room.

"This way I can check things out for myself," Susan's young ob/gyn explained. "I'll take a quick look. Then we'll do the ultrasound and meet back here. Did you drink your water before leaving home?"

"Yes." Her patient grimaced.

"I know." Janie chuckled. "Still, it's a necessary evil." She picked up a file from her desk and gestured for them to follow her along the hall.

Twenty minutes later, Jack stood beside an exam table, watching gel being spread onto his wife's swollen belly, barely able to contain himself.

Had his parents felt this level of excitement prior to his own birth? Somehow, he doubted it.

Certainly, they had found it easy enough to reject, despise and ignore him once he had come into the world, clearly exhibiting for all to see the dark hair and eyes of his mother's Cherokee ancestry that she had striven so hard to keep secret.

Still, while this explained her inability to accept him, it didn't allow for his father's. He couldn't envision turning away from any child produced by him and his Susie as a result of their love, carried to term within her and then placed in his arms.

"Ready?" Susan smiled up at him.

"Ready." He squeezed her hand, once again amazed by everything she so willingly endured for him and their baby.

In the short time they had been at this office, she had been poked, prodded, squeezed, stripped, placed in stirrups, bared and smeared with goo. There was no way he could ever do too much in return for her, the child she had brought to him or the one she now carried.

"Looks like we have a strong heartbeat." The middle-aged tech pointed to a spot on the screen, and Jack felt his throat tighten. "Do you two want to know the sex, or would you prefer a surprise?"

"We'd like to know," Susan replied.

"You understand this interpretation is not a perfect science, right?"

"Yes," Jack said.

"From what I'm seeing with the fetus in this position, I believe we have a girl." The tech glanced his way, pleased when his dimples deepened as a grin split his face.

"Just like you wanted." Susan blinked back tears, relieved not to have disappointed him.

"I'll be fine with either one, as long as he or she is healthy," he assured her, "but I would like to watch a little Susie grow up."

"We may have one little problem with that," his wife informed him, a twinkle in her eye. "You see, I'm doing my best to make sure she'll have dark hair and eyes just like yours."

## CHAPTER XLVIII

"So which is it?" Larry asked as he and Kate hurried along the hall from the parlor, Jeff a few steps behind them, in response to sounds of the front door opening.

Jack looked to Susan and nodded that it was hers to reveal.

"A girl." She smiled back at him as Daniel flew forward and hugged her knees.

"Now, we can work on our baby's room," her son stated, his face filled with excitement. "She'll need books and toys, and girls play with dolls, too."

"Guess I have to pay up." Larry removed a hundred dollar bill from his wallet and dropped it into a crystal bowl on the bombe chest.

"As will Chase." Jack didn't bother to hide his elation. "The two hundred you two have lost due to your own errors of judgment will make a nice donation to my favorite charity in the name of our daughter."

"Beats me how you knew," Larry continued.

"Probably, I picked up some sort of visual clue by watching wizened, old women in primitive jungle villages that enabled me to subconsciously arrive at the correct conclusion," the world-traveled author spun a tall tale.

"Speaking of names." Kate drew their attention, writing off her brother's words as the nonsense it was. "Have you picked out a name for the baby yet?"

"At this point, we've settled on Olivia Elizabeth after your maternal great-grandmother and my mom," Susan informed them.

"Although, I'll call her Pipsqueak like I did you." Jack gave his sister a bear hug.

"Congratulations, Cuz." Larry lifted Daniel into the air and then positioned the boy on his left hip. "You have the little sister I always wanted, although your mom was a pretty good substitute sister."

"That makes two of us who envy you." Jeff patted the boy's back.

"I'll have to watch out for her," Daniel stated solemnly. "Jack and I already take care of my mama. Now we'll have to take care of Olivia, too."

"Yes, but the love she gives you in return will mean the world to you." Jack dropped a kiss on the top of Kate's head and released her.

"I'm going to shower and get ready." Susan headed for the stairs.

"Don't rush," Jack called after her. "We have plenty of time, and the Lear won't take off without us." He turned to his sister.

"Would you mind going with Susan in case she needs help?" he asked. "She's a trouper, but she's been through a lot this morning. And, don't either of you lift that last suitcase off the bed. One of us will do it."

"I'll be glad to." Kate started across the foyer.

"Larry and I loaded my luggage and as many of the suitcases you had waiting here in the office as we could into his SUV, when he returned from taking the dogs to The Cove," Jeff spoke up. "Should I put the rest in the back of yours?"

"That would help." Jack passed his keys to the younger man.

"This one feels empty," Larry commented as he held one of the larger suitcases suspended from one finger, and Kate paused on the steps, wondering if she should take it the rest of the way with her.

"It's to hold anything we purchase while we're there," Jack explained.

"What a great idea." Kate's glance fell on Larry, but then transferred to her brother.

"Buying out a few dress shops while we're there, Sis?" Jack teased, even as he joined her on the stairs. "I'll see if I have another one I can lend you."

"I have a feeling there are plenty more," Kate gave back a smidgen of what she had received, already having heard from Susan about his extravagant purchase.

An hour later, the group's small caravan turned onto the ramp that led to the main terminal at Captain's Point Airport.

"There it is!" Daniel pointed excitedly from his child's seat in the back of their SUV. "I can see the 60XR on the side."

"Looks like you're right." Jeff gazed past his small charge towards the waiting Lear, his own excitement level rising as their vehicle came to a halt.

"Why don't you stick with Kate and your mom, Son, and take care of them, while the rest of us oversee getting our luggage loaded?" Jack suggested as he disembarked.

"I'm fine," Susan answered his unspoken question when he opened her door a minute later, already carrying his performance violin – a valuable antique – in one hand.

"Still, let's get you settled comfortably first thing." Jack escorted her towards the plane, Jeff and Daniel quickly joined to their rear by Kate and Larry.

"Good to see you again, Mr. Jefferson," a uniformed steward greeted them at the top of the stairs, a patch on the left breast of his jacket identifying him as an employee of the drilling equipment company.

"Charles, I'd like you to meet my wife Susan and my son Daniel," Jack introduced his new family, "and this is my sister Kate Sinclair, my cousin-in-law Larry Chesterton and my business associate Jeff Stuart."

"Nice to meet all of you." The middle-aged man stepped back and allowed them to enter.

"Why don't you sit here, Susie?" Jack indicated the first of six comfortable looking individual seats, which would put her within reach of additional couch seating for two that was also available. "Daniel, you take up residence across the aisle and one back from your mom, so she can see you over her shoulder."

"Would it be okay if the little guy took a look around my area first?" A tall, suntanned man joined them from the cockpit.

"Can I?" Daniel looked at his stepfather with hope-filled eyes.

"Sure." Jack held out his hand to the pilot, who shook it. "I'd requested you, but you know how that is with the consortium. Jerry, I'd like you to meet…" He again went through the litany of introductions.

"I see why your husband waited until he found you." The pilot leaned forward and shook Susan's hand as well. "Congratulations on your marriage. We all think Mr. Jefferson's the best, but I'm sure you already know that."

Fifteen minutes later, the luggage loaded onto the plane by two teenagers Jack had commissioned from the teen charitable workgroup at their church and everyone strapped into their seats, Daniel filled them in about the wonderful sights housed in the plane's forward area.

Through his microphone, the pilot announced they were cleared for takeoff, and the jet's engines came to life.

Jack reached over from where he sat on the couch next to his sister and took Susan's hand.

"Here we go," he said. "Excited?"

"Yes." She smiled back at him. "I'm looking forward to hearing you play *Alpine Spring* with the group, and this is certainly the way to travel."

As they taxied along the runway, Jeff stared at the familiar landscape through the window beside him, then felt the aircraft pick up speed and the slight lift as they headed skyward, the Atlantic spreading eastward beneath them as the Lear turned and headed north.

In no time, they would land in New York City, where Becca would arrive on Friday morning for a spring break visit with Angel and her family. He was, as Daniel had advised him to do, taking advantage of an opportunity, surrounded by people that he admired, respected and just plain old liked.

All was right in his world.

## CHAPTER XLIX

"You were right." Jack rejoined Susan several hours later in their bedroom in the two bed two bath Plaza suite, where he had established his family and Jeff. "My bag and Daniel's were swapped. I may have to order us personalized luggage tags."

He deposited a small case on a footstool and took a seat next to his wife where she sat, half-dressed, on the side of their bed, one of her flannel nightgowns clutched to her chest.

"Earth to Susie," he said, surprised to have received no reply. "Are you okay?"

"I will be." She turned her head slowly and met his gaze. "I'm merely processing."

"At least, put on your gown and get under the covers for your nap, so you don't catch a chill." He put his arm around her. "Is something troubling you?"

"Troubling's too strong a word." She stood and began to comply with his wishes.

Not convinced that all was as it should be, he stepped into the central living room and drew Jeff's attention, where the younger man was lounging on a couch on the other side of the common area, his computer open on his lap.

"There's been a slight change of plans," Jack stated. "Daniel might as well benefit from a good nap, and you seem settled in. Would you ask Nigel to let Len know that we won't need the limo for at least another hour and a half?" He referred to the butler who attended their suite and their assigned driver.

"Sure." Jeff set his laptop aside.

Shutting himself in with his wife, Jack was pleased to see she was now ready for the nap that her ob/gyn had ordered that morning for each day of their trip.

"What are you doing?" Susan asked, when he returned from their walk-in closet with a suit hanger in his hands and began to undress.

"Exactly what I always most want to do," he replied, as he finished and joined her in the bed, where she still appeared to be doing some serious thinking.

Once settled, he gathered her into his arms, taking the fact that she hugged him to her as a good sign.

"I didn't realize you were planning on afternoon love as well as evening," she teased him, almost but not quite sounding like her normal self.

"I wasn't," he said, "but I'm open to suggestions. What I always want most is to spend time with my wife, and since she's currently lying between the sheets in this bed, I decided that's where I should be, too."

"That's sweet." She snuggled her head against his shoulder.

"Are you going to tell me what's wrong?" He twirled one of her blonde waves around his finger.

"Nothing's wrong," she began after a slight pause. "I've had my eyes opened to some things that made me think, that's all."

"Go on."

"You called forth the name of Charles's new grandson on the plane, and you asked after Jerry's wife," she pointed out. "Then, when we got in the limo, you inquired about how Len's oldest was doing at Harvard, and it was clear that you had somehow smoothed the boy's path."

"I found myself in a position to do so and saw no reason not to follow through, yes." He wasn't at all sure where she was headed.

"I've only been with you in Captain's Point and on our honeymoon in Key West," she continued. "I woke up this morning next to my husband, who I thought I knew through and through, but by the time I arrived here at the Plaza, I wondered if I knew even half of you. You've spent most of your life away from me, and you have so much history behind you."

"Susie, I've never lied to you, and I've answered every question you've asked me completely." He tried hard to hide his surprise at the direction her thoughts had taken. "I've bared my emotions, my story, my body and soul to you, inside as well as out. Don't you know that?"

"Yes, and it's the same with me in regards to you." She searched his face. "This isn't about trust. I'm not even sure why it bothers me, so I can't explain how I'm feeling."

"I've shared things with you that no one else in the world knows, not even Kate," he sought to reassure her further. "Certainly, I had a life here in New York City and another one the last several years in Geneva, but in neither of them did I find what I was looking for."

He felt her body relax slightly against his.

"Remember when Robin asked me if I'd spent much time in New York City, when we were sampling food items at the Sheffield Place Inn before it opened?" He drew on a memory of when they were dating.

"Yes."

"Do you recall my answer?"

"No."

"I said I'd spent no more time in New York than I had to, and I meant it," he reminded her. "Part of me realized at that moment how glad I was that I had made Captain's Point my permanent home, and my mindset hasn't changed.

I can enjoy a city like this one for a short time, but at heart, I'm not a big city guy."

"Really?" She lifted her face to his. "You don't miss all of this?"

"Not at all." He tightened his hold. "And if I ever do, we can come and visit. I'm grateful to the friends I've made over the years, especially the ones who opened their homes to me, because if they hadn't filled my life with warmth and caring, I would've been terribly lonely."

"I'm grateful to them, too, then." She again snuggled against his shoulder, absentmindedly sending her hand across his chest where it settled at his waist, sending waves of desire through him.

"Now, though, I have my own home and family," he pointed out, "and I don't want to return to the past. I consider myself blessed when I'm working from our big, happy house, often with you by my side, and most of the time, I can handle my responsibilities to both my publisher and the drilling equipment firm quite competently via computer or phone.

"Does knowing that help?" He nudged her chin until she faced him again.

"Yes, I was being silly," she admitted. "Our life together is such a dream come true that part of me still fears I'll wake up, yet again, to a harsher reality."

"I value what I have in Daniel, our little Olivia and you too much to risk it," he reassured her. "Despite the rich lifestyle and many good friends that I had, I was incomplete without you and our children. There's no reason I would ever want to be that way again."

He bent and covered her lips with his, then slanted the kiss and deepened it further, pleased when she responded to him in the same way that she always had.

"Remember when you thought I was intending to make love to you?" he muttered.

"Yes."

"If it still stands, I'd like to follow through on your offer." His hand found the hem of her gown and slid up her bare leg beneath it.

"I believe my mind would be put completely at ease if you did," she said, knowing he would take her to the one magical place where there was only ever the two of them, grateful for his love that, in the end, was all she needed.

# CHAPTER L

Left to their own devices, Kate and Larry decided to enjoy some of the opportunities that New York City afforded them, after they had enjoyed lunch served in their host's suite.

"Since you're escorting all of us ladies shopping on Friday, why don't we visit some stores with you in mind?" she suggested once they were settled in the back of the limo that Jack had said would take them anywhere they wanted.

"Sounds like a plan." Larry stretched his arm along the back of the seat behind her, not quite believing his luck. "I could use a new suit, since I demolished the one I was wearing when you fell on top of me during that Frisbee game," he referred to an episode that had occurred shortly after they had met the previous fall.

A whole afternoon, just Kate and him on the town, he rejoiced, and other wonderful things planned for their enjoyment throughout the rest of the week. The best part, though, was that they were no longer in Captain's Point, where everyone knew them and they were constantly striving to keep their relationship private.

"Normally, I love every minute spent in my hometown, but I felt a huge weight lift from my shoulders the moment the wheels of that jet left the ground." He beamed down at her.

"I know." She patted his thigh and then left her hand there, fighting the urge to lightly massage the muscles that rippled beneath her fingers whenever he moved. "It almost feels naughty."

"I love being naughty with you," he whispered into her ear, getting a kick out of making her blush, even when he received a playful jab in his ribs from her elbow in return.

Smoothly, Len guided their limousine to the curb in front of the Fifth Avenue store they had chosen as their starting point.

"I've just received a text from Jeff Stuart saying that they won't require me back at the Plaza for a while," he informed his passengers. "You have my number, so touch base when you're ready to move on. I may be able to attend to your needs then as well."

"Will do," Larry stated as he disembarked, thinking that Fifth Avenue had never looked so good during any of his previous visits.

Suddenly, overcome by the freedom and love that he felt, he twirled Kate around and into his arms, where he kissed her soundly in front of a steady stream of passersby, many of whom exchanged knowing smiles.

"Sorry," he apologized. "I couldn't resist. I'm just so thrilled to be here and have you all to myself."

Not waiting for a reply, he put his hand on the small of her back and steered her through the revolving doors onto the main sales floor, where he swerved immediately towards a nearby perfume counter.

"They're having a sale on the line that you use," he pointed out. "We should take advantage and get you one of the free gifts that go with it."

Forty minutes later found them discussing whether she needed a new black or brown leather handbag more, Larry finally deciding that the purses were such a good buy there was no need to choose.

Before she could stop him, he had whipped out his credit card once again and purchased both of them, along with a tiny, silver and blue rhinestone-studded evening bag that had drawn his attention from within the glass counter against which he had been leaning.

Determined to at least make it to the Menswear department, Kate soldiered on towards the escalator, only to discover that her companion had abandoned her for a display of watches, realizing that she didn't yet own a Rolex.

"We'll take one of those." He pointed to a white gold classic, embellished by a ring of diamonds around the dial and tiny blue stones embedded in the numeral VI.

"Are you sure?" Her eyes focused on the price tag. "We aren't even engaged yet."

"Absolutely sure." He hugged her to him, his blue eyes outsparkling the watch's diamonds. "It matches both your tennis bracelet and your earrings, and I want you to have something nice to commemorate our first vacation together.

"Besides, we'll be engaged and a whole lot more in a matter of weeks." He sent her a look so filled with trust that it took her breath away. "And it's important that you know exactly what time it is at the office."

Thinking that her computer screen did a highly competent job of fulfilling the role he had just described, Kate merely sent him a smile, not wanting to spoil his fun and suddenly feeling a little worried.

Despite the fact that she had always lived in a wealthy environment, no one except her brother had ever pampered her this way before, and while it felt wonderful to know that Larry wanted to do so, she wasn't sure she should let him. What would Jack think, when he found out?

But then, she remembered the dozen designer dresses her brother had bought his own wife on their honeymoon, not to mention the expensive shoes to go with them, and she felt herself relax a little.

"We aren't buying anything else until we've purchased your suit," she stated firmly, wondering if she should offer to buy it for him and then deciding that, no, that would only make matters worse.

"If you insist." He grinned down at her, barely able to contain his excitement at having the opportunity to openly spoil her. "But first, let's get this fastened on you."

Relief filling her that, between the tennis bracelet and the watch, both of her wrists now had their needs met, Kate stepped onto the escalator, holding the grip on one side and Larry's hand on the other, refusing to let him be sidetracked again.

Reaching the desired floor, they were greeted by comparative silence, this being the middle of the afternoon on a weekday when most men were at work.

"May I help you, sir?" A rather haughty-looking, middle-aged salesman with thinning hair combed back from a high forehead greeted them as they approached the area clearly designated for the Armani collection.

"We would prefer to browse for a few minutes," Larry replied, "but then, I'm sure I'll try on a few selections."

Two hours later – six suits readied for hemming and a mound of shirts, several silk ties, and two belts now scheduled for delivery to their suite at the Plaza, attention Nigel – Larry suggested that they retire to the tearoom for some light refreshment. Once seated, he ordered two cream teas and then texted Len while they waited for their order to be served.

"The limo's free," he advised her, quickly texting back a desired time for pickup. "Apparently, the others have taken advantage of what was available at the hotel. Your brother's probably concerned about my gorgeous cousin overdoing it, and I can't blame him given her condition, although we Chestertons are not known for getting too carried away."

Thinking back through the time they had spent together since leaving the Plaza, Kate worked hard not to giggle. There was no way she could agree with the man she loved more than life itself on that last one.

Meanwhile, in his law office back in Captain's Point, Chase put a big checkmark by the names of Herb and Jewel Stuart at the end of a long list of phone calls he had just made on behalf of Jack Jefferson. Except for when he was with Adrianna, he realized, he hadn't felt this alive in years.

## CHAPTER LI

"I'm going to have fish and chips with chocolate milk to drink," Daniel announced to his mother when she entered the living area of their suite, dressed to accompany his father to dinner at the condo of his business partner in the drilling equipment firm, his friend from his Navy days, Seth Cox.

"That sounds yummy." She ran her fingers through his blonde waves, straightening them.

"Jeff said we could both have Key lime pie for dessert." His chin lifted.

"Jeff would be right then," Jack stated as he crossed to where the others were gathered and, unaware of his wife's endeavors, ruffled their son's hair that she had just combed into place.

"It's almost enough for me to wish I was staying to have dinner with you." Larry high-fived his short cousin and then took Kate's hand in his.

"Do yourself a favor and order some of the lobster hush puppies," Jack addressed Jeff. "I also recommend both the ribs and the New York strip, but order as much of whatever you want throughout our visit. If you need anything, Nigel is your first resource, but feel free to call us."

"We'll be fine," Jeff assured them. "Daniel's already picked out a movie for us to watch while we eat, and then it'll be bedtime."

Attentive as always, Jack helped Susan on with her wrap, and the group made their way down to the lobby and from there into the waiting limo.

Disembarking a few blocks away, Susan noted that Seth and Lucia Cox's condo overlooked Central Park in the same way as their suite at the Plaza, even as she sought to control the butterflies in her stomach. After all, it wouldn't do for her to have a recurrence of her morning sickness this evening.

All of her husband's friends and acquaintances that she'd met so far had been warm and friendly. Why was she so worried about the impression she would make at this gathering? Was it because she was pregnant?

Jack had assured her in their room that she looked beautiful in her new dress, purchased with Adrianna and Kate's approving smiles, but then, he never seemed to see her any other way. Love and, she thought, a hint of pride had shone from his eyes as well, though, before he had kissed her in the tender way that most spoke of his feelings.

It wasn't as though she wouldn't know what to say to his friends either. During her years in D.C., she had spent many hours comfortably conversing at social events, both as a result of her legal career and invitations to her brother's gatherings that often included powerful Washington insiders.

But, as Jack always said, this was now the two of them, and the last thing she wanted was to embarrass him. At least, Larry and Kate were along for the ride, which would help to dilute any wrong impression she might make.

"I see you own one of Luciano Oliveira's works that were put up for auction by the Ruth Stanford estate," Larry commented, as he nodded towards a large painting that hung over the fireplace, when they were ushered into the main room of the Cox's condo a few minutes later.

"Yes." Seth Cox beamed with pride at his wife. "Lucia has always been drawn to his efforts, and it meant the world to me to be able to surprise her with this one. Are you a collector as well?"

"In a small way, yes," Larry admitted, "although I only own one Oliveira. Chase Sheffield, a business associate of Jack's and mine back in Captain's Point and Susan's law partner, was his aunt's heir."

"Larry spent several months sorting through the financial aspects of the estate, overseeing the sale of her Beacon Hill home and Oliveira's artwork, and moving a complete library as well as other fine interior furnishings to our hometown," Susan filled them in.

"My, but it is a small world," Lucia responded. "If I recall, Mr. Sheffield retained a number of the paintings for himself. Do you know if he plans to relinquish anymore of them?"

"I doubt it," Jack stated with an uncustomary firmness that surprised Susan. "Two now hang in Chase's childhood home, which houses an upscale inn and serves as a meeting place for local functions. The rest are prominently displayed in his wife's ancestral mansion, and it's my understanding that she helped him decide which ones to keep and which ones to auction."

"That's right." Larry nodded his agreement.

"What a shame." Lucia lifted one lovely shoulder in a small shrug as her lower lip developed a pout. "Although it relieves me of having to twist Seth's muscular arm in an effort to convince him to buy another."

As conversation continued around her, Susan drifted closer to the large windows that overlooked the city and the park below them. Thank goodness for Larry, she thought. He had broken the ice.

"Penny for your thoughts." Seth Cox joined her, his piercing blue eyes holding hers.

"I'm afraid they're rather mundane," she replied. "I was merely thinking what a magnificent view you have from this vantage point."

"I wanted to congratulate you on your marriage to Jefferson." The businessman turned slightly, so they now stood side-by-side like comfortable allies, the sparkling lights of the city spread before them.

"Your husband's a remarkable man and a wonderful friend," their host continued. "All the years that I've known him, he's been searching for something, and seeing you two together this evening, the way he looks at you and you look at him, I'm happily convinced that something was you."

"Thank you." She glanced sharply his way and decided to trust him. "Your acceptance means the world to me. I didn't even know about John Jeffers or your company when I accepted his proposal, you know."

"So he's shared with me." Seth recalled the disbelief in his friend's voice as it had come over the phone.

"I merely knew him as the kindest, gentlest man I'd ever met, and I loved him deeply. All of this side of him…" She made a small gesture that encompassed the view beyond the windows. "Has been a bit overwhelming since we left Captain's Point."

A small chime announcing that more guests had arrived, Seth started to make his excuses as he turned to greet them, but then paused.

"Know that you have a friend in me should you ever need one," he said softly. "Jack didn't just buy into a fledging business. His generosity to a wet-behind-the-ears Navy buddy saved my marriage and set the whole course of what has proven to be a wonderful life for me and my family." He gave her upper arm a gentle squeeze with his hand and then hurried to the foyer.

"Jack!" A booming voice issued forth as a fifty-something man with salt and pepper hair entered the room, followed by a woman Susan assumed to be his wife. "It's good to see you, you old so and so."

"Susie…" Jack found her with eyes filled with pride and gestured for her to join them.

"I'd like you to meet Dick and Marguerite Evans, good friends of mine from my Harvard days," he continued the introduction, as he placed his hand on the small of her back. "Dick was teaching one of my classes and allowed me to be beaten by him at chess every Friday evening one summer, while Marguerite followed each of my humiliations with a fabulous meal that made it all better."

"It sounds like I owe you my gratitude," Susan addressed the other woman, whose understated clothes and gentle eyes presented her as more approachable than their hostess had seemed upon their own earlier arrival.

"Not at all." Marguerite returned her smile. "It was a pleasure to cook for someone who appreciated my meagre efforts the way that boy did back then and has continued to do throughout the years."

"The Evans's daughter Angel is Becca Tate's roommate." Jack adroitly shifted their conversation to a new subject. "She'll be visiting with them over spring break beginning Friday, and I've secured tickets for both girls, so they can join us at the concert.

"Becca did an internship under Dr. Elizabeth Chesterton, Susie's mother," he added a further explanation for his friends' benefit. "She's a bright young woman."

"Dinner is served," Seth passed on an announcement that had been whispered into his ear by a young woman whose uniform implied caterer. "This way, please."

"I'm stealing you away from your husband, my dear." Susan felt her hand being slipped into the crook of Dick Evans's arm. "I've promised myself that I would take advantage of this opportunity to get to know the woman who captured Jack Jefferson's heart."

For a moment, Susan felt her stomach tighten, but then he added, "From what I've seen so far, he merely held out for the best."

## CHAPTER LII

Daniel already asleep in the double bed by the window and his own bathrobe draped across the foot of the other bed, Jeff made his way into the main living area of the suite a while later, where he once again sought the couch and his laptop. Opening his email, he hit Compose and entered Becca's address line.

*Hey, girl!*

> *Can't wait to see you!!!*
> *Wish you were here now. Having the time of my life.*
> *Felt like a jetsetter flying here in the Lear, and you should see the suite we're staying in at the Plaza. Limos at our disposal, hot and cold running lobster at every meal, and Captain's Point's finest all around me.*
> *Still, I'd give it all up to be back on that park bench with you by my side.*
> *Wrote the next chapter in the novel and part of another while Daniel was napping. Jack gave the first three chapters back to me earlier with a few suggestions – nothing major. He said I'm off to a good start, the same as you did.*
> *The short story's finished, and once it's cold, I'll begin editing.*
> *I took your advice and told Gabe Palmer that I could only accept his offer as a roving reporter, given my time constraints, and he said that was fine.*

*My first submission to the Gazette? A review of Jack Jefferson's appearance with String Flings!*

*Thanks for the input. Spot on as usual. No surprise there. We've always made a great team.*

*Remember that time we won the three-legged race at church camp? Other folks were falling down all over the place, but we looked at each other and took off across that field like we'd done distance running strapped side-by-side for years.*

*Together, we can do anything, Bec, including overcoming time and distance.*

*Only two days, twenty-one hours left until I'll pick you and Angel up at her house for the evening, and there's one thing you can believe in. Somehow, I'll find a way to get you off by myself long enough to take you into my arms and kiss you senseless. Count on it!*

*Love you,*

*Jeff*

Back in Captain's Point, David Eskar zipped up the front of a hanging bag that held the white shirt and black suit he had worn to his father's funeral, trying hard not to take that as a bad omen.

Glancing around his bedroom, he took stock of his open suitcase and toiletries bag, then picked up a thin volume from his chest of drawers and set it on top of his socks and robe. If only his Karen could see him Saturday night, she would know that he was so much more than a dentist.

Not that there was anything wrong with his profession. He wasn't ashamed of what he did – far from it. His efforts saved his patients' teeth for them every day, and dentures weren't all they were cracked up to be.

Still, his dental practice represented only one side of him. He loved music and studied religious history. He read voraciously, treated others fairly and offered assistance to those who needed him.

He knew now that he loved deeply. There would never be anyone else for him, only his Karen.

Sometimes, he was afraid he would lose his chance of securing her, if he didn't pursue her more aggressively, but then an image of Ira Zobel would rise up in his head.

All his life, he had played chess with his father and uncles, and through them, he had learned the secret to a successful life. Knowing your next move was never enough. Always, your mind's eye must remain on the game's final moments.

Ira Zobel was an impulsive man, who acted out of anger and false pride more often than not. In a game of chess, he would beat the older man any day, but this wasn't a game. This was his fight for his Karen and their lives together.

Slowly, steadily, he must make his way forward into her heart, and then he must be prepared for his final move. Nothing less than a checkmate would do. Life without Karen in it was unthinkable.

In the gatehouse at the end of Chase and Adrianna's drive, Penny Plunk turned down the covers on the bed she had shared with her husband for the best part of forty years and smiled.

"Did you set the alarm?" Otis asked as he entered the room, even as he picked up the wind-up clock that was old enough to vote and checked it himself.

"Who would've thought that the little girl who visited her great-aunt every summer would grow up, come to stay, marry Chase and then whisk us away, first to New York City and then on a second honeymoon to Europe?" Penny dropped onto the edge of the bed, events overwhelming her.

"I suppose it was to be expected." Otis settled beside her and drew her to him. "She is, after all, a Montgomery."

"Still…" His wife fought for the right words. "It's as if we're part of the family."

"I believe to those two orphans we are." He rubbed his cheek against the top of her head. "Chase spent hours of his young life in Montgomery House's kitchen, sampling along with Larry whatever goodies you had left."

"True, I thought I'd never get those two boys filled up, especially when they hit their teen years, and Martha Montgomery never objected."

"And they shared their problems and dreams with you, didn't they?" he reminded her.

"Yes."

"What they should've done with their parents, but couldn't." He stood and rounded the bed to his side, ready for sleep after what had been a long day. "We've been there for all three of them, although Larry had Anders and Elizabeth Chesterton to fall back on.

"That Chase and Adrianna have now cast us in the role of substitute parents doesn't bother me." He turned off the lamp on his side of the bed. "Neither of us will take advantage of them, and frankly, they fill a void in our lives as well. There's a reason why that photo of Adrianna riding Silver Queen as a little girl has stood on our mantel for so long. Now, come to bed."

And as she turned off her own lamp, slipped beneath the covers and snuggled against the man who had loved her well throughout their adult lives, Penny recalled the day she had almost refused his proposal, not sure she wanted to be tied down in Captain's Point.

Thank goodness, she had followed her heart and not her head way back then.

## CHAPTER LIII

Stating that he had an early meeting scheduled at the company's office, Jack made their excuses shortly after what had proven to be a long dinner and herded his party outside to their waiting limo.

Once back at the Plaza, Kate and Larry said goodnight at the Jeffersons' door and continued along to the suite that had surprised them when they had first arrived, both of them having assumed Jack would place them in completely disconnected rooms.

"Want something to drink?" Larry gestured towards the stocked bar after he had helped Kate out of her coat.

"No, thank you. I'm fine." She remained where she was, suddenly feeling shy at finding herself alone with him in their two bed two bath suite with nothing to unpack or prepare for.

"Come here." He held out his hand, and she moved forward eagerly, knowing she would always feel safe and comfortable in his arms.

"It strikes me that we have here both a situation and an opportunity." His face took on the excited little-boy look that she loved.

"Yes?" She felt her heart race and wondered if he could feel it beating through his suit coat.

"First, let me say again that I respect your position," Larry stated. "I'm not suggesting that we do anything we haven't done before, but I wonder if we haven't been provided a golden opportunity in which to enjoy what we have shared in a new environment."

She willed him to want the same thing she did.

"It would mean the world to me if you would allow me the privilege of sleeping with you in my arms." He searched her face. "Although, I'll understand completely and am willing to wait if you would prefer not to. I don't want you to feel pressured by me – not now, not ever."

For a moment, they both held their breaths – her in an effort to contain herself and him as he hoped he hadn't offended her.

"Yes." She worked hard not to fling her arms around his neck in her excitement. "Yes, I'd love to sleep in your room, but we'd have to mess up the covers in mine, too, and leave Do Not Disturb signs on both doors."

"Sounds like a plan." He grinned down at her. "Are we ready to go to bed now, or would you prefer to watch television or read first?"

"I'm feeling a bit tired," she lied, wanting nothing more than to jump up and down with joy.

Suddenly, his face sobered. "I've brought a full set of pajamas that I'll wear, although I don't usually bother with the top, and I want you to know we can return things to how they were at any moment, if you feel the least bit uncomfortable."

"I'll never feel uncomfortable with you." She slid her arms around his neck and pulled him down to her, which led to a kiss that he deepened, followed by another and another.

"Okay." He broke away and took her hand, a grin having taken up residence on his face. "Let's mess up those covers of yours."

Two minutes later, her bed now looking thoroughly used, Larry stood with the piece of chocolate that had been left for her enjoyment on her pillow suspended from his fingers.

"I'll put this on the bedside table in my room, where we'll meet whenever you're ready," he said. "Do you have a side you prefer?"

"I think I'd rather sleep on your left like this." Kate demonstrated where they both stood, snuggling her head against his left shoulder.

"Works for me." He hugged her to him, but then his expression once again sobered. "I love you, Kate. You know that, don't you? I'll never do anything you don't want me to."

"I know," she whispered, pressing her body even more firmly against his, sorry when he released her.

A few minutes later, Larry paused in the process of removing his belt, when a timid knock sounded on his door. Still dressed in his suit pants and socks, he turned the knob.

"I can't." Kate's jaw dropped slightly at her first sight of his magnificent, bare upper body, large tears rolling down her cheeks as her eyes widened.

"Don't cry, Baby." He clutched her to him, almost smothering her against his broad chest. "Please, don't cry. Anything, but that. I didn't mean to upset you. I don't want to hurt you. It's okay if we don't. We're okay. We'll put your bed back like it was. I'll return your chocolate. We'll have plenty of time to sleep in each other's arms once we're married. I'll…"

Kate pushed away from him.

"You don't understand," she wailed as she grabbed his hand and dragged him to her room, where a small pile of lace had appeared on the bottom of her bed.

"Don't you see?" She gazed up at him, her lovely crystal blue eyes awash with tears. "I can't wear any of these to bed with you until after we're married. It'd be asking too much of you."

"Now, let's see." He picked up first one of the tiny, frothy creations and then another, determined to find at least one that wouldn't drive him positively insane with need for her.

"Okay." He dropped the last one onto the bed, a crease having formed between his brows. "I'll concede that these might not provide our best choices tonight, although I'm looking forward to meeting them again in the future."

He sent her a leer, and she giggled.

"Surely, there's an alternative." His face brightened. "I know. I have a jersey I could lend you, or you could wear one of my shirts."

"I knew your brilliant mind would find a solution." Kate threw her arms around his neck and kissed him thoroughly, loving the warm feel of his bare flesh and strong muscles around her. Being married to Larry was going to be the best thing in the whole world.

"I know right where it is." He led her back to his room, rummaged in a suitcase and pulled out the desired object, which he then held up against her. "That should do it," he declared.

"Thank you." She accepted his offering and left him to get ready, returning a few minutes later to find his door open and him sitting up reading a section of the *Wall Street Journal* in bed.

"There you are." He tossed his paper onto the bedside table and flung back the covers on her side.

"It's a little big." She tugged at the soft cotton, first this way and then that.

"You look lovely." His gaze softened as he held out his hand and drew her onto the bed, then turned out the lamp on his side, casting the room into semi-darkness.

"I love you, Kate." He gathered her to him, his right arm finding its way around her tiny waist.

"I love you, too." She snuggled against him, and his jaw tensed, as he recognized the full measure of the hell to which he had committed himself that would only be worth it once the whole experience was over and just the memories remained.

# CHAPTER LIV

Several hours later, Susan let out a small sigh and slowly slid her legs over the side of the unfamiliar bed, trying not to disturb her husband this one time.

"Wait there." Jack's hand caught her arm, proving she had failed in her endeavor yet again. "I don't want you tripping and falling, because you've lost your way in the dark." He helped her across the room.

"Thank you." She squeezed his hand a few minutes later when they returned. "You need your rest, too, though."

"I'll be fine," he assured her, tucking her in and then rounding the mattress to his own side.

Reassuming their new sleeping position, he was surprised to hear his wife smother a giggle.

"Yes, Mrs. Jefferson?" he requested an explanation.

"I was thinking about your having put Larry and Kate in a suite," she admitted. "Whatever possessed you?"

"It kept them on this floor with us, and part of me thought they might appreciate the opportunity." He chuckled. "Although, it was probably the devil that made me do it."

"As protective of Kate as you are, I'm amazed that you were able to sign off on it." She rolled over and faced him.

"Why?" It was his turn to be surprised. "I'll be entrusting her to your cousin for what I hope will be the rest of their long lives together in a few weeks."

"True." She kissed the tip of her finger and placed it on his left dimple. "Thank you for being so receptive to their relationship."

"I'd be a fool not to be," he pointed out. "Kate loves him too much to choose me over him, and I wouldn't want her to. Larry's rock solid. They're perfectly matched, and he'll take good care of her. Anyone can see he adores her. No, the only relationship that concerns me at the moment is ours."

"Ours?"

"Yes, I'm wondering why we aren't taking the opportunity we have to the next level." His lips found her neck before moving downward.

"Nothing else anywhere in the world feels as right as this does with you," he uttered the words she most needed to hear, as he slid into the inner warmth of his sweet Susie and sought her lips once again several minutes later.

Afterwards, instead of drifting asleep in each other's arms, he helped her make her way to the bathroom again, where he waited outside the closed door and enjoyed yet another chuckle.

He had known men who had calmly taken care of their bodily functions in front of others in open desert stretches, atop windswept mountains and deep within jungles, but his own wife, whose entire body he could describe in intimate detail, would always prefer her privacy in such matters.

"Okay?" He took her left hand in his and placed his right arm around her waist when she rejoined him.

"Yes." She was quick to reassure him. "Although I feel a bit more tired than usual."

Back in their bed, he gathered her to him in the recommended spoon position he now insisted they assume as much as possible.

"I don't know how much longer we'll be able to enjoy moments like we just shared before the baby comes," she said softly, and he tightened his hold.

"I know," he whispered into her hair, not wanting her to hear the huskiness in his voice that would announce his continuing need for her. "I understand, but we can still cuddle like this, can't we?"

"Yes." She adjusted her position and snuggled closer, as he simultaneously began counting backwards from one hundred and attempted to focus his mind on a minor issue he hoped to resolve at the company the next day, trying to rein in his wayward body.

Over the years, there had been guys at the office he would visit in the morning, who had joked about staying as far away from their pregnant wives as possible for the duration. He hadn't understood it then, and he didn't understand it now.

Why would he abandon his Susie when she needed him the most, especially since it was her willingness to accept him that had put her in her current condition?

Often, he needed to make love to her so badly it hurt, and it would only be worse when he couldn't have her. Still, as she had said about the morning sickness she had already endured, it would all be worth it when he held their little Olivia in his arms for the first time.

Thinking his wife had now fallen asleep, he located the hem of the gown she had put on again before getting back into bed. Lifting the fabric slightly, he slowly worked his way up until he could spread his hands across her bare belly.

"I love you, Susie Chesterton," he said into the night that surrounded them, when he felt her silently laughing.

"I love you, too, Jack Jefferson, or should I say Daddy?"

But then, beneath the palm of his right hand, he felt a gentle pressure accompanied by a slight movement, and his face broke into a wide smile, even as his throat tightened.

Maybe, just maybe, their tiny Olivia Elizabeth Jefferson would recognize him, too, when she first entered the world.

"Your beautiful, dark-haired, dark-eyed daughter says, 'Hi,'" Susan whispered, and he knew, yet again, that he'd never feel as loved and accepted by anyone as he did by the woman beside him.

## CHAPTER LV

At eight-thirty on Thursday morning, a Learjet sporting the same 60XR designation that Daniel would've recognized from the previous day executed another perfect landing on the upgraded runway at Captain's Point Airport.

Thirty minutes later, Charles sat studying the sheaf of pages that Jack Jefferson had passed to him in a plain white envelope, as he had departed from the Lear a little more than twenty-four hours before.

Glancing up, he watched with satisfaction as a twin of the jet in which he sat taxied along the same runway and approached the main terminal.

In his experience, anything planned by Mr. Jefferson always proceeded smoothly, and he was looking forward to meeting Chase Sheffield this morning. During the phone conversation they had shared the day before, he had been very impressed.

Back in New York, Jack smiled tolerantly at the overly eager intern who placed a mug of coffee in front of him on the polished conference table in a mid-sized meeting room.

"I'll be fine now," he assured her, impatient to check his phone that had signaled a text.

CPoint to Mission Control. Chase had keyed.

How's it going? He replied and then waited while members of his Special Projects staff filed into the room for a now rare face-to-face meeting with him.

Wild. Crazy. It's a zoo.
Luv evry min.

Volunteer to be UR ops manager anytime.
Deprting 15 mins–both planes–all here.

Thank goodness, Chase had been willing to fill in for him at that end, Jack thought. Charles would've done so as a favor, but to burden the older man with the whole process would've been way beyond his assigned duties.

Let me know when you land. He sent one last missive, and then took a mental roll call of those seated around him.

Will do.
CPoint out!

"Looks like we're all here," Jack opened the meeting, not bothering to glance at the agenda his administrative assistant had prepared for him. "Let's begin with a brief report from each one of you. Then I'd like to get opinions on some issues Seth thinks we can resolve if we put our brilliant minds together."

An appreciative laugh circled the conference room, and he nodded at the vice-president who reported to him directly, indicating for the man to begin.

As each staff member in turn outlined progress made on their specific projects, Jack found it difficult to keep his mind on the business at hand, wishing instead that he was with Larry, Jeff and Daniel who were shopping for a tuxedo for the latter, while Susan and Kate made use of the spa at the Plaza.

His phone vibrating in his hand, he glanced at the tiny screen where he had it located just beneath the table's edge.

Tux locatd.
Also 2 suits,2ties,shoes?
L

Correctly interpreting the latter as a request for permission to buy, Jack responded:

Yes & something 4 J
Tie? Belt?

As the thirty-something, Type A on his right began her report, he again glanced at his phone.

Nice tie.
L

"Sounds good." Jack took charge once again. "Shawn, I'd like you to contact a man named Dick Evans and ask his opinion on possible solutions to your problem. Mention my name. Eileen can provide you with his number."

"Yes, sir." The newest member of his team made a note.

"Rosemary, it strikes me that we should include some diversification as we move forward with your plans. Can you send me a list of possible avenues we could take via email by the end of the week?" he asked.

"Certainly."

"Mitch, I think that's a wrap on yours," he addressed the V.P. "Great job as usual."

"Thanks, Jack."

"Let's move on to Seth's and my hopes for our future." He found it easier to concentrate now that Daniel's needs had been met and he still had an hour in which to bring this meeting to a close, before two Learjets full of people arrived in New York City from Captain's Point.

## CHAPTER LVI

"Daddy!" Daniel hurled himself at his stepfather's knees two hours later. "Everyone survived their trip from Captain's Point just fine, and now that you're here, we can eat."

"Good, because I'm starving." Jack hoisted the little guy onto his hip and threw his arm around his wife, who read his lifted eyebrow correctly and sent him a silent message that she was fine.

"I must say that you've put us up in style," Chase commented from where he stood behind Adrianna, his arms wrapped around her. "First a helicopter, then a Lear, now the Plaza. I wonder, will the next stop be the moon?"

"Not for a while yet," Jack replied, his tone the same one he had been using in the meeting room all morning. "Although, we do provide equipment to NASA. One of the tiniest offerings in our catalogue is currently mining the bottom of a crater on Mars' surface."

"That's where I want to go." Larry spoke up from where he stood chatting with Otis at the suite's bar, a plate of hors d'oeuvres on the counter in front of them. "But not until after I've exchanged vows with you," he whispered into Kate's ear as she joined them.

"Lunch is ready, Madame," Nigel announced in a voice just loud enough for all to hear, and the nine adults and Daniel soon found their places at the table.

"As a musician herself, Kate has indicated an interest in attending Jack's rehearsal with the Flings," Larry shared with Jeff a few minutes later, once everyone had begun eating. "Why don't you join them, too, this afternoon? I'm more than willing to stay here with Daniel and Susan. I'll check my emails, while they nap."

"Are you sure?" Jeff asked, and then glanced to where Jack nodded his approval.

"I would be interested as well, if you don't think I'd be in the way," Chase spoke up from where he sat further along the table. "Adrianna's planning on spending the afternoon catching up with Susan and Kate at the spa."

"It was wonderful." Susan reached beneath the table and squeezed her husband's hand.

"Pen and I are looking forward to some sightseeing," Otis filled them in. "We'll be back before five, though, which should give us time to get ready for later."

Jack picked up his phone. "I'll order you a limousine then." He sent a quick text.

"Our own limo." Penny's eyes filled with excitement. "And we have the Broadway musical to look forward to this evening." She smiled at the boy sitting next to her. "You'll enjoy that."

"I have to take an extra long nap, so I can stay awake through the whole thing," Daniel informed her, before turning back to his child-sized order of macaroni and cheese.

"You've made a lot of people happy this week." Susan smiled a while later at Jack, where he sat next to her on the edge of their bed as she prepared to nap. "Do you know how proud I am of you?"

"Most of my life, I buried the emptiness I felt in my work." He added her comment to others he cherished. "I lived simply, often in out of the way places, invested wisely, and waited for you to come along." He smoothed the covers. "It feels good to share the blessings I've received in return with our friends."

"Not everyone would be so generous," she pointed out.

"Others haven't been blessed as much as I have." He bent and found her lips, not ready to leave her.

Sensing his hesitation, she shifted onto her left side. "Would you hand me my wedge, please? It really does help."

"Sure." He lifted the covers and watched as she supported the weight of their little treasure on her Valentine's present, easing the strain on her back, then pulled the sheet and blanket back into position and dropped another kiss on her cheek.

"Dream with the angels, Susie," he said, as her eyes closed. "I love you."

Reentering the main room a few minutes later, he received a thumbs-up from Larry.

"Daniel's asleep, and the others are gathered in the newcomers' suite," the broker said. "You may actually pull this off."

"Thanks to your and Jeff and Chase's help," Jack acknowledged. "I couldn't have done it all on my own."

"I doubt that." Larry's eyes narrowed. "At this point, Chase and I are convinced you can do anything you put your mind to."

"To which I would reply that it takes someone who can do to know another."

"Quite possibly."

"Any word from David Eskar?" Jack asked, keeping his voice lowered.

"A text stating the view from your condo is amazing and thanking you for the use of the third limo," Larry filled him in. "He knows to communicate only with me from now on. Just out of curiosity, how many limousines can we call on?"

"As many as we need." Jack sent him a grin, his dimples deepening as excitement at what lay ahead filled him. "As many as we need."

## CHAPTER LVII

"Another wonderful day." Larry pulled Kate into his arms, once they had closed the door of their suite on the rest of the world shortly after Thursday had turned into Friday. "Did I mention how beautiful you looked this evening?"

"Three or four times." She sent him one of her slow smiles. "I've lost count."

"I mean it, Kate." His voice took on a serious tone. "I've never known anyone as beautiful as you are."

"Beauty is obviously in the eyes of the beholder," she stated, belying how pleased she was with his compliment. "Susan's as gorgeous as they come."

"The two of you, along with Adrianna, drew the attention of every man in the room as we passed through the restaurant to our table," he shared with her, "and I bet not a one of you noticed."

"I certainly didn't." She loosened his tie. "But then, I only have eyes for you. Are we meeting in your bedroom again tonight, Mr. Chesterton?"

"You'd better believe it." He hugged her to him and then sent her to slip into his jersey that had turned into the sexiest piece of cloth in the world when it hung on her.

Changing into his pajamas, he couldn't help but think how natural it had seemed to sleep with her by his side and how special it had been to wake up with her head on his shoulder.

This night and the next and then he'd find himself alone again back in his condo, but he wouldn't think of that now.

"I brought my chocolate with me," Kate announced as she joined him a few minutes later, her fingers working on its foil wrapper. "And I picked up a chilled water from the bar. I don't know about you, but I may be too excited from our evening to sleep right away."

"No problem there, we can snooze in until nine." He took the green glass bottle from her hand, unscrewed the cap and took a swig. "I could get used to going to bed with you and a bite of chocolate." He pulled her to him. "Let's see if yours tasted the same as mine did."

"Silly." She giggled when he let her go a minute later, hoping that they never stopped having as much fun as they always did when together.

Larry plumped the pillows behind them, lounged against them and left the light on, and she snuggled against him.

"Thanks for doing everything you are to help Jack," she said.

"My pleasure." He gave her a quick hug. "I'll always be there for your brother and my cousin. You know that, don't you?"

"Yes, it's one of the many things that I love about you."

"I love that you love me," he stated simply. "There were times, when I was growing up, that things got kind of lonely and I thought nobody cared for me."

"Lonely?" She glanced up, but for once he didn't return her gaze.

"My dad worked day and night at Chester's, probably in an effort to avoid my mother, who spent most of her time throwing her weight around and interfering in the lives of everyone else in Captain's Point," he revealed more of his story.

"I had it better than Chase, though," he pointed out. "I was a Chesterton, so I could hang out at the farm with Uncle Anders' brood most of the time. Still, at some point in the day, I had to go home."

"Big houses can be lonely." She passed her hand across his chest, and he sucked in his breath. "Ours was after my brother left."

"And now, we have each other." He tightened his hold. "I'll take good care of you, Kate. Everything that I have will be yours, including my time and attention. When something's been missing in your life, you value it all the more when you find it."

"I know." Her eyes sparkled with unshed tears. "I've found you."

"Don't ever let me go," he pleaded. "If I do something wrong, promise that you'll tell me. I don't want disagreements between us. I'll do anything you want to make you happy, because I know you'll never take advantage."

"You already spoil me." She slid her left leg over his and turned more onto her stomach, so as to face him. "All I ask is that you love me the best that you can. Like my brother, you watch over those whom you care about."

"And our lives together will be fun," he promised her. "We have fun now, don't we?" He didn't wait for an answer, not needing one. "You said once that you wanted to bear my children. Does that hold true, now that you know me better?"

He held his breath, and she slid her hand around his neck.

"Yes, when there's room in our lives for one or two little Chestertons, or do you want to start sooner?" she asked.

"No, I'd like you all to myself for a while, but I do want us to have children."

She lifted her face to his, and he kissed her, touching her lips so gently that the whole world shrank to that one spot of connection between them.

A groan rose deep in the back of her throat, and he tightened his hold further, his tongue tickling her lips until she opened to receive him. He tasted of chocolate and mint, and she never wanted them to separate.

"I think, maybe, we'd better turn out the light now." He drew away slightly, his desire for her making itself clear against her hip. "After all, you need your sleep to maintain all that beauty."

For a moment, they were silent in the darkened room.

"I love you, Kate," he whispered. "You're the best thing that's ever happened to me. I'll never let you go."

"I love you, too." She hugged him to her. "You're the best thing that's ever happened to me, too, even better than Jack. I'll never leave you."

And, as he held her tightly to him and let out a long sigh, she couldn't help but wonder.

What had she been thinking, when she had said they should wait?

## CHAPTER LVIII

The next day flew by for all concerned.

Promptly at ten o'clock, Larry had escorted the three younger women through the lobby and into a waiting limousine, promising to return with them after lunch, while Penny opted to forego shopping and join Otis for more sightseeing.

Jack, Jeff, Chase and Daniel remained behind, Jack taking advantage of the opportunity to practice his violin and Jeff joining him at one point with a pair of drumsticks and two brushes that had appeared magically out of nowhere and were played on the backs of two china plates.

Shortly after their return, Kate and Adrianna both stated they were making use of the gym, as soon as their lunches had settled, but then Kate disappeared along with Chase.

Her workout completed, Adrianna enjoyed a quiet read in their room with Max, who had come along for a long overdue vacation.

Meanwhile, Larry once again spent his afternoon in the Jeffersons' suite in case he was needed, where he received and returned several text messages.

At a few minutes before five, Susan awakened, feeling refreshed after a long nap, glad that everyone else had kept themselves busy.

"Did you have a good sleep?" Jack asked, after he had slipped into their room and found her awake.

"Yes, I did." She stretched in the kittenish way that he loved. "You should be proud of me. I bought another dress and a scarf that caught my fancy this morning."

"Be still my heart," he teased. "Next thing I know, Mrs. Jefferson, you'll be wanting a new cloth coat like Mrs. Nixon."

"How did your rehearsal go?" She snuggled against him when he stretched out beside her.

"Great!" He absentmindedly stroked her hair. "The Flings are fantastic, open and giving when I join them. It isn't always easy to play with a group that's complete in and of themselves, but we spent a lot of time together trying out this and that in Geneva, so we're more used to each other's preferences than sometimes occurs."

"I can't wait to hear *Alpine Spring* played by a group that size," she stated, not for the first time, and he was glad that she had brought an understanding and love of music to their marriage, not minding the sound of his practicing for hours on end.

He would've loved her as much if she had never wanted to hear a note, but it meant the world to him to share his other passion with her. Recently, Daniel had expressed an interest in the piano, another level of enjoyment added to his own.

"What would you say to my asking Edmund if he would take Daniel on as a pupil?" he asked.

"If he thinks he has the patience to deal with a five year old, I think it'd be nice," she agreed. "According to both you and Chase, Edmund did a fine job of mentoring Chase's cousin, but why don't you teach Daniel yourself?"

"I've given him pointers, but there may come a time when he no longer wants to practice enough or take lessons," Jack explained. "When that time comes, if it does, I don't want him to think that he's disappointed me."

"You're a good father." She reached up and kissed his neck.

"Careful," he warned her. "You keep doing that, and my hand may find its way under your gown again, although this time it won't be in search of Olivia."

"Why Jack Jefferson, and here I was thinking you were a man I could take home to my mother."

"That one won't work, my dear." He planted a firm kiss on her lips. "Your mother won't hear a word said against me. It's time for you to get dressed anyway, because I'm taking you and the rest of the crowd to my favorite Italian restaurant. Nothing fancy, you understand, but I think you'll appreciate the food and the ambiance all the same."

"Just in time," Larry greeted the two of them when they entered the main living area a short while later. "Pete Marlborough just called Chase. He's found another house for us to consider purchasing. This one's located next door to his office, so he's familiar with it, and he thinks we can avoid a realtor's fee again."

"Sounds good." Jack took attendance. "Jeff and Daniel appear to be the only ones missing."

"They're ready," Kate spoke up. "Daniel's playing one of his word recognition games, so they're in their room."

At the same time that the group of diners entered the neighborhood Italian restaurant that was their destination, David Eskar buttoned his overcoat and stepped onto the balcony of Jack's spacious condo.

All of this, the dentist thought, taking in the view of Central Park and the city that was spread before him, and the author/composer still seemed content to live in Captain's Point. He, for one, was happy that the man had chosen to do so.

The rehearsals he had attended these past two days had been experiences of a lifetime. Surrounded by so much creative energy, he had learned tons of new things, not all of them about music. There had been friendship and teamwork and giving to others as well.

Glancing at his watch, he turned and reentered the condo. It was time to join his friends for dinner at the French restaurant Jack had recommended to the three of them.

The past two days had been great. Tomorrow would be the best yet. If only his Karen had been here to share this wonderful time with him, then everything would've been perfect.

## CHAPTER LIX

The morning of Concert Day, as everyone in their group now thought of it, Jack and Susan awakened early, the hotel quiet around them.

He smiled down and flashed his dimples that were to her the sexiest things in the world. As a result, she shifted closer and slid her leg along his, followed by a groan issuing from him.

"I love you, Susie Chesterton." The words sounded torn from his throat as his body tensed some time later and he brought their lovemaking to a close. Clutching her to him, he held them together, both on their sides.

Still connected as one, they felt a firm kick announcing the presence of another between them, and they both laughed from the sheer joy of it.

"I love you, Jack Jefferson," she said, and his gaze softened before he took her again – gently, softly – until she felt the strength of the emotion building within him through his skin.

Afterwards, as he held her to him in such a way that, as one, they cradled their tiny other, he whispered into her ear, "I love you, Susie. You're so beautiful, inside and out. So amazing." And then, as he drifted to sleep, "You're my everything."

Quickly, she whispered his final words back to him, but she doubted that he had heard them as his breathing had deepened.

Soon, the alarm announced it was time for her to shower, breakfast and make her way downstairs to the beauty parlor, where he had arranged for all the women in their party to be treated to the full range of offerings.

As the day progressed, no opportunity presented itself during which she could restate the words, and now she was putting the finishing touches on her look for their special evening.

A whiff of his aftershave drifted her way, and she caught his shadowy presence behind her in the full-length mirror.

Looking, she thought, her best under the circumstances in her new, black evening suit with its scallop-topped jacket enhanced by the jewels he had given her, she turned, and his eyes widened in appreciation.

"You've done it again." His words, when they came, wrapped her in velvety warmth and reassured her that he was pleased. "I can hardly believe that anything so lovely can even exist."

Silent, she took in his magnificence as he stood before her – tall, strong, handsome, and powerful – truly a man in his prime, dressed in the tux she knew had been made especially for him by the best tailor in London, her love for him so overwhelming that all she could do was hold out her hand.

As he took it, she held his gaze. "When you're playing the violin this evening, know that you're my everything, too." She made sure that this time he heard the words.

A short limo ride away, Jeff pushed the button on the private elevator that would take him to the Evans's two-story penthouse, his approach already announced to their butler waiting upstairs.

"Good evening, sir," the man's cultured voice greeted him, when he exited the mirror-lined elevator, where he had decided that he rather liked his new black suit and its comfortable fit. "Mr. Evans has asked me to show you into his study."

"Sure." Jeff adjusted his black, silver and gold-striped tie as he followed the other man, his eyes taking in the décor that, while top drawer, still remained comfortable.

"Come in, young man. Come in." Angel's father rose from behind his desk and hurried forward. "It's Jeff, isn't it? Call me Dick. My wife tells me the girls will be ready in no more than ten minutes. If your cab doesn't wait, one of the concierge clerks downstairs will flag you another."

"We have a limousine at our disposal this evening, sir," Jeff replied, in the same tone he would've used had he said he had brought his umbrella.

"A limo?" The older man chuckled. "My Angel will be thrilled."

"I want you to know that I won't be remaining with your daughter and Becca throughout the concert." Jeff took advantage of the pause. "At some point during the intermission, Mrs. Jefferson's cousin, Larry Chesterton, will take over the responsibility of seeing them back to their seats."

Jack had already told him this at the Cox's dinner party three evenings before, but Dick found no reason to embarrass the younger man by letting him know.

"Once the concert is over, both Larry and Adrianna Sheffield, another business associate of Jack's and mine in Captain's Point, will be with them until I'm free to rejoin them," Jeff continued. "From then on, Becca, your daughter and I will be together, either in the limo or at the restaurant.

"The girls are on their way down," Marguerite Evans announced from where she was now poised in the room's doorway, then turned and disappeared.

"We mustn't keep the ladies waiting." Dick gestured for Jeff to precede him into the penthouse's entrance hall, where they arrived at the bottom of a broad spiral staircase as Angel appeared at the top, dressed in a frothy blue dress that set off her eyes.

Remembering his manners, Jeff sent her a smile, keeping his eyes on her until she was closer. "That color really suits you," he commented, and her face lit up with pleasure.

Unable to hold back any longer, he slid his gaze a few steps upwards, where Becca followed behind, and he knew he had never seen her looking so gorgeous.

The black dress she wore revealed her slim figure to perfection. Her dark hair was arranged in an upsweep that framed tiny, gold ball earrings, her only other jewelry the heart pendent and charm bracelet he had given her, the simplicity of her look allowing her own natural beauty to shine through.

Angel now beside him, he explained that their limo was waiting, gratified to see that Becca appreciated the added touch to their evening as well. He had done her proud.

"It was nice to meet you," he took his leave of the Evanses, then stood aside and allowed the two young women he was escorting to enter the elevator first, whispering as Becca passed him, "You look stunning."

Once the elevator had whisked their daughter on her way, Dick turned to his wife.

"Marguerite, we should consider the purchase of a summer home in Captain's Point," he stated thoughtfully. "Our Angel deserves a young man as nice as that one of Becca's, and I'm beginning to think the place where Jack Jefferson now lives is filled with nothing but the best of them."

## CHAPTER LX

As the penthouse's elevator made its way to the lobby, a limo carrying David Eskar arrived at the door of the world famous concert hall that would host the group String Flings that evening, and the dentist disembarked, a violin case in his hand, glad that he'd only eaten a light supper.

Had his great-grandfather felt this excited when he had played the very violin he himself carried in the concert halls of St. Petersburg, Warsaw and Vienna, before his ancestor had made his escape to America, taking with him only his small savings, his new bride and his musical instrument? He imagined so.

Just being asked to join the Captain's Point Chamber Music Group had been an honor. To assist Jack Jefferson with his plans had been a rare opportunity. To play in this hall with world-class musical talents such as the group String Flings and the man he now considered a friend was a once in a lifetime experience.

If only, his father and great-grandfather had lived to see this moment. If only, Ira Zobel could appreciate how far both his talent and his professional skills had taken him. If only, his Karen could've been in the hall this evening to hear him.

Back at the Plaza, Jack and Susan made their way through the lobby with their now sizeable group, Jack holding his wife back with him before they reached the doors, her hand nestled in the crook formed by his left arm as he carried his performance violin in its case on his other side.

Chase and his group left them for their limousine first, followed a few minutes later at Jack's request by Larry and Kate, along with Daniel in his tux, the latter three taking their places in a second limo and soon leaving the hotel behind.

"You're the most beautiful woman in the world, and I love you," Jack said for Susan's ears only.

Finally, Len waiting by the third limousine, the two of them passed into the open, where first one and then another camera flashed. Jack paused, placed his hand at the base of Susan's spine and allowed the hopeful group a clear shot of them as understanding dawned within her.

Daniel had appeared to the paparazzi as Kate and Larry's, safe and protected from the staring eyes of the crowd as an unknown, and Susan marveled at the vision of the man beside her, who loved her and their children so much.

A smooth ride in their own limo, Len opening the door and Jack's free hand assisting her, impressions ran through Susan's mind. This time, many more flashes – a rare sighting of a celebrity in two world arenas with his now pregnant wife by his side.

Glad for the designer outfit and fine jewelry that presented the right appearance, she straightened her shoulders and remembered to smile, relieved that her husband hadn't reminded her of what lay ahead, knowing she would've only worried.

Once inside the building, familiar to her from trips before she had known him, Jack saw her to their seats – one on the aisle that he took for a moment, another for her, then Daniel, filled with excitement next to Adrianna, Chase, Larry and Kate.

Beside the latter, a pretty young woman Susan assumed was Angel Evans sat next to Becca, her dark beauty at its best. Jeff's face filled with pride as he gazed at the girl on his left, while Otis and Penny finished out their row, taking it all in.

The Evanses, she knew from their first dinner, were absent hosting an annual charitable event in their home that evening, but the Cox family was in the hall somewhere and would join them after the show for supper, along with the Flings.

"I have to go." Jack leaned over, again keeping his words to themselves. "You were wonderful, Susie. My wonderful everything."

And then, he was gone, and she was grateful for the hint of his aftershave that he had left behind on her fingertips, a reminder of the love that they shared.

As the composer of *Alpine Spring* made his way backstage to join the group with which he would play it, his chosen driver sauntered along the sidewalk from where he had parked the limo, thrilled but not surprised to have been presented a ticket to the concert. Jack Jefferson was the best.

As he neared the main entrance, two cabs pulled to the curb.

From the first one, a neatly coifed, middle-aged lady disembarked, followed quickly by a younger woman in her mid-twenties with brown hair and hazel eyes, who Len mistook for the older woman's daughter, although she wasn't.

Obviously as excited about attending the concert as he was, they quickly made their way inside chatting gaily, and he found himself hoping that the people who would surround him as he listened would all be as nice as these two women seemed to be.

Then the second cab disgorged its passengers a few feet ahead of him.

A man in his sixties with clipped, blond hair streaked with silver emerged first and cast a furtive glance at his surroundings, but whether he wanted to be noticed or preferred not to be seen, the limousine driver couldn't have said.

Next, a woman appeared and stood ramrod straight beside the man Len assumed was her husband, her own blonde curls now the result of a box, somehow contriving to look down at the world from her five foot eight inches.

"Well, come on," she snapped as he shortened the distance between them, and the limo driver felt a surge of relief that he had chauffeured the musician who would be playing and his wife instead of the twosome before him.

One good thing about his current position was that he never associated with anyone even remotely related to the likes of the female he had just witnessed.

And, as Len entered the famous hall behind the couple to whom he had taken such an instant dislike, he had no way of knowing that, for the second time since he had begun observing the cabs' occupants, he was badly mistaken.

# CHAPTER LX!

"The most remarkable thing has happened," David greeted Jack backstage a few minutes later, when the composer took a seat in a comfortable folding chair next to his. "Unfortunately, as a result, I'll have to excuse myself from your dinner party after the performance."

"Is something wrong?" Jack's face filled with concern.

"No, but I wasn't aware that Karen had arranged to visit her aunt here in New York this weekend. She texted me a few minutes ago as they were riding here in a cab," the dentist explained. "They're attending the concert and have asked if I would escort them to supper afterwards. I'm to meet them in the lobby."

"I'm glad Karen will have the opportunity to see you perform in this famed hall," Jack replied, "but there's a simpler solution. I've arranged a private room for our party, and I'm sure the restaurant will have no problem adding two more places for us. I'll contact them now if you're agreeable."

"Karen and her aunt will both be thrilled." David couldn't believe his luck, knowing the two women couldn't help but be impressed by an invitation to join them at the premier New York City destination for supper after a concert or show.

"There'll be plenty of room in the limousine for two additional passengers as well," Jack pointed out. "Drop the others off first, and then feel free to continue using it as long as you need to take your guests home and return to the condo."

For the first time in his life, the dentist felt the need to pinch himself in an effort to insure that he wasn't dreaming. How could so many unbelievable things happen in such a short time?

"They'll be lowering the lights soon," Pierre, the Flings' lead violinist, let them know as he joined them. "Time for you and me to take our places." He rested his hand for a moment on the composer's shoulder.

Jack rose from the folding chair, unaware that a slim man of about his own age had just slipped into the empty seat by his wife.

"Susan Jefferson?" The man in a tuxedo didn't wait for a reply. "I'm Jules Fauré." He held out his hand, shook hers and then glanced to the next seat. "And this must be Daniel. I understand you're starting to learn the keys on the piano."

"My Daddy's teaching me," Daniel replied.

"There's no one better to do so," Jules stated and then turned his attention back to Susan. "The concert is being taped this evening, and I need to ask if you would be willing to assist me briefly during the second act."

"If I can." Susan couldn't think of a thing she could do that would be in any way helpful.

"I knew I could count on you." Jules smiled with what could only have been described as relief. "Only an exceptional woman could've captured the heart of Jack Jefferson. If I need your help, you'll have no problem following my directions. I'm afraid I must get backstage." He reached across her and shook Daniel's hand. "Good luck with the music lessons."

"What did he want?" Adrianna asked once the musician had hurried to take his place onstage.

"Frankly, I'm not sure." Susan gave a slight shrug. "The lights are dimming, Daniel, so it's time to sit still." She put her arm around her son, part of her hoping that he might sleep during some of the concert, although he was used to being quiet when music was played.

Finally, the lights in the grand hall dimmed completely, and a hush fell over the audience. A spotlight fell on the center of the velvet curtains, and the cellist who had just left them appeared to a ripple of applause.

"Good evening, ladies and gentlemen," he said. "My name is Jules Fauré, and it's my privilege to welcome you to our String Flings' concert this special evening. I say special for several reasons.

"First, we are honored to be appearing in this magnificent venue. Second, the concert this evening is being broadcast to a live audience and taped for later showings, and third we have with us tonight a special friend."

Surprised to hear that the performance was being broadcast, Susan wondered if her husband had known.

"Some of you are familiar with either our friend's Anderson detective series or his literary novels written as John Jeffers," Jules continued. "Others of you may know him as Jack Jefferson, a talented musician who has appeared with us onstage on several occasions, most recently in Washington, D.C., in December as a favor when Pierre, our lead violinist, suddenly decided to have his appendix removed.

"Not wanting to cancel our scheduled appearance at a large charitable event, I contacted Jack completely out of the blue. He immediately agreed to drop everything, fly his personal helicopter at his own expense up to D.C. from his home in southern Maryland and fill the void with one codicil, which is the reason why the final number is listed merely as Surprise on your program.

"After all, one can hardly refuse the sort of man who not only owns, but flies his own helicopter."

A ripple of laughter circled the room.

"Mr. Jefferson will be playing with us throughout the evening, including during our first piece – Rimsky-Korsakov's *String Sextet in A Major*. So, without further ado, let there be music."

At which, the curtains parted to reveal the String Flings with Jack added to their number.

"That's my Daddy!" Daniel's young voice called out clearly.

Onstage, Jack's face broke into a grin as he quickly saluted his stepson with his bow, but then gave his full attention to Jules who was conducting the first number.

Relieved that several of the musicians had chuckled at the outburst, Susan whispered an admonishment into her son's ear, and then relaxed into her seat, prepared to enjoy the rich sounds pouring forth from the stage.

All too soon, it seemed to her, the piece was over, and she was pleased when the audience burst into enthusiastic applause.

"They're wonderful." Adrianna leaned over Daniel and whispered, before giving her attention back to the stage where another member of the group was announcing a selection by Mozart that was followed by a work by Borodin.

Each piece had been introduced along with the telling of a short anecdote about either its premiere or its composer, the Flings obviously bringing a mischievous sense of humor as well as skill and appreciation to their work. No wonder Jack enjoyed playing with them, Susan thought.

Once again, the stage lights were lowered and a spotlight shone on Jules as he prepared to introduce the next number.

"Four years ago, we Flings were lucky enough to be lent two spacious apartments overlooking Lake Geneva for a bit of summer rest and relaxation, as well as some serious planning for our next tour," he began. "Thrilled, we were a bit concerned about disturbing the owner of the penthouse apartment above ours.

"Upon arrival, I discovered this card in the kitchen written by the owner of the upstairs unit we were using. Translated, it reads:

*At some point, you will find yourselves desperate to meet the owner of the penthouse. When that moment comes, you will recognize it with certainty. Call the number below immediately, introduce yourselves, mention my name, and you will be welcomed to join him.*

"Needless to say, we were intrigued, but for two days, we heard no sound from above. Then, as we were preparing for bed, we heard footsteps overhead," Jules continued. "The next day, we practiced as usual, but no complaints were forthcoming.

"That evening, as the sun was setting and we were enjoying our fruit and cheese at the end of a supper served on our deck, the strains of a single violin floated to us from above – haunting, lilting notes that made our hearts sing, but which not one of us recognized.

"You can imagine the looks that passed around our table." Jules' eyes widened at the memory. "It was as if Heaven itself had opened its doors and allowed an angel to play for us. The moment described in the note had come, and I dialed the number."

A second spotlight now fell on the group's special guest.

"Jack Jefferson answered," Jules continued his story. "The melody we had heard was from his recently completed composition *Alpine Spring*. As promised, we were welcomed upstairs, and by the end of a summer of collaboration, it was agreed that we would premiere the new work with Jack playing the solo parts.

"We, of course, were both honored and thrilled," the musician brought his tale to a close. "*Alpine Spring* is now a regular part of our repertoire, and tonight you will be privileged to hear the composer himself play the solo parts once again – a rare opportunity indeed."

As Jack stood, Susan realized she was holding her breath and released it.

Was he nervous? She certainly would be, although he appeared completely at ease.

How handsome he was, her talented husband. How lucky she was that he had chosen her to be his wife.

Jules raised his baton, and then brought it down as Jack's violin, lent to him by a museum in Bern for concert performances, sounded the first solo notes of *Alpine Spring*.

As other instruments entered in, Susan found herself amazed by the richness and depth of the piece when played by the full complement of instruments for which it had been written in a hall with amazing acoustics.

The notes rose and fell, louder and softer, richer and then distilling to only one melody played solo and impeccably, until Jack's bow drew across the strings a final time and the last note faded into a memory.

The audience rose to its feet in wild applause, as the composer and the Flings took their bows and the curtains closed.

In that moment, Susan knew she would never hear anything more beautiful in her life, but like Len the driver, she was wrong.

## CHAPTER LXII

The lights in the hall now on, Daniel turned in his seat. "Is it over?" he asked his mother.

"Not yet." Susan absentmindedly straightened his blond waves with her fingers. "First, we have intermission, and then, there's the second half of the concert."

To their right, Chase and Larry both stood, anxious to stretch their long legs.

"Are you planning to go to the lobby, or would you prefer to stay here?" Adrianna asked Susan. "Chase and I will be glad to oversee Daniel's getting around some if that would help."

"Janie said I should move a bit, if I could," Susan replied, "but I'd appreciate it if Chase would take him into the men's room."

The aisle now clear, the group made their way to the lobby, where she handed her son over to her law partner and headed for the ladies' room herself.

Returning a few minutes later, she was unable to locate anyone from her own party in the crush, but then she spotted her sister-in-law, who appeared to be lost in the crowd as well.

"Have you seen any of the others?" Kate asked as she neared. "You'd think we could pick out Larry, Chase and Jeff, even in a swarm like this. They're so tall."

But, before she could answer, Susan watched as her companion sucked in her breath, her face freezing into a shocked expression.

"What is it?" Susan's question, uttered as her glance settled on a middle-aged, blond-haired man and his wife who wore a deep scowl on her face as she argued with her husband, effectively brought Kate's attention back to her.

"Promise me you won't tell Jack." Her sister-in-law grabbed her arm and headed them into the thicker part of the crowd. "It would only upset him, and there's no reason he needs to know."

"I promise," Susan answered reflexively, her immediate concern Kate's obvious discomposure. "What exactly is it that I'm not telling him?"

"Did you see them?" Her sister-in-law's crystal blue eyes locked on hers. "The blond-haired couple who were looking down their noses at everyone else?"

"I caught a glimpse of a couple that might've been them." Susan thought she could see Larry and Jeff up ahead. "Who are they?"

Kate brought them to a halt. "Jack's and my parents."

"Here?"

"They've come to New York so my mother could shop for years, and they often attend concerts when they visit," Kate filled in her brother's wife. "I used to come with them, hoping each time that I'd somehow be able to slip away and see Jack."

"Do you think they knew he'd be playing this evening?" Susan asked, not sure what answer she wanted.

"I doubt it." Kate shrugged. "My mother wouldn't have come if she'd known, although my father might have decided to stick with the program. The one thing he did right by Jack and me was to encourage our talent with music, something that runs in his family."

"I'm assuming you don't want Larry to know either." Susan found herself feeling sorrier for her husband and his sister than ever before.

She couldn't imagine a world without her loving and supportive family, and yet, Chase and Adrianna were basically alone in the world except for each other, while Jack and Kate might as well have been. No wonder Jack's love for her and their children was so strong.

"Larry's spotted us." Kate's voice filled with relief. "Let's get you back to your seat."

Everyone else apparently deciding the same thing at that precise moment, Susan clutched Daniel's hand in hers as soon as she located him and Adrianna. Their small group made their way down their aisle, while the Plunks, Larry, Angel and Becca edged along the one on the other side of the rows.

Once settled back in their seats, Susan listened attentively to Daniel's excited comments and answered his childish questions, until finally the lights blinked overhead, announcing the intermission's approaching end.

"Daddy will play his violin some more now, won't he?" Daniel asked, this time his words carrying only to those in their immediate surroundings – many of whom, Susan noted, smiled.

As the hall darkened, a spotlight once again settled upon the velvet curtains, drawing her attention as Pierre appeared to announce the next number, this one by Beethoven.

The selection that had been chosen was one of her favorites. Still, Susan found it hard to concentrate, her heart filled with a new understanding of the level of hurt that surely had been metered out to the man she herself loved so deeply by the haughty, blonde-haired woman whose eyes were the coldest she had ever seen.

# CHAPTER LXIII

As applause sounded for the Beethoven, the velvet curtains once again closed, effectively shortening the audience's response as anticipation grew.

Sounds of chair legs scraping and heavy objects rolling against the stage could be heard from behind the cloth by those waiting in the darkened hall.

A shadowy figure slipped through the curtains, the spotlight returned, and Jules was revealed.

"Who doesn't like a surprise?" he began and received whispered replies from seats scattered throughout the hall.

"I know I do," he continued, "and believe me, I was surprised as were the rest of the Flings, when Jack Jefferson revealed the terms of the codicil to his emergency appearance with us in December. Surprised and, I might add, thrilled.

"Unbeknownst to us, he had composed a new piece – a work inspired by the news that he and his wife Susan were expecting a child."

An excited murmur circled the hall as the audience realized they were indeed in for a treat – the premiere performance of a new offering by an internationally celebrated composer.

The left hand curtain opened, revealing the Flings and Jack, who shrugged an apology and flashed his dimples for the audience.

From where she sat, Susan could see that two rolling dividers now separated whatever stood behind the right hand curtain from the players on the left.

"Jack's wife, to whom this piece is dedicated, and their son Daniel are with us this evening, and I'd like for them to stand, so you can see them." Jules held out his right arm in Susan's direction as a spotlight bathed her and Daniel in its light.

Her eyes on Jack, she saw his face fill with surprise at the request as she took Daniel's hand and complied, remembering to smile, relieved when she heard Adrianna whisper to her son, "Climb up. I'll hold your seat still for you."

Onstage, Jack stood as well, his face filled with love as he brought the fingers of his right hand to his lips and then slowly extended his hand, palm down, with a slight uplift at the end, as if to send it gently their way, effectively drawing much of the attention away from them to the stage.

Taking her husband's resuming his seat as a cue, Susan sat down as well.

"It's time for your daddy to play now," Adrianna whispered to Daniel.

"He plays the best," the five year old announced in a stage whisper as he sat down.

"All the Flings and your daddy are extraordinary," Adrianna adroitly diffused his loyal words.

"You came this evening prepared to hear only strings, but Jack's new piece requires a bit more," Jules filled them in. "For a man who writes award-winning novels and flies helicopters, this wasn't an issue. He merely called upon his talented friends back in Captain's Point, Maryland. I give you a selection of the membership of the Captain's Point Chamber Music Group."

Susan watched in amazement as the right hand curtain opened and stagehands efficiently removed the dividers, placing them side by side at the back of the stage.

Two grand pianos manned by Chase and Edmund were revealed, along with David Eskar who walked a few paces and took Jack's seat with the other violins. Jeff sat behind a full set of drums on the far right.

All the Captain's Point men wore black suits, white shirts and black, silver and gold-striped ties.

Jack crossed and stood next to Kate, who was dressed in a floor-length, black-sequined evening dress, placing them both center stage.

As a welcoming round of applause filled the huge hall, Susan couldn't help but wonder what her in-laws must be thinking as they viewed both their son and daughter making a huge mark in the musical world.

In this rare moment, were they proud of Jack and Kate, or did they care? Would either of their parents congratulate their talented son or daughter after the concert, or would they ignore one or both of them altogether?

"Ladies and gentlemen, it is with a great sense of honor that I give you *Susan's Song* by Jack Jefferson." Jules resumed the conductor's spot and raised his baton.

"You knew all along," Susan whispered to Adrianna, who merely grinned back. "How in the world?"

"Your husband is amazing."

Jules brought his baton slowly down, and the rich notes of a single cello softly sounded. Jack's violin joined in, followed by Jeff's soft brushes from the right.

Gradually, the piece grew as more instruments added their notes, the two bass players plucking what could be taken as a gentle heartbeat underneath. The work took on color and texture as the melody developed.

Then a musical conversation began between Kate's flute and Jack's violin, and Susan found herself wondering if this represented her New Year's Eve announcement. Next, Kate's flute fell silent, and Jack's violin wove brief references to her favorite pieces by Massenet and Fauré into his own melody, taking them to a whole new level of poignancy.

As she blinked back tears at the beauty her husband had created as a reflection of their love, Susan felt the flutter of a soft cloth on her right wrist, realized that Adrianna had passed her a large, black cotton handkerchief and smiled. Her detail-oriented husband had thought of everything.

Folding the cloth into a small square, Susan surreptitiously blotted her eyes as one by one the instruments faded, until all that was left were Kate's flute, Jack's violin and a single bass heartbeat softly completing the work's structural arch as they drifted away.

As one, the audience leaped to their feet and applauded as the musicians on stage rose from their seats and bowed in response.

Jules grabbed Jack's hand and led him front and center, where the composer took a bow and gestured for Kate to join them. Another bow, and he lifted his left hand in which he held his violin to give credit to those from Captain's Point. This done, he gave the same courtesy to the Flings and, finally, blew another kiss to Susan and Daniel where they sat in the audience.

As Jules indicated for the listeners to resume their seats, he made another announcement, "The composer and his friends have agreed to join us in the playing of two encore pieces for you in a minute," he shared with them as Jack resumed his place with the Flings.

Left alone, the cellist continued, "To commemorate this event and still maintain the surprise until the last minute, we have printed an insert for your programs outlining the piece, a biography of the composer and the names of those who joined us onstage that you can pick up on your way out."

Turning, he returned to his own seat as Raphael Barreau, of the Flings, announced that he and Jack would play Danyel's *Passemezzo* for two lutes, a piece they had enjoyed together on soft summer evenings overlooking Lake Geneva.

As the lilting notes wrapped around her, Susan's face beamed with pride as her husband sought her eyes. His evening, she recognized, would be reported as nothing short of a triumph.

# CHAPTER LXIV

Once the curtains had closed for the final time and the hall's lights had come on, Adrianna leaned towards Susan. "Jack said we should stay seated until the aisle clears, and then we can join him backstage if he hasn't already appeared."

Shortly thereafter, the Captain's Point musicians began to make their way from behind the curtains, Kate and her brother bringing up the rear as they approached those who had watched the performance and were now gathered together in an aisle.

"What did you think?" A beaming Edmund was the first to reach the listening group, his wife Marissa behind him, carrying a thick spiral notebook.

"You were all fantastic, and the piece was amazing," Adrianna declared.

"Marvelous!" Larry hurried forward and hugged Kate to him, heedless of the additional witnesses from their home town.

"I stayed awake through the whole concert and listened, because you're the best," Daniel pointed out as Jack hoisted him onto his hip.

"Your saying so means the world to me, Charger." He kissed his loyal fan on the cheek and threw his arm around his wife.

"Are you upset with me?" he whispered into her ear. "I didn't know Jules was going to do that."

"Not at all," she assured him as she pressed nearer, her eyes shining with pride. "He had asked me beforehand if I would assist him, although he hadn't offered specifics. I can't believe that you did all of this for me. *Alpine Spring* was everything I had hoped it would be, and my song…" She blotted her eyes again. "My song…"

"*Susan's Song* is my gift to you." He squeezed her to him as he handed their son off to Larry and Kate once again.

"Who's running the Sheffield Place Inn, so that Edmund and Marissa could participate?" Susan asked as they followed the others to the four limousines that were now waiting outside.

"That worked out well," Jack shared with her. "Herb mentioned at one of our business meetings that Jewel made the best homemade cinnamon rolls he'd ever eaten. I told Chase, and he asked them if they'd fill in. All Jewel had to do was take reservations, check guests in and cook them breakfast in the morning. Housekeeping staff did the rest.

"We really needed Marissa." He held the door to the lobby for her. "She managed the instrument rentals up here and made sure everyone knew where to go and when. She also dealt with the catering that we utilized for practice sessions."

Once in their limo, Jack left the dividing glass down and leaned forward. "So what did you think?" he addressed their driver, claiming he was his toughest critic.

"Your best yet," Len stated emphatically. "You should've married your lovely wife a long time ago."

"I agree." Jack hugged her to him. "The only problem was I hadn't yet found her."

"Obviously, you should've tried harder." The driver gave his employer no quarter.

"That's a bit unfair when I'd traveled the world and looked in all the odd corners," Jack retorted as if his wife wasn't with them.

Relishing this glimpse of another, lighter side of her husband, Susan relaxed against him, until they arrived at the restaurant for the next leg of what had turned into an unbelievable evening.

Two hours later, the fourth limousine dropped Edmund and Marissa off at Jack's condo, where they had been staying with David Eskar who remained inside the vehicle with Karen and her aunt.

"What an amazing experience," Karen said, once the three of them were alone. "I was so proud of you and all the other Captain's Point musicians."

"I couldn't believe my ears when Jack told me what he needed me to do for him," the dentist shared.

"You obviously deserved his trust," Miriam Zimmerman stated. "There wasn't a single wrong note played during the entire concert, and the dinner afterwards provided icing for the cake."

"It was my pleasure to arrange for you to attend that as well," David assured her as the limo pulled to the curb in front of a large brownstone. "I'll see the ladies to their door and then be right back," he addressed their driver once he had alighted from the vehicle.

"It was nice to meet you, David." Miriam turned towards him for a moment before entering her home. "I hope to see more of you in the future."

"Will you be jogging on Monday?" Karen paused briefly.

"You can count on it." He leaned forward and kissed her cheek. "It was a wonderful surprise to learn that you were here. Our sharing this experience has meant the world to me."

He waited until she closed the door behind her and then returned to his ride, feeling as if he were walking on air.

As the dentist resumed his seat in the fourth limo, Jeff, Becca and Angel stepped into the private elevator that would whisk them to the Evans's penthouse.

"I'm glad Becca drew you as her roommate," Jeff addressed the owners' daughter. "I can see why you two get along so well."

"We were lucky," Angel agreed as the elevator came to a stop, and Jeff took Becca's hand, keeping her next to him.

"Would you excuse us for just a minute please?" he addressed her friend. "I have something I'd like to discuss privately with Becca before I head down."

"No problem." Angel's eyes twinkled as they swung from him to her roommate.

Once the elevator door closed behind her friend, Becca wasn't surprised when Jeff drew her to him and kissed her with a possessiveness that left no room for doubt as to his feelings. After all, he always kept his promises.

"You'll call me as soon as you arrive in Captain's Point on Monday, right?" he asked, his voice husky as he held her close.

"Yes, and I've made a decision," she announced. "This time, there will be no hiding who it is that I'm dating."

"I'm glad."

And with that, he had to be content as he released her and opened the door, wishing with every fiber of his being that he could take her with him.

## CHAPTER LXV

"Our little guy was asleep before his head hit the pillow," Jack informed his wife as he undid his cummerbund and began removing his studs. "He was certainly a hit with everyone at the restaurant. Several of the Flings offered to adopt him, if we ever tire of him."

"It probably helped that he slept in the limo on the way there," she pointed out. "I couldn't believe that you'd had Larry and Jeff shop with him for a tux, although he did look cute in it."

"On the other hand, his mother was a thing of beauty." He placed the last stud with the others.

"As was his father." She released her blonde waves, allowing them to fall softly against her shoulders. "Not everyone can pull off that look."

"Having a great tailor helps, and I can't play as well if I'm uncomfortable." He slipped his feet from his shoes. "Did I mention that I've been called upon for assistance by Angel?"

"No, you didn't." Susan handed him the small boxes containing the jewelry she had worn that evening. "With what?"

"Apparently, she believes I can do anything, so it will be nothing at all for me to insure that Jeff and Becca get married." He set the shirt he had worn to the side. "Exactly how I manage this has been left up to me."

"After what you pulled off this evening, a mere marriage between two young people who are obviously in love with each other shouldn't provide you with too much of a challenge."

Susan draped her wet washcloth over a towel rack, then felt her husband's arms come around her from behind and leaned against his warm wall of strength.

"Thank you for not being upset about the spotlight and cameras." He rested his chin on the top of her head. "You were wonderful, and part of me can't help but want the whole world to know that I'm the one you chose to marry."

"I was proud to stand up for you as your wife." She closed her eyes and breathed in his scent – a mixture of sandalwood, male and fresh air. "Although, I was glad you had thought to send Daniel with Kate and Larry."

"Tired?" he asked.

"A little." She opened her eyes and smiled at him in the mirror, not wanting him to worry.

Returning his tux to its special hanger a few minutes later, Jack was glad Susan had finally made it into their bed, the shadows under her eyes a sign that for her it had been a long day.

Still pumped from the evening's success, he wanted nothing more than to make love to her throughout the night, but even an idiot could tell that would be out of line. This was one time when he must put her needs first, allowing her to get her rest, and there would be more such times now that they were headed into the home stretch of their pregnancy.

Sliding between the sheets a moment later, he leaned over and kissed her, surprised when she hugged him tightly to her.

"You seemed so relaxed onstage during the concert." Her hand slid its way from his waist to his chest. "I would've been a nervous wreck in the same situation. Are you exhausted now that it's over?"

"Not really." He began to count backwards from one hundred in his head, willing to talk if she wanted, but still determined to allow her to sleep as soon as she was ready.

"You were…," she paused. "I don't have any more words to use. Wonderful, amazing, fantastic, extraordinary have all become terribly mundane since this evening began."

"If you don't stop, I'll end up horribly conceited, and you'll use up a whole new list." He chuckled, again surprised as an intent look entered her eyes.

"I'm afraid it's your evening for women to come to you for assistance," she said, as she absentmindedly began making slow circles on his abs with her palm. "I need to ask something of you, too."

"Anything." He wondered if he should be concerned, even as he revised his counting and started over at one thousand. "How can I help?"

"Played by such a talented group in this evening's awesome venue, *Alpine Spring* was more than I could've imagined," she continued.

"On the other hand, my song…" Her eyes sparkled with tears. "My song took me to a whole other world, a world to which only you and I travel together."

"Then I succeeded as a composer." He kissed her gently. "I love you, Susie."

"I love you, too," she whispered against his lips. "I want to return to that world in your arms. I need you to make love to me before we sleep. I need you to play the song you wrote for me with my body in your hands instead of your violin."

"I'll play anything you choose on whichever instrument you desire, any time that you want," he assured her as he proceeded to make her wishes come true, even as he stopped counting and thanked God that the extraordinary woman in his arms had been gifted to him.

# CHAPTER LXVI

"I meant what I said earlier." Larry shot the bolt. "You were amazing."

He let out a small 'umph' as he turned, Kate flung her arms around his neck and his back struck the door to their suite.

Believing her to be excited still from their evening, he held her to him and continued, "I'll never forget how beautiful you looked in that gown, center stage, with the soft light shining upon you, and you played your flute like an angel.

"I almost cried out that you were my girl, like Daniel had with Jack's being his daddy. That's how proud I was of you." He changed the subject. "Do you need help getting out of your dress?"

She nodded her head against his chest, and he lessened his hold, following her to her room.

Earlier, he had been called upon to zip her up, since she was afraid she would catch the sequins in the zipper if she attempted to do so unaided.

What had appeared at first glance to be a simple task, though, had ended up being far more difficult than he would've imagined, as the mobile sequins had seemed bent on thwarting him.

Still, he had managed, and once he'd gotten the hang of it had even made a game of kissing her bare back a few inches higher than the point the zipper had yet reached, which had resulted in a passionate kiss in the end.

Kate flipped on the bedside lamps using a switch by the door and then took several steps forward towards the bed, where she gathered her hair in her hand and curled it around her neck, so it was out of his way.

Where going up earlier had been difficult, Larry found that he now faced a different challenge, when a widening V formed between the two sides of the dress as he held his left arm around her waist and his lips traced her spine downward.

She let out a moan, and, like a cat that had turned in its skin, he found her suddenly arched over his arm, her face lifted to his.

Reflexively, he sought her lips, tightening his hold as she took a step backwards that brought her against the foot of the bed.

As he deepened the kiss, she melted in his arms, and he felt them leaning even further over the mattress as a freight train full of passion roared through him, until a tiny voice deep within his brain shouted the word, "No!"

Straightening sharply, he brought her with him and then dropped his hands to his sides, recognizing that while she might want it to be 'yes' this evening, she would wish it had been 'no' in the morning.

"I'd say that we've demonstrated we won't have any trouble getting things started once we're married." He sent her a wry smile. "You should be okay with your dress now, and I'm taking a quick shower, after which I hope we'll once again meet in our accustomed place."

She nodded her agreement, and Larry hurried to his room where he shrugged out of his suit and locked himself in the bathroom. It wasn't until the cold water hit him that he realized Kate hadn't uttered a word, since they had returned to the Plaza.

Toweling himself dry, he slipped into his pajamas and entered his bedroom, his concern deepening as he discovered her already under the covers, the lights out and his side of the bed turned down.

"Are you okay, Sweetheart?" He slid into place beside her, propped up the pillows and drew her to him.

In response, she once again locked her arms around his neck, almost choking him.

"There's something I have to tell you," she said, her breath tickling a spot just beneath his right ear, sending waves of desire washing through him. "We shouldn't have secrets between us, but I don't want my brother to know."

"I'm listening." He couldn't imagine where this was going.

"My parents were at the concert this evening," she blurted out. "I saw them in the lobby."

"Did you speak to them?" He wasn't sure he wanted an answer.

"No, and I didn't want to thrust them on you either," she replied. "It was a shock seeing them there out of the blue, and I needed to keep my head straight. Jack was counting on me, and that had to be my first priority."

"Were you ashamed of me?" He had to know. "Is that why you didn't introduce us?"

For the first time, she looked him straight in the eyes. "Of course, not. You're worth more than both of them put together, but you have no idea what they're like. I didn't want them ruining Jack's special evening, nor did I want yours ruined."

"So you put everyone else first." He marveled at how much harder it must've been for her to perform, knowing their parents were watching and unsure as to what might happen after the concert was over.

"Myself included," she admitted. "I didn't want to deal with them either, and they hadn't seen me."

"Then, for what it's worth, I think you did the right thing," he stated, only to feel her let out a sob.

"Baby, don't cry." He tightened his hold, unsure what to do as he once again faced his worst nightmare. "It's over now. You played beautifully, Jack's evening went perfectly, and your parents missed out on enjoying a bigger part of it because of their own past behavior."

"I'm just being silly." She hiccupped lightly. "Please don't be mad because I didn't introduce you. It's our last evening together like this, and I don't want you to be angry."

"I've never once felt the slightest bit of anger towards you." He stroked her hair gently. "And I'm certainly not mad at you now. All I'm feeling is a whole lot of love and a little concern.

"I'll meet your parents when and if a good time ever arrives, and in the meantime, I'm quite content merely having their son for a friend and their daughter right here in my arms."

"You're so incredible." She once again sobbed into his neck. "Tomorrow we'll return to Captain's Point, and we won't sleep like this anymore. You'll drop me off at Jewel's, and then you'll go back to your condo."

"Only for a few weeks, a few days really," he reminded her, lightly massaging her back. "Do you want a tissue?"

"Please." She sniffed as he reached to his bedside table and retrieved several of them, not sure how many would be needed.

"I'm sorry I've made such a fool of myself," she apologized. "It's just that seeing them this evening, underlined how wonderful having you in my life really is."

"It isn't foolish to value what we have," he pointed out as he blotted her tears and then waited while she took care of her nose.

"Do you want me to take over payment of this suite?" he asked. "We can stay here, away from prying eyes until April 15, and then we can get married either here in New

York or back in Captain's Point. I'll do anything you want, Kate – whatever will make you happy."

"No, Jack and Susan have already gone to a lot of trouble arranging things for our wedding, and I want it to be special for us to remember." She sounded more like herself.

"So, we're back on track, and everything's okay?" He wanted to be sure.

"Not exactly okay." She let out a small sigh. "I'd rather sleep in your arms, but it's only for a few weeks. You do still want to marry me don't you? I haven't ruined everything by being ridiculous, have I?"

"A few tears because you've been hurt and upset aren't going to stop my loving you." He found her lips, his kiss filled with tenderness.

"My love for you isn't that shallow, Kate." He sought to reassure her further, remembering how abandoned she'd been by the man to whom she had entrusted her life before. "Besides, I can manage to sleep without you for a few weeks, since you feel we should, but I'd never make it through a whole lifetime."

"I love you, Mr. Chesterton." She snuggled her head against his left shoulder in their normal way, suddenly exhausted.

"I love you, too, Mrs. Chesterton-to-be." He held her warm, soft body close, counting his blessings that he was able to do so for this one more night at least, even if the entire top right side of his pajama top felt terribly damp and cold.

## CHAPTER LXVII

Early the next morning, Kate returned to semi-consciousness and immediately recognized two things. Larry was still sleeping beside her, and sometime during the night, his right hand had found its way beneath his jersey and now pressed against the bare skin of her back, holding her to him.

Smiling, she snuggled closer and drifted back to sleep, not ready to face the day.

An hour later, Larry floated from a dream, half awake, and immediately realized two things. Kate was still asleep in his arms, and his right hand now pressed against her back. He'd never felt anything as soft as her skin in his life, and try as he might, he couldn't make himself pull away.

Maybe, he told himself, he was only dreaming. If so, he wished to continue.

At ten o'clock, Larry opened his eyes and watched as Kate opened hers.

"Good morning, Mrs. Chesterton-to-be." He smiled at her.

"Good morning, Mr. Chesterton." She suppressed a giggle. "You did some exploring while we were asleep."

"Do you mind?" For the moment, he left his hand where it was.

"No, I love the feel of your fingers on my skin," she assured him. "I'm looking forward to their exploring a whole lot further in the future."

"I love you, Kate." He passed his wayward hand over her back as he kissed her.

"I love you, too, Larry." Her left hand slipped under the cloth of his pajama top that he hadn't realized she'd unbuttoned, and he stilled his own as another part of him prepared for action.

"If nothing else, you know now that you have nothing to fear from me once we're married." He dropped a kiss on her forehead, thinking that might be safe.

"I've never been afraid of you," she replied. "I've only ever feared the damage that being mistreated and hurt like I was can do to someone, and it isn't in you to treat anyone like he treated me," she referred to her soon-to-be ex. "You don't have a mean or cruel bone in your body."

"Still, I'd fight to the death to keep anyone or anything from harming you, if need be." He made his position clear.

"Which is another reason why I love you." She drew his face down to hers, and the freight train he had experienced before rounded the curve and dragged him along with it.

"Whoa, girl!" He released her and rolled onto his back. "I want you to respect me when this morning is over."

"Silly." She giggled, rolling onto her stomach next to him. "These past days have been the best of my life."

"Mine, too." He stroked her cheek with the back of his fingers. "And the good news is that we'll have many more of them. Now, though, we'd better order breakfast, get packed and join the others."

A while later, she rejoined him, his folded jersey in her hands, and he placed it gently in the suitcase he was packing with the certain knowledge that he would sleep with it beside him for the next several weeks.

"Can I help you?" she asked.

"Not really," he replied.

But then, seeing her disappointment, he added, "Not here, but you could check my bathroom to see if I've remembered everything."

A moment later, she returned, the tiny bottles of women's shampoo, conditioner and lotion in her hand. "If you don't want these, I'm keeping them as a souvenir," she said, and he held open his own toiletries case.

"Drop them in here, and I'll put them in your bathroom at the condo, all ready for you." An idea immediately entered his head and then another, followed closely behind by a third.

Why hadn't he thought of this before? It would certainly help the next few weeks pass more easily, and Kate would enjoy it, too.

"That's it here." He hoisted his suitcase off the luggage rack. "Let me gather mine and yours both in the common area, and then we'll pop over to your brother's and check on my gorgeous cousin."

"It's about time you two showed up," Jack greeted them a few minutes later. "All ready?"

"We're packed and waiting in the main room." Larry joined him as Kate gave Daniel a hug. "Thanks for everything." He placed his hand on his soon-to-be brother-in-law's upper arm.

"My pleasure." Jack grinned at him as Kate approached.

"I've moved to the next level." Daniel held up his game and drew Larry to him, as Kate slid her arm around her brother's waist and received a hug in return.

"Thanks for everything," she whispered into his chest. "These past few days have been really special."

"I can't believe that we filled that whole empty suitcase and spilled over into two others." Susan joined them as Kate crossed to where Larry stood and slipped her arm around his waist in the same way she had done with her brother.

"Is everything okay?" Susan turned her back on them to keep her words between herself and her husband.

"More than okay, I think." He winked at her. "I've just been thanked by both of them for 'everything,' but what exactly that means, beyond my having put them in a suite, I have no idea."

"Which may be for the best." She stood on her tiptoes and kissed his cheek, as the rest of their group arrived from the third suite.

As wonderful as their visit in New York City had proven to be, it was time for all of them to return to their favorite place in the whole world – Captain's Point.

# CHAPTER LXVIII

Mid-afternoon found everyone in various stages of boarding the three Learjets that would fly them home, as an impromptu meeting of Sheffield and Montgomery Enterprises, Inc., was being held on the tarmac.

Max, wearing a canine version of a navy blue suit, white shirt and red tie, watched over the proceedings as he sat beside Adrianna's leather jewel case, inherited from her great-aunt, that looked for all the world as if it was the rescue's briefcase.

"Paul says they would like to move in April 1, and they're willing to sign a two-year lease with a moving clause if the rent's right," Chase passed on the message he had received on his phone in the limo from the assistant minister of their church, who rented the former caretaker's cottage on the grounds of Montgomery House.

"Sounds like a good deal to me." Jack provided his two cents worth. "You've already vetted them when he applied to be our new Youth Minister, and they should make good neighbors for Herb and Jewel, who can keep an eye on the place."

"In the meantime, the property's value will probably increase over the next two years with no harm done to the improvements we've made," Larry added.

"So we're all in agreement?" Adrianna asked. "Among us, we form a quorum, and it's no surprise that they want an answer this afternoon before they return to Kentucky. Thank goodness, Herb had a key and could show them around."

"I move that we rent the Tuttle Avenue property to Jonathan and Mary Fitzpatrick for the period of two years for the sum of $500.00 per month, which we all understand is much less than the going rate, but agree is the right amount to charge this young couple," Larry stated.

"I second the motion," Otis spoke up from where he stood with his arm thrown around his wife's shoulders.

"All in favor raise your hands." Adrianna glanced from one to the other. "Let the record show and I'll record once I can access our minutes that the motion has passed unanimously. Chase and I will meet with them at Montgomery House as soon as we arrive home and get the lease signed. We have rented our first property."

"Now all we have to do is get the finishing touches done," Otis pointed out, "but things should be wrapped up by Friday."

"A job well done." Chase beamed at all of them.

"I do love doing business the Captain's Point way, although I missed the plate of molasses cookies that usually accompanies our meetings." Jack drew the lawyer aside and handed him a thick mailing envelope.

"This contains directions, introductions, phone numbers and some additional sightseeing suggestions," he explained. "Henri will meet you at the apartment, and you're to call on him for anything you need. He can be very helpful." He referred to his European publicist, who resided in the Geneva penthouse apartment in the author's absence and moved in with his parents as needed.

"I can't express how much we appreciate your arranging for another Lear to return the four of us to New York on Thursday," Chase stated. "Lending us your home in Geneva for the month was more than enough for the little that we did to assist you, especially since all of us would've helped you for free."

"Nonsense." Jack brushed away his comment. "I lend the apartment to friends all the time, and Henri could care less. He has more privacy at my place, but his mom feeds him better at his parents'. Either way, he's content."

"We'll bring his box and supplies by your condo Wednesday evening," Adrianna addressed Larry a few feet away, as she nodded towards Max. "Are you certain that you want us to bring him by Chesterton and Chesterton on our way to the airport?"

"Absolutely," Kate assured her. "Have him dressed in that outfit. He'll fit right in. Don't worry about him while you four are in Europe either. I plan to spoil him rotten."

"Too late." Chase wrapped his arms around his wife from behind. "Adrianna's already done that."

"The luggage is all loaded," Jack joined them. "Time for lift off."

"Pen and I want to thank you again." Otis held out his hand to the author. "Your hosting our trip to New York and those two young'uns taking us along for a second honeymoon in Europe are dreams come true."

"My pleasure." Jack shook the older man's hand and then took his leave of them, eager to board his own family's jet and check on his Susie and Daniel.

As much as they had all enjoyed the trip, he could tell Susan was tired. It was time to pamper her in their own comfortable home until their Olivia arrived.

Unaware that three 60XRs were landing at Captain's Point Airport as he spoke, Gabe Palmer looked over the screen of his laptop to where Beth was rolling out pastry for a cherry pie on her kitchen table.

"Did I mention that I received Jeff's first article, a summary and review of the premiere of Jack Jefferson's new composition in New York on Saturday night?" he asked.

"No." She wrapped the circle of dough around her rolling pin and then unrolled it into an oversized, glass pie plate. "How did he do?"

"It's exactly what I'd hoped for." His eyes sparkled. "He's combined a travel piece full of big city lights with the story of our talented, small town musicians performing on an equal basis alongside the internationally renowned in a world-famous concert hall."

"Folks around here will swell with pride, as well they should," she pointed out. "Your friend Jack has done a good job of putting Captain's Point more on the map than it ever has been, without endangering the good that we have here."

"Which shouldn't hurt him when he makes his bid for the ad hoc city councilman position." He watched as she deftly crimped the edges of the two crusts together, cut decorative slits in the top and then popped the pie in the oven. "How long before that will be ready?"

"An hour and fifteen minutes, if you don't want to burn your tongue, and that takes into account that you'll want yours with vanilla ice cream on the side." She laughed softly, pleasure filling her face.

"Come here." He rose and held out his arms, and then rested his chin on the top of her head as she snuggled against his chest. "Do you have any sense at all of how much I love spending time in this room with you?"

"No, I only hope that it's half as much as I enjoy having you here with me." She smiled up at him, responding eagerly to his kiss when it came, certain in the knowledge that she would willingly bake a hundred cherry pies every day for the man who now held her in his arms.

## CHAPTER LXIX

"I don't see anything wrong." Janie Jackson, M.D., tapped the file folder opened before her with the tip of a slim finger as she looked across her desk Wednesday morning at her friend Adrianna. "How long did you say you and Chase have been trying to get pregnant?"

"Three and a half months." Her patient's face retained its worried gaze.

"Not so very long," the ob/gyn assured her. "Sounds to me like it's early days yet. I'll give you some literature that will explain ways you can determine when you're ovulating, so you can make better use of your, shall we say, pleasurable interludes. How would you describe your sex life?"

Adrianna sent her a shy grin as the words poured out. "Wonderful! Chase is wonderful! I can't imagine ever growing tired of his making love to me. He's gentle, passionate, tender, considerate, playful, kind, and the way he…"

"I wasn't asking for a full report." Janie threw back her head and laughed. "Just relax and enjoy all of that, and you should be fine."

"I…"

"Yes?" The doctor's professional antennae went on the alert.

"I don't think we could do it any more often." Adrianna's face filled with anxiety.

"Trust me." Janie's voice took on a firm tone. "This isn't a race, and it certainly isn't a competition. I meant what I said – relax and enjoy Chase's obvious talents as they are offered to you.

"You're both healthy and strong. Let Nature take her course. If you're still concerned in another six months, there are tests I can suggest, but I think it's much more likely that we'll be discussing a due date before then."

"Thank you." Adrianna stood, sensing her time was up. "You've been very reassuring."

But when she left the office behind, three pamphlets now contained within her purse, she failed to notice a bevy of early butterflies flitting around the beautiful daffodils blooming alongside the sidewalk that led to the parking lot, her face once again carrying a worried expression.

As Adrianna steered her car between the gates of Montgomery House, a line of kindergarteners, all wearing white surgical masks, were ushered into the Emergency Room of Captain's Point General Hospital by Bev Lockhart, Head ER Nurse.

"As you can see, if you ever come to visit us, you'll be treated by one of the ER doctors in your own curtained room." She demonstrated by moving a white curtain. "This way, if you have an injured arm or leg and need an x-ray, we can simply roll you to Radiology, so that you don't have to move."

"Daniel, is that you behind the fourth mask on my right?" Dr. Pug Brownley entered the area through the doorway that led to Observation, immediately recognizing an opportunity to help the boy's parents with some concerns they had voiced to him. "I had no idea we had a celebrity visiting today, Nurse Lockhart." He sent his glance along the row of wide-eyed children.

"Why my *World Famous Casebook* is filled with references to Daniel's amazing escapades," he continued.

His favorite patient's eyes sparkled as he grinned beneath his mask. "Tell them I've always been brave," he requested.

"That you have, Son. That you have," the ER doctor stated soberly. "The first time I met Daniel, I was required to remove a plug of wax the size of the Empire State Building from his ear. Now, most folks would've raised Cain, but your friend here didn't even let out a whimper."

Daniel nodded his head in agreement as his small shoulders straightened.

"Imagine my surprise when, only a few short weeks later, your friend's father rescued him from a cliff by making Chase Sheffield jump down to him from a helicopter that Daniel's dad then used to lift them both to safety," Pug continued, his eyes widened at the mere memory of such an exciting event having happened in Captain's Point. "It was like a scene in a movie."

Excited murmurs rippled along the row of spectators that stretched on either side of the ER's former patient.

"Thinking I probably wouldn't see Daniel again, I sent him home the next day, only to have him pop up a few months later – his cousin Larry Chesterton and his new aunt, who was in tears, rushing him here with a huge fishbone stuck in his throat." The doctor's arms stretched out on either side of him.

"I still have it in my room at home," Daniel informed them.

"That last one was a bit touch and go, but with Nurse Lockhart's assistance, we managed to remove the bone without our patient experiencing any further discomfort as he maintained his composure throughout." Pug leaned forward and looked the subject of his story up and down.

"I trust this is purely a social call today." The doctor pulled an instrument from his pocket, used it to examine Daniel's ear, and then declared, "Clean as a whistle."

Pulling a pad from another pocket, Pug made a few scribbles, tore off a page and passed it to the head nurse with a flourish. "I prescribe a sucker for everyone," he announced, turned on his heels and exited through the same doorway he had used to join them a few minutes previously.

Unaware that his stepson's school visit to the ER was being enhanced by a dramatic rendition of his having utilized his helicopter to effect a rescue, Jack stuck a pitchfork into the earth leading to his home's garage and turned a chunk over.

"Have you decided which roses to plant?" Jeff asked from where he was doing the same, as they worked to aerate the soil before mixing in a mound of compost that was waiting at the back of the property.

"I want a climbing Queen Elizabeth on that wall, two Peace roses, a John Kennedy, and some David Austins in a variety of colors for starters," Jack filled him in. "We'll put the fountain here, so we can hear it in the library if we open the windows, with a small bench on either side of it."

"Susan should be happy with those choices."

"So far she hasn't noticed anything, because this isn't in your direct line of sight as you're coming or going." Jack straightened. "I think she'll be pleased with the garden as part of her Mother's Day present."

"Which will be extra special this year with Olivia on the way," Jeff pointed out.

"Yes, it will," Jack agreed, thinking as he watched the younger man work beside him that he hadn't done anything yet in response to Angel's request at the restaurant in New York.

Perhaps, it was time to make his first move.

# CHAPTER LXX

Tired after a full day of classes followed by a long evening at the library, Becca plopped onto her bed and checked her email one last time, pleased when she found a new entry from Jeff in her Inbox.

Always newsy and often funny, his daily communications with her offered a unique view of Captain's Point as seen through his eyes that differed greatly from the jaded impressions living with her parents had left in her mind.

How had she been born in the same hospital, attended the same schools, walked the same streets and still lived as if they existed in different worlds?

Eagerly, she opened his latest only to be surprised and then concerned as she read:

*Hey, girl -*

*Attended a Gazette staff meeting this morning. Gabe mentioned my piece on the debut of Jack's "Susan's Song" and the part the Captain's Point Chamber Music Group had played in it. Called it a positive new direction for the paper.*

*Jack led those of us who are currently in Captain's Point through a final walk-through at the Tuttle Avenue project today. Lots of pats on the back for yours truly outside, and then we entered through the front doorway.*

*It wasn't long before everyone else paired off in couples, including my dad who had invited Jewel to join us.*

*Left alone, I wandered along with the crowd, seeing a shadow cast by your graceful movement out of the corner of my eye, hearing your light laughter just around the next corner.*

*Refurbished and updated, I realized immediately that this, Becca, was a house we could live in. It's exactly the kind of place in which I hope, one day, we'll start our lives together, and I missed you so much.*

*I miss you day in and day out, of course, but this was worse. Part of me hurt so badly at your absence that it was all I could do to stay where I was and not jump into my truck and drive to Virginia.*

*You know me. I'm not a depressive kind of guy, but during those few minutes, I needed to pull you into my arms more than I needed to breathe in the air around me.*

*I needed to hold you and kiss you and feel your soft warmth. I needed to know that you were alive and okay. I needed to believe you would love me forever in the same way I love you.*

*Take care of yourself, Bec. Be safe. Think of me now and again, because as much as I support you and your dreams, I do miss you.*

*I love you more than life itself.*

*XOXOXO*

*Jeff*

Putting a finger to her lips she placed it over his name as if somehow it could connect her to him.

Glancing at the bottom right of the screen, she confirmed what she had already known. It was way too late to call him, especially since he had a big test first thing in the morning.

Hitting Reply, she pulled her thoughts together and then moved her fingertips around the keyboard. Finished, she reread her message to him:

*Jeff –*

*I miss you, too. Day in and day out. More than you know.*
*This evening I ate my supper sitting on the bench under the grapevine arbor where we sat on Valentine's evening. For a moment, I closed my eyes and believed you were still there, almost able to smell your aftershave in the air.*
*I'll fall asleep in a few minutes, thinking of you and all the wonderful moments we've shared, in the hope that I'll spend my night with you in my dreams.*

*XOXOXO*

*Becca*

First thing the next morning, she checked her email, not surprised to discover a new message from him that contained only a few short words, which she eagerly read:

*Thanks, Bec*

*You were with me in mine.*

*Always!*

*Jeff*

An hour later, fresh from dropping Daniel off at kindergarten, Jack gave a perfunctory knock on the front door of The Cove and then let himself in.

"Anyone home?" he called.

"In my office," his mother-in-law responded, and he hurried forward.

"Do you have a moment?" he asked from the room's doorway.

"For you, anytime." Elizabeth gestured for him to take a seat in one of the visitors' chairs. "Nothing's wrong is it?"

"Everything's fine," he assured her.

"Then to what do I owe the honor?"

"My wife would tell you, if asked, that I'm a closet romantic," he began. "I've decided to come out of the closet with you."

"Ah…" Elizabeth removed her black-rimmed glasses and relaxed in her own chair. "Are you planning another surprise for our Susan?"

"Not at this moment." Jack sent her a mischievous grin. "Although I haven't ruled that out as a possibility."

"So are you wanting to help Larry and Kate along in some way?" She moved further down her list.

"Those two don't need any help." He chuckled. "All they need is for time to fly, and even you and I can't make that happen."

"True." She watched as his face sobered.

"I've come because you're in a unique position to assist the course of true love," he stated in the same tone he might've used if he had asked her to pass him the butter. "I have a friend…a young friend…who needs our help, as much as we're in a position to give it."

"Jeff Stuart?" She surprised him with her question.

"Yes."

"I'm assuming you want me to influence Becca Tate somehow." Elizabeth rested her elbows on the arms of her chair and made a tepee with her fingers.

"Yes."

"How?"

"I'm not sure," Jack admitted, "but I do know that those two are meant to be together. Furthermore, I believe they would be happiest over a lifetime here in Captain's Point."

"I agree."

For a moment, he watched as his mother-in-law's index fingers tapped out a beat on one another as if keeping pace with her thoughts. Then she smiled as her eyes refocused on him.

"My church circle has been studying the roles of women at various stages of our lives," she filled him in.

"Yes?"

"As a middle-aged woman, my role is to mentor younger women who are just beginning their adult lives," she explained. "Becca Tate is a member of our church and a former intern of mine at the college. I believe I should, as part of my role, email her and reestablish contact."

"Definitely," he agreed.

"Perhaps, she would be interested in helping me with the cataloguing and packing of the Underground Railroad materials that have been found in the cellars of Montgomery House," she continued. "After all, she was present when they were discovered and has an interest in the period. I might even be able to work out some sort of credit for independent study that would transfer towards her degree."

"Now you're talking, Mom." Jack rose, not wanting to take up too much of her time. "I knew I could count on you to see the need. Keep me posted as to how you're progressing, and I'll make sure you know anything I do." He rounded her desk, dropped a kiss on her cheek and took his leave.

# CHAPTER LXXI

Larry and Kate arrived at The Cove's former carriage house that evening with Max in tow, where one of them was surprised to find a rather large box waiting for them in the inset area tastefully marked as being for package delivery that resided next to the second-floor condo's built-in mailbox.

"Looks like it's finally arrived," Larry announced as his face took on its excited little boy look.

"What's arrived?" Kate felt her own spirits lift as she gathered her purse and a small bag of groceries to carry inside, since he would be dealing with Max in his carry cage.

"I ordered something that should keep us busy for a couple of hours over the weekend," he answered, revealing nothing. "If you'll hold the Open Door button on the elevator after I put Max's cage in there, we can get everything upstairs in one trip."

"Sure." She obliged, determined to read the box's label on the ride up, only to be disappointed when he set the even larger than it had looked before carton down with the return address turned away from her.

"Here you go, Max." Larry released the dog, set his carry cage to the side in the foyer and then hoisted the box from the elevator's floor, before Kate could check it out.

"Let's get comfortable, and then we'll open your surprise," he teased as he led the way to the master bedroom, where he deposited the new arrival in his own dressing room.

Thwarted again, she hastened into what would soon be hers, where she quickly changed into a pair of jeans and one of the T-shirts that he had insisted she keep there, ever since their return from New York.

"Ready?" He tapped on her dressing room's door, obviously as eager to see her reaction as she was to see her surprise. "You'll need these." He handed her a large pair of scissors, once he'd set the box on the floor. "Cut the tape carefully."

Receiving no clue from the box, even though she could now see the label, she took her time as she cut the reinforced tape, Larry and Max supervising her progress. Lifting the flaps, she revealed a stretch of pink plastic as the light scent of her favorite perfume greeted her.

"Here, let me help you." Larry reached along one side and strained as he lifted the huge bag, its contents morphing into a lopsided mound as he placed it atop the large island of drawers that filled the room's center.

"Nothing's going to jump out at me, is it?" she joked, as her fingers untied the satin bow holding the contents in check and then pulled one of what felt like rolls of thick paper from inside. "Drawer liners!"

She turned and flung her arms around Larry's neck, her eyes sparkling. "How did you know that I wanted these?"

"I didn't. It was a lucky guess." He smiled at her. "Why didn't you tell me you wanted them? Don't you know that I'll buy anything you wish?"

"I would've ordered them myself once I moved in," she replied. "These are perfect. It'll take me forever to get all the drawers lined, though."

"Then we'd better eat our supper and get started, don't you think?" He planted a firm kiss on her lips. "I want you as moved in here as we can get you, as soon as we can possibly manage it."

Monday evening, two more boxes were awaiting them – both smaller and thinner than Friday's surprise, both marked FRAGILE.

This time, Larry made her wait until after supper to open them, saying he was counting on them as a centerpiece during their meal.

Max appeared to be as excited as she was by the time they were settled in the den with their coffee, although Kate suspected it was because he was hoping for another treat.

Two oval vanity mirrors, rimmed with gold filigree, appeared a short time later – one each for her built-in dressing table and her bathroom vanity.

"There." Larry placed the three tiny bottles from the Plaza on the latter and smiled at her. "Now your area looks more like home."

Tuesday and Wednesday, nothing was delivered, and Kate stopped looking as they pulled into the drive – part of her relieved that he hadn't gotten too carried away and part of her wishing that he had.

Thursday, there was nothing in the inset outside, but when they entered the condo, Max began barking and running to and fro, then dropped his long nose to the floor and made a beeline for her dressing room, where she discovered a wall-mounted television had been installed.

"Maggie Daniels let them in." Larry beamed at her. "Max probably recognized her scent from her regular days at Montgomery House." He referred to the cleaning woman who assisted the owners of homes on the Point.

Friday, he took her to Montgomery's for dinner, since it was their five-month anniversary, and as they watched the sunset color the sky, they toasted the fact that it was now only two weeks until her divorce would be final.

Saturday, she helped Susan line and arrange the drawers in the room slated to be Olivia's nursery, and the two enjoyed lunch at Tea, Crumpets and More afterwards.

"Would you like to come see what Larry's been up to?" Kate asked her sister-in-law, when Susan drove her to the carriage house on the way to Blue Wolf Manor, only to be surprised herself when they entered the condo.

"How was lunch, Twinkle Toes?" Jack called forth one of his childhood nicknames for her from where he was lounging on the couch with Larry – Daniel stretched out asleep between them.

"The scones were delicious." Susan sat on the arm of the couch and gave her cousin a hug. "Thanks for treating."

"You treated us?" Kate's eyes narrowed as guilty looks suddenly plastered themselves on both men's faces.

"We had to keep you away somehow," Larry explained as both of them stood. "Come see what we've done for you."

This time, instead of heading to her dressing room, Larry paused at the door to the room he used as a gym that now boasted a mirrored wall at one end with a dancer's bar stretched across it.

"I knew your brother had installed one for you at his house," he said, "and when I asked him for the particulars of what you needed, he insisted on going in halves with me on this one."

"I don't know what to say." Kate blinked back tears as she gave each of them a hug and a kiss on the cheek. "This is so sweet of you."

"It wouldn't be your home without one." Larry hugged her to him.

Monday evening's offering was a carved, pink marble Cupid that boasted its antiquity.

"He'll look perfect centered on your deep window sill." The man who had gifted the expensive statue to her placed it with care on the shelf area behind her tub, where she could enjoy it at the same time she overlooked an unencumbered view of the ocean beyond.

A crystal atomizer, a complete line of her favorite perfume, loofahs, bath crystals, bubble bath, scented candles, a sterling flower vase, even a waterproof radio to hang in her shower – one by one items appeared as Larry surprised her.

On the Wednesday before her divorce would be final the following Monday, he put his fork down once he had finished eating supper, reached over and took her hand in his.

"There's something I want to ask, but I don't want to offend you," he said.

"I can't imagine your being offensive." She gave him her attention. "What is it?"

"When we first dined at Montgomery's, you mentioned that you hadn't taken much in the way of things from your marriage, but I wondered if you might have a few items in storage, either here or back in Virginia," he said. "If so, it's time we retrieve them and bring them here."

"I have a small storage unit near my parents' house," she admitted. "Do you really want to bother with that?"

"Taking care of you will never be a bother to me, Kate." He pushed his chair back from the table and gestured for her to sit on his lap. "Will your stuff fit in my SUV, or do we rent a truck?"

"We'll need a small truck or a trailer," she filled him in. "It's mainly boxes of shoes, clothes and coats, plus some things I had purchased for myself or were gifts from friends. There's also an album of photos that I'd like to retrieve from my parents', if my mother will let me."

"Contact her and see," he suggested. "We'll drive over and back on Saturday. I love you, Kate, and I want us totally moved in together once we're married."

And, as he kissed her, she knew more than ever that she wanted the same thing.

## CHAPTER LXXII

"It won't be long before the Montgomery House folks will return from Europe." Larry started their conversational ball rolling Saturday morning, once they had pulled from the rental lot onto the main road heading out of Captain's Point.

"It was nice of Jack and Susan to keep Max." Kate put on her sunglasses. "He's well-behaved at the worst of times, but it would've been hard on him to spend a long day in his carry cage."

"This way, he'll enjoy Daniel, Casey and Lady," Larry agreed and then changed the subject. "You know, I haven't pulled a trailer since I drove back from grad school."

He then proceeded to amuse her with stories from his college days until they arrived at her rental unit, where he made quick work of emptying it into the trailer and the back of his SUV.

"That's it." He held her door for her, once he'd settled her account over her objections. "Did you reach your mother about the album you wanted?"

"She never responded to my email or phone messages."

"Do you want to go by the house, just in case?" He ran his index finger along her cheekbone. "It seems silly not to try, since we're this close."

"Will you come to the door with me?"

"Of course, I'll go anywhere you want."

"It's the next drive on the right," Kate instructed several minutes later. "What's that piled along the roadside?"

"Someone's put out the trash."

"Pickup isn't until Tuesday," she filled him in. "Pull into the drive and stop, so I can see what's going on."

"There's been a clean out," he commented as he brought the SUV to a halt, and Kate immediately disembarked.

"She's thrown them away – all our family albums, Jack's high school trophies and everything else from his room." Kate pointed from one box to another as he joined her. "Can we load all of this into the trailer and SUV?"

"I can try." He hurried to unlock the trailer and then began stuffing smaller items on top of what was already inside.

Thirty minutes later, they were back on the road, loaded to capacity, neither of them having noticed the middle-aged, bleached blonde who had watched them from the shadows behind an upstairs window of Kate's childhood home, clutching a brown pill bottle in a claw-like hand as she had done so.

"Why would my mother throw them away?" Kate sniffed as she dried her cheeks on the back of her hand. "How could she be so hurtful to her own child? How can she not love Jack?"

Unable to bear it any longer, Larry turned into a convenient rest area and brought them to a halt in the shade of some trees at the far end.

"Come here." He drew her to him, ignoring the console pressing into his ribs. "I can't explain her, or offer excuses. Knowing you and Jack, nothing she's done makes sense to me, and I don't understand why your father goes along with it. I'll be thrilled if our children turn out half as well as you two did."

"Thank you for bringing me here." She looked up with watery eyes. "If we hadn't come today…"

"But we did," he pointed out. "All that matters now is the life we'll create together going forward. It doesn't make the other right, but I love you, Kate. I always will."

He kissed her gently. "Now, let's get this stuff back to Captain's Point, where you'll soon be married to me and can put all this behind you, like your brother has done quite successfully."

He turned the key in the ignition, wanting to put as much distance between his Kate and those who had hurt her as he could.

Two days later, on April 15, Kate awoke to her phone ringing on her bedside table.

"Happy first day of the rest of your life, Sleepyhead." Larry's strong voice came through clearly when she answered. "I've never been so excited about the arrival of Tax Day in my life." He chuckled.

"Don't be silly." She giggled, even as she rejoiced at the great weight that had been lifted.

"How soon can I pick you up?" he asked. "I'm taking you out for breakfast, and we're spending the day together. I've already cleared it with Uncle Anders and Glenda. Wear jeans and shoes that you don't mind getting wet, and put on sunscreen. It's gorgeous outside."

"Can I carry anything?" she offered a while later, as he parked in one of the Montgomery slots at the marina.

"Grab those two canvas bags if you don't mind." He lifted a cooler from the back and headed them away from the stores and restaurants and towards the rows of boathouses, entering a larger one that housed his sailboat and a fair-sized, motorized fishing boat.

"I'm assuming you're like your brother and don't get seasick," he stated as he helped her onboard the latter. "Put on a life jacket. We'll be on our way in a jif." He undid the boat from its moorings and started the engine.

A short ride later, he dropped anchor, and they breakfasted on melon wrapped in prosciutto, along with croissants, orange juice and coffee, accompanied by the lilting notes of *Alpine Spring's* European premiere as it had been captured on CD.

"This is Heaven." She smiled at him as the breeze lifted her hair from her neck. "I'm learning to love the water as much as my brother."

"Good, because I want to share this type of outing frequently with you and our children." He put his arm around her. "Do you realize that we can now be official?"

"It was the first thing that entered my head when I heard your voice this morning." She relaxed against him.

The rest of their day was magical as they enjoyed a leisurely cruise up the coast and back, during which they discussed the two week honeymoon they planned at Chase and Adrianna's Cape Cod house, since they didn't want to venture too far away until Olivia arrived.

Larry planned to rent a boat and teach Kate to sail, they would breakfast watching the sunrise and eat their way through a menu that included every type of homemade pie ever made at a small restaurant along the road.

It would be two long, lazy weeks filled with nothing but time spent with each other, and they were thrilled by the idea.

Returning to land, they lunched on lobster rolls at Montgomery's outdoor annex, then stopped at the condo where he insisted she enjoy a long bubble bath, before they went to see a new movie.

Finding themselves the only ones in the theater, its being an afternoon on a work and school day, Larry proceeded to fulfill what he referred to as 'every teenaged boy's dream,' wrapping his arm around her shoulders and kissing her repeatedly as they shared a large tub of buttered popcorn.

"We'll have to rent the video once it comes out and actually watch the movie." He grinned down at her as they left the theater, her hair a bit more mussed than it had been when they'd entered.

Back at the condo, they took Max for a long walk along the Point. Then Larry grilled flounder stuffed with crabmeat for their supper, keeping her in stitches throughout as he shared one funny story after another before popping a cork from a bottle of champagne to make their evening seem even more like a celebration.

"To us." He clinked his crystal flute against Kate's, where they sat side-by-side on a pillowed bench on the deck overlooking the ocean once they'd finished dinner.

"To us." She smiled back as the sun sent streaks of pink and rose across the sky from behind them and he lit two candles on the low table in front of them.

"Thank you for making this such a wonderful day," she added.

"It isn't over yet." He took her flute from her and placed it on the table. "I know we've already planned everything for our wedding in two weeks, but today I'm making it official."

He retrieved a small box from his pocket and opened it, revealing a ring composed of a large sapphire surrounded by diamonds all set in platinum and accompanied by matching wedding bands.

"Make me the happiest man alive." He took her left hand in his. "Live with me here at the condo where I can hold you in my arms and make love to you all through the nights and, someday in the not too distant future, bear my children. I'll always love and take care of you, Kate. Everything I have will be yours as we grow old together. Marry me now that you're free."

"Yes," she whispered, not trusting her voice further as he slipped his ring on her finger.

"Tiffany's engraved our initials and the date of our marriage inside the wedding bands," he shared with her.

"Pretty sure of yourself, weren't you?" she teased.

"No, I was sure of you," he replied, his tone sober. "I knew you would never break my heart as others have before you."

He tightened his hold on her, and as they enjoyed the sunset with her wrapped in his arms, they both breathed freely for the first time since the cold December evening, when he had declared his love for her on her brother's broad porch.

# CHAPTER LXXIII

Having told Penny that he and Adrianna planned to try out a new French restaurant in Captain's Point for dinner as a way of carrying their European trip forward, Chase wasn't surprised when no one greeted him in the kitchen Wednesday evening after his first day back at work.

When neither Max nor his wife had appeared by the time he had glanced through a small stack of mail on the foyer table, though, the quiet that pervaded the house concerned him. A quick search of the downstairs rooms failed to discover either of them, and worried, he took the steps of the broad staircase two treads at a time.

Relieved to find them both in the tower sitting room, he knew immediately that something was wrong – Max only acknowledging by a small wag of his tail his master's presence from where he sat next to Adrianna on one of the room's window seats, a worried expression on the dog's small face.

Pink and mauve reflections from the sky beyond the room provided the only illumination. Moving quietly forward, Chase flipped on a table lamp and took a seat beside his wife, wrapping his arm around her and drawing her close.

"What's wrong?" he asked, surprised when she dried her eyes with a wad of tissues as she handed him a sheet of stationery held in her other hand.

A quick glance showed him the letter had been written by Mary Ellen, his wife's friend in Seattle, and he read:

*You're happily married to Chase now, but I felt you should know that Brad was killed last Saturday, when the single-engine plane in which he was a passenger crashed into the Amazon jungle. He and another doctor were flying to a remote village, where they planned to inoculate the children.*

*I don't know exactly what transpired when he visited you that last time in Captain's Point, but whatever you said or did then was the making of him.*

*Gone was the cocky, frankly self-centered man you had wasted so much time on, replaced by someone who was determined to make a difference, first volunteering in free clinics here in Seattle and then signing on for international aid missions. I found myself actually liking him for the first time, and we were dating occasionally before he left.*

The letter then went on to tell of another friend's engagement before closing.

Adrianna blew her nose softly as he finished reading and looked up. "I'm sorry," she said as fresh tears filled her eyes, and he gathered her to him.

"You have nothing to be sorry about." He held her close, rocking her gently back and forth. "You said it yourself, while Brad was flawed, he had his good points, and he meant a great deal to you for a long time. It's perfectly normal for you to feel sad that he's gone."

"Thank you." She drew back and wiped the last of the tears from her eyes, before putting her hand on his cheek. "Each time you interact with me in any way, my choice of you over him is reaffirmed."

"Glad to hear it." He kissed her gently. "It's supper time. Why don't I make us some salads? We can try the new restaurant tomorrow night."

Nodding in agreement, she stood, but instead of walking away, she drew his head onto her breast, whereupon he again wrapped his arms around her. "He was a good man deep down inside," she whispered.

"Yes, and he died a good death, trying to help others," he acknowledged. "I'm not surprised that you saw his promise when others didn't."

At which, she released her hold, as did he. "I'll freshen up, and then I'll meet you downstairs," she said. "Max has been fed, so don't let him get the best of you."

"I won't," he promised as he watched her leave them behind, not quite convinced that everything was as yet alright.

Later that night, when Adrianna turned off the bedside lamp and joined him beneath the covers, his suspicions were confirmed as she turned away from him.

Respecting her need for time to process her loss, but still wanting her to know he was there for her, he passed his arm around her waist and drew her to him until they were nestled like two spoons. He kissed her softly on the neck and then drifted off to sleep, hopeful that all would be well in the morning.

## CHAPTER LXXIV

All had not been well the next morning, although Adrianna had tried hard – too hard – not to show it, and when she once again turned off the bedside lamp, slid under the covers and turned her back to him, Chase determined that the time had come to get to the bottom of things.

Shifting into more of a sitting position against the bank of pillows behind them, he pulled her beside him, so he could see her face in the muted glow from the fireplace.

"What is it, love?" he asked softly, not surprised when she didn't immediately answer, but rather gathered her thoughts first, this being her way.

"If I had been a better person, Brad wouldn't be dead," she said.

Shocked by the direction her thoughts had taken, he, too, took a moment to reply, recognizing the weight his response would carry with her. "Why do you say that?" he asked, thinking it best to gain a better understanding.

"When Brad showed up here, he pointed out that I hadn't been engaged in our relationship for some time," Adrianna explained. "Pamela, the nurse he turned to in response, had filled the void in his life that had been left by my disinterest. This didn't excuse his actions, but it did show me that I had a share in the blame for what had happened."

"What did you say to him?" Chase asked, not sure that he agreed with her accepting even partial blame for Brad's having run off with another woman when he could've approached Adrianna with his need first.

"At the time, all I said was that I was sorry, both for my having created a distance between us and for not being willing to take him back," she told him. "He left it that he would check out of the inn at eleven o'clock the next morning, and if he hadn't heard from me by then, he would know that it was over between us. You know the rest. I didn't call, and he left."

"Do you wish now that you had called?" Chase asked, not sure he wanted to hear her answer, but knowing that he needed to.

"No, not at all." She sat up cross-legged on the bed and met his gaze, taking his hand and nestling her cheek against its palm. "My feelings for you by then had shown me that what I had felt for Brad had never been love, and I also recognized that you were twice the man." She hung onto his hand, even as she lowered it and sat up straighter. "How can I explain?"

"One word after another," he said. "Take your time."

Again she thought for a minute. "Let me give you an analogy. Brad was like a piece of chocolate cake from a mix covered in store-bought frosting," she continued. "Not bad, but nothing when compared to a slice of Penny's from scratch chocolate cake smeared with a thick layer of homemade butter cream."

"So, my queen thinks of me as nothing but a bite of dessert." He attempted to lighten the moment. "I do get your drift, and I'm glad you find me on a level with Penny's cake. It's delicious. I'm still not seeing how any of this would make you responsible for Brad's death, though."

"If I had been more in touch with my feelings back then, if I had been less absorbed in my career and more engaged in our relationship, I would've recognized the change in my feelings and broken up with him. Then none of what followed would've happened." Adrianna hung her head. "He would still be alive and practicing medicine in Seattle."

"Come here." Chase opened his arms, glad when she moved over, nestled her head against his shoulder and passed her arm around him.

"Brad was a grown man who made his own decisions," he pointed out. "I sensed a tiny space between us for twenty-four hours and faced you with it, not being willing for it to remain between us. He allowed a shift in your feelings to create a void. And then, instead of approaching you with it and giving you an opportunity to recognize the honest change in your feelings, he ran off with another woman."

"That's true." Her voice held a note of hesitant acceptance.

"It appears to me that Brad did his own soul searching after his trip here, during which he found himself to be lacking," Chase continued. "You were not a part of that, and while the decisions he made eventually led to his death, they were his own choices made without input from you.

"Brad had found within himself a desire to make a difference," he stated. "Who knows? Perhaps a child he saved before he died will someday find a cure for cancer or develop a cheap way to distill drinking water from sea water."

Feeling he had said enough, Chase gave his wife a quick squeeze and then merely held her, again giving her time to process her thoughts.

"When did you become so wise?" she asked, when she finally looked up after several minutes, her face cleared of the cloud that had hung over it.

"I was born wise," he joked, "but I've learned a few tricks along the way." He lowered his lips onto hers, glad to receive her normal healthy response. "Would you like for me to demonstrate one or two of them now?"

To which, she sent him one of her shy smiles as she replied, "Please do, sir."

## CHAPTER LXXV

At precisely five o'clock the following afternoon, a woman, who could've fallen anywhere between an old thirty-something and a young fifty-something, disembarked from a dented two-door that had left an odor of burnt oil in its tracks as it had made its way into the parking lot near the offices of Chesterton and Chesterton.

A short, tight, black leather skirt revealed a good portion of her long legs that might once have been lovely, but were now covered in blue veins. Stumbling slightly in her stiletto heels, she took her first step.

Her psychedelic pink blouse was cut low in a V. Deep lines ran perpendicular to her upper lip and, along with an air of stale smoke and a gravelly voice, proclaimed her to be a heavy smoker.

Kate's eyes widened as the newcomer entered the brokerage firm a couple of minutes later and approached Glenda's desk.

"Ms. DiMarco to see Larry Chesterton," she announced herself.

"Yes, he's expecting you." Glenda sucked in her breath as she started to rise, thought better of it and reached for the intercom button on her phone.

"Yes?" Larry's voice carried through clearly.

"Your last appointment of the day is waiting out here, if you'd like to come greet her." Glenda's smooth tones gave no hint as to how uncharacteristic her words were.

Sensing that all was not right, Kate kept her ears open as she appeared to be busy, but as soon as she detected motion in Larry's doorway, she gave up all pretense of work.

"Ms. DiMarco?" Larry strode into the room, his right hand extended, but then he came to an abrupt halt as his jaw and hand dropped simultaneously. "Candy...?"

"I thought you'd be surprised to see me after all these years." His high school sweetheart, whom he had once hoped to marry, attempted unsuccessfully to close the gap between them, as he stepped backwards and turned to Kate.

"Ms. Sinclair, please bring a pad and pen with you as you join us." His eyes begged her to understand.

Gathering her wits about her, Kate rose from her desk and followed along behind them.

Larry gestured for each of the women to take a seat at his desk.

"What can I do for you today, Candy?" he asked and then made a quick note of who she actually was in his computer.

"My mother passed away four weeks ago, and we're selling the house," the apparition seated across from him began. "I want you to handle the investment of my half of her estate. You always did know how to turn a dime into a quarter. Frankly, I would've done better if I'd stuck with you all along."

"Yes, well, that's all water under the bridge now, isn't it?" Larry found he was having trouble breathing, unsure if it was because of shock, embarrassment or the sour odor emanating from the woman who now sat next to his Kate.

Kate...

What must she be thinking? He didn't know what to think himself, except that he must've been an idiot all those years ago. Was it possible for someone to be as blind as he must've been?

"You never know." Candy sent him a come hither smile that revealed a gold tooth into which a small diamond had been set. "Embers could rekindle as we work together on my portfolio."

"Ah...your portfolio." He struggled to think straight, part of his brain recognizing that this was his means of escape.

Should he stick her with Uncle Anders? No, that wouldn't do. His uncle had always been good to him.

"I'm afraid it won't be possible for me to represent your interests, given our history." He hoped he sounded sane. "Some would perceive me as having a conflict of interest."

Once again, his fingers found their way around his computer's keyboard. "Ms. Sinclair, if you would write down this name, address and phone number for Ms. DiMarco, I'd appreciate it." He read off the name of a rival firm in a neighboring town.

"I believe they have a wonderful reputation." He prayed for forgiveness, even as he uttered the lie, doubting that Candy would contact them anyway. "I'm sorry to hear of your mother's death. Please express my condolences to your sister as well."

He stood and gestured for the two women to go first, disappointed when Kate sent him no sign of the thoughts that must be filling her mind as they passed into the empty main office as a group, both his uncle and Glenda now gone for the day.

As soon as Candy had exited onto the sidewalk, Larry turned the lock, took Kate's hand, and led her into the small break room at the back of the building, where their actions wouldn't be overlooked by passersby.

Here, he closed the door behind them, pulled her into his arms, covered her lips with his and kissed her as if he were a starving man and she was a steak.

"Spend the evening with me like we had planned," he begged as he clutched her to him. "I need to hold you in my arms, breathe in the soft scent of your perfume and hear your sweet voice in my ear, until the memory of the woman who just left us is obliterated.

"We can order Chinese takeout, since we'd planned to dine at a restaurant, but please don't make me face these next few hours alone."

"I'll stay." Kate pulled back slightly while still allowing him to maintain a hold on her. "But I need to know what you're thinking."

"How stupid I've been all these years," he replied immediately. "How could I have believed myself to be in love with someone like that? What was I thinking?

"And then, when she'd shown her true colors and run off to Vegas, leaving me high and dry, what did I do? I kept her up on a pedestal, holding her memory between me and reality until you found your way into my heart and replaced her. What a fool you must think me."

"You're no more a fool than I am," Kate pointed out. "You were the same age when she broke your heart as I was when I married what's his name. Both of us were young and inexperienced. You don't hold my disastrous marriage against me, and I don't hold your past love for Candy against you."

"But you had the sense to recognize your mistake and put it behind you," he reminded her.

"Because I was rattling around in a great big house all on my own," she responded. "On the other hand, you were attending graduate school, building a career and actively engaging in community affairs."

"Still…"

"No, I know you, Larry," she interrupted him. "Most days during those years, you left your condo in the morning and didn't return until time to fall into bed, having largely spent the intervening hours in the service of others.

"You didn't take time to process what had happened, grieve for the loss and move on, which is why you first came to me with your heart still so damaged."

For what seemed like an hour, but was in reality only a minute, she remained silent as he considered her words. Then his shoulders sagged.

"You're right," he admitted. "How did you get to be so smart?"

"My brother would say that I learned my lessons well in the School of Hard Knocks." She smiled at him. "I will say one other thing, if you'll allow me."

"Feel free." He sent her a wry smile. "I owe you big time."

"That same School of Hard Knocks taught me well what to look for in a man," she continued. "Humor and intelligence, kindness and gentleness, a good work ethic and a strong sense of family – these are what mean the most to me along with unselfishness and a caring attitude – all things that I recognized immediately in you, which is why I love you so much."

"Even now?" His face filled with hope. "Even after this debacle?"

"Especially now." She cupped his cheek in her hand. "Especially after this debacle.

"You could've taken her into your office and declared your undying love, but you didn't," she pointed out. "Instead, you allowed me to see for myself your reaction to this nightmare from your past as well as the kind, generous way in which you handled it.

"What did I do to deserve someone like you?" He drew her to him once more.

"You opened your heart to me." She slid her arms around his waist. "You took an interest in me, helped me find a home, offered me a job and listened when I needed someone with whom I could share my innermost hurts and fears.

"You were there every time I needed you and sometimes when I wasn't even aware that I had a need," she reminded him. "You became my best friend, and then one day you slipped even closer until I recognized that I could do without food or water or even air easier than I could do without you."

"I love you, Kate." He held her tightly to him.

"I love you, too," she breathed into his chest. "Now, don't you think we would be more comfortable continuing this discussion at your condo?"

"I think we would be more comfortable continuing this discussion at *our* condo." He bent and kissed her thoroughly before leading them to the main office area and steering her towards the front door. "I suppose there's only one question remaining," he stated as he locked the office behind them once they stood on the sidewalk.

"What's that?"

"Who gets to choose their fortune cookie first?"

And with that, he threw his arm around her as they headed towards his SUV, both of them laughing at the sheer joy of being together and so in love with each other.

The following evening, as Kate was preparing salad to accompany their dinner, the tone sounded that meant visitors were requesting permission to ride up in the elevator.

"I believe that's for you." Larry grinned, and then hurried to arrange two more place settings on the kitchen table, once she'd rushed to press the button that would allow access to whoever it was.

"Special delivery from Beth's Buds for Ms. Kate Sinclair," Gabe announced as he preceded Beth into the condo, bearing a philodendron planted in a cut-crystal bowl in each of his hands.

"Perfect," Larry approved. "Bring them in here."

He led them to what would be Kate's bathroom and helped the newspaper owner place them on either side of the Cupid on the window ledge, before herding them all back to the kitchen.

"To our first dinner guests as an official couple." Larry raised his wine glass and then clinked it against Beth's once they were all seated at the table.

And, for the first time since she had set eyes on him back in October, Kate believed that the dream she had been experiencing ever since she'd come to Captain's Point might actually be real.

## CHAPTER LXXVI

Finally! It had arrived.

Larry entered a bold, black X into the last square on his bathroom calendar as if to cinch the deal and then removed it from the wall, tore it into tiny pieces and threw it in the trash.

Today, he and his Kate would become man and wife, and tonight he would hold her in his arms and make love to her for the first time.

But then, his thoughts sobered. Her ex had turned their wedding night into a nightmare. If he never did anything else right in his life, he must keep his mind on Kate's needs this evening.

"Are you awake, Aunt Kate?" Daniel whispered the words six properties away, his breath tickling her nose, and she opened her eyes to find his face a mere three inches from hers. "We're having blueberry pancakes for breakfast, and they're your favorite. You don't want to miss them, do you?"

"No, of course not." She managed a smile. "Are they ready now, or can I wake up slowly?"

"I can snuggle with you for a minute like I do with my mama and Jack, if you want me to." He climbed onto the bed and slid between the covers as he had often done before.

"It's only 76 more days until we can see Olivia," he reported. "She kicked my hand this morning, but she didn't know it was me."

For a moment, Kate wondered if she had ever kicked Jack's hand, while still in their mother's womb. If so, she should apologize to him, but then she realized that was silly. Their mother would never have let Jack touch her in such a way.

As bad as her parents were, though, Larry's had their downside, too.

"I told Gertrude this was our only child's wedding and she was going to attend, no matter what her garden club was doing." She had heard his father brag to a noncommittal Anders Chesterton the evening before, and so far, Gertrude Chesterton hadn't even acknowledged her future daughter-in-law's presence.

On reflection, though, that might be a good thing.

"Edmund and Marissa are coming, Pete and Julia are coming, Jim and Bev are coming, Jason and Ginny are coming, Arthur and Edwina are coming, Uncle Andy and Aunt Courtney and their families are coming, Gabe and Beth are coming, Herb and Jewel are coming, Jeff and Becca are coming – I like them.

"Chase and Adrianna are coming, Otis and Penny are coming, Max is coming – he'll wear his tux like me. Grandma and Grandpa are coming…" Kate realized that, beside her, Daniel was going through his litany of their invited guests.

"Paul Lynch is going to marry you," her nephew pointed out, moving on to more important things. "He marries everyone."

"Tell me that my son didn't wake you up," Susan said from the doorway, a soft, full-length cotton robe doing nothing to hide the fact that she was almost seven months pregnant.

"Aunt Kate doesn't want to miss blueberry pancakes," Daniel spoke up.

"Why don't you join us?" Kate patted the queen-sized mattress.

"If you don't mind." Susan stretched out on top of the quilt and took her sister-in-law's hand in hers. "Late nights get to me more than they used to. Nervous?"

Correctly interpreting the last word as a question directed at her, Kate answered, "Not at all. Being with Larry makes everything right."

"I know what you mean." Susan shifted onto her left side. "It's the same way with me and your brother. Life with him in it is magical, but then, you know that."

"So here's where you all are." The object of their conversation strode through the doorway and took a seat on the foot of the bed. "Are any of you joining me for breakfast, or should I feed your pancakes to the birds?"

"Come on, Mama." Daniel jumped off and rounded the bed. "We started a new sheet on the refrigerator. Olivia will see us in only 76 days."

"And I won't get any sleep for the next 76." Susan laughed as she allowed herself to be pulled from the room.

"Is everything okay?" Jack waited for Kate to tie her robe and then gathered her to him for a hug.

"Absolutely." She nestled her head against his broad chest that, before Larry, had been her only refuge in the world. "This time, I'm getting it right."

"I agree." He lifted her chin with his finger, so she faced him. "I wouldn't give you away to him if I didn't believe that, but I'll always be here for you if you need me."

A short time later, the antique doorbell announced the arrival of the first delivery from Beth's Buds. Next the long tables that would extend along the broad back porch and be covered in white tablecloths for the sit-down reception appeared, along with their chairs, followed shortly by Adrianna who had walked over to see if there was any way she could help.

"It's only 76 more days until our baby can see us, and I'm staying out of the way," Daniel greeted her.

And so, the day progressed quickly for all but Larry who, not wanting to spend any more time than he had to with his parents, abandoned them to his aunt and uncle, took a last look around his condo to make sure all was as it should be for his bride, and then passed a few reflective hours alone on his sailboat.

"You look lovely," Susan pronounced in her dressing room as six o'clock approached.

Kate stood before her in a pastel blue, mid-calf dress comprised of an embroidered satin bodice set above a flowing chiffon skirt over a matching satin liner.

A headband covered with miniature white orchids secured the uplift the bride had achieved with her blonde curls. A mixed bouquet of white roses, lilies of the valley and more orchids for her to carry waited in a vase on the island next to which Adrianna stood.

"Beautiful," the latter agreed. "Larry's going to be thrilled."

"Larry'll be a wreck, if we don't get you down there." Jack grinned at his sister from where he had appeared in the room's doorway, then turned to his wife. "Everyone's here, so you two ladies should go ahead."

As she took a last glance at herself in the cheval mirror, Kate recalled how lovely the large parlor downstairs had looked and then pulled up a picture of how nice her groom would appear in the navy blue Armani they had picked out together in New York.

"Ready?" Jack passed her the bouquet and then closed her other hand around his arm.

"Ready." She stood on her tiptoes and kissed his cheek. "Thank you for being you. You're the best brother in the whole world."

"It takes the best sister to know one." He returned the compliment as he accompanied her from the room, down the stairs and along the main hallway to the notes of Mozart being played by Edmund on the grand piano.

As they entered the room, her eyes locked onto her intended's, his filled with his love for her as they approached him, all of their closest friends and family present in the large room.

"We are gathered here today…," Paul Lynch began the service as she and Jack drew even with Larry. Susan took her bouquet and stepped back, and Kate slipped her hand into the crook of her groom's arm.

"Who giveth this woman to this man?" Paul asked.

"I do." Jack smiled at the couple and then joined his wife, who leaned against him as he put his arm around her.

Their vows exchanged and the engraved rings placed on each other's fingers, the service came to a close as Paul stated, "I now pronounce you man and wife." And then, to Larry, "You may kiss the bride."

"I love you, Kate." Her new husband smiled and gathered her into his arms for a kiss.

Congratulations filled the room as they separated, and Daniel hurried forward in his tux to shake his tall cousin's hand.

"Now, you're my uncle and my cousin," he stated proudly. "We're double special."

"You two are as special as it gets." Kate smiled down at her nephew.

Several hours later, a Surf and Turf dinner of individual Lobster Thermidors served alongside slices of filet mignon drizzled with Béarnaise sauce and accompanied by broiled green and white asparagus catered by Montgomery's had been enjoyed on the broad back porch, and the wedding cake had been served.

Kate faced the front door and tossed her bouquet over her shoulder to the group of single women behind her, the guests bursting into applause when it was caught by a blushing Bev.

"I know you two are going to be as happy as Jack and I are." Susan slipped her arm around Larry's waist and hugged him. "You deserve it."

"I'll take good care of her." The groom held his hand out to Jack.

"I know you will." His new brother-in-law sent him a grin as he shook his hand. "I know where you live."

Larry hurried to his bride and escorted her to his SUV that Chase had just driven forward from the home's garage, its only decoration a garland of white flowers draped inside the back window.

"Next stop, our condo." Larry reached over and squeezed Kate's hand once he'd made their right turn.

And, as they drove the short distance along the road, she found it hard to believe that she was finally going home.

## CHAPTER LXXVII

"Let's change into casual clothes and watch the sunset from the deck," Larry suggested as they exited the condo's elevator, in what he hoped Kate would feel was the same comfortable way he had every evening for months after work.

"I'd like that." She suddenly felt shy, glad for a few minutes alone in her dressing room in which to catch her breath after the excitement of their wedding and reception.

But then, she took in her clothes hanging on their padded hangers, the vanity mirror with its gold filigree border, and all the other thoughtful things Larry had done to make this their home, and she felt herself relax, surrounded by so many reminders of his love for her.

Opening the door, she discovered the bedroom to be empty and headed for the deck, where he was lounging on the bench upon which he had proposed, a bottle of champagne and two flutes – each with three raspberries nestled in them – on the low table before him, candles already lit as the colors in the sky overhead deepened.

"Nature's giving us a lovely show," he said casually as he popped the cork, poured and handed her a flute.

"Yes, she is," Kate agreed and sat beside him.

"It isn't as lovely as you were this evening." He put his arm around her. "I'll never see anything more beautiful than you were when we exchanged our vows." He clinked his glass lightly against hers. "To us."

"To us." She took a sip of her champagne. "I can't believe we're actually married. I get to stay in your condo tonight, and tomorrow we'll drive off on our honeymoon."

"Tonight, you'll stay in our home for the first time," he corrected and drew her closer, pleased when she rested her head on his shoulder. "Was everything like you wanted it?"

"It was perfect." She held out her left hand and marveled at the wedding band that now resided there, then glanced at its mate where it gleamed softly on his ring finger.

"You should've seen Jim's face when Bev caught your bouquet." He chuckled.

"They seemed like, I don't know, more of a couple this evening," she shared, wishing them the best if it was what they both wanted.

"Our being a couple is now official in every sense of the word." He rested his cheek on the top of her head.

"Yes." She pulled away slightly and set her flute on the table as the sky darkened above them. "Why don't you kiss me?"

"Kate…," he whispered her name, as he found her lips, not having to be asked twice. "I love you so much." He tightened his hold and kissed her again, then dropped a line of feathery brushstrokes down her neck, pleased when she arched her back slightly and gave him better access.

"I love you, too," she breathed as the fingers of his left hand pushed the fabric of her top aside and his lips continued on their downward path.

"I want you so badly." His breath warmed the hollow at the base of her neck before he lifted his head, his face only inches from hers. "Will you come to my bed and make it ours, by allowing me the pleasure of making love to you?"

"Yes." She found his mouth and kissed him hungrily. "Oh, yes."

At which point, he stood and took her hand. Lifting her into his arms, he carried her over the threshold and to what was now their room, where he set her feet on the floor and then kissed her again.

"Take all the time that you need, Kate." His finger traced her jaw gently. "Like in New York, I'll be waiting here for you whenever you're ready."

Once she'd disappeared into her dressing room, he hurried to close the door to the deck, secured a green bottle of chilled water from the fridge, slipped into his pajama bottoms, lit three candles, withdrew two wrapped chocolates from the drawer of his bedside cabinet, slipped beneath the sheets and propped the pillows behind him.

Taking a deep breath, he prepared to wait, but she entered the room a few moments later, wearing a long, flowing gown of powder blue, her blonde curls shining in the soft candlelight.

"You're so beautiful." He found it difficult to get the words past his throat as he held out his left hand to her as had been their habit, thinking it important that she come to him at her own pace.

"I have your chocolate all ready." He retrieved one of them from the cabinet's top and held it out to her as she joined him.

"And a chilled bottle of water, too." A smile graced her face as she nodded its way, her fingers working on the foil wrapper as he popped his own chocolate into his mouth and then unscrewed the cap from the water and took a swig before passing it over to her.

"It was a wonderful wedding." She snuggled against him as she had when they had slept together previously, once he'd returned the green bottle to the cabinet.

"The best ever," he agreed. "This time, you married me."

He drew her to him, kissing her gently at first, but then seeking admission as she opened her lips to him. She tasted of chocolate and champagne, and he felt his need for her rising within him.

"I love you, Kate," he muttered against her lips, "and now I'm going to make love to you, only you, always you, my sweet wife."

His hand found the hem of her gown as he sought her lips again, and he felt her fingers on his chest. Holding himself in check, he allowed her to explore his body as he did the same with hers – her gown and his pajama bottoms eventually making their ways to the floor.

"I love you, Kate," he cried in response to her calling his name as he brought their first lovemaking to a close, clutching her to him as he rolled them onto their sides still connected.

"I love you, too." She hugged him to her. "I love the way you love me, the way you make love to me, the way that you care for me and take care of me."

"I always will, Kate," he promised. "I always will."

# EPILOGUE

Susan awoke the next morning to find Jack smiling down at her.

"How can you sleep through that?" he asked. "Olivia kicked me awake, and she's inside of you."

"I'm either more used to it or more exhausted." She stretched in her kittenish way and then turned back to him.

"Why don't we give our daughter something to think about in return, while we still can?" He suggested and drew her to him.

Three properties away, Chase looked over to where Adrianna was finishing a last bite of croissant from the breakfast tray he had prepared and served them in bed after a round of lovemaking.

"Listen to this from the *Post*," he said and proceeded to read aloud:

*Close on the heels of the successful premiere last month of Jack Jefferson's newest musical work, 'Susan's Song,' followers of his literary novels issued under his pen name, John Jeffers, can now purchase his latest offering titled Home At Last, either online or at their local bookstores.*

*Yours truly has already read it, and believe me, it's his best yet.*

In the condo over The Cove's former carriage house, Larry opened his eyes and watched as Kate opened hers a few moments later where she lay in his arms.

"Good morning, Mrs. Chesterton," he greeted her.

"Good morning, Mr. Chesterton." She beamed back at him.

"Ready for some breakfast before we head out on our honeymoon, or would you rather have coffee and then pick up something somewhere along the road?" He tucked a lock of her hair back into place.

"I'd rather start with another serving of you." She surprised him as she lifted her face and molded her body to his.

Lovemaking with her new husband, she had discovered after the sweet tenderness of their first time, was as fun-filled as everything else they did together.

Separating briefly a few minutes later, he grinned down at her.

"Being married to you is the best thing ever," he stated, unaware that, even as she returned his kiss, she disagreed with him.

The best thing ever, she knew with certainty, was being married to Larry.

# Coming Soon!

## The Fifth Novel in the Captain's Point Stories Series

# Love's Second Chance

Adrianna's matchmaker instincts are on high alert, but how well will she do as she attempts to encourage the developing relationship between Jim and Bev as well as Pete's new feelings for Julia?

Will Edwina and Arthur find their way forward?

Will David's courtship of Karen bear fruit?

What new secrets will Montgomery House reveal during its second round of renovations?

Can Daniel get through a novel without a visit to Pug?

Discover the answers to these and other questions posed by series readers in this next romantic women's fiction/family saga tale of true love and personal growth from Charlotte Kent.

# New to the Captain's Point Stories?

# A Special Treat for You!

## From

## Charlotte Kent

# A Clue for Adrianna

## Chase and Adrianna's Courtship

### Chapter One

Viewing the tarmac beneath her, Adrianna Montgomery could see Chicago's Midway Airport's ground crew loading last minute luggage and truly relaxed for the first time since her arrival home to her condo in Seattle the previous evening.

"Is this seat taken?" a shy, cultured voice asked from the aisle to her right.

Turning, she found herself looking into a pair of worried blue eyes. Reflexively, she straightened the seat belt and lowered the arm that would separate them as she replied, "No, it's free. Help yourself."

"Thank you." The elderly woman joined her. "I don't often fly, and I've been dreading hours spent aloft beside a crying child." With the toe of a tiny shoe, the newcomer pushed a large patent leather handbag beneath the forward seat before fastening her seatbelt.

A light fragrance of honeysuckle wafted its way towards Adrianna, reminiscent of early childhood summers spent playing in the gazebo behind her great-aunt's seaside mansion, breezes blowing off the Atlantic lifting her dark curls. Despite her parents having left her behind as they had traveled the world in search of archeological treasure, those had been happy times.

But then, she had grown old enough to accompany them, and the summer visits had ended. As promised, she had written to her great-aunt of her travels, her childish script filling pages with stories of her adventures – a camel ride in Egypt, a mosaic at a dig in Turkey, a Minoan vase her mother had uncovered on a Greek isle – the list had gone on and on.

"My name's Edwina Foster." Her traveling companion broke through her thoughts. "I'm flying to visit my grandson and his wife."

"This trip is strictly business for me," Adrianna replied.

"Actually, it's more than a visit." The blue eyes now twinkled. "They're in their mid-thirties, and Ginny is expecting their first child. Jason has to attend a long conference in New York and didn't want to leave his wife alone this close to her due date. They've just moved to Captain's Point, Maryland, and haven't had time to make friends."

"Captain's Point?"

"Do you know it? I hear it's lovely."

"I haven't been there for any length of time since I was seven – almost twenty years ago, but I liked it back then. The town was full of little shops, but my favorite memory is of looking for shells on the beach."

With a start, Adrianna realized she had just lied. Her favorite memory had nothing to do with the beach, but rather with the wind-tossed woods behind the giant house.

One day during the early part of her last summer visit, she had found an old butterfly net stuffed between the croquet sticks and badminton racquets that were stored in a deep closet beneath the staircase. Not wanting to disturb her great-aunt's pre-dinner nap, she had gone outside to play with it, neglecting to tell the housekeeper where she was going. Happily chasing a bevy of yellow and white butterflies, she had left the manicured lawn and entered the cool quiet of the woods.

Other paths covered in pine needles had crossed, joined and then separated from the one that she had followed, and as the sun had set, she had realized that she was lost. A twig had snapped sharply somewhere behind her, and she had started to run, her way partially revealed through the leaves of the trees by a full moon rising overhead. Inevitably, she had tripped on a root and fallen to her knees, her right one striking the corner of a sharp pebble as she had let out a cry.

"Who is it?" A voice had called out up ahead.

"Adrianna," she had responded, forgetting her great-aunt's careful instructions about speaking with strangers.

"Stay where you are," the voice had commanded. "I'm coming."

A light rounded the bend ahead and came towards her, at first blocking her view of the boy who was carrying it. "What are you doing out here?" He had dropped a backpack onto the ground. "Miss Martha will be fit to be tied."

"You know my great-aunt?"

"Everyone knows Martha Montgomery." He had shrugged, calmly pulling a first aid kit from his pack and cleaning the cut on her knee with water from a Boy Scout canteen. "These woods aren't safe at night for a little girl."

"You're here," she had pointed out.

"But I'm older, and besides, I'm collecting specimens for my merit badge."

At the time, she hadn't known what a merit badge was, but it had sounded important. Silently, she had watched as he had applied an adhesive bandage to the cut by the light of his flashlight.

"I'll walk you back." He had held out his hand, and she had taken it gladly.

As the aircraft's engines roared to life, Edwina's voice broke through Adrianna's long ago memories. "I'm sure I wasn't the first person my grandson called on, but still, it's nice to be needed," Edwina admitted.

"I know they'll appreciate your help," she assured her traveling companion.

Turning towards the window, Adrianna watched as the runway flashed by, wondering if she had ever been needed by anyone – certainly not by her bright, shining parents, who had left her at a Swiss finishing school just two weeks before they had plunged to their deaths from one of the infamous curves along the Amalfi coast. And yet, here she was, flying from one end of the country to the other in response to two letters – one that had been more a command than a request and one that had broken her heart.

# OTHER TITLES AVAILABLE FROM ANNIE ACORN PUBLISHING LLC

## By Annie Acorn

*Chocolate Can Kill*

*Murder With My Darling*

*Love's Third Chance*

*Christmas By Design*

*Valentine Goodbye*

*Love's Plan*

*Love Heals (8/14)*

*A Stranger Comes to Town*

*The Young Executive*

*When to Remain Silent*

*On the Road*

*The Magic Sand Dollar*

*One More Christmas Past*

*One Last Gift To Go*

*A Haunting Christmas*

*Too Busy for Christmas*

*A Christmas Rescue*

*An Afghan of Many Colors*

*A Tired Older Woman: Loses Weight and Keeps It Off!*

*How to Survive Your New Home Purchase*

*How to Survive Your 203K Mortgage*

**Annie Acorn writing as Charlotte Kent**

*A Clue for Adrianna*

*A Man for Susan*

*Love's Journey*

*Love's Surprise*

*One Sweet Christmas*

*A Christmas Kiss*

*A Valentine Surprise*

<u>By Susan Jean Ricci</u>

*Dinosaurs and Cherry Stems*

*The Sugar Ticket*

*A Super Sandy Christmas*

*The Christmas Cardinal*

*Twilight and Chickadees*

*Heart Marks the Spot*

<u>By Beverly J. Crawford</u>

*A B-17 Christmas*

*The Christmas Child*

*The Best Homemade Christmas*

*While Shepherds Watched*

*The Stockings Were Hung*

*Towards the Sun*

## By Peggy Teel writing as denise hays

*Niki Knows the Dirt – A Niki Edgar Mystery*

*Monkey Business – A Niki Edgar Mystery*

*Merry Christmas Minus One*

*Walking for Weight Loss*

## By Peggy Teel

*God and Grandma*

*Christmas in Tartan Glen*

*The Best Worst Christmas*

*A Merry Mary Christmas*

*Twelve Bells for Christmas*

## By Juliette Hill

*Pink Lemonade Diary*

*Finding Christmas Love*

*Two Beaux for Christmas*

*Christmas Shoppe Magic*

*Christmas Shoppe Magic Revisited*

*Christmas Shoppe Magic Continues*

*Country Cabin Christmas*

*The Christmas Spirit of Starlight Cove*

**By Angel Nichols**

*Christmas in the Mojave*

*Christmas Love Exchange*

*Jolly Old Spook*

**By Sheila Lawrence**

*The More the Merrier*

*A Silent Night*

*Ho Ho Ho and a Bottle of Rum*

*The Angel in the Mirror*

**By Billie Thomas**

*Murder on the First Day of Christmas*